THIS ANGEL FOR HIRE

Trent smiled, reaching out a hand to her. "Detective. Good to meet you."

Trent's hand closed over hers with a surge of power that jolted through her, searing every nerve, every fiber; flooding her with an energy that was not her own, but belonged to her in a way she did not understand. An energy that made her more aware in that instant of Jacob Trent than of life itself. That tried to repel her even as it drew her into its source.

And then . . . then she saw the wings. Rising from Jacob Trent's shoulders, spread in fiery, golden glory behind him. Wings, like those of a giant bird.

Or an angel.

She might never have seen this man before, but somehow she *knew* him . . .

SINS OF THE ANGELS

THE GRIGORI LEGACY

LINDA POITEVIN

ACE BOOKS, NEW YORK

THE BERKLEY PUBLISHING GROUP
Published by the Penguin Group
Penguin Group (USA) Inc.
375 Hudson Street, New York, New York 10014, USA
Penguin Group (Canada), 90 Eglinton Avenue East, Suite 700, Toronto, Ontario M4P 2Y3, Canada
(a division of Pearson Penguin Canada Inc.)
Penguin Books Ltd., 80 Strand, London WC2R 0RL, England
Penguin Group Ireland, 25 St. Stephen's Green, Dublin 2, Ireland (a division of Penguin Books Ltd.)
Penguin Group (Australia), 250 Camberwell Road, Camberwell, Victoria 3124, Australia
(a division of Pearson Australia Group Pty. Ltd.)
Penguin Books India Pvt. Ltd., 11 Community Centre, Panchsheel Park, New Delhi—110 017, India
Penguin Group (NZ), 67 Apollo Drive, Rosedale, Auckland 0632, New Zealand
(a division of Pearson New Zealand Ltd.)
Penguin Books (South Africa) (Pty.) Ltd., 24 Sturdee Avenue, Rosebank, Johannesburg 2196,
South Africa

Penguin Books Ltd., Registered Offices: 80 Strand, London WC2R 0RL, England

This is a work of fiction. Names, characters, places, and incidents either are the product of the author's imagination or are used fictitiously, and any resemblance to actual persons, living or dead, business establishments, events, or locales is entirely coincidental. The publisher does not have any control over and does not assume any responsibility for author or third-party websites or their content.

SINS OF THE ANGELS

An Ace Book / published by arrangement with the author

PRINTING HISTORY
Ace mass-market edition / October 2011

Copyright © 2011 by Linda Poitevin.
Cover art by Michael Heath.
Cover design by Annette Fiore DeFex.
Interior text design by Kristin del Rosario.

ISBN: 978-0-441-02091-1

ACE
Ace Books are published by The Berkley Publishing Group,
a division of Penguin Group (USA) Inc.,
375 Hudson Street, New York, New York 10014.
ACE and the "A" design are trademarks of Penguin Group (USA) Inc.

PRINTED IN THE UNITED STATES OF AMERICA

10 9 8 7 6 5 4 3 2 1

For Mom and Dad.
Wish you could have been here for this . . .
and for so much more.

ACKNOWLEDGMENTS

So very many people have made this book possible. These are the ones who deserve special mention.

My husband, Pat, for his love and unfailing belief in me. Chloé, Emilie, and Mikhaila, for inspiring me to lead by example. Maureen Daly, for the wonderful kitchen chats that fanned a spark of imagination and inspired me to delve deeper into angel mythology. Paty Rutenberg, for being so much wiser than me and saving the one and only draft of a story that became the seed for this series. Isabelle Michaud, RCMP officer extraordinaire, for the enthusiasm and the many reads to make sure I had my details right. Karen Docter, for taking the time to write to an unknown contest entrant a letter of such encouragement that I carry it with me still. Isabelle and Lyne and the staff of their coffee shop, for allowing me to stake out a corner in which to write. My agent, Becca Stumpf, for raising the bar and then helping me reach it. My editor, Michelle Vega, for taking me under her wing and believing in me and my story.

See? Angels really do exist.

PROLOGUE

I t was done.

There could be no turning back.

Caim stared down at the destruction he'd wrought and held back a shudder. They would come after him, of course, as they had the first time. They couldn't allow him to succeed. Couldn't risk him finding a way back and opening a door to the others. They would send someone to hunt him, try to imprison him in that place again.

His breath snared in his chest and for a moment the awfulness of the idea made him quail inside, made his mind go blank. An eternity of that awful, mind-hollowing emptiness, that nothingness. His belly clenched at the thought. It was a miracle he had escaped, and whatever happened, he couldn't go back. Could never go back.

He focused his thoughts, made himself calm. He could do this. He could find the right one and return to where he belonged; it was just a matter of time. A matter of numbers.

Caim gazed at the corpse by his feet. It was also a matter of being more careful than this. He crouched and touched a withered fingertip to the crimson that welled from the gash in the mortal's chest. He rubbed the viscous fluid between thumb and forefinger and studied his work, displeased at the lack of control he saw there. The haste.

He scowled at the frisson of remembered, wanton pleasure that even now edged down his spine, making his heart miss a beat. He so disliked that side of himself, the part that thrilled at the destruction. He had never wanted this, had tried so hard not to give in to what *she* had claimed to see. He wished he'd had another choice; that she'd given him another choice.

But whether he was here by choice or not, he would do well to maintain better control. If one of her hunters had been near just now, his search would have been over before it began. He'd been so caught up in his task, he wouldn't have felt an approach until it was too late.

No, to stay ahead of her, ahead of the hunter she sent for him, Caim needed to rein himself in, to contain the blood-lust that clouded his mind. To be disciplined. He lifted his head and breathed in the alley musk, scented with rain and death. He needed to be faster, too. Finding one of the few he could use among the billions that existed now—the task seemed nothing short of monumental.

He wiped his bloody, clawed fingers on the corpse's clothing, and then, on impulse, reached over and spread the corpse's arms straight out, perpendicular to the body, and crossed the ankles over one another.

Pushing to his feet, he surveyed his handiwork with bitter satisfaction. Perfect. Even if she never saw it herself, she would know of his contempt, know what he thought of the esteem in which her children still held her.

He drew a breath deep into his lungs and stretched his wings over his head, letting his body begin to fill out again, taking on flesh and warmth. He reveled in the fierce pleasure of his own aliveness; the pull of wet cotton against his skin; the remains of the fierce summer rain dripping from his hair; the thick, sullen night air, unrelieved by the storm that had proclaimed his return. The sheer gratification of *feeling*.

Then, folding his wings against his back and casting a

last, dispassionate glance at the remains on the pavement, he turned and started down the alley toward the street. His mind moved beyond the kill to other matters. Matters such as finding a place to stay. Somewhere to hide, where a hunter wouldn't think to look for him.

Caim emerged from the alley onto the sidewalk and looked up the deserted pavement to his left, then his right. Somewhere—

He paused. Stared across the street. Smiled.

Somewhere . . . interesting.

ONE

That was the thing about a murder scene, Alexandra Jarvis reflected. It would be difficult to drive past one and later claim that you couldn't find the right place. No matter how much you wanted to.

She wheeled her sedan into the space behind a Toronto Police Service car angled across the sidewalk. Alternating blue and red spilled from the cruiser's bar lights, splashing against the squat brick building beside it and announcing the hive of activity in the dank alley beyond. Powerful floodlights, brought in to combat the predawn hours, backlit the scene, and yellow crime-scene tape stretched across the alley's mouth.

And, just in case Alex needed further confirmation she'd found the right place, a mob of media looked to be in a feeding frenzy street-side of a wooden police barricade, their microphones and cameras thrust into the faces of the two impassive, uniformed officers holding them at bay. One of the uniforms glanced over as she killed her engine, acknowledging her arrival with a nod.

Alex took a gulp of lukewarm, oversugared coffee and balled up her fast-food breakfast wrapper. She'd bought the meal, if it could be called such, out of desperation on her way home, as a combined supper and bedtime snack. The nearest she could figure, it was the first food she'd had in almost twenty hours, and she hadn't made it past the first bite before she'd been called to this, another murder. Even knowing what she'd have to view when she arrived at the scene, she'd gone ahead and eaten it. Working Homicide had that effect after a while.

She dropped the wrapper into the empty paper bag, drained the remainder of her coffee, and tossed the cup in to join the wrapper. Then she slid out of the air-conditioned vehicle.

The early-August humidity slammed into her like a fist, rising from the damp pavement and the puddles that lined the uneven sidewalk. Alex grimaced. After a storm like the one that had raged from midnight until almost three, knocking out power to most of the city's core for the better part of an hour, surely they'd earned at least a *brief* respite from the sauna-like weather.

She fished in her blazer pocket for a hair elastic, checked that her police shield was still clipped to her waistband, and raised her arms to scrape back her shoulder-length blonde hair as she kneed shut the car door and started toward the alley.

The media piranhas, scenting new prey, engulfed her.

"Detective, can you tell us what—?"

"Can you describe—?"

"Is this death related—?"

The questions flew at her, fast and furious, and became lost in each other. Alex elbowed her way through the throng and shouldered past a television camera, wrapping the elastic around her fistful of hair. If they knew how many coffees and how little sleep she operated on, they wouldn't be so eager to get this close.

She patted her pockets in an automatic check. Pen, notebook, gloves . . . Lord, but her partner had picked a fine time to retire and take up fly-fishing. Davis was a hundred times more diplomatic than she was, and she'd always counted on him to run media interference for her at these times. She hoped to heaven his eventual replacement would be as accommodating.

"Don't know, can't say, and no comment," she replied, and winced at the snarl in her voice, glad her supervisor wasn't there to overhear. "We'll let you know when we have a statement for you, just like we always do."

The uniform who had acknowledged her arrival lifted the tape so she could duck beneath it.

"Yeah," he muttered, "and the sharks will keep circling anyway, just like *they* always do."

Alex flashed him a sympathetic look and headed down the alley, her focus shifting to the tall, lanky man silhouetted against the floodlights, and to the scene he surveyed.

Her stomach rolled uneasily around its grease-laden meal. Even from here, she could see the remains of a blood-bath: telltale shadows darkened the brick walls on either side of the narrow passageway; rivulets of the night's rain, stained dark, pooled on the alley floor; crimson reflected back from puddles lit by the floodlights.

She flicked a glance at a sodden cardboard box, cata-logued it as nothing out of the ordinary, strode deeper into the narrow passageway. A numbered flag, placed by Foren-sics, marked a blurred shoe imprint in a patch of mud. Another sat beside a door where nothing visible remained, perhaps the site of something already bagged and tagged.

Alex drew nearer to the scene and inhaled a slow breath through her nose. She held it for a moment before expelling it in a soft gust. If this was the same as the others, if it was another slashing . . .

She drew her shoulders back and lifted her chin. If it was another slashing, she would handle it as she did any other case. Professionally, efficiently, thoroughly. Because that was how she worked. Because her past had no place here.

She stepped over the electrical cables powering the flood-lights. Staff Inspector Doug Roberts, in charge of the Homicide

Squad where Alex worked, turned. A smile ghosted across
his lips but didn't reach his strained eyes. Alex made out the
vague shape of a human body beneath a tarp stretched out
just beyond him.

"Have a good sleep?" Roberts asked. Even raised over
the guttural thrum of the generator powering the lights, his
voice held a dry note. He knew she'd never made it home.

Alex produced a credible return smile. "Nah. I figured
the concept was highly overrated, so I settled for caffeine."

She ran a critical eye over her staff inspector's height,
noting the two days' growth along his jawline. Perspiration
plastered his short-cropped hair to his forehead and she felt
her own tresses wilt in mute sympathy. If the air out in the
street had been heavy, here in the alley it was downright
oppressive. The man looked ready to drop.

"What about you?" she asked.

"Ditto on the sleep, but I missed out on the caffeine."

That explained it. Given enough java in his or her system,
a homicide cop could run almost indefinitely, but without . . .

Alex's gaze slid to the tarp. "Well?" she asked.

"We won't know for sure until the autopsy."

"But?"

Silence. Because he didn't know, or because he didn't
want to say?

"Chest ripped open, throat slit, posed like the others," he
said finally.

"Damn," she muttered. She scuffed the toe of her shoe
against a weed growing through the pavement. Four in as
many days, with the last two less than twelve hours apart.
One of the floodlights gave a sudden, loud pop, and the light
in the alley dimmed a fraction. Underneath a loading dock,
someone bellowed for a replacement bulb, his voice muffled.

Alex pushed a limp lock off her forehead, scrunched her
fist over it for a moment, and said again, "Damn, damn,
damn." She released her clutch on her scalp. "Is Forensics
finding anything?"

"After the rain we had? We're lucky the body didn't float
away."

"Maybe the killer's waiting for the rain," Alex mused. "Maybe he knows it will wash away the evidence."

"So what, he's a disgruntled meteorologist? How does he know it will rain hard enough?" Roberts shook his head. "The weather's too unpredictable for someone to rely on it like that, especially lately. None of these storms this week were even in the forecast. I think it's just bad luck for us."

She sighed. "You're probably right. So, has the chief called for a task force yet?"

"Not yet, but my guess is that it's about to become a priority. I'll put in a call and get the ball rolling. The sooner we get a profiler working on this psycho, the better. You have a look around here, then go home, okay? I've put Joly and Abrams on point for this one. You've been on your feet longer than anyone else on this file so far, and you need some sleep."

Alex rolled her eyes. "If this guy keeps up at the rate he's going," she muttered, "I can pretty much guarantee that won't happen."

"If this guy keeps up at the rate he's going, I'm going to need you on your toes, not dropping from exhaustion. So let me rephrase that: *get* some sleep."

The head of Homicide Squad stalked away. Alex watched him cover the distance to the end of the alley in remarkably few long-legged strides, dodging a police photographer who looked to be performing a weird kind of dance in an effort to catalogue the scene's every angle, and then bulldoze his way through the waiting scavengers. With a sigh that came all the way from her toes, she turned back to the bloody, rain-washed alley.

Roberts was right. The others *were* getting more downtime than she was on this case. They always did on slashings, because as much as she liked to pretend that her past had no bearing on her present, no one else brought the same unique perspective to these cases that she did. The kind of perspective that made her drive herself a little harder, a little longer . . .

That made sure she wouldn't sleep much until it was over.

* * *

THE DOMINION VERCHIEL, of the Fourth Choir of angels, stared at the Highest Seraph's office door for a long moment, and then raised her hand to knock. As much as she didn't look forward to delivering bad news to Heaven's executive administrator, she could think of no way to avoid the task, and standing here would make it no easier.

A resonant voice, hollowed by the oaken door, spoke from within. "Enter."

Verchiel pushed inside. Mittron, overseer of eight of the nine choirs, sat behind his desk on the far side of the book-lined room, intent on writing. Verchiel cleared her throat.

"Is it important?" Mittron asked. He did not look up.

Verchiel suppressed a sigh. The Highest knew she would never intrude without reason, but since the Cleanse, he had taken every opportunity he could to remind her of her place. In fact, if she thought about it, he had been so inclined even prior to the Cleanse, but that was long behind them and made no difference now. She folded her hands into her robe, counseled herself to ignore the slight, and made her tone carefully neutral.

"Forgive the intrusion, Highest, but we've encountered a problem."

The Highest Seraph looked up from his work and fixed pale golden eyes on her. It took everything Verchiel had not to flinch. Or apologize. Her former soulmate had always had the uncanny knack of making her feel as though any issue she brought before him was her fault. Over the millennia, it had just become that much worse.

"Tell me," he ordered.

"Caim—"

"I am aware of the situation," he interrupted, returning to his task.

Irritation stabbed at her. She so disliked this side of him. "I don't think so. There's more to it than we expected."

After making her wait several more seconds, Mittron laid aside his pen and sat back in his chair, giving her his full attention. "Where Caim is concerned, there is always more than expected. But go on."

"The mortals have launched an investigation into Caim's work. They're calling him a serial killer."

"A valid observation."

"Because the police officers involved will be more likely than most mortals to put themselves in his path, I thought it prudent to warn their Guardians. Have them pay particular attention to keeping their charges safe." Verchiel hesitated.

"Yes?"

"One of the officers doesn't have a Guardian."

"Every mortal has a Guardian."

"Actually, not every mortal has."

"Rejected his, has he?" Mittron shrugged. "Well, he has made his decision, then. He is of no concern to us."

"That's what I thought at first, but I thought it prudent to make certain and—well, *she* is of concern. Great concern."

The Highest Seraph frowned. He sat up straighter and a shadow fell across his face, darkening the gold of his gaze to amber. Then the creases in his forehead smoothed over.

"She is Nephilim," he said.

"She is descended from their line, yes."

"That does complicate matters."

"Yes."

"What do you suggest we do?"

Verchiel shook her head, no closer to a solution now than she had been when she'd first heard the news herself. She moved into the study and settled into one of the enormous wing chairs across from him.

"I don't know," she admitted.

"How pure is she?"

"We're not sure. We're attempting to trace her, but it will take time. Even if the lineage is faint, however—"

Mittron nodded even as Verchiel let her words die away. "There may still be a risk," he agreed.

"Yes."

Mittron levered himself out of his chair. He paced to the

window overlooking the gardens. His hands, linked behind his back, kept up a rhythmic tapping against his crimson robe. Out in the corridor, the murmur of voices approached, another door opened and closed, and the voices disappeared.

"What about assigning a Guardian to her?" he asked, his voice thoughtful.

"None of the Guardians would stand a chance against a Fallen Angel, especially one as determined as Caim."

Mittron shook his head. "Not that kind of Guardian."

"What other kind of Guardian is there?"

"A Power."

"A Power? One of my Powers? With all due respect, Mittron, there is no way a hunter would agree to act—"

"Not just any Power," Mittron interrupted. "Aramael."

Verchiel couldn't help it. She snorted. "You can't be serious."

Mittron turned from the window to face her, his eyes like chips of yellow ice, and Verchiel's insides shriveled. She paused to formulate her objection with as much care as she could. She needed to be clear about the impossibility of Mittron's suggestion. She had allowed him to sway her once before where Aramael and Caim were concerned, and could not do so again. And not just for Aramael's sake.

"Hunting Caim very nearly destroyed him the first time," she said. "We cannot ask him again."

"He is a Power, Verchiel. The hunt is his purpose. He'll recover."

"There must be some other way."

"Name one angel in all of Heaven who would risk a confrontation with a Fallen One to protect a Naphil, no matter how faint the lineage."

Verchiel fell silent. The Highest knew she could name no such angel, because none existed. Not one of Heaven's ranks had any love for the Nephilim, and Verchiel doubted she could find one who might feel even a stirring of pity for the race. The One herself had turned her back on the bloodline, a constant reminder of Lucifer's downfall; had denied them the guidance of the Guardians who watched over other mortals, and left them to survive—or, in most cases, not—on their own.

But where this particular Naphil was concerned, surviving Caim was essential. For all their sakes. Verchiel felt herself waver. She rested her elbow on the chair's arm.

"It will consume him," she said at last.

"Caim already consumes him, which is why we will ask him. The moment you mention Caim's name, Aramael will do anything necessary to complete the hunt, even protect one of the Nephilim." Mittron left the window and returned to his desk. Apparently having decided the matter was closed, he lowered himself into the chair and picked up his pen. "See to it. And keep me informed."

Despite the obvious dismissal, Verchiel hesitated. The Highest's logic made a certain kind of sense, but sending Aramael after Caim for a second time felt wrong. Very wrong. He was already the most volatile of all the Powers, barely acquiescing to any standard of control at the best of times. How much worse would he be after this?

The Highest Seraph lifted his head and looked at her. "You have a problem, Dominion?"

She did, but could think of no way to voice her elusive misgivings. At least, none that Mittron would take seriously. She rose from her chair.

"No, Highest. No problem."

Mittron's voice stopped her again at the door. "Verchiel." She looked back.

"We will keep this matter between us." He put pen to paper and began to write. "There is no need to alarm the others."

MITTRON HEARD THE door snap shut and laid aside his pen. Leaning back, he rested his head against the chair, closed his eyes, and willed the tension from his shoulders. He was becoming so very tired of Verchiel's resistance. Every other angel under his authority obeyed without question, without comment. But not Verchiel. Never Verchiel.

Perhaps it was because of their former soulmate status, when, out of respect, he had treated her more as an equal. A mistake he'd realized too late and had paid for ever since. The Cleanse had been intended to provide a clean slate between them, between all the angels, but it hadn't been as effective in every respect as he would have liked.

Not for the first time, he considered placing the Dominion elsewhere, where they wouldn't need to be in such constant contact with one another. Also not for the first time, he discarded the idea. She was too valuable as a handler of the Powers, particularly where Aramael was concerned, and particularly now.

Mittron sighed, straightened, and reached again for his pen.

No, he'd keep her in place for the moment. As long as she followed orders, however grudgingly, it would be best that way. If she didn't . . . well, former soulmate or not, he was able to discipline an uncooperative angel. More than able.

TWO

Alex studied the scene in detail for several long minutes before she admitted to herself that she avoided the inevitable. The admission wasn't easy. In six years of homicide detail, she'd seen just about everything there was to see, and had witnessed far worse than what they dealt with now. But this one unnerved her. This one, and the three before it.

She eyed the tarp-covered corpse with distaste. She knew why slashings bothered her, of course. She didn't need a shrink to tell her that what she'd seen twenty-three years ago had left its mark. She had learned to deal with it, however; learned how to shut off the memories and disregard the initial horror that threatened to swamp her whenever she viewed such a victim. She'd had no choice—not in this career.

But this case, with so many of them so close together, and the near certainty that there would be more . . .

Alex pulled up her thoughts sharply. After thirty-six straight hours on her feet, her resistance was bound to be a bit low. She'd just have to be careful. She swallowed, steeled herself, and then started toward the body, pulling on latex gloves to protect the scene from contamination, steadfastly placing one foot in front of the other. She paused at the tarp. Every time she had a case like this, the memories threatened. Sometimes she could hold them back. She crouched and lifted a corner of the plastic sheeting.

And sometimes she couldn't.

Alex's breath hissed from her lungs. Despite her best efforts, images bombarded her: vivid, horrifying, resisting all attempts to push them away. She squeezed her eyes closed and gritted her teeth. Made herself think only of her mental door, made her mind force it shut again on the past. Waited for the heave of her stomach to subside and the nausea to recede.

Seconds crept by. At last, her grasp on her dinner still precarious at best, she opened her eyes again, careful to focus beyond the victim. She wiped her sleeve across her forehead, removing moisture she couldn't blame on the stifling air. Footsteps approached from behind. Mud-spattered black shoes entered her peripheral vision and stopped at the edge of a murky red puddle.

Alex looked up to find fellow detective Raymond Joly standing beside her. "Christ," she said softly, "do you ever get used to seeing this, do you think?"

"Some say they do." Joly shrugged, his face a closed mask as he viewed the remains. "I think they're kidding themselves."

Alex tasted a faint metallic tang and realized she'd bitten her lip hard enough to draw blood. She licked away the droplet and, aware of Joly's presence at her side, forced herself to do her job and lift the tarp clear of the lifeless, wrecked young woman on the pavement.

Under control once more, Alex examined the victim: the single, bloody gash that ran from ear to ear across the throat, and the other slices across the torso—in groups of four, equidistant from one another—that had gone through clothing, skin, and muscle alike to expose pale bone and now-bloodless organs.

Roberts had been right. It was exactly the same pattern as the three previous killings and, like the ones before it, it wasn't an ordinary murder—if murder could ever be ordinary.

Alex chewed at the inside of her cheek as she studied the young woman's waxen features and the way she had been posed on the pavement, arms outstretched perpendicular to the body, legs together, feet crossed at the ankles.

Simple death did not satisfy whoever had done this, whoever had done the same to the others. There was more here than mere disregard for human life, more than a desire to kill. This was . . . Alex paused in her thoughts, searching for the right word. Obscene. Depraved. Another word jolted through her mind, and she shuddered.

Evil.

She dropped the tarp and struggled to her feet. Then, to cover her discomposure, she flipped open her notebook and put pen to paper.

Joly plucked the pen from her grasp. "Go home."

"Excuse me?" Alex looked at him in surprise.

Six inches shorter than she was, but with an enormous handlebar mustache that somehow made up for his lack of stature, Joly waved his cell phone under her nose. "Roberts called and said that if you were still here, I was to kick your ass for him." He stuck the cell phone back into its holster on his belt. "He also said that this was a limited-time offer. The task force meets at eleven."

Alex glanced at her watch. That gave her six hours including travel time, first to home and then to the office. Given the fact that she lived a good forty minutes from work—without traffic—the allotment wasn't nearly as generous as it first seemed. "Lucky me," she muttered.

"Take it." Joly handed back her pen. "If this lunatic keeps up this pace, none of us will be going home again for a while."

Recognizing the truth of his words, Alex slid the pen into her pocket and closed the notebook cover. "Do we have enough people for the canvass?"

"We'll manage. We won't exactly be tripping over witnesses around here at this hour." Joly stepped around the tarp-covered body with the unspoken respect they all gave the dead and strolled away to join his partner, tossing a last disheartening comment over his shoulder. "I hate to be the one to break it to you, Jarvis, but you won't miss a thing. This is one I'll guarantee we won't solve today."

"NO." ARAMAEL DIDN'T turn around to deliver his refusal. Didn't care that nothing had been asked yet. He'd sensed Verchiel's approach long before her presence filled his doorway, and knew why she was there.

He wouldn't do it.

"Warmest greetings to you, too," Verchiel said dryly. "May I come in?"

Aramael shrugged and selected a slim volume from the shelf in front of him. Poetry? The flowery verses might be just what he needed to soothe his battered soul. Or they might drive him over the edge into outright rebellion. Kill or cure, so to speak—and perhaps not the best choice in his current frame of mind. He slid the book back into place and, from the corner of his eye, saw Verchiel join him, her pale silver hair glowing against the rich purple of her gown. He ignored her.

"This is rude even for you," she commented at last, mild reproof in her voice.

Aramael reminded himself that she was only the messenger, and that snarling at her would serve no purpose other than to alienate one of the few angels with whom he shared any kind of civility. He gritted his teeth, looking down and sideways at her. "I'm sorry. And you're right. I am being rude. But I'm still not doing it."

"You don't even know why I'm here."

"There is only one reason a Dominion visits a Power, Verchiel. Why any of the others would visit us, either, if they bothered at all." Aramael ran his finger down the title on the spine of a massive volume, paused, and moved on.

Too heavy—in the literary, as well as the literal, sense. "So, yes, I do know why you're here."

Verchiel fell silent for a moment, then admitted, "I'd never thought of it quite like that. I suppose it is rather obvious."

"Rather."

"You're right, of course."

"Of course. And I've told you, I'm not doing it. I've only just come back from the last hunt. Find someone else."

"There is no one else."

Aramael met the other angel's serene, pale blue gaze for a moment before he turned away. "Ezrael is in the garden. Send him."

"There's more to it this time. Mittron wants you to go."

Aramael caught back an unangelic curse and pulled a book from the shelf. "I'm tired, Verchiel. Do you understand? I'm tired, and I'm empty, and I've just finished four consecutive hunts. I'm not doing it. Send Ezrael."

"There's a woman—"

"A what?" He pushed the book back into place without glancing at its title and eyed her narrowly. "What does a mortal have to do with this?"

"She—well, she—" Verchiel floundered, avoiding his eyes. Her hands fluttered in a way that reminded him of a trapped bird. Any hint of serenity had vanished. "She's important to us," she finished.

"And?"

"We think the Fallen One might attack her."

He wasn't sure if he found it more unsettling or annoying that she seemed to have lost her capacity to give him a straight answer. "And?"

"We'd like you to watch over her."

That was straight enough.

"You want me to *what*?"

"To look out for her. Make sure that the Fallen One doesn't reach her—"

"I'm not a Guardian."

"I know." Verchiel's hands fluttered faster. "We know.

We don't expect you to protect her in any other way, just to keep . . ." Her voice trailed off.

"I am not a Guardian," he repeated. He turned his back on her and glared at the row of books, but their titles had become a meaningless jumble of letters.

"We know that."

"Then you shouldn't be asking."

Verchiel muttered something that sounded like "I know that, too," but when Aramael glanced over his shoulder, she had closed her eyes and begun massaging her temple. He regarded her, toying with the idea of asking her to repeat herself, but decided to let it go. Whatever she'd said had no bearing on a conversation he would prefer not to be having in the first place. A conversation he now considered finished. He turned his attention to the bookshelf once more.

She didn't leave.

Long seconds crawled by.

Aramael's impatience surged and he rounded on the Dominion. "I don't know why this woman is so important to you, Verchiel, and I won't even pretend to care. But I will *not* be sent on another hunt right now. Especially one where I have to act—without explanation, I might add—as a Guardian! Now, if you don't mind—"

"She's Nephilim."

Aramael almost choked on the rest of his outburst as it backed up in his throat. He stared at the Dominion. "She's *what*?"

"Nephilim. The bloodline is very faint at this point, of course, but—"

He held up a hand, cutting off her words, and narrowed his eyes. "You want me to act as Guardian to a Grigori descendant."

The Dominion slid her hands back into the folds of her robe. She nodded.

Aramael left the bookshelves and began pacing the room's perimeter. His mind raced. *Nephilim.* The very name tasted bitter on his tongue, as it would on the tongues of all those who remained loyal to the One. He paused at the window, bracing a hand on either side of the frame, staring out without seeing.

Nephilim. Seed of the original Fallen Angels, the Grigori, who were cast from Heaven for interference with the mortals they were to watch over. Reminder of all that had been lost in the ensuing exodus from Heaven, and of the enduring, irreconcilable split that remained between angel-kind.

And now Mittron wanted one of those reminders protected from a Fallen One? His belly clenched. His fists followed suit. He knew of only one former angel who would target a Naphil, who could raise the concern of Heaven's administrator, the highest of the Seraphim.

"It's him, isn't it?"

He willed Verchiel to acknowledge that he was right without speaking the name. If she didn't say it, if *he* wasn't named, maybe Aramael might still escape. Deny the hunt. Retain his soul.

Verchiel cleared her throat. "Yes," she said.

Aramael closed his eyes and braced himself, knowing what would come next.

"It's Caim."

Ugliness rose to engulf him, a dark fury as timeless as the One herself. A pulsing, nearly living thing that wanted to consume him, to become him. The harder he fought it, the more he struggled, the more of himself he lost to it.

The rage was as familiar to him as it was hated. It was what set him apart—set all of the Sixth Choir apart—from the others. What made them Powers. Hunters. Now it had awakened in him and would drive him, relentlessly, until he found the prey that had been named to him.

And not just any prey.

Caim.

No other name could have triggered a wrath of quite this depth; no other Fallen Angel could have aroused this passion. He knew that, and in a blinding flash of clarity, he understood that Verchiel and Mittron had known it, too. More, they had counted on it.

"Then you'll do it," Verchiel said, her voice seeming to come from a very long way off, hollow and flat. "You'll accept the hunt and protect the woman."

Aramael wanted to deny it. He wanted with all his being to tell Verchiel that she and the Highest Seraph had misjudged him, that he didn't care in the least about the hunt, and that he cared even less about the woman.

But he wanted Caim more.

More than anything else in his universe.

His voice vibrated with the anger that now owned him. "You knew I would."

"Yes."

"You promised I would never hunt him again."

Verchiel's hands disappeared into the purple folds of her robe with a soft rustle. "I know."

He wanted to shout at her. To rage and yell, and fling himself around the room. To demand that she release him from the hunt; that she hold to the promise she had made four thousand years before. But it was out of her hands now. She had already inflicted the damage: she had designated his prey, and he had no choice but to complete what had begun, even as his every particle rebelled at the knowledge.

Caim had escaped. After all that pain, all that torment, he walked the mortal realm as if none of it had ever happened, as if it had not torn Aramael nearly in half to capture him in the first place and would not destroy him now to do so again.

Aramael gritted his teeth until his jaw ached. "Then know this, too, Dominion," he snarled. "Know that I hate you for what you've done. Almost as much as I hate him."

Almost as much as I hate my own brother.

THREE

Alex closed the coffee room door, muting the din of Homicide behind her. The noise didn't usually bother her, but today it put her teeth on edge—and it would only get worse once the media learned about the serial killer. The phones would ring nonstop then, and the usual commotion would escalate into chaos. Not that she'd be in the office much at that point. None of them would. They'd be too busy running down the leads called in by the ever-so-helpful public. Spending endless hours following up on crank calls, hoaxes, and runaway imaginations in the hopes that just one tiny clue would emerge. One truth.

Making a face at the thought, she yawned, not bothering to cover her mouth, and headed for the counter on the opposite side of the room. She debated whether she felt better or worse after the sleep Roberts had ordered, and decided it was an even split—worse for the moment, but, with luck, better once she'd had a coffee and finished waking up.

She took a cup down from the shelf and lifted the thermal pot from the coffee machine. Empty. Her mood nosedived from irritable to outright bad tempered.

"Jesus fucking Christ," she growled.

"Really, Jarvis, it's only a coffeepot," a woman's dry voice commented.

Alex jumped at the realization she had company in the room. God, she hadn't even noticed. Rather unnerving, given her line of work. She rubbed the back of her neck as she turned to the elegantly suited woman seated at the table.

"Sorry, Delaney, didn't see you there."

Detective Christine Delaney arched a brow. "You almost tripped over me on your way in." The fraud detective's cool brown gaze swept over Alex, pausing once at the same dress pants she'd worn for the last two days and again at her plain white shirt, and then settled on her face. The under-eye circles Alex herself had noticed in the mirror suddenly felt the size of overstuffed grocery bags. Delaney flipped the page in her magazine and selected a celery stick from the plate in front of her, her glossy pink nails a perfect foil for the pale green vegetable. "Roberts told everyone you went home to sleep. You don't look much like you did."

Alex mentally counted to three and then favored the other detective with as sour a look as she could summon around another yawn. "Thanks."

"Don't take it personally. You all look like hell when you're working one of these cases. One of the reasons I don't work Homicide."

Biting her tongue—literally—Alex refrained from commenting on Homicide's good fortune and turned her attention to rummaging through the cupboards in search of a fresh coffee filter. "So how come you're slumming it today? Don't you have your own coffeepot in Fraud?" she asked over her shoulder as she stretched on tiptoe to retrieve the package from the top shelf.

"I'm killing time until I head out to Oakville. Some hoity-toity complainant who thinks he's too good to come to the office. Our coffeepot was empty, so I came here." Delaney eyed her over the rim of the mug she'd raised. "Relax, Jarvis. I'm not the one who finished off your precious elixir. You'll have to blame your visitor for that. Guess no one told him the rules."

Alex rocked down onto her heels. "Visitor?"

"Mm." Delaney sipped her coffee and wrinkled her nose. "Ick. Whoever makes the coffee here could do with a lighter touch."

"Or you could make your own," Alex suggested through her teeth. She spooned coffee into the filter and considered asking more about the visitor, but hesitated. Christine Delaney had perfected the art of office gossip, and after having found herself the subject of the grapevine three years before, when her relationship with another officer had soured, Alex tended to avoid anything to do with the woman.

She rinsed out the pot and filled it with cold water. It would be easier to resist being drawn in, however, if Delaney didn't keep glancing in her direction, looking like a cat who'd made off with a whole cage of canaries. The woman knew something, and from that expression, Alex guessed it to be significant.

At last, after she'd poured the water into the machine, set the pot in place, and flipped on the switch, she caved. "All right, what?"

"Nothing." Delaney hesitated, then shrugged. "I was just admiring you, that's all."

Yeah, right.

The fraud detective's guileless gaze met her own. "I mean, you seem to be taking it so well. I know I'd be a lot more upset if I were you."

Upset? Now, there was a word that didn't bode well. Alex glowered at the other detective and felt herself waver. She supposed she'd eventually find out what Delaney was talking about, but then again, forewarned might mean forearmed.

She dropped a teaspoon into her waiting mug with a loud clatter and retrieved the cream from the nearby refrigerator. Then she cast an irritated look Delaney's way. "Fine, I'll bite. What am I taking well?"

Delaney's perfectly lipsticked mouth curved with satisfaction and Alex tried to ignore a fishhooked feeling. "Jacob Trent. Your new partner," the fraud detective said. She shook her head. "Poor you. It'll be hell training someone in the middle of something this big."

Was that all? God, for two cents—Alex summoned up a saccharine smile and reminded herself that cops had a moral obligation not to commit murder.

Granted, she wasn't thrilled with the idea of babysitting someone new in the middle of a case of this magnitude, but she could hardly complain. With her partner now retired and wading through rivers, the brass had been making increasingly unhappy noises about her working solo; a new partner had been inevitable.

She had to admit surprise, however, that no one had given her any warning. Roberts could have at least mentioned it at this morning's scene. Behind her on the counter, the coffee machine hissed and gurgled its progress.

"I didn't know about it, but I'm sure I'll have no problem working with Detective Trent. When does he get here?"

"He's already here. I told you, he had the last of the coffee." Delaney nodded out the window overlooking the Homicide Squad office. "That's him beside Roberts. The guy in the gray pinstripes."

Alex's gaze found her staff inspector, his head just a few inches shy of scraping the top of his office doorway, with the slightly gaunt look that had made his desk a receptacle for anonymous food gifts ever since his separation. Then she turned her attention to the man beside Roberts—and felt her jaw go slack.

Oh.

Jacob Trent stood almost as tall as Roberts, but nothing about the man could be described as gaunt. From the powerful set of his wide shoulders to the narrow taper of his hips, right down to the poised, balanced ease with which he shifted his stance, his strength emanated clear across the office. Strength, and a raw, unmitigated magnetism that made Alex's mouth go dry and her heartbeat kick up a notch.

Oh my.

Her gaze traveled over him a second time, lingering on the thick, dark hair that fell in an unruly wave across Trent's forehead, the bold lines of a profile as harshly beautiful as it was classic . . .

Delaney cleared her throat and Alex jolted back to reality. "Are you all right?" Delaney asked. "You look flushed."

Alex glanced at the other woman's smirk. If she wasn't careful, the fraud detective would have her in bed with Trent before she'd even shaken his hand. She turned from the window.

"Fine," she said. "Thanks. I think I just need that coffee."

Delaney nodded at the pot sitting in the now-silent machine. "Don't let me stop you."

Alex poured her coffee, stirred it, and dropped the spoon into the sink. Seeing that Delaney had returned to her magazine, she risked another peek at Jacob Trent, but he was hidden from view. Just as well. She could probably use a few seconds to deal with certain unruly hormones before she went out there to introduce herself.

She picked up the mug, straightened her spine, and headed for the door, barely registering Delaney's laconic farewell.

CHRISTINE WATCHED ALEX Jarvis step into the Homicide Squad room, narrowly missing a file-encumbered clerk on her way toward the group clustered around Staff Inspector Roberts.

There but for the grace of God, she thought, taking in the appearance of every sleep-deprived detective in the place and remembering how she'd very nearly accepted a transfer to this section instead of Fraud. She shuddered. Jarvis was right. She'd never have survived. Not that the homicide detective had ever said so outright, but Christine knew the other woman's opinion of her. She'd long ago given up being insulted—about the same time she realized that Jarvis really was the superior cop. By far.

Not that she herself was a bad one; she just wasn't driven

the way Jarvis was, and she certainly didn't want or need the kind of pressure that came with working Homicide. She took a celery stick from her plate and nibbled at it. No, Fraud offered ample challenge, and it let her go home to sleep on a regular basis, too.

That didn't mean her job didn't have its own special moments, however. Like this morning's call. Talk about a bullshit complaint from an overprotective parent. Christine had known it the moment she'd answered the phone, and still couldn't believe she'd let that jerk pressure her into opening a file. The guy's kid was twenty-one, for God's sake, plenty old enough to decide for himself if he wanted to give away his entire inheritance to some mission or other. Without proof of coercion of some sort, the police could do nothing about it.

Unless Daddy played golf with the mayor and opening a file wasn't so much a courtesy as it was a career move. As in wanting to *keep* her career.

Christine grimaced and rose from her chair. CYA, she reminded herself: cover your ass. If she went through the motions, she could at least say she'd done her job. She carried her dishes to the counter and dumped the remainder of her lunch into the trash. So she'd meet Daddy first, then get the son's side of the story, and then, just to be on the safe side, she'd even interview the accused "money-grubbing missionary."

Leaving plate and cup sitting beneath the sign that ordered her to wash her own dishes, she stepped out into Homicide, where she was grateful all over again not to be a part of the tension driving her colleagues.

HALFWAY ACROSS THE office to join the group clustered around Roberts's door, Alex glimpsed a pin-striped shoulder and her heart skipped another irritating few beats. She paused beside a desk and set down her coffee, and then wiped damp palms, one at a time, against her pants.

He's just another cop, she told herself. *A very hot other cop, maybe, but a cop all the same.*

And if Delaney was right about him being her new partner, she'd do well to remember past lessons. She'd done the office romance thing once, and the repercussions had reverberated through her life for nearly a year after the fact. It wasn't a scenario she was anxious to repeat.

Alex picked up her coffee again, composed her features into what she hoped was professional welcome rather than drooling idolatry, and approached the others. Weaving her way to Roberts's side, she cleared her throat.

"Jacob Trent?" She smiled. "Alex Jarvis. I understand you're my new partner."

Trent turned his head. Cold eyes ran over her and then lifted to meet hers, their depths filled with an intense dislike that bordered on loathing. Alex blinked and took an involuntary step back. *What the hell—?*

She'd barely registered her new partner's reaction to her greeting, however, when a shutter came down over his expression, turning it bland. Impersonal.

Trent smiled, reaching out a hand to her. "Detective. Good to meet you."

Still reeling from what she'd thought she'd seen in his eyes, what she had to have imagined, Alex stared at her new partner's outstretched hand. She pulled herself together with an effort, dredged up another smile, and reached to accept the handshake.

Her world imploded.

Trent's hand closed over hers with a surge of power that jolted through her, searing every nerve, every fiber; flooding her with an energy that was not her own, but belonged to her in a way she did not understand. An energy that made her more aware in that instant of Jacob Trent than of life itself. That tried to repel her even as it drew her into its source.

A lightning bolt, Alex thought. *I've just shaken hands with a lightning bolt.*

The grip on her fingers tightened and pain shafted

through her bones, until, after what seemed an eon, Trent released her. The energy did not. It swelled between them, linking them, holding her immobile, squeezing the breath from her lungs.

And then . . . then she saw the wings. Rising from Jacob Trent's shoulders, spread in fiery, golden glory behind him. Wings, like those of a giant bird.

Or an angel.

The coffee cup dropped from Alex's hand and shattered across the thinly carpeted floor in a shower of scalding liquid and ceramic shards. All around her, people scurried into action. One called for paper towels; another took her arm and tugged her away from the steaming mess.

In the sea of chaos that surrounded them, that isolated them, Alex looked again into Trent's eyes. Dark gray and turbulent, like Lake Ontario at the height of an autumn storm, they riveted on hers. Stunned. Disbelieving. Angry.

Earthshakingly angry.

On some instinctive level, Alex thought she should be afraid. Knew anyone else on the receiving end of that fury would have quailed in their shoes. But the quiver running through her—swift, stunning, shockingly familiar—had nothing to do with fear and everything to do with recognition. Alex sucked in a ragged breath, fighting for an existence she sensed being ripped from her.

She might never have seen this man before, but somehow she *knew* him.

FOUR

Aramael clenched his fists at his sides, fighting the instinct to protect himself. The rage that defined his existence roared in his ears and surged with every beat of his heart, demanding everything he had to contain it. His wings quivered under the strain of holding back, pulsing with unspent power. If he lost his grip, if he slipped for even an instant . . .

The activity around him faded into a background haze of muted voices and blurred movement. For long, agonizing seconds, there existed only himself and the savagery—and the woman.

The woman whose touch had imprinted itself on his very core. Whose eyes, bluer than a hot summer sky, had seen the impossible, and even now held a thousand questions in their depths. A thousand questions and an impossible, unequivocal recognition that ignited a whisper of response within him.

Aramael wrenched his thoughts back to his efforts, tightened his grasp on the tumult within him, and, at last, felt it yield. Slightly, reluctantly. His very center shook with the effort. In all his existence, he had never had to catch back the fury like this, never had to seize hold after it had begun. Never felt it surge to the surface on its own, independent of him, with neither warning nor provocation.

The anger ebbed, stilled, subsided. Aramael exhaled the air burning in his lungs and forced his hands to uncurl and his wings to flex and then stretch. The activity around him filtered through, and he became aware of the cleanup operation near his feet as someone picked up pieces of shattered cup and blotted up coffee. Still the blue eyes never wavered, never left his.

He fought back the urge to seek out Verchiel on the spot and demand an explanation for this crisis. An explanation of how a mortal could have seen a Power in his angelic form and damn near set off his full wrath.

Ten minutes ago he wouldn't have hesitated to increase his energy vibration to its normal level, to step out of the mortal realm and into the heavenly one. Ten minutes ago, he'd been confident his disappearance into thin air and his absence for the barest flicker of mortal time would go unnoticed. Now the awareness in a mortal's eyes had changed the very parameters of his world.

Someone jostled his arm.

"Damn," he heard a man mutter beside him. "Would you look at that?"

Doug Roberts stepped forward, moving between him and the woman, severing their eye contact and allowing Aramael to take a breath he hadn't known he needed. Aramael watched the police supervisor stoop and pry something loose from the woman's clenched fingers, then straighten and hold it aloft.

Roberts whistled and shook his head. "The whole bloody handle gave way," he said to the woman. "You're lucky you weren't burned. You are okay, aren't you?"

Aramael saw her blink, focus on the cup handle in Roberts's hand, and blink again.

"Lucky," she echoed in a tight, hollow voice. "Yeah."

She'd never know how lucky. Unleashed against a human, the Power could have caused a lot more than a coffee cup to explode, and all the Nephilim blood in the world wouldn't have saved her. Aramael shoved his fists into his front pockets. Verchiel had one hell of a lot to answer for.

The woman's stare returned to him and he stiffened, self-preservation stirring in him again. Rigid and watchful, he waited as her slow gaze moved over him, resting briefly on his shoulders. After a moment, she raised her eyes to his, wariness written across her features. Aramael waited for her to speak. Braced himself for the questions.

But instead, the woman's expression turned bleak. He watched as her mouth tightened, her throat convulsed, her chin lifted. Watched as she looked away and focused on empty air.

"Excuse me," she whispered. "I should—I have to—excuse me . . ."

She walked away, her back stiff and her movements jerky. Beside him, Aramael heard the police supervisor grunt.

"Huh. What the hell got into her?" Roberts murmured. "Why don't you wait in my office, Trent? I'll make sure she's okay and then we'll get down to business."

Aramael nodded. "Take your time," he told Roberts. "I'll just get another coffee."

And see about raising a little angelic hell.

ARAMAEL SLAMMED OPEN the solid oak door with little regard for its antiquity and even less regard for the nerves of those on the other side of it. A startled shriek greeted his entry. He towered over the diminutive female Virtue who had just dropped an armload of files onto the marble floor, scattering paperwork across the office foyer.

"Where is she?" he demanded. He scowled for emphasis, but his fierceness only seemed to rob the Virtue of speech. He studied the five closed doors that ringed the reception room. He'd never been here before—never had reason to be—and had no interest in playing find-the-Dominion. He cinched in his temper a few notches.

"Verchiel," he grated. "Where is she?"

The Virtue opened her mouth but emitted no sound. She hastily extended an arm, pointing to a door on the left. He brushed past her, ignoring the alacrity with which she jumped away from physical contact with him, and pushed into Verchiel's office.

Two long strides took him across the room. He slammed his palms onto the paper-strewn desktop and leaned across to thrust his face into that of the Dominion seated on the other side. "What in the *hell* is going on? Do you have any idea what nearly happened? Do you know what I almost did? What the repercussions would have been?"

An obviously shaken Verchiel swallowed hard. "That's enough, Aramael."

He curled his fingertips around the edges of the dark-stained oak and just barely restrained himself from dumping the entire desk, contents and all, into her lap. "Enough? I haven't even begun yet."

"I know you're upset—we all are. But we won't find the answers by slamming doors and yelling."

The wood beneath Aramael's fingers heated, blackened, began to smolder. Verchiel blanched and removed her own hands from the desktop, tucking them into her lap.

Aramael's voice softened with a menace he made no effort to hide. "You dare to lecture me, Dominion? You, who cannot keep a promise, who conspired against me in order to serve your own needs? *You* would lecture *me* on how to comport myself?"

Verchiel's face turned a shade whiter. "I told you—"

Aramael cut across her words. "She saw me, Verchiel. Not as a man, but as an angel."

The Dominion regarded him in silence for a long moment, truth struggling with denial in the pale depths of her eyes.

She sighed. "Yes."

"I very nearly destroyed her."

"I know."

"Then tell me what went wrong."

"I can't. I don't know."

Aramael released his grip on the desk and straightened to his full height, towering over her. With a monumental effort, he lowered his voice to a snarl. "Nephilim or not, she is still a mortal. If I hadn't stopped—"

"I'm aware of the consequences, thank you."

"Consequences? War between Heaven and Hell isn't a *consequence*, Dominion. It's the end of the mortal realm. And I'm damned if I'll be the one to start it." Aramael paced the room, returned to the desk. "Find someone else to watch her."

"But Caim has been named to you—you cannot leave the hunt."

"Not for the hunt. For the woman."

Verchiel shook her head. "There is no one else. You were the only one—" She broke off and her gaze slid away from his.

Aramael's mouth twisted. "The only one desperate enough to agree to this?"

The Dominion didn't answer. Aramael didn't need her to. The very mention of his brother's name had stirred anew the vortex in his center, and the instinct to return to the hunt clawed at him. Instinct, and a darker, bleaker something that thrilled at the idea of taking on Caim a second time.

Of making him suffer.

Aramael's chest went tight. He would not think those thoughts. Would not be drawn down the same path his brother had chosen. And he dared not let the Dominion know the depth of the conflict raging within him.

As if sensing victory in the matter, Verchiel stood up from her chair and folded her hands before her. Brief pity flashed across her expression before it hardened.

"You cannot leave her side again," she said. "Caim cannot find her."

She was right, but the knowledge did nothing to ease

Aramael's resentment. He wheeled and stalked to the door, leveling a last, livid glower over his shoulder.

"Fine," he snarled. "But find what went wrong and bloody well fix it."

VERCHIEL WAITED UNTIL the outer door had slammed shut behind the departing Power and then sank back into her chair, hating herself for the tremble that overtook her. Nagging apprehension, omnipresent ever since Mittron had first suggested this entire fiasco, took on a new, urgent edge. This—all of this—was such a bad idea.

The scent of scorched wood drifted through the room, punctuating her unease. No mortal, not even a Naphil, should have been able to see an angel like that, without invitation or intervention of any kind. It should have been impossible—*was* impossible. Yet it had happened, and not to just any angel, or even any Power.

Verchiel rested her elbows on the desk and cradled head in hands, feeling her misgivings rise again. Aramael was the most volatile of an already explosive choir. If he hadn't been able to regain control, if he had— She lifted her head. But he hadn't. Not this time, anyway, and she would just have to make sure there wasn't a next time.

Verchiel stood and paced the perimeter of the office. A breeze stirred the curtains at the open window and wandered into the room, heavy with the scent of the gardens beyond. It seemed unlikely that the woman could be to blame. The first Nephilim, direct descendants of the Grigori, had displayed some interesting traits, but their abilities had diminished with each generation, becoming more and more diluted until nothing remained. So unremarkable had the line become, in fact, that Mittron had ceased having them tracked almost three millennia ago. Had they relaxed their vigil too soon?

A darker concern nagged at her. What if the fault lay with Aramael? For all his volatility, he'd always been as careful with regard to protocol as any of the others, and had never had an adverse incident. But what if she'd been right about this hunt pushing him over the edge?

What if he wasn't in control anymore?

She stopped by the window and pushed the linen panel to one side. The gardens beyond lay peacefully, reflecting no trace of the turmoil that had just shaken the realm. Or the perpetual threat of war that overlay it.

Verchiel tightened her lips. No. Whatever had gone wrong between Aramael and the woman, she would, as he had said, have to find it and fix it. When war did come, it wouldn't be because of anything as preventable as a mortal's unexpected glimpse of an angel. Not if she could—

She stopped, her free hand raised to cover her mouth. The treachery of her thoughts reverberated through her.

If war came, she corrected herself. Not when. If.

FIVE

Alex splashed a handful of tepid water over her face and worked to still the churning in her belly. She turned off the single-lever faucet with a shaking hand—the one that didn't jangle with the vestiges of raw, unfettered energy—and then raised her head to study her dripping reflection in the mirror over the sink. A sudden image of turbulent gray eyes replaced her own and she inhaled sharply. Her reflection's nostrils flared and the angry eyes disappeared, but the memory, and its effect on her, remained.

She released the breath she hadn't intended to hold. A hundred questions crowded her thoughts, all vying for her attention. All centered on Jacob Trent. Who was he? Where did she know him from? Why had he looked at her like that, with such anger, such fury?

Why did I see wings sprouting from his back?

Alex's stomach lurched again. She squeezed her eyes shut and rested her hands on the cool, porcelain edges of the sink. For the second time that day, long-buried memories stirred along the fringes of her mind—this time accompanied by the faintest whisper of a lifelong fear. What if . . . ?

Enough. It's not that. You're not her. And you didn't see wings.

Inhale.

Exhale.

The shifting memories slid beneath the surface. She opened her eyes and stared at her reflection again. It scowled back, anger replacing panic. No wings. A trick of the light, maybe. Or glare from the overhead fixtures, combined with way too little sleep and way too much imagination. But no wings.

As for Trent's reaction to her—and hers to him, well, they'd just been mistaken, that's all. Both of them. It was that simple.

Or just simplistic?

The bathroom door cracked open beside her, making her jump.

"Shit!"

"Alex?" Staff Inspector Roberts's voice asked. "You all right in there?"

"Yeah," she replied. "I'm fine. I'm coming."

She tugged a sheet of brown paper towel from the dispenser and scraped it over her face, any pretense of preserving her makeup long since gone. She *was* fine. Apart from a general lack of sleep shared by everyone in the department right now, there was nothing wrong with her. Nothing.

Especially not fucking wings.

Alex scrunched the damp paper towel into a ball and dropped it into the garbage can. She pulled opened the door. Roberts's gaze probed her face with wary concern. She forced a smile. "Is everyone waiting for me? Sorry about that."

Her supervisor gave a soft, noncommittal grunt. "You sure you're all right? You looked like you saw a ghost out there."

Despite her best intentions, Alex flinched. She curled her hands into fists at her sides and saw Roberts's all-too-perceptive eyes track the movement. A tiny crease appeared in his forehead.

"I'm no worse off than any of the others after this last week," she assured him. "We'll all be a whole lot better once we've caught this prick."

Roberts stared at her for a long second before nodding. "Right. Then let's get to it."

"TRENT."

"Detective."

The task force meeting had ended, and Alex faced her new partner across a few feet of carpet that felt more like the Grand Canyon. She shifted from one foot to the other. Back again. Tapped her clipboard against her thigh. Looked everywhere but directly at Trent and still managed to notice the fit of his suit jacket across broad shoulders.

"Hell," she muttered.

"Pardon?"

"Nothing." She sighed. "Let's get you settled. Your desk is over here with mine. I'll have one of the admin assistants put in a requisition for your computer this afternoon, but it'll take them a day or two to get one for you. You'll have to share mine in the meantime. You'll need to order cards, too."

Alex led the way across the office as she spoke. Her desk was at the epicenter of Homicide, her preferred location. In the midst of the noise and activity, it made paperwork a challenge sometimes, but it also let her keep her finger on the pulse of everything going through the unit.

"Cards?" Trent asked behind her.

"Business cards. You're there." She stopped and pointed at the empty desk abutting her own paper-strewn mess. "I'll have someone make copies of the files for you."

"Whatever. So now what?"

Halfway into her chair, Alex paused. She eyed the other detective. "Um, now you read the files, familiarize yourself with the case—"

"A waste of time."

"I beg your pardon?"

Dark eyebrows met in a slash above eyes that flashed with impatience. "We need to be out there."

"Out where?"

"There." Trent gestured toward the windows on the far side of the office. "Looking for him. For the killer."

Sudden suspicion reared in Alex. She straightened again and assessed her new partner with a critical eye. In his mid- to late-thirties, he had to have been on the force for at least a decade to make detective. Long enough that he should know how an investigation ran. An unsettling thought occurred to her.

They wouldn't dare.

"How long were you on the streets, Detective?" she asked.

"What?"

"How many years were you in uniform, on patrol?"

Trent hesitated. Looked annoyed. "I don't see how that matters."

Alex's heart hit the floor. Good God. They did dare. They'd given her a career paper pusher as a partner. A desk jockey who didn't have the first clue about investigative procedure.

Was this why Delaney had been so sympathetic? Had she known? Alex closed her eyes. She began a slow count to ten and made it as far as three before her temper got in the way. The brass could not seriously expect her to train this man in the middle of a serial-killer case, and if they did, they could bloody well think again.

She leveled a hostile look at her new, about-to-be-ex part- ner. "Excuse me," she said through gritted teeth. "I need to talk to Staff Inspector Roberts."

Alex didn't knock, and didn't wait for an invitation. She simply thrust open Roberts's door and, hands on hips, squared off against him. "What the hell is going on?"

"Apart from a media nightmare and every politician in the city snapping at my heels?" Roberts tipped back in his chair and linked his hands behind his head. "Why don't you tell me?"

"Assigning me as babysitter," Alex snapped. She wondered if she might be overreacting because of her earlier encounter with Trent, but pushed past her misgivings. "Where the hell did they dig up this clown, anyway? Fucking accounting or something? Has he ever even *been* on the street?"

Roberts aimed a pointed look at the door and Alex pushed it shut with her foot. She saw Trent watching from her desk, his face dark with annoyance. *Tough.* She turned her back on him and faced her supervisor again.

Roberts settled forward in his chair again. "I have no idea what you're talking about, Alex, and no time for guessing games. Start from the beginning and keep it brief. I have a meeting with the chief in five minutes."

"Trent. He's a goddamn paper pusher. I can't believe you'd let them saddle me with him, especially without warning."

"Careful, Detective." Roberts's voice went cold. "I'm sure Detective Trent has worked his way up the ladder in his own way."

"You mean you don't know? How could you not know? What does his file say?"

"I haven't seen it yet. It's being transferred over from staffing."

Alex almost shook her head to clear it. This made no sense. They wouldn't have transferred someone onto the squad without advising the staff inspector in charge . . . would they?

"You really didn't know? And you're okay with that?"

Roberts glared. "In case you haven't noticed, it's been a little busy around here lately. I'm sorry you're not happy with Trent, but you can't keep running around the city on your own, especially with this asshole on the loose. You need a partner."

"A desk jockey isn't a partner, he's a liability."

"He's another body on the street when we need all the bodies we can get."

"He thinks reading files is a waste of time," she growled.

"Deal with it, Detective."

"Damn it, Staff—"

The phone on Roberts's desk rang, stopping Alex mid-objection. And possibly pre-official-reprimand, she thought, watching her supervisor's frown turn to a glower. She clamped her mouth shut and waited for him to answer his call.

"Roberts." He listened for moment, then said, "Hold on, would you?"

He put a hand over the receiver, lowered it from his ear and grimaced. "Look, I know it's not ideal, but we're all struggling right now. Just do what you can with Trent. Keep him close and don't take chances, and forget the files for now. Take him over the scenes with you—a fresh perspective can't hurt, and maybe he'll surprise you."

Alex crossed her arms. "Is that an order, *sir*?"

Roberts sighed. "Yes, Detective. That's an order."

ARAMAEL WATCHED THE woman leave the police supervisor's office, her face reflecting the same unhappiness he felt. Whatever she'd discussed with her superior had not gone well. She started across the office toward him, determination palpable, and Aramael tensed with the certainty that Verchiel's mess was about to descend from unacceptable to intolerable.

Damn it to Hell and back, protecting this woman was wrong on more levels than he could count. He was a Power, not a bloody Guardian. And for any angel to remain near a Naphil like this, conversing, interacting—the very idea galled him.

Aramael met the woman's gaze and saw the deep flare of recognition in her eyes once again. Felt the same flare within himself. The woman's steps faltered and he bit back a curse. *The hunt,* he reminded himself. *Think about the hunt.* With an effort, he forced his focus away from the approaching woman.

Speed would be his greatest obstacle. Caim's decline from Fallen Angel to monster had stripped him of the ability to escape the mortal realm, but he could still accelerate his energy vibration enough to move at phenomenal velocities within its boundaries. To track him, Aramael needed to be able to move with at least the same speed, if not faster. The simplest of feats, rendered impossible if he had to remain at the woman's side, exist at her vibration level. He'd never even make it to the scene of an attack before Caim's energy trail went cold, and if Caim decided to take his search global—

The woman stopped in front of him. She crossed her arms and jutted out her chin.

"You get your wish," she said. "I'm supposed to take you with me and go over the scenes again. But first we need to get a few things straight."

Aramael raised an eyebrow. Was she *scowling* at him?

"I don't know what section you're from," she continued, "but it is glaringly obvious you don't know the first thing about running an investigation. So here's how it's going to be. I call the shots. You watch, you listen, and you keep your mouth shut. You do what I say, when I say it, or your ass is in the car. Are we clear?"

Shock rendered him speechless for several seconds. Wrestling with a foreign pride took several more. No one less than an Archangel—not even the Highest Seraph himself—spoke to a Power like that. Ever. While one of the Sixth Choir might never use their powers against any other than a Fallen Angel, the potential to do so was there. The ability obvious. Palpable enough to command a certain level of respect that Aramael hadn't even known he expected until now.

Until this woman dared to defy him.

"You presume a great deal, Detective Jarvis," he said through clenched teeth, only just refraining from calling her *Naphil.*

She slid into her jacket, checked her sidearm, and gave him a stony look. "As do you, Detective Trent. Now, are you coming or not?"

SIX

Alex shot her passenger a filthy look as she jabbed the key into the ignition and twisted it. *She* presumed? That was rich, coming from a pencil pusher who thought he could play at being a detective in the middle of a serial-killer case. Who was he trying to kid? Better yet, who did he know to make this whole situation even possible? Whoever it was had to be high up on the ladder. Talk about connections.

She made a mental note to go after staffing for his file when they got back to the office, then jerked the gearshift into drive, jammed her foot onto the gas pedal, and pulled out of the parking space with a squeal of tires.

She'd meant it when she told Roberts that Trent was a liability. Apart from the time and effort it would take to train him, she also had to worry about keeping him in one piece if anything went down. And make sure he didn't endanger anyone else. *And* put up with that goddamn superior attitude he had going on.

If Trent was aware of her simmering displeasure, however, he gave no sign, and fifteen minutes later, Alex wheeled the car into the mouth of the alley where the previous night's body had been found. While the wooden barriers were gone, yellow tape still fluttered in the faint breeze, waiting for the city workers to clean up the residual gore. Alex shuddered. For all the grimness of her own job, she didn't envy them theirs.

She shoved the gearshift into park and switched off the ignition, then opened her door and climbed out into the humidity that lay like a damp, woolen blanket over the city. Leaning down, she peered in at Trent. "Are you coming?"

He didn't move and, for a second, hope flared. Maybe he'd refuse to follow directions and Roberts would have no choice but to—

Trent pushed open his door and slid out. In silence, Alex locked the doors, pocketed her keys, and joined him at the front of the car. Together they ducked under the drooping crime-scene tape and, separated by about as much distance as the alley's parameters would allow, walked into the gloomy depths. The pungent aroma of rotting garbage, overflowing from two Dumpsters, assailed her.

She kicked a plastic water bottle out of her way. "So, how familiar are you with the case?"

"Familiar enough."

"Have you looked at *any* of the files?"

"No."

Accounting, she decided. If he didn't have any street smarts and he didn't believe in reading files, he'd most likely been a number cruncher in his prior post. Great. Now she had to train him in the field *and* in the office.

"All right, just tell me what you know about the case so far. Start with the victims."

Trent frowned. "What do they have to do with anything?"

Alex closed her eyes and promptly stumbled into a pothole. She staggered, regained her balance, and flashed Trent a look of dislike. This was shaping up to be a very long afternoon.

"A lot," she said through her teeth. "Trust me. Why don't I just summarize for you?"

"If you want."

She felt certain he meant *if you must*, but she crammed her hands into her front pockets, hunched her shoulders, and forged ahead. If nothing else, she consoled herself, reciting the facts would further solidify them in her own mind.

"Martine Leclaire was the first," she said. "Seventeen years old, street kid, no fixed address. No job, no friends, no record. She'd been in town for about three weeks, as far as we can figure. We're still trying to track down her next of kin."

Alex studied the brick walls hemming in both sides of the alley. "Walter Simms was two days later. Fifty-three, widower, lived alone. Semiretired, a few close friends, quiet social life. We found no connection to the first victim."

A tremor started in her center. Despite her careful recitation of *just the facts*, images from the crime scenes of the last two weeks crept back, scarlet gashes as vivid in recall as in real life.

"Detective?" Trent asked.

Alex's chest tightened. The scent of garbage mingled with the remembered one of death, clawing at the back of her throat. Annoyance sparked in her. Slashing or no slashing, it wasn't like her to be this on edge. She forced herself to continue.

"The third victim was a day after Simms. Connor Sullivan, twenty-two, university student. Active social life, lived at home with his parents. Again, no connection to the others. We found our fourth"—she waved vaguely at the alley in which they stood, then tucked her hand back into her pocket—"last night, less than twelve hours after Sullivan. Another female, approximate age twenty to twenty-five. We haven't identified her yet, but it doesn't look like she was from the street. So far there's been no pattern with regard to time of day or location, but all the vics died the same way, and they were all posed to look like they'd been hung from a crucifix. That's why the psych profiler suggested a religious connection in the meeting today. Not that it helps much if we never get any bloody evidence."

Alex shrugged her shoulders with the impatience they

all felt at the complete absence of leads. "Anyway, right now we're looking for anything that might tie the victims together, no matter how obscure it seems. Staff Inspector Roberts thinks you may offer a fresh perspective." Unable to resist the challenge, she added, "So? Any insight?"

Trent's expression turned flat. "They were all human."

Alex watched him stroll to the center of the alley, uncertain how she should take the bald statement. A poor attempt at cop humor? Trent turned in place, his gaze moving over the graffitied walls and littered roadway and then settling on the massive bloodstain near his feet. She considered joining him, but the memory of the tarp-covered victim held her back. She pulled her hands from her pockets and crossed her arms. Staying professional and focused was one thing, subjecting herself to unnecessary suffering quite another.

Trent looked over at her. "You're uncomfortable here."

"Murder scenes aren't my favorite place to be."

"You're a cop. You're not used to this?"

She recalled a similar conversation with Joly the night before. "Are you?"

"You'd be surprised at what I'm used to, Detective."

He walked away, farther into the alley's depths, moving with the grace of the very fit and giving Alex the sudden, unsettling impression of a predator. Desk jockey or not, the man kept himself in shape. She wouldn't want to meet up with him in a dark alley. She shot a look at her surroundings and pulled a face. Wow. Talk about a bad choice of cliché.

Trent paused beside a battered metal door several meters away and Alex watched him pivot, his sharp gaze probing the alley's nooks and crannies. Pencil pusher or not, at least he *looked* like a cop examining a crime scene.

She sighed. Maybe Roberts was right. Maybe she should give the guy a chance. Maybe, if he was willing to learn and could keep that attitude of his under control, he might be trainable.

Maybe if she toned down her own attitude, his might follow.

Damn, but she hated being professional sometimes.

Clenching her teeth and pasting a tight smile to her lips, Alex stalked down the pavement toward Trent's entirely too broad back. When she reached him, she stopped, shuffled her feet, and cleared her throat.

Play nice, she reminded herself.

ARAMAEL'S FOCUS SLIPPED as the woman halted behind him and he felt her impatience, her tightly leashed annoyance. Her heat.

He shoved the latter thought away and considered ignoring her, but even if he did manage to reconnect with Caim's fading energy, it would serve little purpose. A fresh trail was difficult to follow; a cold one nearly impossible.

He wheeled to face the woman. "We're done."

One of her eyebrows shot up. "We are?"

"There's nothing here."

Her eyebrow descended again, met its companion above her nose. "I see. Apart from the fact that Forensics has already been over the scene, you would know this because . . . ?"

"I just know." Aramael waved an impatient hand. Even if he could have explained himself to this Naphil, he had no desire to do so.

"Right. Because of your extensive investigative experience, I suppose."

He glared at her. First she challenged him and now she *mocked* him? The pride he hadn't known he possessed flared anew. Damn it to hell, he'd never had to engage in actual discussion with a mortal—everything he had ever said to one of them had been accepted without question, without effort, helped along by a Guardian's influence.

Apparently the Ninth Choir had a use after all.

The woman's lips thinned. "Look, Trent, when I said I call the shots, I meant it. I'm not happy about having to train you in the middle of a serial case, but I'm willing to do so. *If* you cut the crap." She met his eyes squarely. "So. Truce?"

Aramael stared at the hand she held out to him and, in

the space of a single heartbeat, a single sharp inhale, felt reality shift beneath his feet. Shift, and then turn inside out as the Naphil he'd been sent to protect became the very center of his universe.

He stepped back from the woman, struggling to regain his bearings. An ache began, low in his belly, spread outward to claim his entire being, became a desire to reach out to her and make himself complete. For an instant, he hovered on an unfamiliar, dangerous edge, and the universe itself seemed to hold its breath.

Then an entirely new survival instinct surfaced, screaming at him to put space and time—however inadequate—between himself and Alex Jarvis. Space to buffer him from feelings he couldn't have; time to recover from having those feelings in spite of their impossibility. He obeyed without question, turning on his heel and striding out of the alley's confines, his jaw clenched and his fingers curled so tightly inside his pockets that his forearms went into spasms. He forced himself to focus on each measured step, trying to put his head together, to figure out what in all of creation had just happened.

Because angels didn't feel what he'd just felt.

Not ever.

And sure as hell not about a Naphil.

Aramael arrived at the car and then tensed anew at the sound of firm footsteps behind him. The stitching around his pockets threatened to give way, and for the first time in his existence, he felt the damp of perspiration across his forehead. The footsteps halted. With no escape and no other choice, Aramael turned and met the woman's seething glower. Several threads popped against his fists.

"Right," his charge greeted him tightly. "Obviously you have a problem. Care to share it?"

He had no reply.

"Damn it, Trent—" A trill interrupted the woman. She hesitated, seeming torn between answering the cell phone at her waist and finishing what Aramael was sure he didn't want to hear. To his everlasting relief, she chose the phone. "Jarvis."

Distracted by the call, the woman crossed the few steps to join him beside the vehicle. She braced her elbows on the car roof and leaned her forehead into one hand, her sleeve whispering against Aramael's arm.

The ache exploded, scattering its searing fragments throughout his body, spreading until it claimed every corner of his being as its own. Then, before Aramael had recovered from the first blow, the woman flipped her phone closed and turned to him, and her lingering annoyance turned to alarm.

"Trent? Are you all right?"

He saw her reach for him. Knew he should pull away. Knew he couldn't allow her to touch him. Too much happened inside him, too much that left him raw and out of balance and entirely uncertain of his ability to control himself.

But his new instinct for self-preservation seemed to have deserted him, and he could do nothing but watch in mixed fascination and dread as Alexandra Jarvis's hand came to rest on his arm. Stand, frozen, as her eyes widened and the curtain of angelic illusion between them thinned once more.

ALEX JERKED HER hand from Trent's arm, but too late.

Energy jangled through her, unstoppable, unfettered. Making her see again that which could not be. A man who looked as shell-shocked as she felt, and who was possessed of wings rising from his back.

Magnificent, powerful, golden wings.

Panic twisted in Alex's gut. She stumbled backward, recoiling from Trent—and from her own reaction. Most of all her reaction. She did *not* see wings, and she sure as hell didn't feel myriad emotions woven into the brief touch they had shared, either here or in the office. Didn't feel those emotions vying for her attention, each as improbable as the one before it, all underlined by utter confusion.

"Detective Jarvis—"

At the sound of Trent's voice, the wings rising beyond his shoulders disappeared. Alex blinked, swallowed, and felt cold fingers of dread brush against a mind that terrified her with its sudden fragility.

No. Not that.

Never that.

With careful movements defined by their very deliberateness, she took the keys from her pocket and replaced the cell phone in its case at her waist. Then, with equal precision, she locked away the image of a winged Trent with the memories and the gut-congealing fear with which she'd lived a lifetime.

"We have another body," she said. "Staff Roberts wants us at the scene."

SEVEN

Christine Delaney pushed the buzzer for a third time and stood back to peer up at the windows of the stately home. Not so much as the twitch of a drape. She checked her watch again. Three o'clock. Exactly on time. So where the bloody hell was Arthur Stevens, overbearing parent extraordinaire? Christ, she detested the way the wealthy set figured the world would fall in with their own personal schedules.

She scowled at the glossy black front door. She should never have agreed to drive all the way out to Oakville for the moron's statement, just so the staff in his downtown office wouldn't know about Daddy's difficulties with his son. It would have been so much more sensible to have the Halton Regional Police Service do the interview for her. Oakville fell within their jurisdiction, after all. She gave a soft snort. Maybe she was the moron, not Stevens.

She gazed down the long, empty sweep of driveway. Well, she was here now, so she might as well check around back to see if anyone was there. With a place this size,

Stevens had to have hired help kicking around somewhere. Maybe they'd know when he was expected home.

Heading down the stairs and across the lawn, she cursed as her designer shoes sank into the soft turf. Great. Now she'd have to have them cleaned, all because the mayor's golfing buddy couldn't let go of his adult son. Asshole.

Speaking of the son, she still needed to get his side of the story, too. Daddy Stevens might not think it necessary, but Christine planned to err on the side of extreme thoroughness on this file. She had no intention of having it come back to bite her in the ass.

She pulled out her cell phone, punched the Recent Calls button, selected Mitch Stevens's name, and hit Auto Dial. If she could meet him on her way back to the office, her day might not feel like such a colossal waste. As she rounded the corner of the house, however, Mitch Stevens's voice mail kicked in yet again.

"Damn it, doesn't anyone answer the phone anymore?" Christine waited for the tone and left another message, terser than the first two. She hung up as her shoe landed in something too soft to be lawn. Groaning, she froze. "You have got to be fucking kidding me."

She stared at the dog crap under her foot for a moment and then raised a baleful face to whatever deities might occupy the sky. "If you're trying to tell me this case is a pile of shit, I already figured that out," she muttered. "You don't have to rub it in."

ROBERTS TURNED AS Alex climbed out of her car. His forehead creased. "What happened to you?" he asked. "You see that ghost again?"

Alex recoiled from her staff inspector's ill-chosen words. Her hand, still quivering from its encounter with Trent, tightened its grip on the top edge of the driver's door. "I'm fine."

"You don't look it."

Alex shrugged off his concern and reached into the car for the sunglasses she'd left on the dash. A hot wind, scented by exhaust fumes from the city four stories below, gusted across the rooftop parking lot and lifted the hair from her neck.

Trent got out on the other side of the car. Alex eyed his stiff posture, turned her back on him, and slid her sunglasses into place on her nose.

Roberts raised an eyebrow. "Something I should know about?"

Still smarting from the dressing-down she'd received in her staff inspector's office, Alex shook her head. "Nothing more than we already discussed."

Roberts grunted and turned back to the scene. "So has the circus started yet?"

Alex knew he referred to the gathering of media she'd come through on the street below. She slammed the door and joined her supervisor beside the coroner's vehicle. The sun's harsh rays radiated back from the concrete at her feet. "Four more than I counted last night, including CNN. They've set up for live broadcasting this time."

"Fucking hell."

Alex turned her attention to the tarp-covered victim. In his cryptic phone call, Roberts had said the body looked to have been there for about a day, which meant it had been out in the rain and the scene had likely been washed clean. Again. She looked askance at her staff inspector.

"We're sure it's the same guy?"

"We're sure."

That put the count at three in the last twenty-four hours. Their killer was escalating. Alex heard the scuff of a shoe against concrete and braced for Trent to join them.

They hadn't exchanged a word since she'd told him the subject of Roberts's phone call. Eighteen minutes to maneuver through traffic and not a word, not a glance. Only a cold anger emanating from him like the chill from an iceberg, defying the day's heat. If he'd been anyone else, she wouldn't have hesitated to confront him, to demand an end to the bizarre behavior and tell him to take a flying leap off the nearest building if he couldn't get his act together and behave like a decent human being.

But he wasn't anyone else.

He was the man who had grown wings before her eyes.
Twice.

The man who'd left her reeling from a simple touch. Also
twice.

Alex pressed her lips together. "Has anyone run the plates
yet?" she asked Roberts. When he shook his head in the
negative, she took her notebook from her pocket and held it
out to Trent. Her partner made no move to take it.

"What's that for?"

"License plates. All the cars on this level."

She saw a muscle twitch in Trent's jaw, but refused to
back down. She continued holding out the notebook, silently
defying him not to take it, and at last he reached out a hand.
Alex maintained her grip, careful not to let his fingers touch
hers, until he met her eyes.

"Don't forget to record the province if it's not Ontario,"
she said.

Trent stalked over to the first parked car. Alex extracted
her nails from her palms, then turned to her staff inspector.
"Any word on that file yet?"

"What file?" Roberts asked absently, his attention on his
own note-taking.

"Trent's service record."

"Oh. That. Not yet."

"But you're looking into it."

Temper flared in Roberts's expression. "Was I not clear
enough about this the first time around, Detective? I'd rather
they sent us someone with experience, too, especially right
now. But unless this asshole eases up, the administrative
stuff isn't going to happen and you're just going to have to
deal with it."

She knew he was right. Knew that, in his shoes, she'd
expect her to deal with it, too. But she didn't have to like it.
She eased her neck from side to side against the tension
building there.

"Fine," she said. "So what do you want me—us—to do?"

"I gave Troy and Williker the file. You can check with them to see if they need you to follow up on security cameras or anything, but otherwise just finish up the plates with Trent and have someone pull up the drivers' licenses for comparison to the vic's photo. Maybe we'll get lucky." He nodded toward the surrounding buildings and the hundreds of windows looking down on the parking lot, too many to canvass with resources already stretched thin. "We'll ask the media to put out a public appeal and see if anyone out there saw anything."

They both looked over as the head of Forensics passed by, clipboard in hand. Frustration was etched into every line of the man's face and he shook his head in response to the unspoken question hanging in the air.

"Of course not," Roberts muttered. "How could I have possibly imagined they'd find something?"

"He has to slip up at some point," Alex said. "Maybe they'll get something on the autopsy."

After five scenes without a scrap of evidence, however, her words sounded as hollow to her as she knew they did to her supervisor. Without responding, Roberts turned and headed for his own vehicle, parked near the top of the ramp. When he was gone, Alex settled her hands on her hips and stared at the covered body on the pavement beyond the barriers. Fingertips poked out on either side, and she didn't need to see the familiar pose to know it was there: arms outstretched, ankles crossed. Neither did she need to see the gashes; deep, livid, exposing parts of the victim never meant to be seen.

A familiar knot formed in her belly.

Of all the weapons in the world, the killer had to use a blade. Couldn't have just strangled his victims instead, or blown their faces off with a shotgun—just as messy, but so much less personal and, for her, so much less complicated.

Alex looked down the parking lot at the other complication in her life. She ran her gaze up Trent's lean, powerful body, letting it come to rest on his profile. Her partner.

A partner who inspired imagined wings and wild energy, and a certainty that he despised her on a level she'd never encountered.

Along with a visceral response she'd never had to any man in her life.

The knot in her belly snarled a little tighter. Fuck, she didn't need this right now. Any of it. Not the case, not the memories, not the hormones, not the imagination gone berserk. She didn't need that last one *ever*, but especially not now.

Another year and she would have made it. Been in the clear. She would have passed that magic milestone in her mind, the age her mother had been when the madness had won. She could have begun to relax, to believe that maybe she wouldn't be the same as her mother after all, that she wouldn't inherit the voices, the delusions.

The insanity.

FROM THE CORNER of his eye, Aramael saw Alex's determined, hands-on-hips approach. He suspected that even if he hadn't seen her, he would have still felt the space between them closing; he had become that tuned in to her presence, that aware of her every move.

He clutched the pen until it dug into his knuckles.

He *should* be focused on the hunt. Should be directing all his energy toward tracking Caim, following the taint of evil that lingered, drawing ever closer to the confrontation with his brother. The capture.

Instead, he was writing down license plate numbers. On the orders of a mortal. A Naphil whose very existence was a slap in Heaven's face. Aramael jabbed pen against paper hard enough to dig through to the underlying sheet. A Naphil he'd been sent to defend and who had instead put him on the defensive and awakened a response that shouldn't exist. Couldn't exist.

Alex's steps neared. Aramael's neck knotted.

It had been bad enough the first time they had touched

and she had seen him. Even then he'd felt a response to the recognition flaring in her eyes, a tug of something that had acted as a brake on his instinct to lash out.

But the second time had been worse. So much worse. No urge for self-preservation had come to his defense. Not even a hint of one. Only that need to complete a connection between them. To reach out to her, to the descendant of a Grigori, and—

Alex cleared her throat at his elbow.

Aramael dug deep and found the edge of purpose that drove him. Clung to it as he turned to his charge.

"Are you just about done?" Alex asked.

He flipped the notebook shut in answer and held it out to her. She took it from him and tucked it back into her jacket pocket.

"So," she began.

Bloody hell, he couldn't continue like this.

"We need to talk," he said.

Alex studied him with guarded reservation. "About what?"

"The killer."

"What about him? Or them?"

"Him."

Alex lifted an eyebrow. "We have to consider the possibility there's more than one—"

"Him," Aramael repeated.

"You sound awfully sure of yourself, Detective. Care to share why?"

"Not here." He looked over her head and out across the city. He shouldn't do this—shouldn't even be considering it—but he had to do *something*, and Mittron and Verchiel had left him little choice. "Can we go somewhere else?"

A pause. Then a scowl. "Fine. I'll just see if they need us for anything here first."

"No."

Alex stopped in mid-swivel. Slowly turned back to face him again.

"I beg your pardon?"

"This is a waste of time."

"Excuse me?"

"You're not going to find him this way."

"All right," she said, "then how will we find him?"

"We need to talk," he repeated. "But not here."

He saw her waver, her sense of duty warring with curiosity. At last she fished the car keys out of her pocket.

"We'll get a coffee," she said. "You're buying."

EIGHT

Alex slid into the red vinyl booth across from Trent and righted her overturned cup to await coffee from the approaching waitress. Trent did not follow suit.

"Not a coffee drinker?" she asked.

"Not really."

"Tea?"

"I'm fine. Thanks."

Alex slid her cup to the edge of the table. She watched the waitress pour coffee, shook her head at the offer of a menu, and watched the woman depart again, headed for another booth near the door. Across the table, Trent stared out the window, jaw clenched, fingers drumming on the worn tabletop. Alex suppressed the urge to reach across and smack his hand into silence, partly because it would be rude, mostly because she didn't dare touch him again.

She picked up the sugar dispenser, dumped a rough tea-spoon's worth into her cup, and stirred her coffee. Then she set the spoon on a napkin she pulled from the dispenser. Determined to follow through on her decision—arrived at on the drive over—to try once again for a fresh start with her new partner, she cleared her throat.

"So. Nothing like coming into a new section in the middle of chaos," she said. "Talk about trial by fire."

"Are we going to talk about the killer or not?"

For a moment, Alex was speechless. Then, when words threatened to return, she opted to drown them in a gulp of stale, lukewarm brew so she wouldn't say something she probably shouldn't.

Like *Kiss my ass.*

She scowled at the pedestrians passing by on the sidewalk, deciding she liked this man less and less with each of their encounters. Even without taking into account his propensity for sprouting feathered appendages or setting her soul on fire with the slightest touch.

Maybe she should just flat-out refuse to work with him and take her lumps. Roberts wouldn't be happy, but facing his displeasure couldn't be any worse than this.

Then again, how much worse could *this* get? If she and Trent could get past circling one another with raised hackles, and she could get past her unruly hormones, surely things would improve.

If.

"Look," she said. "I'm sorry if I offended you earlier, but I was just calling it like I see it, and what I see is someone who doesn't know the first thing about investigating one murder, let alone a serial case. If I'm wrong, feel free to correct me; if I'm right, let it go. And if you can't let it go, then for chrissake, ask Roberts to put you with another partner. Please."

Trent turned his face to the window. A muscle twitched in his jaw. "I don't want another partner."

Something in the way he grated the words made Alex study his profile with a fresh eye. It had nothing to do with her, she thought with sudden insight. He didn't want *any* partner. He didn't want to be here at all. She set down her mug with a determined *thunk.*

"That's it. I've had it," she informed her partner. "Just what the hell is going on? Why were you assigned to Homicide? You don't even want to be here—"

Ferocity flashed in the gray depths of Trent's eyes, so fast Alex almost missed it. So awful, she wished she had. For a millisecond, she remembered the rage she had seen in a winged man in the office. She swallowed. *Thought* she'd seen, she corrected herself. *Only thought.*

Just as she'd only thought she'd seen wings, too.

"Why?" she asked again. "Why are you here?"

"Because I can catch him."

Alex might have laughed if the hairs on the back of her neck hadn't been standing on end. She lifted a hand to smooth them down. Outside the window, a flare of lightning illuminated a street gone gloomy beneath clouds she hadn't noticed until now. She glared at the man across from her.

"Let me get this straight. We have an entire police force out looking for this prick, we're using every forensic procedure at our disposal, every profiler, and you think *you're* the one who will find him? And just how, pray tell, are you planning to do that?"

"I can feel him."

Well. What this guy lacked in experience, he certainly made up for in balls. Alex picked up her coffee again and shot him a look of exasperation. "Newsflash, Detective Trent. You don't hold the monopoly on a cop's instinct."

"It's not instinct," Trent said, his voice deadly quiet.

Alex's hand froze with the cup hovering near her mouth. She so didn't like the way this man's reality seemed to operate. Or the way it skewed her own.

"It's fact." Trent leaned over the table. His glare bored into her, held her immobile. "When he stalks a victim, I feel him. When he kills that victim, I feel him. I feel his hunger, his need, his desperation. And it's just a matter of time until I'm close enough to catch him."

Alex was sure she must look as stupid as she felt, with her jaw hanging slack and her eyebrows raised so high that her forehead felt stretched. But she couldn't help it. Because she didn't know how else to look when her new partner suddenly announced his psychic ability.

And she'd been worried about her own sanity?

With great deliberation, she set her cup back in its saucer. "You know," she said, reaching for her car keys, "I think we're done—"

Trent lifted a hand in a sudden, imperious gesture.

Alex raised just one eyebrow this time. "Excuse me?"

"Quiet."

Trent had gone rigid, his whole attitude one of intense concentration, alert to something she couldn't see or hear. Thunder rumbled faintly through the glass beside them, vibrating down Alex's spine alongside a sudden chill.

Her partner bolted from the booth. "He's near."

Alex's hand jerked, overturning her coffee cup. "Shit!"

She hastily righted the cup, then pulled a wad of napkins from the dispenser and dabbed at the stain spreading down the front of her white cotton blouse, then at the coffee spilling over the edge of the table. She tried to remember if she had a clean shirt in her locker and jumped anew as Trent plucked the napkins from her hand.

She opened her mouth to object, but the ferocity in his eyes stopped her cold.

"Didn't you hear me?" he snarled. "He's near. Now."

People in the diner turned to look at them, some frowning, others only curious.

"Who's here?" Alex motioned at the napkins in his hand. "Can I have those back, please?"

The napkins sailed past her to land in a soggy lump by the sugar dispenser. Alex watched their progress, then turned a dumbfounded gaze on Trent. Christ, was normal conversation with this man even possible?

"What in the hell is the matter with—" she began.

Trent thrust his face down to her level, inches away. "He's near," he grated. "Not *here*, but near. And he's about to kill again. And I will not lose him because of you, do you understand?"

He seized her arm and pulled her unceremoniously from the booth. Too astounded to object, Alex found herself towed out of the restaurant, across the sidewalk, and into the middle of the street. Trent stopped there, in the center of four lanes of city traffic traveling in two different directions, and tilted his head as though listening.

Or sensing.

Car horns blared around them and Alex started, tugging without success at Trent's grasp on her arm and noting that, for once, his touch was just that. A touch. With no hallucinogenic effect. Which made her theory that she had imagined the prior incidents all that much stronger—and her mental state that much more questionable. Shoving away the misgivings inherent in the thought, she pushed back a dripping lock of hair. It was raining, she realized. Hard.

"Damn it, Trent—"

"There." He whirled to face down the street, oblivious to the rain and Alex's attempts to free herself. "He's there."

Thunder cracked overhead. The rain came harder.

Trent advanced down the center line of the street, silent, watchful, towing her behind him toward the heart of Chinatown. Alex shivered with a chill that had nothing to do with the weather. He was serious, she thought. The man was serious—and seriously nuts.

They stopped in front of an Asian grocery store, its front sidewalk cluttered with an array of produce on makeshift tables and stacked high with empty cardboard boxes. A narrow passageway stretched between the store and neighboring building, shadowed beneath the afternoon's clouds.

Alex shot a look at Trent and found him focused on the passage. One hundred percent focused. She fought another shiver. Nuts, she thought again. Right off his rocker. Maybe now Roberts would listen. A cab swerved around them, horn blaring.

But what if he was right?

Against all reason, her free hand settled on her gun.

"You're sure he's in there?" she whispered.

Trent looked down at her as if he'd forgotten her existence

and was surprised to find her still there. Without replying, he pulled her through a break in the traffic and thrust her into the midst of the boxes in front of the grocery.

"Wait here," he ordered.

"Are you kidding me?" Alex scrambled out of the sodden cardboard. "I'm not letting you go in there alone." *No matter how much I don't like you.* "I'm coming with you."

"No."

Trent's growl was so fierce it startled her into a step back. Seeming to take this as submission, he nodded his satisfaction. "Good. Now, whatever happens, do *not* come in after me. Do you understand?"

"No, I do not—"

Trent took hold of her shoulders and shook her. "Do you understand?"

A frisson of real fear crawled across Alex's shoulders. She wanted to deny him, to tell him to go straight to hell, but something in his face, in the urgency of his grip, held her back. Something she didn't want to identify.

She looked at the passageway again and the fear solidified, settling in her gut. She didn't understand. Didn't think she wanted to. But she nodded anyway, and in an instant, Trent released her and disappeared down the passage. She stared after him, the heat of his touch lingering on her skin, unsure whether she should be more shocked at his behavior or hers.

A sudden tap sounded beside her and she spun to face the store window, gun in hand, thumb reaching for the safety. A wide-eyed storekeeper stared back at her through the rivulets running down the plate glass, raising his hands above his head along with the phone he held. Heart pounding, Alex lowered her weapon and flashed the badge she wore clipped to the belt at her waist. The storekeeper backed away from the window, looking unconvinced, hands still in the air.

Alex drew together the tattered remnants of adrenaline-ravaged nerves and peered around the corner of the store, down the passageway. Nothing moved in the rain-blurred depths. The blood in her veins chilled. Nutcase or not, there was no way Trent should have gone in there alone. No way she should have let him.

So much for keeping him out of trouble.

"Fucking hell," she muttered. She shifted her grip on her gun, clambered over the collapsed boxes, and stepped into the stale, sour gloom.

NINE

Aramael emerged from the passageway into a wider alley, perpendicular to the first. He paused to take his bearings. *Close. So very close. But where?* A muffled sound reached him, far down the laneway. He turned, waited, and then felt it again. Caim, in a niche between two buildings, hidden from the world. Too caught up in his task to be aware of his hunter.

He began to walk, stalking his quarry with silent focus, oblivious to the rain, his surroundings, the mortal whose life slowly drained onto the dank earth at his brother's feet. With each step the rage unfurled a little more in his belly, hot and bitter, mixed with the betrayal he had carried for almost five thousand years, ever since his brother had chosen Lucifer's path. He shrugged away the pain and stopped.

"Caim," he said.

The creature his brother had become froze but didn't turn. Instead, it stared down at what remained of the human life in its withered, clawed hands. Then it shook its head and let the corpse slump to the ground.

"It wasn't the right one," Caim murmured, his voice guttural, twisted by the same hatred and bitterness that had changed his physical form. Underlined by an infinite sadness.

Aramael spread his feet wider. Readied himself. "You know why I'm here."

Caim nodded. "I wondered if they'd send you. It can't be pleasant, hunting your own brother. Again."

Fresh pain uncoiled in Aramael's chest. He made himself detach from it, noting instead the blood that soaked the arm and shoulder of his brother's otherwise pristine white shirt, a garment revoltingly out of place on the skin-clad skeleton who wore it. "If you'd stayed where you belonged, hunting you again wouldn't be necessary."

"Have you any idea what it is like in that prison?" Caim's voice was clearer now as the bloodlust faded from his veins. He began shifting form again and turned to face Aramael, the front of his shirt and jeans dark with crimson, his face still half-foreign but becoming eerily familiar. His wings, faded and ragged with neglect, rustled behind him. "The emptiness—no sound, no touch, nothing but your own thoughts. *Nothing.* An eternity without so much as a whisper." His eyes darkened to the color of obsidian. Became distant. Empty. "It is beyond endurance."

Aramael suspected the truth in his brother's words. He had dragged a hundred Fallen Angels into Limbo and the few seconds he'd spent there each time had seemed endless in their nonbeing. He couldn't begin to imagine spending the rest of his existence there. That was why it had been so awful to abandon his twin to it the first time. Why he recoiled from doing so again.

"You cannot send me back," Caim said. "I cannot survive there."

Aramael pushed away the unwanted compassion that twisted in his heart. "Damn you, Caim," he growled. "You knew the consequences if you followed him. You knew what would happen if you interfered with the mortals. You made a choice."

"As did you," Caim retorted bitterly. "I wanted to return. I begged her forgiveness. But you—you chose to betray me."

Aramael's nostrils flared. "I chose to speak the truth, to remain loyal to the One. Your soul was not pure. You knew it and I could feel it. I could not lie for you."

"Then have mercy, Brother. You can choose differently this time—you can spare me."

"I cannot."

"You *can*."

Suddenly Aramael understood what his brother asked. He recoiled from the idea—and from the question that whispered through him in response. Could he?

Caim dropped to his knees, bottomless misery staring through his eyes. "Kill me," he whispered. "Please."

"*No.*"

The single harsh word hung in the air between them, ripped from Aramael's soul. An angel's duty to the One. A brother's denial. Aramael grappled for mastery over a seething mass of conflicting emotions. It was time to finish this. To return Caim to his prison and end the struggle between them. To end the struggle within his own breast.

He flexed his wings and readied the power in his core. Rain dripped from the roof of the building beside them and puddled on the ground, murky red near his brother's feet. The universe stilled with expectation. Hope faded from Caim's expression.

"Trent? Are you okay?"

Aramael heard Alex's words behind him in the same instant he felt the shift in his brother's focus. Felt Caim zero in on the mortal presence that joined them. Felt him desire it.

His reaction came blindly, from a place inside him he had never known. He whirled and grabbed Alex's shoulders, pushed her back, extended his wings to hide her from Caim. He felt her startled, soft warmth beneath his hands, his own primal response. For a fraction of a second, all thought of his purpose slid away.

He realized his mistake instantly. Knew before he put Alex from him and turned back to Caim that the space his brother had occupied would be empty. That he had let the impossible happen. The unpardonable.

Because of a Naphil.

ALEX STAGGERED UNDER the assault on body and senses. Flashes of impressions burned into her brain: the merest glimpse of a hazy form through the pelting rain; massive wings aflame with golden fire; Trent's fingers digging into her arms, their touch burning, going beyond the mere physical.

Her mother's face.

Alex swallowed the sudden bile of memories. Trent snarled something and released her, and then turned away, his form still blocking her view. She didn't ask him to repeat his words.

Instead, she stared at his smooth, suit-clad back. She rubbed her arms where they had gone cold in the absence of his touch; tried to remember how to breathe, to forget what she thought she'd seen. To put the feel of his hands out of her mind.

She realized she still held her gun and fumbled it back into its holster. Then she saw the bloody rivulets of water trickling past her feet and traced them to their source. Her reason for following Trent into the alley crashed back.

Fuck. He'd been right. There was another one.

Alex started toward the crumpled, shredded body by the wall, tugging the cell phone from her belt. Trent's hand snagged her arm, held her tight. No heat this time. Only purpose.

"We have to go."

Alex's jaw dropped. "Excuse me?"

"We have to go. Now."

"We're cops, Trent, we don't leave a crime scene." She tugged at his grasp, but he didn't let go. "What if she's still alive?"

"She isn't. There's nothing you can do here, but if we leave now, while the trail is fresh, we might still find him."

"Find—you saw him?" Her free hand pushed aside her jacket, drew her gun again as she searched the alley for another presence. Tried to recall details of the figure she thought she'd glimpsed: clothing, hair color, height—

Envisioned fiery wings instead.

Shit.

"He's gone," Trent said.

She flipped open her cell phone and dialed 911. "Well, if you saw him, he can't have gone far. We might still find him if we get enough cars in the area—"

Alex broke off as Trent's grasp tightened. She stared into eyes gone flat and frighteningly cold.

"You'd better hope to Heaven that you don't, Alex Jarvis. Because you don't stand a chance against him. Not you, and not your entire police force."

Alex's mouth opened, but she couldn't find her voice. And even if she'd had a voice, surely there were no words with which to respond. Long seconds passed. A trickle of rain dripped from the end of her nose.

"Hello? Hello! You've reached nine-one-one. What is your emergency? Hello?"

The insistent female voice in Alex's ear penetrated at the same time two officers burst from the passageway behind her. Alex whirled.

Chaos ensued.

Guns drawn, the uniforms screamed at her to drop the weapon and put up her hands. A marked car hurtled into the far end of the alley. Red and blue streaks shattered the gloom. A siren died mid-wail.

Behind Alex, footsteps scuffed. Trent. Her heart stalled and a warning formed in her throat. *"Don't—"*

Two shots cut her off, their reports echoing off the brick walls. Alex jerked at the sound, instinctively bracing for pain. Nothing. Ice water washed through her gut as the gunshots faded into silence. *Nothing.* Not even a whisper of sound from behind her to signal another's presence.

Trent.

She threw her arms wide, away from her body. Away from misinterpretation.

Where the hell is Trent?

"We're cops!" she yelled. "Jesus Christ, hold your fire! We're fucking cops!"

The uniform shouted back, his words running together, mingling with the pounding in her ears. Alex couldn't understand him, but his intent was clear. She dropped to her knees in a puddle. Two shots fired at point-blank range, two cops upset well beyond the ordinary.

Sweet Jesus, they've shot Trent.

Her heart clawed its way out of her chest into her throat.

She strained to hear her downed partner. A moan, a gasp, anything. The police car skidded to a halt somewhere to the left. Car doors opened. Continued bellows from the uniformed officer hammered at her ears. Still no sound from behind her.

They fucking shot Trent.

Alex felt her control slip. She tightened her grip on it, met and held the uniform's gaze, forced herself to speak past the rawness burning in her chest where her heart was no more. "I'm with Homicide. My badge is on my belt. It's right there—you can see it."

Point-blank, two shots. Why the hell isn't the other cop moving? Trent needs help. They have to stop the bleeding, call for help—

The uniform facing her ignored her words. "I said down! On your stomach, hands out!"

A new voice joined the fray. "Back off, Kenney—she's Homicide!"

Footsteps approached from the side, and hands raised Alex to her feet. She stumbled, caught herself, shoved away the help. Water trickled down her shins and into her shoes. Her mind parted company with her body and watched from a distance as she turned to look down on the unimaginable awfulness of a fallen partner. She stared at mud-spattered shoes. Raised her eyes up a suit-clad length. Met Trent's wary, but still very much alive, gaze.

Deep in her brain, disbelief spawned a small, ominous bubble of hysteria.

TEN

Caim gripped the sink jutting from the wall and tried to still his shaking. His heart pounded in his ears, drowning out the rest of the world. He raised his gaze to his reflection, to the fear in his eyes.

The abject, primal terror that came from his very center.

His hands tightened around the porcelain and shame churned in his belly and rose to burn in his throat. He had begged. Prostrated himself before the brother who had betrayed him, and begged.

Like a coward.

Like a sniveling, spineless, pathetic coward.

He hadn't even *tried* to argue his side, hadn't once tried to reason with Aramael, to convince him that the killings were nothing, that they were only a way to get home again, nothing more. That if he could just return to Heaven, all this would end.

No matter that Aramael hadn't understood the first time, that he'd spurned Caim's arguments, Caim should have at least had the backbone to try again.

But no. Faced with imminent capture, he had begged instead. Not for another chance, but for death. For anything but Limbo. Caim quivered at the thought, cringed at his weakness. He felt the sink begin to give way beneath his hands and willed himself to relax, to remember reason. Things were different now. He was wiser, more cautious, and fully capable of evading his brother if he stayed in control. He knew how Powers hunted—he'd been one of them for long enough, before he'd fallen—and he'd learned much control since his last encounter with Aramael. He could still do this, still find the soul he needed to be able to return.

But not here. No matter how many assurances his benefactor had given him that a Naphil lived in this hunting ground, and no matter how confident he felt in his control, it wasn't worth the risk. He wouldn't take the chance of coming that close to capture again—or to feeling that edge of terror. Another quiver rippled through him. If it hadn't been for the mortal woman's interruption just now—

Caim's mind ground to a standstill.

Seized on its last thought.

Aramael had been interrupted by a mortal. He had allowed himself to be distracted by—Caim paused, working furiously to recall the details of his narrow escape. No. His hunter hadn't just been distracted. Aramael had turned to shelter the woman. To protect her.

From Caim.

He watched his reflection's expression change, lighten with dawning comprehension. They'd sent a Power to protect a mortal.

They could have only one reason for doing so.

Nephilim.

The woman was Nephilim. Descendant of the Grigori. A tainted soul that would not go on to be reabsorbed into the One's life force as other mortals were, but would be drawn back to its roots in Heaven before it was discarded, cast aside as its ancestors had been. But not before it took Caim with it.

Elation sang through him. He'd done it. He'd found one.

He locked his knees against an ancient desire to kneel in gratitude. No. That kind of obeisance had belonged to the One who spurned him, not the benefactor who had made it clear he wanted only Caim's success. Success Caim could now almost assure him.

But wait. It couldn't be that easy. Something was wrong. Caim held himself still and made his thoughts go quiet. A Power protecting the descendant of a Grigori? It would never happen. Too much hatred existed between the two lines of angels. He remembered how painful the Grigori betrayal had been to all of them, and how much he, too, had hated the Tenth Choir when he'd stood beside Aramael rather than in opposition to him.

No, Aramael would never protect a Naphil. He might use her as bait, perhaps, but he would never protect her.

Yet he'd done exactly that.

Caim wrestled the urge to rip the sink from its moorings and throw it through a wall. He glared at his reflection. Damnation, was she Nephilim or wasn't she? Aramael would have no reason to protect her either way, so why had he? Why had he let himself be distracted, chosen a mortal over his prey, let Caim escape?

Caim groaned. He knew he should just let it go, move on, find a new hunting ground, continue his search. Should, but wouldn't. Not when it meant turning his back on a near certainty to continue a random, perhaps fruitless quest.

He set his jaw. It wouldn't be easy. He would have to be patient. Cunning. He couldn't risk another confrontation with his brother, so he'd have to find a way to separate Aramael from his charge. The risk would still be enormous, but worth it.

He'd watch them, he decided. See how close the Power stayed to the woman, try to figure out why he protected her in the first place and how difficult it might be to distract him, to pull his attention from her long enough to strike.

Caim stripped off his soiled shirt and let it fall over the corpse of its owner, still splayed across the bathroom floor where he'd left it three days ago. He eyed the mangled human whose life he'd appropriated. He'd have to do something with it soon. He could prevent mortals from seeing or smelling it as long as he was here, but he couldn't guard the thing around the clock, and now that he'd decided to stay, its discovery would be hellishly inconvenient.

He bent to his ablutions. So many details. So many ways he could yet fail. He thought of the woman sheltered in his brother's wings and smiled into his soapy hands.

Such a good reason to persevere.

"OKAY, LET'S GO over this one more time," Roberts said wearily. His tone warned Alex he held on to his patience by a thread. He stopped pacing the perimeter of the mud puddle in front of the car and faced her. "You come down the alley after Trent. You think you see someone standing by the wall, but whoever it is disappears without a trace and you don't get a good enough look for a description. Have I got that right?"

Alex shifted her weight on the car hood where she sat. She wrapped her hands around the Styrofoam cup of coffee someone had given her and tried to ignore the soaked knees of her pants. Tried harder not to think about the blood that had mingled with the water in the puddle. Or the other time in her life when she'd knelt in a pool of blood.

She felt the Styrofoam begin to buckle and eased her grip. "Yeah. That's about right."

"Trent didn't see anyone."

Alex scowled. "What the hell does that mean? You think I'm seeing things?"

"It means I think the stress is getting to all of us," Roberts replied carefully, "and that you have good reason to be more stressed than anyone."

Cold settled in Alex's gut. Not once in thirteen years had anyone intimated that her past might interfere with her ability to do her job, and now her supervisor questioned whether it might have turned her into a hysterical eyewitness? She couldn't even come up with a response, let alone speak through teeth clenched so tight they made her head ache.

She glared across the alley to where Trent stood, watching the scene from the exact place he'd been when she'd looked ten minutes ago. Looking as angry as he had ten minutes ago, too. The ice in her belly began to spread. She'd been fine up until this morning, she thought. Right up until Jacob Trent had entered her life with golden wings and electrical charges and a presence that reached into her center and twisted her very reality.

He thought *he* had a reason to be angry?

She realized Roberts still watched her, concern etched into the lines between his brows. She slid off the car and tossed her cup, coffee and all, into a Dumpster. Then she met his gaze with a stony one of her own.

"Fine," she said. "Maybe it was a trick of the light. Or the shadows. Or my fucking imagination. It was raining, it was cloudy, I saw whatever it was from the corner of my eye for a split second, and then all hell broke loose. I'm sorry I even mentioned it."

Roberts's lips thinned. Then he shook his head. "Look, let's just forget it, all right? Like I said, we're all under stress."

Alex bit the inside of her cheek to keep further comment to herself. She changed the subject. "How's the kid doing?"

"The rookie? He's pretty shaken up, but he'll survive. His trainer is apoplectic, however."

Alex would be, too, if her partner had been that quick to fire. Or if he'd missed at that range.

Two shots, both buried harmlessly in the wall behind Trent, wide of their mark. If she hadn't seen it with her own eyes, she wouldn't have believed it. She hugged her arms around herself.

Still wasn't sure she did.

"Remedial firearms training?" she hazarded.

"Oh, yeah."

They fell silent for a moment, watching the latest victim being zipped into a body bag and then loaded onto a gurney.

Roberts cleared his throat. "Whether you saw him or not, Alex, we came close this time. Any closer and we'd have had him."

"Yeah. Sure."

Roberts looked down at her. "He's getting cocky. Killing in broad daylight in an alley off a busy street—if he keeps up like that, we *will* get him."

Alex's palms turned clammy. She remembered Trent's flat, cold expression; his colder words: *"You'd better hope to Heaven that you don't, Alex Jarvis. Because you don't stand a chance against him. Not you, and not your entire police force."*

She stared again at Trent. He didn't look in her direction, but she felt his attention on her all the same. His awareness of her, echoing her own sensitivity to him. Her heart stuttered in her chest. Roberts had continued speaking, and now something he said snagged her attention.

"What did you just say?"

"I said, even with this rain, we got here soon enough that we might actually find some evidence."

"Before that."

"What? The part about Trent having such good hearing?"

"Is that what he told you? That he heard something?"

Her staff inspector's forehead creased. "Is there a problem with that?"

Alex hesitated. Was Trent's claimed sixth sense something she wanted to share? She glanced at her partner again and noted the tension that had crept into his posture, as if he knew what they discussed and didn't want her to continue. Which gave her ample reason to do so. She straightened her shoulders.

"We were sitting in a coffee shop two blocks away," she told Roberts. Trent turned his head and Alex recoiled under his fury. Then she lifted her chin, met his anger glare for glare, swallowed hard, and made herself continue. "He said he could feel the killer. Physically hauled me out and brought me here. Told me to wait while he went into the alley alone."

Silence met her words. She saw a muscle flex in Trent's jaw and she deliberately hardened her own expression and turned her back on him and looked up at her staff inspector.

"It was raining," she said harshly. "And thundering. There was traffic and we were *two blocks away*, *inside* a building. Trent didn't *hear* anything."

Doubt mingled with outright skepticism on her supervisor's face, and he looked in Trent's direction. "You're telling me you think the guy's psychic?"

"I'm telling you what happened. What he told me. He said he could feel the killer. Feel him stalk the victim, feel him kill . . ." Alex trailed off and shivered. "You had to be there, Staff, it was downright weird."

"You're sure that's what he meant."

"We're here, aren't we?"

Roberts said nothing for a moment, then muttered, "Shit."

Oh, she'd second that, all right.

"Now can we ditch him?" she asked, her tone light but not entirely kidding.

"You know I don't hold much stock in the whole woo-woo thing," Roberts said.

She counted on it.

"But nothing about this case remotely resembles normal, and right now, I don't care if the guy's a card-carrying member of the fucking Magic Wand Society," her staff inspector continued. "He came within a hair of nabbing our killer, and if there's any chance he can get that close again—"

Alex swallowed bitter disappointment. "You're serious."

"With six bodies? You bet your ass I'm serious."

God damn it to hell.

"Well, then, can we at least put him with someone else?"

"I'm not going to start screwing around with partnerships in the middle of this, Alex. You're a big girl. I'm sure you can figure out a way to work with the guy."

"That's it? That's all you have to say?"

"Unless you need another direct order, yes. That's all I have to say."

* * *

ARAMAEL WATCHED THE dozen or so people swarming over the scene, collecting every particle that hadn't been swept away in the storm of Caim's strike. Behind him, he felt the tug of Alex's presence, sensed her every move as though a cord ran between them.

Between a Power and a Naphil.

With an effort, he restrained himself from putting a fist through the brick wall at his side. The very idea he could feel any connection to a descendant of the Grigori—worse, let that connection interfere in a hunt—was insupportable. Unforgivable.

It flew in the face of Heaven itself.

Aramael felt Alex's approach and knew he'd become the subject of her attention again. The thought sent a tingle along his limbs. His breath locked in his lungs, denied exit by the heart lodged at the base of his throat. Bloody hell, he couldn't let this continue. Not if he wanted to catch Caim.

He heard her stop behind him and clear her throat. Hated himself for the sudden damp of his palms. He drew the shreds of defeat about himself, using them to rekindle the anger he needed to stand against her.

He turned on her. "I told you not to follow me. I told you to stay on the sidewalk."

Aramael watched her flare of surprise give way to annoyance. Good. Anger was good. Familiar. Better by far than the vulnerability he had glimpsed following his survival of the shooting. A vulnerability that had, in turn, stirred in him a feeling that had taken several long minutes to identify.

Because Powers didn't feel compassion any more than they felt connections. Not for any mortal, but especially not for a Naphil.

Alex crossed her arms, responding to his challenge. "Are you telling me you actually expected me to let you go it alone? You've been watching too much television, Detective Trent. Real cops don't work like that. You and I are *partners*. We work together. As a team."

Aramael scowled at her. "You don't understand."

"Then enlighten me. You can start by explaining why the hell you told Roberts you didn't see the suspect."

Too late, Aramael tried to hide his surprise. She'd seen Caim? He'd been so caught up in the frustration of losing his brother, he hadn't considered the possibility.

She nodded, as if she'd read his thoughts.

"I only caught a glimpse before you shoved me back, but yes, I saw him. Because you told Roberts you didn't see anyone, however, he now thinks stress is interfering with my judgment. So I repeat: why did you lie to him?"

"It's complicated."

"Then fucking uncomplicate it."

Aramael hesitated. Damn it to hell and back, it would be so much easier if she knew at least some of it. But what? The fact she was in danger and he'd been sent to protect her? He'd known her only a few hours and was already certain she would never let him stop there. She would demand more, much more than he could reveal under the cardinal rule against interfering with a mortal.

"I can't."

Alex's face went dark with anger. In spite of himself, a small admiration glimmered in Aramael. He'd never dealt this closely with a mortal before, never come to know one this intimately. He couldn't help but wonder if they all had Alex's courage, her capacity to stand up to something she so obviously didn't understand. To challenge it despite the underlying fear he sensed in her. Perhaps the One's faith in her mortal children wasn't entirely misguided after all.

He watched her hands clench at her sides.

"Detective Jarvis?"

Aramael went still at the interruption. He knew that voice; it was as unmistakable as it was out of context. Impatience sparked from Alex as she turned to the woman in uniform who had joined them.

"What?"

"Staff Inspector Roberts wants to see you again."

"Now? Can't it wait?"

The uniform shrugged. "I'm just the messenger, Detective. Sorry."

Alex closed her eyes for a second. "Fine," she snarled. She leveled a ferocious look at Aramael. "I'll be back in a minute," she said. "And just so we're clear, you and I are nowhere *near* done."

Aramael watched Alex stalk away, waiting until he was certain she was out of earshot before he rounded on the uniformed cop who had remained at his side. Glared into familiar, pale blue eyes.

"It's about bloody time I got some help on this."

Verchiel sighed. "I know it's difficult, Aramael—"

"You know nothing, Dominion."

The other angel's expression clouded with what looked like guilt, but Aramael was unmoved. He spread his hands wide. His empty hands, because he had not captured Caim.

"Did either of you stop to consider how impossible this would be?" he demanded. "In your great wisdom, did you or Mittron give a single thought to how I might hunt without leaving Alex's side? How I could stay with her and not explain what the hell I'm doing? I had him, Verchiel. I had him, and I had to let him go."

Verchiel quirked an eyebrow at that. "Had to?"

"You're the one who sent me to protect her," he pointed out, hearing his own evasiveness and hating it.

"That's what you were doing? Protecting her?"

"What I'm doing," Aramael enunciated between clenched teeth, "is the best I can. I told you I am not a Guardian, and shackled as I am by your lack of foresight, I'm not much of a bloody hunter, either."

Verchiel glowered back at him, her own frustration evident in the crease between her brows. "What would you have us do, leave the woman to Caim?"

The idea hit Aramael like a fist to the center of his chest. He struggled for air, and to keep his reaction from the Dominion. He had seen what his brother was capable of, and the thought of Caim wreaking that kind of damage on Alex—

"Wait," his handler said, her frown deepening. "You

called her Alex just now. When did you begin thinking of her by name?"

The sharp question delivered a second blow. Wrung a reply from him he'd rather have kept to himself. "I didn't realize I had."

But he knew, immediately and instinctively. It had been when Alex had answered her cell phone that afternoon, when she had reached out to him, irrevocably altering his entire universe. He met Verchiel's too-perceptive gaze. Felt it reach into his very soul.

"Aramael, why didn't you finish the hunt when you had the chance just now?"

"I told you."

"I know what you told me. Now I want the truth."

The truth? The truth was that the moment Caim's attention rested on Alex, the hunt had ceased to matter. Everything had ceased to matter except protecting Alex. Shielding her from Caim's very sight.

Verchiel almost certainly did not want that truth. Hell, *he* didn't want that truth.

The Dominion seemed to reach the same decision. She cleared her throat. "Well. Never mind. The important thing is, what can we do to make this easier?"

Release me from the guardianship. Find someone else to protect Alex and let me hunt Caim.

It was the obvious solution, but try as he might, Aramael could not speak the words. No Guardian could stand up to Caim, and even if another Power consented to protect Alex, Aramael could not give over that protection to someone else. Neither could he examine his reasons.

"I don't know."

His handler sighed. "Think about it. I'll see if Mittron has any ideas. And, Aramael—"

Down the alley, Alex had turned and was heading back in their direction again, her stride determined, her head held high. Aramael looked at the Dominion wearily.

"For what it's worth, you're right," Verchiel said. "We didn't think this through. I'm sorry."

ELEVEN

"What is it?" Alex peered at the thing resting in the stainless steel tray, seven to eight centimeters long, curved, black, and indisputably lethal. The light glinted from it as Jason Bartlett, the coroner, shifted his grip on the tray. Alex felt her skin crawl.

"It's a claw."

"A what?"

"A claw. At least, that's what we think." Bartlett dropped the tray onto the steel countertop with a loud clatter. "My best guess at this point is that it's from some kind of big cat, or maybe a bear, but I haven't been able to match it to any of the pictures I found. We're still waiting for results on the DNA, but I figured this was a rush, so I have someone coming in from the Toronto Zoo tomorrow to give us an expert opinion. You never know—we might get lucky."

"A claw," Alex echoed, staring down at the object. From the corner of her eye, she saw that Trent had remained by the door, showing no interest in their reason for coming to the coroner's office. That figured. "In one of the victims."

"Victim number four." Bartlett peered at a chart beside the tray. "Still a Jane Doe."

The door beside Trent opened to admit an assistant medical examiner along with Raymond Joly and his partner. Alex flashed them a tight smile of acknowledgment and plucked two latex gloves from a box. She looked askance at Bartlett. "May I?"

"Be my guest. Careful, though. The thing is razor sharp."

She lifted the claw gingerly from the tray and grunted in surprise. "It's cold," she said. She held it up for Joly, who had come across the room to join her.

"I know. Like ice. It doesn't warm up no matter how long you hold it, except—" Bartlett paused.

"What?" Alex asked. "You have something else?"

"Maybe. But damned if I can explain it. We measured the actual temperature of the thing at twenty-one degrees Celsius."

"But that's—"

"Room temperature. I know. Like I said, I can't explain it."

The claw's cold suddenly pierced all the way to Alex's bones. She shuddered and dropped it back into the tray. Peeling off the gloves, she leaned around Joly and dropped them into the garbage bin beside Trent, meeting her partner's flat gaze before turning back to Bartlett.

"Anything else?"

Bartlett leaned back against the autopsy table in the center of the room and crossed his arms. "Just that it was lodged in the anterior side of the scapula. The shoulder blade."

"Anterior—you mean the front of it? As in—?"

"As in it had to get there from the front of the body. Through the chest cavity. And when I say it was lodged, I do mean lodged. It took me almost twenty minutes to pry the thing loose. Whatever put it there has one hell of a swing. Which reminds me: given the strength it would take to inflict this kind of damage, I think we can safely rule out any possibility the killer is female."

Alex stared at the coroner. "He cut through *bone*?"

Bartlett nodded.

"Maybe we should rule out the possibility he's human, too," she heard Joly mutter as he followed his partner and the assistant examiner into another room.

Alex sensed Trent's sudden stiffness from across the room, but ignored him in favor of glaring after Joly. Great. Now she'd be up all night with nightmares of some bizarre cat creature roaming the city. She massaged the back of her neck.

"All right. I'll let Roberts know about"—she waved her hand at the tray—"whatever it is. Call me when you have something more on it."

A CLAW.

Alex climbed the steps to the exit door and stepped out into the shadows of the buildings that blocked the evening sun's rays. A silent Trent followed close behind her, but to her everlasting relief, she felt no tingle at his nearness, no heightened awareness. The alley episode might have been hell on her nerves, but it seemed to have done for her hormones what no amount of internal lecturing had been able to achieve. Thank God.

A *claw*.

No such thing had been mentioned on the list of possible weapons for any of the murders. It had never even been hinted at. Probably hadn't been thought of. She opened the driver's door of the car and reached inside for the unlock button.

What was next, fucking Catwoman?

She leveled a hostile look at her partner across the roof of the sedan. And what the hell was with Trent's complete lack of reaction to all this? He hadn't displayed the slightest interest in either the claw or Bartlett's observations. Hadn't reacted at all until Joly's flip suggestion that the killer might not even be human.

Trent glowered back at her. "What?"

"Nothing." She slid behind the steering wheel. They'd

finished the task Roberts had set for them—well, she had, anyway—it was seven o'clock, she'd passed exhausted three days ago, and she refused to extend this day by a single second. Certainly not by participating in another of *those* conversations with Trent.

"So where am I dropping you?" she asked as he closed the passenger door behind him.

"Dropping me?"

"Roberts said we were done for the day once we'd seen the coroner. Is your vehicle at the office, or do you need a ride home?"

Silence met her query. Alex switched on the ignition, put the car into reverse, and looked sideways. Trent stared out the windshield, his face like carved stone. She squashed her curiosity like a bug.

Don't ask, her inner voice growled. *Don't you dare ask.*

She backed out of the parking space, drove to the exit, and then, when Trent still didn't seem prone to respond, prodded, "Well?"

"You shouldn't be alone."

Alex braked, sat for a moment, and then slid the gearshift into park. Maybe she should just resign herself to every exchange with this man turning into one of *those* conversations. Maybe expecting it would somehow make it easier.

"And why would that be?"

"If you did see the killer, then he saw you."

Alex's hands tightened on the steering wheel and she bit back a reminder that he had denied anyone else's presence in the alley. "So?"

"It's not safe for you to be alone."

The hard plastic grips imprinted ridges on Alex's palms. "I appreciate your concern, but even if he did see me, he doesn't know who I am or where to find me, and there's no reason to think he'd come after me specifically. His victims are random. He—"

"Trust me," Trent interrupted. "Once he realizes wha— who you are, he will come after you. You can't be alone."

She suddenly found herself replaying that afternoon's

scenario: the way Trent had turned as she'd come up behind him; had grabbed hold of her arms; the way he had shoved her back, away from the scene; the way he had sheltered her with his own body.

Stop, she told herself. *Stop now.*

But her voice took on a life of its own.

"You don't know that," she said. "You don't know him."

A harsh inhale from Trent's side of the car made her turn. She flinched a little from his white-hot fury, felt the iron control he wielded over himself, and, in a flash of intuition, recognized the anguish that underlay both. That underlay the man himself.

Because he did know the killer.

And it was personal.

Before the cop in her could react to the realization— before she could muster her thoughts or phrase her questions or demand answers—another part of her hijacked her thought process. A part that felt ageless and timeless, and made her earlier response to him pale into insignificance as she reached for his shoulder. Reached to comfort him, to relieve him of even a tiny part of the burden she sensed he carried.

Reached—and connected with something invisible. Soft. Warm.

Unmistakably feather-like.

The blood drained from her face. She snatched back her hand, clenched it into a fist in her lap, tore her gaze from Trent's, and turned again to the windshield.

Shit.

Fuck.

Fucking shit.

Nausea rolled in her gut, began to spread. Panic fluttered in its wake.

"Detective—" Trent began.

"Get out."

"Listen to me."

"Shut up. Shut up and get out." She bit down against the sickness rising past her chest, into her throat. *"Now."*

Trent hesitated for another second, and then opened his door and silently slid from the car.

BEFORE ALEX PULLED away, leaving him standing on the street, Aramael had already considered and discarded the idea of putting himself back in the vehicle without her knowledge. He didn't trust himself to stay hidden from her, or her not to sense his presence despite his best efforts. Neither could he allow her to be out there in the city on her own.

A touch of his hand unlocked the door of a dark gray sedan parked at the curb. Another touch fired the ignition. He didn't hesitate, didn't consider his actions. Knew only that he had to follow her. Caim would seize on an opportunity like this, might already be watching for it.

Aramael pulled off the side street and into the traffic, heading in the direction he'd seen Alex take. For a moment, he couldn't find her, and his heart turned to lead in his chest. Then he felt again the connection between them, the gossamer thread that ran from his soul to hers, fainter than it had been in the alley, but there. He traced it and found her car turning left at the intersection ahead. Sliding into the line behind her, he made it through on the same green light, and settled back into the driver's seat.

Only then did he think about the consequences of what he had done. He tightened his grip on the steering wheel and pressed down harder on the gas pedal as Alex accelerated ahead of him. Car theft. Another first for a Power. Maybe now the Highest Seraph would see fit to—

To what? The only possible option might be to have another Power join the hunt, and Aramael rejected the idea with a vehemence that threatened the wheel in his hands. It was too late for that. He could never tolerate another hunter going after his brother. Caim was *his*.

And so, Heaven help him, was Alex.

TWELVE

Alex stared at the tea cooling in the delicate, rose-patterned porcelain cup on the oak table before her, certain her cell phone would begin shrieking at her any minute now, a precursor to the Wrath of Roberts. As valued a detective as she knew herself to be in the unit, she harbored no illusions about how little her past performance would mean after the stunt she'd just pulled.

And abandoning Detective Jacob Trent at the coroner's office had been quite a stunt.

She moaned and dropped her head onto her forearm. Away from him, here in the haven of her sister's kitchen, her behavior took on even more bizarre overtones. She'd just left him there. Without a word of explanation or an offer to call another ride for him, she'd ordered him from the car and driven off. Let her paranoia get the upper hand and imagined—

What? What had she imagined? Wings on a man she didn't know but somehow recognized anyway? An electrical something that had shattered her reality when she reached out to him in that alleyway? The rage that flashed into his eyes, its awfulness overshadowed by the anguish that followed?

Or maybe she'd just imagined a desire to reach out to a stranger, to hold and be held, to chase away his demons along with her own.

Alex shuddered. None of what she'd seen or felt, or *thought* she'd seen or felt, made any sense. None of it was possible. Not in the context of the real world, anyway.

But in her mother's world . . .

A gentle hand ruffled Alex's hair. She kept her head down, absorbing Jennifer's quiet, healing presence as she had so many times before, trying to focus on the immediate problem instead of the cold fear that had replaced her core.

"Roberts is going to crucify me," she mumbled.

"Seeing as how you've been sitting here for twenty minutes and still haven't told me what happened, I'm hardly in a position to dispute that," came her sister's tolerant reply.

"You wouldn't believe me if I did tell you."

"So you keep saying."

Alex heard Jennifer set down the basket of laundry she'd brought from the laundry room, then pull out a chair from the table. From the corner of her eye, she watched her sister sit and take a T-shirt from the top of the pile, folding it with practiced ease.

Jennifer dealt with a half dozen items before she touched Alex's arm. "Come on, Alex. The last time you arrived on my doorstep looking like this was when what's-his-face told you he was married. What on earth is going on?"

"Thanks so much for that little reminder," Alex muttered. "And his name was David."

"It was three years ago. Water under the bridge. Now, are you going to tell me what happened or not?"

Head still down, Alex peered warily past her elbow at her sister. "Promise you won't go all psychologist-y on me?" she asked, referring to Jennifer's current studies at the University of Toronto. Proud as she was of Jen's decision to return to school after the divorce, she dearly wished her sister had chosen a program other than one that made her want to delve into others' psyches. Not that she blamed Jen for the choice. It was probably as much her sister's way of dealing with the past as Alex's work was for her. A past that, by some unwritten agreement, they never discussed.

Never needed to.

Until now.

"Scout's honor," Jennifer replied to her question.

"You weren't a Scout."

"Whatever. I promise. Now, out with it."

"I have a new partner—"

Jennifer slammed her fist down on the table, making the teacup dance in its saucer and Alex jump and raise her head. "Outrageous!"

"Jennifer."

"Sorry. Couldn't resist. Go on." Her sister snagged a pair of shorts from the laundry basket. "I take it you don't like the guy?"

Alex snorted. "He's an arrogant ass."

"But that's not the problem."

"No."

"You do know that having a conversation with you is a little like pulling hen's teeth, right?"

"Sorry." Alex lifted one foot onto the edge of her chair and rested her elbow on her knee, then threaded her fingers through her hair and watched the strands slide between them. "There's just something about the guy that rubs me the wrong way. And he seemed so angry with me when we met."

"Why would he be angry with you? Do you know him from somewhere?"

"No. Yes. I don't know."

Her steady brown gaze serious now, Jennifer sat back to regard her. "You either know him or you don't, Alex. You can't have it both ways."

"I don't. But I feel like I should."

In the silence that followed Alex's words, the clock numbers on the aged stove rolled over from 8:19 to 8:20 with a loud click. Forty-five minutes since she'd dumped Trent.

It felt like a lifetime.

"I see," Jennifer said at last. "Anything else?"

Alex stood and paced the hardwood floor from the table to the blue-painted cabinets and back again. "The guy keeps changing," Alex muttered.

"Excuse me?"

"I know it sounds ludicrous, Jen, but I keep seeing . . ."

"What?" Her sister's voice had gone tight.

Wings, Alex tried to say. But she couldn't. Couldn't bring herself to admit aloud the undeniable parallel to their mother. She couldn't do that to Jen. Wasn't ready to do it to herself.

"Nothing," she said. "It's nothing."

Jen visibly gathered herself, looking determined. "It must be something, or you wouldn't be here acting all weird and jumpy. Just tell me what's bugging you, for heaven's sake. It can't be *that* bad."

Alex wanted to tell her. Desperately. She needed to talk to someone before she went nuts just from thinking she was *going* nuts, but protectiveness surged in her as she looked into her sister's wary face. Several years Alex's senior, Jennifer had taken her in after their parents' deaths, and she hadn't just set aside her own life to raise her little sister, she'd also become the rock that anchored Alex through some pretty horrific years. She deserved better than to have her foundation shaken by Alex's sudden insecurities—at least until Alex knew for sure what was going on inside her own head.

So Alex made her shoulders shrug and her lips curve upward. "It's nothing. Really. I just think this case is getting to me, that's all. I'm sure a good night's sleep will help."

With luck, it would also provide inspiration on how to deal with the massive abandonment-of-her-new-partner problem she'd face in the morning.

"Well, if you're sure."

The relief in Jen's voice belied the concern that remained etched on her face, telling Alex she'd made the right decision. She picked up her cold tea and carried it to the sink, then turned to give Jen, now standing, a quick hug. "Thanks, Sis."

"I don't know what for, but you're welcome." Jen returned the hug. "Call me tomorrow and let me know how you're doing, all right? Better yet, come for dinner if you can. You haven't seen Nina in weeks."

"She'll be home on a Friday night? How'd you manage that?"

"We had a little incident and agreed it would be best if she took a couple of weeks off from some of her friends."

Alex held back a snort. She knew how difficult things had become recently, with Jen's divorce and the hormones running rampant through Nina's sixteen-year-old body, and she could just imagine the tone of such an *agreement*. "Something I can talk to her about?"

"Not right now, thanks. It was just a few missed curfews, so it's not even that serious, really. She's just testing me, that's all." Jen shook her head and sighed. "Hell, it was even church related, in a way, so how bad can it be?"

Church related? Alex wanted to ask more of her strongly atheist sister, but Jen's hard face told her now wasn't the time. She walked down the hall to the front door, Jen trailing in her wake, and paused there, hand on the knob. One question, she told herself. Just one to reassure herself.

"Jen?"

"Mm?"

"You don't think—"

"No." Jennifer cut her off, soft brown eyes darkened by the heavy, unnamed cloud that hung over them both. "Don't say it, Alex. Don't even think it. You're nothing like her. *Nothing.* Do you understand? You're just tired. You'll be fine."

Far from imparting reassurance, however, Jennifer's vehement denial sat, cold and heavy, in the middle of Alex's chest.

Right beside the realization that Jen had answered the question before Alex had even asked it.

* * *

ARAMAEL SHIFTED HIS weight against the tree trunk. The rough bark scraped through his suit jacket, chafing at his body even as the inactivity chafed at his mind. This standing about, this idleness, was interminable. Unforgiveable. He should be stalking the city streets, homing in on his prey, finding Caim.

He should not be standing here waiting for Alexandra Jarvis to emerge from the tidy, two-story house into which another woman had admitted her almost an hour ago. Shouldn't be wondering what she was doing in there. Who it was she spoke to. What she was saying.

Would she talk about what happened back there in the alley? Or the recognition that had flared between them? Or the way her hand had brushed his wing? Aramael resisted the urge to reach up to the spot she had touched, where a tingle still warmed the flesh beneath the feathers. He wrenched his thoughts back to the question of how much she might have figured out. If only she had a Guardian he could ask—

He ruffled his wings irritably. Hell, if she had a Guardian, he wouldn't be in this mess to begin with. Wouldn't be shackled by an obligation he'd wanted no part of in the first place and now found himself unable to surrender.

Wouldn't be torn between his purpose and a desire he should not—could not—feel.

His purpose. Did he even remember what that was? Did he remember that he existed only to hunt the Fallen Ones, to do what the rest of Heaven couldn't do, what none of them had the stomach for?

A tiny bird, black-capped and bright-eyed, flitted onto a branch near his head and regarded him with interest. Overhead, the evening sky darkened with premature gloom. Aramael glowered at the gathering clouds. A natural weather occurrence, or Caim at work again? His mouth twisted. He shouldn't need to even ask that question, damn it. He should be so attuned to his brother's energies that he knew exactly when Caim became active again, the very instant his brother targeted another mortal.

He should be, but he wasn't. Because a woman, a Naphil, had become more important.

The front door of the house opened and the bird departed in a flutter of feathers. Aramael drew back behind the tree as Alex emerged and descended the stairs toward the driveway, her jaw set and her face clouded. She passed by on the flower-bordered walkway, unaware of him, a bottomless weariness in her eyes. Reaching her vehicle, she stopped, back turned to him, and inserted a key in the door lock.

Notice me.

The thought slid through Aramael, unbidden, making his breath catch in his chest. The gossamer thread of awareness that stretched between them suddenly took on the strength of spider's silk, wrapping around him, entangling him in steely softness. The thought came again.

Notice me. See me.

He stared at Alex's abruptly taut back. Disbelief joined the seething mass that had once been coherence. She'd heard him.

But she couldn't have. He hadn't spoken aloud, couldn't have said what he hadn't even known he felt—

He stepped farther behind the tree as Alex turned. Felt her puzzlement, her indecision, the faint uneasiness that ran through her. He held himself rigid, waiting for her to decide she had been imagining things, to get into her car and leave so he could follow, undetected—

And then he felt Caim.

THIRTEEN

Caim watched the bloody heart quiver into stillness, life fade from blank, staring eyes. Distaste sat thick and bitter in his throat—not for what he'd done, but for how he'd done it. Killing without the rush of anticipation, the expectation that this might be the one he sought—fuck, what a letdown.

He scowled.

Fat raindrops began to fall, making tiny explosions in the blood pooled at his feet. There had to be a happy medium. Something between the passionless act he'd just committed in an effort to needle his hunter, and the impassioned one that would bring that hunter down on him in a heartbeat. He shook his head and wiped his hands on the mortal's jeans. He'd never before killed for the sake of killing. Never gone about the act without real purpose.

Sure as hell had never dreamed doing so would bring so little pleasure.

Caim turned his face toward the sky, squinting against the rain's increasing onslaught. *See? I'm not entirely beyond redemption,* he thought to her. *You would have known that if you'd just let me come home.*

No answer came. He hadn't expected one. She had never answered. Not once since he'd left. Not when he had begged her forgiveness; not when he'd professed remorse; not even when he had sworn his undying loyalty . . . if only she allowed his return.

Such was her love.

Unconditional, my ass.

He cocked his head to one side and made his thoughts go still. Nothing. No sense of impending pursuit. No frisson along his spine warning him of a Power's approach. Right, so now he had a baseline. Knew how much control was too much. He'd let go a little on the next, a little more each one after that, until he found the perfect balance: enough passion to incite Aramael's hunting instincts, and enough control to allow himself to withdraw to a safe distance before Aramael arrived. Enough that his brother wouldn't feel him watching, waiting for—

"Hey! You! What the hell are you doing?"

The shout ripped through Caim's skull, shredding his thoughts. A hand grabbed his shoulder and spun him around. Caim staggered, caught his balance, straightened to his full height, and extended his wings, bringing his focus to bear on his attacker. The man's eyes went wide. Caim reached for his throat. Then more loud voices. Clumsy, heavy steps. Grotesque shouts.

The man turned and fled. Caim saw a cluster of people running toward him. He hesitated. He could easily kill them all, but he could already feel his control slipping into the state where he would be unable to feel Aramael's approach and might not escape in time.

Hell.

He clenched his muscles against the urge to pursue the man. Flicked a last look at the approaching mob. Then, with a snarl, ramped up his energy vibration and left the scene.

ALEX FELL BACK against the car door as Jacob Trent exploded from behind the giant maple tree in her sister's front yard.

Even as her heart stuttered its shock, however, part of her wasn't surprised. Pissed, yes. But not surprised.

She focused on pissed.

"What the hell are you doing? Stalking me?"

"He's made another kill."

Alex's heart stalled. Christ, not again.

"Did you hear me?" Trent demanded.

Alex rubbed her hip where it had connected with the side mirror. She didn't want to answer him. Didn't want to believe him. Hell, if this kept up, she didn't think she even wanted to be a cop anymore. Not on this case, anyway, and sure as shit not with this partner. She stooped and snatched up her keys from where she'd dropped them. Metal ridges bit into her fingers.

She glared at Trent. Later, she'd have questions about how he'd followed her. Why he'd followed her. Why in God's name she felt a frisson of pleasure at the idea in spite of her anger. Right now, however, she *was* a cop, and no matter how much she might dislike his uncanny ability to feel the killer, she couldn't deny its existence. Not after this afternoon.

She unlocked the car. "Where?"

Heading around the vehicle, he pointed west. "And no, I can't be more specific," he growled. "Just drive."

Alex's cell phone trilled at her waist. Ignoring Trent's mutter of impatience, she pulled the phone from its case and flipped it open. "Jarvis."

"We have another," Joly's voice told her. "With witnesses. Lower Sherbourne at the Gardiner underpass."

Due west of where she and Trent stood. A spatter of rain hit Alex's cheek, another the hand she rested on the car. She met Trent's eyes across the car roof.

"Jarvis, you there?" Joly asked.

Nope. She really, really didn't want to be on this case anymore.

"We're on our way," she said.

Twenty minutes later, Alex pulled up beside a cluster of police vehicles, turned off the windshield wipers and the engine, and climbed out of the sedan into the exhaust-scented, headlight-lit underpass. She scanned the heavy equipment parked beside the scaffolding rigged for repair work on the hulking structure.

Trent slid out of the passenger seat. Alex turned her back on him. She'd made no effort to break the silence between them on the drive over and wasn't ready to do so now. Given the kinds of questions looming in her mind, it just seemed safer that way.

Not to mention saner.

She spotted Joly examining the ground beside a massive concrete pillar and headed toward him, leaving Trent behind.

"Well?" she asked. "Do we really have witnesses?"

The radio chatter on the way over had been fast, furious, and frustratingly conflicting. One witness, several witnesses, victim still alive, victim DOA—by the time she'd made it halfway here, she'd been ready to rip the radio out of its housing and toss it out a window.

"Witnesses, forensic evidence, guy running from the scene."

"Dogs?"

"For all the good it will do in this rain. They just got here."

"Where's Roberts?"

"Over there."

Joly nodded in the direction of the taped-off crime scene and Alex saw her staff inspector in conversation with one of the dog handlers. She looked down at Joly, who was crouched to turn over a clump of soil with his pen.

"You okay here?"

Joly straightened again and wandered around the pillar. He waved her off. "Go," he said. "Find clues. Catch the prick. Make sure he suffers in the catching thereof."

Roberts was alone when Alex joined him. He looked up from his notes and jutted his chin toward Trent. "So how's it going?"

That would have to be his first question. She thought

about how she'd abandoned Trent earlier and averted her gaze. "Fine," she lied.

Her staff inspector raised an eyebrow. "You are clear on the working it out part, right? I don't need a personality conflict getting in the way of this case, Alex. Especially not now."

How about a psychotic break with reality instead?

She nodded. "I know. We're good. So, where do you want me?" She saw his eyebrow lift again. "Us," she corrected. "Where do you want *us*?"

"The dogs are trying to pick up a trail, but it's not looking good. We're working on compiling a description from the witnesses, but so far our perp is every color from black to green, could be anything from an elf to a giant—"

"Elf?" Alex interrupted. That was a new one.

"Don't ask. About the only thing anyone can agree on is how he left the scene." Roberts scrubbed his hand over his short-cropped hair, a tension in his manner that she hadn't seen before. "Poof."

"Poof?"

Her staff inspector's gaze slid past hers and his mouth pulled another fraction tighter. "According to seven eyewitnesses," he said flatly, "our perp vanished into thin air."

The day before, Alex would have responded to that kind of statement with complete contempt. After lightning bolts and wings, however, she swallowed and kept her attention on the scene and very carefully did not look in the direction of her new partner. "I see," she murmured.

"I'm glad one of us does. Anyway, I put Bastion and Timmins in charge of the canvass—you and Trent can work with them. I'm heading back to the office to work on a press release. I don't want to see any of you until you've hit every door within ten blocks."

Wonderful. A canvass of that magnitude should only take them the better part of the night, Alex thought. But one look at the strain in Roberts's face and she decided to keep her opinion to herself. If she and the others were feeling the demands of this case, it was a thousand times worse for their

supervisor, who had to coordinate the investigation, keep a
rein on the press, and answer to every higher-up and politician in the city, if not the province. If Roberts wanted
a ten-block canvass, then that was what they'd give him.
Besides, it would keep her and Trent occupied. Perhaps
enough so that they wouldn't have to speak to one another.
She shivered.

Or touch.

CAIM STOOD TO one side of the group that had gathered
roadside to stare down on the murder scene. A gray car had
pulled up beside the police vehicles, and he watched first a
woman emerge, and then a man. His heart skipped a beat,
then began to race. It was him. It was Aramael—and the
woman from the alley.

The Naphil.

Anticipation lanced through his veins and his breathing
quickened. Beside him, a young woman looked at him
uneasily. Caim glared at her, then caught himself.

*Restraint. You can't draw attention to yourself. Espe-
cially not his attention. Not yet.*

He made his wings relax and formed his expression into
one of concern and compassion—or as close as he could
come, never having felt either—and then turned back to the
scene in the underpass below. The woman beside him settled
again.

Stupid bitch. Her Guardian would be doing backflips
right now, screaming at her to move, to get as far away from
Caim as she could possibly manage. But like most mortals,
she would have been taught to value thought over internal
voice, reason over instinct. Seeing no sign of the blood and
gore on Caim that he hid from human eyes, she would decide
no threat existed and shut out the immortal guide that might
one day save her life. Perhaps from someone like Caim.

He snorted. Really, he almost did the One a favor, taking
the lives he did. Useless, every one of them. A waste of
energy, better off returned to her greater life force. So arro-

gant in their presumption of their superiority, their invinci-
bility. Pathetic in their ignorance of the multiple layers of
the world they inhabited, the role they would play in their
own inevitable downfall.

Below, in the underpass lit now by floodlights, Caim
watched Aramael move away from the Naphil and pace the
taped-off police perimeter. Knew his brother searched for
lingering traces of energy. A tremor ran through him. He
thought again of the risks inherent in coming back to the
scene like this. If Aramael sensed him, if he looked up here
and saw him—

Caim stepped to the rear of the cluster of people and
paused to steady himself. It would never occur to the Power
that he might remain at a kill like this. Caim just needed to
stay calm, remember why he was here, stay focused on his
goal. He watched the woman stalk away from his brother.
How much did she know? Had Aramael told her she was
Nephilim? Did she know the Power protected her?

He studied the rigid, defensive lines of the woman's body
and the way she didn't look in Aramael's direction. He gave
a soft snort. Damned if she didn't look downright antago-
nistic toward his beloved brother. How intriguing.

Feeling a sudden shift in the energies around him, Caim
cast a sharp look in Aramael's direction and saw that the
Power had looked up toward the crowd with an expression
too watchful by far. Without hesitation, Caim turned and
walked away. He had more questions now than when he'd
started, but if there was one thing he had learned, it was
patience.

The thought made him smile. How ironic that the lessons
from his years in Limbo should stand him in such good stead
now. Even more ironic that Aramael had been responsible
for him learning those lessons.

He strolled down the roadway, shifted his energy vibration upward, and, in a blink, continued along an entirely
different sidewalk in the neighborhood of his residence. He'd
have to give some thought to his next move, he decided.
Random killings held limited benefit and, as he'd just dis-

covered, even less satisfaction. He needed a strategy. A way to make things more fruitful, more interesting, and definitely more enjoyable.

Caim rounded the corner onto the street leading to his appropriated residence. His steps slowed and he frowned at a car parked in front of what he'd come to think of as his home. An umbrella-sheltered female stood on the sidewalk beneath a streetlamp, with the air of someone who had knocked and waited now for a response to her summons.

Wings tensing, Caim hesitated. He could just bypass whoever it was and let her wander off when no one answered, but then he risked having her return. He could also simply deal with her—another murder this soon after the last might even irritate Aramael into lowering his guard, giving Caim some of the answers he needed.

Even as he debated the possibility, however, the woman turned toward him, moving the umbrella so the light from the streetlamp fell across her face. An unexpected heat tightened his groin. Oh, my, but she was lovely. He ran his gaze over her, from the confident tilt of her head to the way her suit followed the lines of a body that invited a man's attention. Demanded it.

Relaxing his wings again, he resumed his stroll, giving himself time to observe her. Admire her. Appreciate her. And consider a third option. He smiled and took his hands from his pockets, and then stepped up to greet her with a warmth not entirely feigned.

She wasn't quite what he'd had in mind when he'd thought to make things more enjoyable, but she would do nicely.

FOURTEEN

A lex found Trent standing to the left of the cordoned-off scene, his attention on a group of people clustered behind a concrete barrier at the roadside above them. No, not just his attention. That weirdly intense focus he had.

He turned his head as she walked toward him and, for a moment, his gaze seemed to skewer her in place, making her heart flutter in her chest like a captured butterfly. Alex's steps faltered. Then, eyes hardening, Trent turned back to the onlookers.

Damn, but she hated how he could do that to her.

Alex took a moment to remember how to breathe, watching her partner study the crowd. *Personality conflict, my ass.* Whatever there was between her and Trent, it was no mere conflict. Not that it mattered, because regardless of the issue—and whether it was real or imagined—she was still going to have to suck it up and deal with it.

And somehow find a way to keep it separate from the chaos that had become her psyche.

She adjusted her gun where it pressed into her hip bone, gathered her resolve, and picked her way across the uneven ground to Trent's side. She looked up at the vultures watching them, as always a little sickened by the way her fellow humans were drawn by another's tragedy. They should do her job for a while and see how fascinating they found death then.

"See anything?" she asked.

Trent said nothing for a second, then turned from his study. "No."

She hadn't thought he would. Their killer, if he had been in the crowd, would have caused a considerable stir, covered in blood as he had to be. Alex watched the cluster of people for another moment. Then, driven by a perversity new to her, she asked casually, "Feel anything?"

She sensed Trent's stiffening beside her.

"Are you making fun of me?" he asked.

The very quietness of his question sent a quiver down her spine. She swallowed.

"Of course not. I was curious, that's all."

"Then yes, I feel him."

"Ah." Alex turned her attention to a nearby Forensics member planting a numbered flag beside a shoe print.

Like I can feel you.

She jerked her head around to stare at Trent, startled at his boldness. "Pardon me?"

Trent's eyebrows twitched together. "I didn't say anything."

"You said— I thought I heard you—" She stammered to a halt. She'd thought she'd heard his voice back at her sister's house, too, just before he'd jumped out from behind that tree. Shit. That was twice. Winged hallucinations were bad enough—but voices?

A sickness stirred in her belly.

"Detective?" Trent's voice held an edge that might have been concern, but his face remained distant and watchful.

"Nothing," she said. "Roberts wants us to help canvass the neighborhood. I'll check in with Bastion and then we can get started."

She ducked under the yellow tape and strode toward a

closely shorn, rumpled detective standing over a body. *No voices,* she told herself. *You're not her. No way will you allow voices. Now, concentrate on the case and do your goddamned job.*

She arrived at Bastion's side. "Roberts said you're running the canvass. Where do you want me?"

Bastion flashed her a surprised look, then went back to his notes. "Greetings to you, too," he said dryly.

He was right; that had been pretty rude. Christ, she was tired of feeling so on edge that she couldn't function normally anymore. Alex grimaced. "Sorry. Long day."

The older detective shook his head. "Don't worry about it. We're all in the same boat. I was just giving you a hard time." He tucked his notebook into his inside jacket pocket and swiped his sleeve across his forehead. "This shitty weather isn't helping. Do you know that it was forty-three degrees Celsius with the humidity this afternoon? They're calling for even higher tomorrow."

With surprise, Alex noted the sweat trickling down her neck beneath her hair. She'd been too caught up fretting over Trent to pay attention before. "Gotta love Toronto summers," she agreed.

Bastion tugged a battered map from an outer pocket. "So. You and your partner want in on the canvass, huh?" He used his teeth to uncap a red felt pen. "I go' Penn an' Smiff workin' dish"—he slurred around the marker cap, stabbing at a circled area and leaving a red dot in its center—"an' Ab'ams and Joly ovah he'ah." Another red dot. "An' Timmins an' I wi' take dish." He dotted a third circle.

Lifting his left leg, Bastion braced the map against his knee and swiped a fourth circle, nearly toppling over in the process. He stood straight again, removed the cap from his mouth, and held the map out to Alex, his index finger hooked over it to point at another spot. "That leaves you and your partner with this neighborhood over here."

Alex peered at the wobbly circle, noting the streets that formed the generous boundaries. "Great," she said. "I'll see you back in the office in what, a week or so?"

"Now, now, Jarvis," Bastion chided. "If you're letting this case get to you already, it's going to be a long haul."

Alex forced a smile. He had no idea. "I know. I'm not nearly as bitchy as I sound, honest."

"Uh-huh." Bastion stuffed the crumpled map and the marker back into his pocket and ambled away.

Alex rolled her shoulders, trying to ease the tightness across her back. She knew without looking that Trent hadn't moved from where she'd left him. Nor had he once taken those intense gray eyes off her. She stretched until her shoulder blades almost met, feeling the crack and crinkle of things sliding back into—or perhaps out of—place.

She didn't want to rejoin him. Didn't want to face that accusatory glare with its strange vulnerability, didn't want to feel the responding flutter in her chest—or anywhere else on her person—didn't want to find herself searching his back and shoulders for evidence that she wasn't going mad. Or that she was.

She glanced absently down at the body by her feet: a man in his forties, just beginning to gray, his eyes staring up at nothing, his throat slashed as the others had been, his torso ripped apart.

A man in his forties.

Warning prickled up the nape of Alex's neck. In less than a heartbeat, she realized her mistake. She'd forgotten to brace herself, to take her usual precautions, to block out what she couldn't face again, what she should never have faced in the first place. Her throat closed. Memories shifted in the long-ignored recesses of her mind, then began rising to the surface. *Shit.*

She tried her damnedest to stop what she knew was coming, but her attempts shredded like tissue-paper boats adrift in a hurricane. Ruthless images stabbed at her, each leaving a new hole in her decades-old defenses.

"Bye, Jess!" she yelled, waving from the back door as *Jessica ran down the alley behind the house. She watched until her friend caught up with a group of girls, her heart twisting inside her. She'd wanted so much to invite Jess in*

today, wanted to bring her up to her bedroom to do home-work together and share her secret stash of bubble gum . . .

The girls looked back at her as one and dissolved into giggles. Alex felt her face burn. She pasted on a smile and made herself wave at them all, then turned and pushed the door open into the enclosed back porch. She'd wanted to ask her friend to stay, but she hadn't dared. She never dared. She knew what the giggles were for, knew what the others said about her—the kid with the crazy mother.

But Jess was different. Jess sat with her sometimes at lunch, and chose her for partner in class, and sometimes walked her home like she had today. Of them all, Jess was the only one Alex might consider bringing into the house. But not today. Not the way Mama had behaved this morning.

She'd known the minute Mama came into her room that it was a bad day. Mama had made her recite four psalms before allowing her to dress, and she'd been so rough with Alex's hair, pulling it into braids tight enough to cause tears, and all the while, she'd been talking to them.

Her angels, she called them. She even had names for them. Samuel, Rachel, Ezekiel. There were others some-times, but mostly just those three. Like this morning.

Alex slipped her sandals from her feet and tucked them beneath the bench. She'd been going to stay home—one of them always did on bad days, just in case Mama tried to do something silly, Daddy said, though he never told her what that might be. But this morning had been worse than usual, bad even for Mama, and Daddy had looked out from behind his paper and told Alex to hurry or she'd be late for school.

Even then she had hesitated, knowing it meant Daddy would have to take the day off work. Knowing they couldn't afford for him to do so. But Daddy had smiled and winked, and called her pumpkin, and slipped her some lunch money. With a kiss and a wave, she'd gone, although not without a stab of guilt.

A stab that returned now as she hung her school bag on the hook beside the back door. She hoped the day hadn't been too awful. Maybe she'd play chess with Daddy before dinner. He liked chess, especially when she managed to beat him, which she found kind of weird. Nice, but weird.

Alex opened the door between the porch and the kitchen, pausing by the basket of peaches ripening on the bench. "I'm home!" she called. No answer came and her hand hesitated, hovering over the peaches. "Daddy? Mama? I'm home."

The house waited for her, too still. A shiver went down Alex's spine. She withdrew her hand, leaving the peaches untouched, and stepped into the kitchen—

—and stumbled over her father's body and skidded in a puddle of cold, sticky blood and fell to her knees and stared into his vacant eyes and then, after almost forever, raised her gaze to the horror that had once been their kitchen.

Blood was everywhere. Soaking her father's shirtfront, pooled beneath him, streaked across the floor. A handprint stood in crimson contrast to the white-painted door frame and cheerful yellow wall where a round, indifferent clock marked the time at 3:45 p.m. Streaks of red led like a trail of bread crumbs toward the living room.

Alex climbed slowly to her feet and followed the trail. Past her father, past a chair overturned beside a smashed coffee cup, past the knife block and its scattered contents on the floor by the stove, down the hallway. She stared at the shoe-clad feet sticking out from the living room. At the legs, covered in blood, with a bright floral dress tangled about them. At the gaping slashes in the pale, pale wrists of arms reaching up for her, seeking an embrace, gore-streaked knife still in hand.

Her gaze moved up her mother's prone form to the fading, beatific smile, the lips forming words that came from a long, long way away.

"It's all right now, baby, it's all over. Mama fixed everything. You're safe now. Come pray with me, Alexandra, come pray with your mama."

A strong arm encircled Alex's shoulders, turned her away from the body, steered her insistently along a path she could not see, did not care about. Hands urged her back against a rough surface and guided her head toward her knees as the first wave of nausea hit. Held her there when she struggled to escape.

"Take your time," Trent said, his rumbling voice coming from a far-off place.

Alex resisted for a brief second, then gave in to the all-consuming roil in her gut. Great, wrenching spasms wracked her—finally, blessedly, derailing the memories. Allowing her to stop thinking, stop reliving.

Letting her avoid, for a little longer, the black hole yawning at her feet.

She remained doubled over long after the nausea receded, leaning against the concrete pillar, her hands resting on her knees. Gingerly she tested her spent body and her battered mind, surprised to find she still existed, might still be coherent, if not quite sane.

A handkerchief appeared before her and she stared at it. He would carry a handkerchief. With a shaking hand, she accepted the cloth, wiped her mouth, folded the fabric over, and dabbed at the water streaming from her eyes. Then she straightened, stepped away from the stench of vomit, and tucked the soiled wad into her jacket pocket. She lifted her gaze to Trent's, wanting to flinch from the too-astute watchfulness she met there, from the curiosity mingled with compassion, but refusing to do so.

She could survive this, she told herself. If she was careful to keep things where they belonged. Each issue in its own place, separate from the others.

Very, very careful.

"Thank you," she said, inserting into the two little words every note of warning she could manage. *Don't ask questions. Mind your own business. Don't you dare feel sorry for me.*

ARAMAEL HEARD THE defiance in Alex's voice as clearly as he did the embarrassment. He studied her for a long minute without responding, debating the wisdom of pursuing the matter. Every rigid line of her body screamed defensiveness, making him inclined to spare her further stress, but he read lingering torment there, too. In the protective droop of her shoulders; in the shadows underscoring her hollow eyes; in the tremor she could not conceal; in the way she tilted her head and looked away from him.

He scowled. This wasn't his forte. It wasn't his job. Hell, it wasn't even his business. He couldn't help wondering, however, if his presence here—and Alex's awareness of him—had somehow contributed to the meltdown he'd just witnessed. The possibility left him feeling a whole new level of responsibility for this fragile mortal woman.

Hell.

He shoved his hands into his pockets and looked down on her bowed head. "Want to tell me what's going on?" he asked quietly.

Alex looked up at him for an instant, and then away. "I'm sure you've seen this happen before," she said. She forced a hollow laugh. "I'm not the first cop to do it, and I doubt I'll be the last."

"No. This was about more than a body."

Alex was silent for so long he thought she wouldn't answer; swallowed so often he found himself watching the movement of her slender throat in fascination. Then her shoulders lifted in a quick shrug. The shrug of a child trying to pretend that life had no impact on her; of an adult denying the child had ever existed.

Aramael waited. If she chose not to answer, he'd leave it alone, he told himself. He had his hands more than full already. He didn't need to take on the role of psychologist as well, and chances were he'd just foul things up further for her if he tried. His kind weren't well-known for their temperate approach.

To anything.

"When I was a kid, I saw one similar to that," Alex said at last. She jerked her head toward the scene but fixed her attention on the ground before her. "I usually manage to block it out, but this one got to me. That's all."

She hunched her shoulders again and Aramael felt another tug of compassion for her. *Leave it alone,* he reminded himself. *Leave* her *alone.* Powers didn't deal with humanity on this level. Others did that. Others who didn't hunt. Who didn't carry out the One's dirty work so the mortal world could survive.

Others who were forever out of Alex's reach because of her Nephilim bloodline. Aramael sighed. Hell, he couldn't leave her like this. He had to at least try. "Detective—"

Alex's fair brows scrunched together. "That's *all*, Trent."

Part of Aramael didn't want to let the matter drop, suspected the importance of breaking through the barriers he sensed rising around her. A larger part of him, governed by his very nature, finally—belatedly—asserted itself. He stared into the dark beyond the floodlights. He would let it go, as Alex asked. As his existence demanded.

He'd just prefer he didn't have to cut away a vital element of his soul to do so.

FIFTEEN

Alex cast a weary look at her wristwatch and groaned. Almost eleven thirty. She and Trent had been canvassing their assigned sector for more than two hours without a break. No wonder her feet hurt and her belly grumbled.

She plucked at the shirt clinging between her breasts. Despite the earlier rain, the heat hadn't abated in the least and thunder growled again in the distance. She glowered at the bluish glimmer of sheet lightning behind the clouds, and then looked down the sidewalk.

Interior lights had gone out in most of the homes, but a glow still crept out from behind curtains and blinds in some. Apart from her and Trent, who stood bathed in neon orange beneath an all-night corner store's sign, the only other person out of doors was an elderly man waiting patiently for his terrier to complete its business at the base of a garbage can. For all intents and purposes, the neighborhood's rhythm had continued as if the evening's murder had never occurred, as if two homicide detectives hadn't just wasted an entire evening pursuing wishful thinking.

About the only good thing to have come of this exercise,

Alex reflected, was the time it had given her to get her act together. It had been far easier to put things back into perspective here, tramping up and down endless, narrow flights of stairs in elevatorless buildings, than it would have been alone at home with too much time to think.

She'd managed to return certain demons to the mental closet where they belonged, but she didn't delude herself that the peace would last. Like it or not, at some point she'd have to deal with what she'd spent the last twenty years trying to ignore. For now, however . . .

She shot a dark look at Trent, who had turned aloof after her embarrassing display at the crime scene, and then proceeded to grow ever more surly as their evening wore on. At last her patience had reached its limits and she told him, as pleasantly as she could manage through gritted teeth, to just wait for her while she knocked on the last few doors at the end of the street. Now that she'd finished, however, she would have preferred to face a hundred more doors rather than drive back to the office with him.

Her eyes lingered on Trent's broad shoulders and she felt a tingle at the memory of the hard, muscled arm that had gone around her at the construction site, leading her away from the victim, holding her against a solid, sculpted chest. She let her gaze slide lower, until it rested on Trent's flat stomach. Wondered if his stunning musculature extended to that part of his anatomy . . . or any other.

Heat flared low in her belly and scorched her cheeks, like the aftermath of a slap in the face. A well-deserved slap. Fantasies about her partner? Christ, that was all she needed. Next thing she'd be imagining the two of them—

Stop.

Gritting her teeth and shoving her unruly hormones as far from mind as she could manage, Alex scanned the quiet street a final time, noting that the man with the terrier was gone, leaving the street deserted between her and Trent. Footsteps hollow in the night air, she started toward her partner. The sooner they headed back, the sooner she could get away from Trent and get a few hours' peace, if such a thing were possible after her little episode. So many memories after so many years . . . Her insides jittered and she cinched her self-control a little tighter.

Over and done with, Alex. You remembered, you survived, now let it go again.

A barely there sound caught her ear.

Alex stopped midstride, cocked her head, and listened.

A hundred normal summer noises floated through the muggy, ozone-scented night: the steady hum of dozens of window air conditioners, a distant siren, the rumble of a truck the next street over, a baby's wail, a television. Against the familiar soundtrack, however, there had been something else. Something that hadn't belonged.

One by one, she filtered out the ordinary sounds until nothing remained. Waited.

Heard it again.

A soft scrape. A rustle. She whirled and scanned the sidewalk behind her. Her gaze settled on a narrow, inky-dark gap between buildings. She retraced her steps, stopping at one side of the opening. A quick glance around the corner showed nothing except the blaze of a floodlight at the opposite end of a long, narrow passageway—maybe four feet wide at most, and impossibly black.

Thunder rolled again, closer, more menacing, and the hairs on the back of Alex's neck lifted. She patted her pockets on the chance she'd stashed her mini-flashlight in one of them, but found no familiar metal cylinder. Damn.

She listened. Not a sound. It was probably nothing. An animal, or a kid avoiding curfew, maybe. The possibility their killer had remained in the area this long was almost nil. The guy was far too cautious for that kind of mistake.

But she couldn't take the chance.

She looked over her shoulder. Besides, this would be the perfect opportunity to show a certain someone the *right* way to handle going into an alley: as a team. She gave a short, low whistle to get Trent's attention.

Her partner turned his head and she held a finger to her lips, pointing with her other hand toward the passageway.

Trent took his hands from his pockets, his posture straightening as he came alert. He started toward her.

Alex divided her attention between listening for more movement and watching Trent's approach. When only a few feet separated them, she rested her hand on the grip of her nine-millimeter pistol and stepped into the inkiness, the musty odor of old, damp building foundations rising around her. She stood for a few seconds to let her eyes adjust to the dark, but the brilliant floodlight at the other end continued to blind her.

Trent's footsteps stopped behind her. Instantly, her entire body tuned to his presence, burying her cop's instinct under an avalanche of tightened skin, heightened pulse, and quickened breath.

"Shit," she muttered. So much for sensing anyone else who might be near.

"Detective?" Trent's voice sounded muffled and oddly flat.

"Quiet for a second," Alex whispered back. She felt her way along the narrow passage, the brick rough beneath her touch. If she put some distance between her and Trent, maybe—

A shoe scraped against loose stones and then she heard the unmistakable, metallic *snick* of a switchblade. She flung up her hand, unable to see the attack, but knowing it was coming.

"Knife!" she yelled. White heat seared her forearm. She lunged to the side, grunting as cheek and palms impacted the brick wall. Thrusting upright again, she fought for her bearings against a wash of pain and fumbled for her gun. Struggled to see her invisible assailant, a shadow among shadows.

She heard him grunt and braced herself for another attack, and suddenly felt herself lifted from her feet and flung aside. Her head connected with brick and pain lanced through her skull. She forced herself upright, light exploding in the backs of her eyes, and stared in disbelief—tinged with horror—at the scene unfolding before her.

Fire lit the night. Golden flames, so brilliant they almost blinded her, with Trent at their center. Trent, standing in the mouth of the passageway, with powerful wings spread behind him. Trent, raising his hands, palms forward, his face filled with a terrible wrath.

And then a man's body sailing backward, like a rag doll fired from an invisible cannon.

Alex's world went dark.

"VERCHIEL!"

Mittron's roar reverberated through the great library, silencing the mutterings and whispers that followed Verchiel up the sweeping staircase. Verchiel paused, her foot on the top step, and looked down at the angels clustered in the main hall. They stared back at her, round eyed and openmouthed. From Second Choir Cherubim to Eighth Choir Principalities, each was as stunned as the next by what had just happened in the mortal realm. By what Aramael had done.

Verchiel pressed her lips together and turned her back on the gathering below her. She eyed the long gallery stretching before her and, beyond that, the hallway leading to Mittron's office. With an uncharacteristic lack of charity, she considered making the Highest wait—and stew—for a few minutes more. After all, she *had* told him that sending Aramael on this hunt was a bad idea, and she wasn't above feeling a little smug about being proved right.

"Ver—chi—el!"

Verchiel winced. Another bellow like that and the venerable old library might very well collapse around their ears. She removed her hand from the stair rail and slid it into the folds of her robe with its partner. The important thing, she reminded herself as she started toward the Highest Seraph's office, was to decide what they would do next, not to indulge in a petty game of "I told you so." Besides, if she were completely honest, she knew that, regardless of her reservations, not even she could have predicted this outcome.

Mittron paced the hallway outside his office, stopping

when he saw her, his amber eyes accusatory. "You felt what happened?" he demanded.

She sighed. "Was there a corner of the universe that didn't?"

Mittron glared at her. "I do not appreciate flippancy, Dominion."

She inclined her head in wordless apology and bit back the impulsive, *Then perhaps you should have heeded my counsel*, that hovered on her lips. After paying so little attention herself to today's earlier warning signs, she had no room to criticize. She could, and should, have done far more than simply consider the problem as she had.

The Highest's eyebrows slashed together. "He attacked a human. Turned the power of Heaven itself against one of the very beings the One has charged us to protect. Need I remind you of the consequences if the mortal does not survive?"

Verchiel leaned against the wall and closed her eyes. "No, Highest."

No angel needed reminding of the consequences should the agreement between Heaven and Hell be broken. They had all witnessed the conflict between the One and Lucifer over the mortals, had seen the love between the universe's two greatest powers ripped apart by jealousy and betrayal. For four and a half thousand years, they had all tiptoed around the fragile contract that stood between those powers and a war that would decimate humanity.

Mittron's footsteps passed Verchiel, turned, approached again, and then stopped. She opened her eyes to find him standing before her.

"What are you going to do?" he asked.

Not what are *we* going to do, Verchiel noticed, but *you*. She tightened her lips. What the Highest lacked in interangelic skills, he more than made up for in his ability to evade responsibility when things didn't go according to plan. The longer she wasn't soulmated to him, the more she wondered how she ever could have been.

"We could recall him."

"You know nothing short of the One's own voice can end a hunt before it is finished."

"Does the One know what has happened?"

"As you so aptly observed, the entire universe knows."

Meaning that the One knew and, for unknown reasons, wished the hunt to continue. Verchiel hoped it also meant the One had far greater insight into the matter than she did, because from where she stood, a decision not to interfere did not bode well. She straightened away from the wall, but couldn't quite coax her shoulders out of the slump that plagued her these days.

"Then I suppose I will have to speak with him," she told the Highest. *Again.*

ARAMAEL HEARD THEM before he saw them. Alex's voice, curt and inflexible. Another woman's response, reverberating with exasperation. Both sliced through his thousandth grim review of the evening's events. The impossibility of what he had done.

A shudder jolted his core. Even as his mind tried to disengage from the memory, his soul could not forget the force of the power he'd released against a mortal. Inconceivable, inexcusable—words could not begin to describe the wrongness of what he had done. His unprecedented, unforgivable loss of control.

Alex's voice drew nearer, and louder. Aramael glanced across the nearly full waiting room to where Roberts stood at the coin-operated coffee machine. He met the other man's resigned gaze. With a wry twist of his mouth, Roberts offered his untasted cup of coffee to an elderly man in a wheelchair, then crossed over to join Aramael.

"Sounds like we're driving her home."

"But she's hurt."

The staff inspector grunted. "You tell her that."

They turned as the doors beside the reception desk swung open and Alex stepped out of the examination area, her face pale and set. She stalked toward them.

Aramael tensed, bracing himself for the worst. He had no idea what Alex had seen in the passageway, and therefore no idea of what to expect from her now. When she'd regained consciousness after only a few seconds—seconds that had felt unnervingly like an eternity—she'd asked only a single, terse question about her attacker. Then, on finding out the man still lived, she had settled into stony silence, her hand clamped over the gaping wound in her left arm, refusing Aramael's assistance. Refusing to so much as meet his eyes.

Continuing to do so now.

Aramael grimaced. He supposed he could hope her hostility stemmed from the day's events in general, but he wasn't that naïve. No, Alex Jarvis had seen more than she should have, and now he needed to find a way to alleviate the harm he had caused.

The additional harm.

A stocky, middle-aged nurse stomped through the doorway behind Alex, clipboard in hand and voice raised in objection. "Detective Jarvis, be reasonable. All we're suggesting is a few hours of observation."

Alex's face darkened. She planted herself in front of Roberts. "Will you please tell this woman I don't need observation?"

Roberts looked over her head. "How is she?" he asked the nurse.

Alex's glare turned murderous.

"I'm fine," she snapped.

"She has a headache—" the nurse began.

"Of course I have a headache. I whacked my head on a goddamn brick wall!"

In spite of himself, Aramael felt the corner of his mouth twitch. He'd barely registered the phenomenon—a Power feeling humor?—when Alex's gaze flicked to him, intensified, and moved away again. He narrowed his eyes. There had been something ugly in that look. Something more unsettling than having her ignore him.

"—and a mild concussion," the nurse finished, setting her hands on her hips and returning Alex's defiant look.

"Plus twenty-three stitches in her arm. We want to keep her here for a few hours just to make sure she's all right."

"Alex?" Roberts asked.

"No." Alex crossed her arms, paled, and uncrossed them again, cradling the bandaged one against her.

"You need observation," the nurse huffed.

Alex's lips compressed. Pain had etched itself into the tight lines about her mouth and cast a haze over her eyes. Apparently it also brought out her stubborn side.

"I *need*," she said through clenched teeth, "to go home."

The two women glowered at one another. Conversation in the waiting area ceased as the other patients watched the argument unfold in their midst.

"What if someone stays with her?" Aramael asked.

Alex stiffened. "I don't need a babysitter."

She directed her words to Roberts, wordlessly rejecting Aramael's very presence, back to behaving as if he didn't exist. Aramael's mouth tightened. Damage control would be challenging.

Roberts looked askance at the nurse. "Would that do? Having someone stay with her?"

"I don't need—" Alex growled.

The nurse turned her back on Alex and spoke to Roberts. "We'd prefer to keep her here, but I suppose that would do."

"Alex?" Roberts asked.

Aramael watched Alex wrestle with her loss of independence, her expression running the gamut from denial to grudging acceptance. At last she heaved a sigh.

"Fine. *Now* can I go?"

"I'll get the discharge papers ready," the nurse said. "You'll have to sign yourself out against our advice."

"Whatever."

The nurse stalked back through the doors by the reception desk, her back rigid with disapproval. With the argument resolved, the other patients in the waiting room lost interest and returned to their own business. Alex glared at Roberts.

"I don't need you to stay with me."

"I'm not. I have to write up the file on this and submit it to the chief before morning. I'll call your sister—"

"No!"

A few heads turned their way again. For the first time, Alex seemed to notice that they weren't alone in the waiting room and lowered her voice. "I don't want to worry Jennifer. A good night's sleep—"

"Forget it, Jarvis. I'm not taking any chances, especially after a head injury. You either have someone stay with you at home, for the night, or you stay here. Your choice. And yes, that's an order."

"You can't make me stay—"

"Actually, I can," Roberts interrupted. "And if I need to, I'll put a uniform outside your door to prove it."

"But—"

"I'll stay with her," Aramael said. He watched Alex go still. Knew she wanted to refuse his offer but had no other options. Waited for her to reach the same conclusion.

Alex nodded, a single, curt incline of her head, and looked up at him at last.

"Thank you," she said.

Her eyes did not echo the gratitude.

SIXTEEN

Alex sat in silence as Trent negotiated the corner onto her street and drove through the sleeping neighborhood. They had exchanged neither word nor glance during the twenty-minute ride from the hospital. Roberts had issued directions to Trent before they left and the man had followed them unerringly, leaving her to sit beside him, separated by a few inches that might as well have been an unbreachable chasm.

Leaving her time to relive yet again the moments in the alley; to try to convince herself that her version of events hadn't happened. Couldn't have happened. Just as Trent couldn't have wings, just as those bullets couldn't have passed through him this afternoon, just as she couldn't keep having that insane, visceral reaction to him.

Alex ground her teeth together. She was tired of going in these same circles over and over again, trying to rationalize what she'd seen and felt, trying to find—or create—an acceptable explanation. Trying to ignore the whisper of possibility that she was perfectly sane, and there were things in play here that were—

She pressed fingertips between eyebrows, slamming the brakes on her unfinished thought as Trent pulled into the driveway. Fuck, ideas like that made her question her sanity more, not less. She tried to think past the pounding in her skull, to find a way out of the endless loop in which she was trapped.

Maybe she should just pretend that none of it had happened. Maybe she could start fresh in the morning, hoping against hope that her world would have returned to normal, that all of this would be relegated to the status of a bad dream. Maybe that smack on the head had been harder than she realized, and—

Alex paused, contemplating the last idea.

As excuses went, that one might actually work. Any hit hard enough to knock a person out was bound to scramble things somewhat. The explanation didn't work for the entire day, but right now she'd settle for rationalizing any small portion at all, and the idea *did* fit with what the others believed had happened in the alley.

Trent slid out of the vehicle.

Lightning, they'd said. A freak bolt that found its way between the buildings to the knife in her assailant's hand, its energy enough to knock her from her feet. Lightning from the sky, not an invisible blow from a man standing amid golden flames, his face dark with anger, his wings outstretched—

Alex suppressed a shiver. Lightning. Just lightning, and the hospital had assured them her attacker would live. Even if the doctors couldn't explain why there hadn't been a mark on him. No hint of a scorch mark, no singed hair. Instead, all the damage had been internal: bruised organs, internal bleeding, massive fluid retention.

All of which he would survive.

The car door opened beside her, making her jump. She stared up at Trent for a moment, then, with a small, tight shake of her head, rejected his assistance and levered herself out of the seat with her good arm. No matter how rational she wanted to be, she still couldn't accept his touch.

Couldn't forget the brush of her fingers against unseen feathers.

She shivered in spite of the night's mugginess. Crossing the lawn, she made the short climb to the unlit, covered front porch that stretched across the face of her older home. The steady trill of crickets filled the night, unbearably loud to a head that already felt like a hundred strong men with sledge-hammers had taken up residence in it. Her arm throbbed ten times worse than her head, and her scraped hands burned like blazes. So did her cheek, for that matter. She hurt in so many places, in fact, that she'd given up keeping track.

And that was just the physical pain.

Alex gritted her teeth. No, she told herself. She would not deal with the other stuff right now. Not tonight. Tonight she had reached every limit she knew she had, and exceeded others she'd never dreamed existed. She'd had enough for one day. Enough voices, enough hallucinations, enough memories.

Enough, in truth, not for a day, but for a lifetime.

Supremely conscious of Trent's presence behind her, she crossed the porch and turned to hold out her hand for her keys. Trent reached past, unlocked the door, and pushed it open.

For a long moment, Alex stood without moving. She wanted to believe it was independence that kept her from going inside rather than trepidation, but a fine film of sweat on her forehead and the jitter in her gut said otherwise. She did not want to spend hours alone in the house with this man. Didn't want him imprinting his presence on her home, leaving behind traces of his warmth, his scent.

"I really am fine, Detective Trent. You don't need to stay." She bit the inside of her bottom lip. Had he heard the same traitorous quiver in her voice that she had?

If so, he didn't comment on it. He didn't say anything, in fact, just stretched his arm into the house and switched on a light, making Alex blink in the sudden brilliance. Then he waited, face devoid of expression, arms crossed. Long seconds ticked by.

Alex's arm throbbed, her imagined chill settled deeper into her bones, and she felt herself sway. She bit down harder on her lip to distract herself, but knew if she insisted on continuing this standoff, she stood a good chance of passing out on the spot. Which would result in Trent staying *and* involve the touching she wanted to avoid.

She stepped past him into the house.

Trent moved into the living room, turning on more lights as he went. Another hundred men joined the sledgehammer ranks inside Alex's head.

Trent returned to the front hall and frowned at her. "You're in pain."

"That generally happens when some asshole slices open your arm and shoves you into a brick wall," she agreed. Then she regretted her sharpness. The man was hardly responsible for the twisted state of her sanity, and he *had* volunteered to babysit her tonight so that she could leave the hospital and come home—the least she could do was be civil.

"I'm sorry," she said.

"Trust me," he replied cryptically, "you're not the one who should be sorry."

She blinked at him, decided he must mean her assailant, and shrugged. "He'll pay the price," she said. "He already has, in a way. You don't get retribution much more divine than lightning, after all."

A shadow darkened Trent's eyes. Guilt? Over what— dishing out the retribution in question? Alex gave an inward sigh. There she went again, blurring reality with the dark goings-on in her psyche.

Trent shoved his hands into his pockets. "Can I get you anything? Tea? Something to eat?"

Her stomach revolted at the very suggestion. "God, no," she muttered. "But thanks. I'm going to take a shower. Help yourself to whatever you'd like. The kitchen is that way." She pointed toward the back of the house. She crossed the foyer to the staircase leading to the second floor and con-templated the climb ahead of her. She desperately needed to wash this day from her body, but that was a *long* way up.

"What about your stitches?"

Hell. Alex remembered the list of instructions issued by the nurse, the first of which had detailed how she was not, under any circumstances, to get her stitches wet for twenty-four hours. Her head drooped.

"Maybe we could cover them," Trent suggested.

The gentle note in his voice surprised her. The sudden lump that formed in her throat in response surprised her even more. She swallowed twice before her vocal cords cooperated enough to tell him where to find a plastic garbage bag, scissors, and tape. Then, when his firm tread had faded down the hallway, she sagged onto the stairs, rested her pounding forehead on her knees, and tucked her arm against her side.

The drugs they'd given her at the hospital had taken the edge off the pain, but that was all, and for the first time, she regretted refusing the additional medication the nurse had tried to press on her as she was leaving. Pharmaceutical oblivion held a certain appeal at this point.

Alex released a shaky breath. No. The last thing she needed right now was drug-induced hallucinations. Her mouth twisted. As opposed to the ordinary ones, for instance.

The hammering in her head settled into the same rhythm as her heartbeat. In the living room, the mantel clock chimed a soft three times. Already? Hell, even with Roberts pushing back the task force meeting until noon, she'd be lucky to get three or four hours before the alarm went off.

Trent's returning footsteps sounded. Alex gathered herself, lifted her head, and held out her hand for the supplies he carried. Trent's eyebrow rose. She bristled, and then slumped. He was right. It would take her forever to wrap her own arm, and she couldn't hope to do it well enough to keep her wound dry. She had no choice but to accept his help.

And that bloody touch.

Trent squatted in front of her, set the tape and scissors on the bottom step, and unrolled the white plastic garbage bag. Alex turned her head away and raised her arm. She wondered if he, too, remembered the overwhelming electricity that had surged between them. Wondered what he would think if he knew how she'd stared at him that evening, what she'd imagined. She braced for the feel of his hand.

Trent slid the bag over her arm, snipping off the bottom to fit it over her hand, his fingers gentle and jolt-less. Alex exhaled in relief. She looked down at his bent head as he unrolled a length of tape and clipped it off. He seemed so normal right now. Like a concerned colleague, and not some angel of wrath—

Trent looked up at her twitch. "Did I hurt you?"

Alex compressed her lips. Why did she keep doing that to herself?

"I'm fine," she muttered.

Trent returned to his task, his movements reassuringly impersonal. Alex watched, still half expecting wings to sprout and send her world somersaulting out from beneath her again, but his shoulders remained solid and unchanging, and a tiny knot of tension unraveled in her belly.

He wrapped a long piece of tape around the top of the plastic and secured it just above her elbow. Everything about him seemed . . . normal. Not ordinary, exactly—no man who looked the way he did could ever be ordinary—but normal in the sense of not weird or bizarre. Normal in the sense of real.

Human.

A wry thought occurred to her. Maybe that whack on the head had been a blessing in disguise. Maybe it hadn't scrambled her brains after all, but had instead knocked some sense into her, made it possible for her to put things in perspective.

Or maybe it was just the drugs.

"You look amused."

Alex realized Trent was watching her. Without thinking, she shook her head, sending an extra crash of pain through her already-aching skull. "Hell—I have to remember not to do that," she murmured, cradling her forehead in her hand and waiting for the reverberations to die down.

"Do you have something you can take for the pain?" Trent asked.

"Upstairs. I'll take it when I go up for my shower." She felt him wrap another piece of tape around her arm and smooth it into place. "Trent—"

"Mm?"

She hesitated. She'd had a sudden urge to apologize to him, but for what? Her imagination? Her paranoia? And what would she say? *I'm sorry I keep seeing you as a really angry angel*? Oh, yes, that was sure to erase any bad impressions made so far. And *I'm sorry I have the hots for you* would be about as good.

"Nothing."

Trent looked up at her, his gaze assessing, then returned to his ministrations. He applied several more strips of tape to seal his handiwork and, a minute later, gathered up the remaining supplies.

"That should hold well enough."

"Thank you."

He rose to his feet and held out a hand to her. Alex hesitated for only the briefest of moments before accepting it and letting him draw her to her feet. A frisson of warmth slid through her, less than the jolt she had experienced from him earlier, but more than she had the right to feel from her new partner. With or without wings, Jacob Trent packed a powerful aura.

Alex withdrew her hand from his grasp and offered him a shaky smile—and herself a stern reminder about the dangers inherent along that particular path. "I mean that, Trent. Thank you. I guess I did need some help tonight after all."

"Believe me," he said quietly, "it was the least I could do."

Alex felt her smile falter. She had the sense that his words held some greater meaning, but her brain shied sideways from any kind of analysis. She'd just started to get things *un*scrambled, and she would very much like them to remain that way. At least for a while. With an effort, she found her voice.

"I think I'll take that shower now."

SEVENTEEN

Aramael placed the tape and scissors into the drawer with careful precision, slid the drawer closed again, and then paused, staring at his outstretched hands. His traitorous, treacherous hands. Hands that had tended a mortal's arm but had wanted—coveted—so much more.

He curled his fingers tightly into his palms and watched his knuckles whiten. Somewhere, somehow, in the process of looking after Alex, his awareness of her had grown. Become more than some ethereal connection. Become . . . physical.

The scent of her hair, the warmth of her breath on his cheek, her proximity itself had triggered a longing in him that set every fiber of his being aflame, touched off an intensity of sensation so acute that the very texture of her skin had imprinted itself on his soul. Aramael's belly clenched and his entire body thrummed with pent-up energy—a foreign, nearly living force he had no idea how to handle.

Physical desire for a mortal. In all his years, he had never experienced an agony quite so complete, quite so . . .

Exquisite.

"Bloody Hell!" His harsh curse echoed in the empty kitchen. He leaned his fisted hands on the counter and hunched his shoulders against the quiver coursing through his center—and the ache underlying it. An ache born of a need so raw he thought it might have the capacity to redefine him.

He eased his head back against the strain building in his neck. At least this time he hadn't been completely caught off guard by his reaction to her, had managed to endure his feelings without projecting them. Doing so had taken a toll, however. A much greater toll than he would have imagined, if he could ever have imagined it at all.

Exquisite agony.

He stared at the ceiling. First his attack on the mortal man, and now this. He dreaded what might come next. Above him, footsteps crossed the floor, and water began to run. Alex, getting into the shower.

A newborn imagination snaked to life, conjuring an image for which nothing in the universe could have prepared him: Alex, her long hair caught up, her slender neck and shoulders exposed, stepping naked under a cascade of water; her skin, smooth, slick, glistening with a thousand tiny water beads. Alex, tipping her head back to let the water cascade over her face, pivoting under the spray, rivulets sliding down her back, her waist, her hips . . .

"Well," a voice said, shattering the image in his mind as suddenly as it had formed. "Of all the things I might have expected from this hunt, this certainly wasn't one of them."

Verchiel.

Aramael whirled to face her and hot, liquid humiliation washed over him at the idea of the Dominion bearing witness to his internal struggle. What had merely clenched in his belly before now twisted into a defensive, angry knot. "My thoughts are none of your business, Dominion," he snarled.

Verchiel eyed him, looking puzzled, and then intrigued. "What thoughts?"

With a rush of irritation, Aramael realized he had misinterpreted her presence and piqued a curiosity with which he preferred not to deal. He put Alex from his mind and pulled together his fractured center, and then leaned against the counter, arms crossed.

"Never mind," he told the Dominion. "You're here about the mortal."

"The one you attacked, yes."

"A mistake."

Verchiel raised a delicate, silver-white brow. "Your second mistake today," she pointed out, her voice no less tart because of its mildness. "The very fact that you struck a mortal, Aramael . . . we'll be lucky if you haven't already precipitated matters."

Aramael scowled at her. He needed no reminding of the One's pact with Lucifer. Or that, if the mortal had died, Aramael's actions would have allowed Lucifer to toss aside the agreement in its entirety, and could very well have resulted in all-out war between the loyal and the Fallen. Might already have done so even if the mortal lived.

But he was damned if he'd take full blame.

"No," he said. "You do not get to pass judgment on me for Mittron's arrogance, or for your own complacence. You know as well as I do that something is wrong here, but rather than find out what it is, you're behaving like a puppet, doing no more than what you're told to do."

"I'm following orders, Aramael. It's what we do."

"Then maybe we need to do more."

Dismay crossed the Dominion's face. "You don't mean that."

His words were tantamount to blasphemy, Aramael knew. No angel had the free will to act on his or her own. Not since so many had exercised that will in following Lucifer. He half expected instant reprisal, the rush of Archangels' wings, but felt nothing but irritation at himself. Of course Heaven's enforcers weren't coming for him. They answered not to Mittron, but to the One, who wouldn't even have noticed Aramael's transgression just now because her presence in her angels' lives had been noticeably lacking for the last several millennia.

Which was why Mittron got away with this arrogance in the first place.

Aramael levered himself away from the counter and stalked toward Verchiel, stopping when she took a step back. He lowered his voice to a growl. "Bloody Hell, Dominion, just for a moment, think for yourself. If I'm to protect Alex and complete this hunt, I need to know what's going on. Have you even tried to find out why she can see me? Is it because she's Nephilim?"

Not only did Verchiel not reply, she wouldn't even meet his gaze. Aramael's irritation surged, and then he realized that the Dominion didn't avoid him but instead stared past him, her eyes wide with dismay. For the span of a heartbeat, Aramael wondered if he might have underestimated Mittron; then, in almost the same instant, he knew he faced something far worse than potential Judgment.

Verchiel withdrew from the room, from the realm, her final words, whatever they might have been, fading with her. With no similar escape available, and because he had no choice, Aramael turned to confirm what his instinct, his heart, already knew.

Alex stood in the doorway to the hall, her skin glowing from her shower, damp tendrils of hair escaping the twist on top of her head to cling to her neck. A white terry cloth bathrobe fell in soft folds to skim her ankles. She looked beautiful, fragile, and utterly panicked.

Aramael felt it then. Felt her awareness of *him*. Keenly. Decisively. Knew she saw him not as another mortal, but in all his angelic glory.

For long, agonizing seconds, he stood frozen, unable to react, bared to Alex in ways he had never imagined, vulnerable in ways he could not explain. Until at last Alex blinked and, far too late, the curtain of celestial duplicity slipped between them once more.

Alex slid to the floor, her shoulder resting against the

door frame. With a mighty effort, Aramael pieced his presence back together, and then roused himself to motion. He strode forward to crouch in front of Alex, trying not to flinch at the hollowness he saw in her eyes. A hollowness he didn't understand but knew he had somehow caused. He sought for words of reassurance and comfort, found none in the inner turmoil he'd once known as his center.

Slowly Alex's expression hardened into something cold and uncompromising, and he saw her withdraw so far into herself that he knew he had no hope of reaching her. Not now, not like this. He rose, stepped back, and waited.

Long seconds ticked by while Alex stared into a place he could not follow, her face an alabaster mask. At last, ignoring the hand he extended to her, she climbed to her feet, met his gaze, and squared her shoulders.

Then, very succinctly, she said, "Get the *fuck* out of my house."

DON'T THINK, DON'T think, don't think . . .

Alex climbed the stairs and lurched down the hallway to the bathroom. She closed the door, fumbled with the lock, and leaned her head against the frame. Only then could she breathe again, gulping air into deprived lungs. She slumped against the wall and willed her legs not to fail a second time, because she wasn't at all sure she could get up off the floor again. Wasn't sure she would want to . . .

Don't think.

Her head pounded. She pressed her fingertips against her eyelids and then pulled herself upright and crossed to the sink, reaching for the mirrored cabinet above it. Stopping when her gaze locked on her reflection. She took in the pale face and haunted eyes. The resemblance was undeniable, but how deep did it go?

No. You're not her. You're nothing like her. Jennifer said so.

But Jennifer didn't know about the wings or the voices or—

Alex opened the cabinet and took out the bottle of acet-
aminophen.

Don't think.

She pried off the cap and shook two tablets onto the
countertop. She hesitated, assessing her pain level, wondering how much medication they had already given her at the
hospital, and then added a third tablet. If the pills had more
than their intended buffering effect, if they made it possible
to sleep, maybe, or to forget what she'd seen in her kitchen
just now—

Don't think.

Alex returned the bottle to the cabinet and ran a glass of
water. She tossed back the tablets, drained the glass, and
looked once more at her reflection.

The image of a hollow-eyed woman stared back at her.
A woman with wild gray hair and piercing blue eyes and a
manic intensity about her, who had been plagued by beautiful, glowing, winged beings that hadn't existed.

Winged beings like Trent.

Glowing ones like the woman with him.

DON'T THINK!

Too late.

She'd heard the voices as she'd come out of the bathroom.
Had known she should ignore them and stay away; known
she didn't want to identify their source. Her feet had taken
on a life of their own, however, and led her downstairs, one
step at a time, until she reached the bottom. Until she tra-
versed the length of the hallway. Until she stood in the doorway and saw the woman, ethereal in her beauty, robed in
iridescent purple, her silvery hair shining with a light of its
own, standing just beyond *him.*

Her partner, but not her partner, at the center of the
kitchen, with massive wings rising more than a foot above
his head and trailing nearly to the floor. Golden wings, their
feathers alive with a fire that seemed to surround each and
every one of them. Shimmering, pulsing, hypnotically beautiful fire.

An eternity had passed before the woman disappeared

and he turned, almost as if he moved in slow motion, to face her. A man in real life, an angel in her mind's eye, merged into one. Gray eyes had clashed with hers, imprisoned her—no, impaled her—and had driven the wind from her body and coherent thought from her mind.

She didn't know how long they'd stared at one another, neither moving, before she had blinked and the wings had disappeared. Before his eyes had taken on the torment that made her want, once again, to reach out to him, as if her touch could heal something in him. Something in herself.

Except whatever was wrong in him existed only in her imagination, and what was wrong in her could not be healed.

Alex turned and hurled the glass at the bathroom wall.

EIGHTEEN

"Well?" Verchiel faced Mittron, her arms crossed in a gesture she knew full well he would interpret as aggressive. With good reason, because she certainly wasn't feeling very passive at the moment. Not after what she'd just witnessed. She watched the Highest Seraph pace the floor behind his desk with slow, deliberate steps and tried to hold on to what little patience she still retained. How could he remain so calm? So—

Mittron turned to face her.

"Did you make our position clear regarding his earlier actions?" he asked.

Verchiel felt her jaw go slack. She'd just told Mittron that she suspected Aramael—the most volatile of an already volatile line of angels—had developed an unheard-of connection to a mortal, and the Highest was more interested in whether or not she'd delivered a reprimand? She added clenched fists to her crossed arms.

"Have you heard a word I've said?" she demanded, ignoring Mittron's raised eyebrow. "Whatever went wrong is getting worse. Aramael is calling the woman by her name—

identifying with her!—and she is seeing him too many times for us to keep ignoring the matter. She even saw *me* just now."

Verchiel shuddered, remembering the shock of having a mortal's gaze rest on her as an angel. It had been nothing like when she had met the woman earlier . . . not unpleasant, quite, but certainly unique, and without doubt an experience she was not eager to repeat. She brushed away the memory and returned her attention to the Highest.

Other than a hint of annoyance in his amber eyes, the Highest Seraph's expression remained impassive. "Given what I know of Aramael, I suspect he may simply be overreacting to the situation," he observed.

Verchiel's already slack jaw fell open and she stared at Mittron in disbelief. "And me? Am I simply overreacting, too? I was *there*, Mittron. I know what happened."

"Your sense of responsibility toward Aramael is somewhat overdeveloped, Verchiel. It is no wonder that you imagined more than is actually there. I do not blame you, but neither can I allow your flawed perceptions to influence my judgment."

Mittron returned to his seat behind his desk and picked up a quill, his writing instrument of choice when signing divine decrees. He glanced up at her briefly. "This experience has obviously been traumatic for you. I suggest you allow yourself time to regain your perspective, and then we will speak again."

Now that Verchiel's mouth had dropped open, she seemed incapable of closing it again. "You can't be serious."

This time, both of Mittron's eyebrows ascended. "I am quite serious."

"But there must be something we can do. Something more we can find out. Aramael questioned whether the woman's ability to see him is due to her lineage. What if he's right? What if she's seeing him because she's Nephilim? Maybe that's why she saw me, too."

"There are tens of thousands of Nephilim descendants, Verchiel. If lineage allowed them to see any of us, we would almost certainly have faced a situation like this long ago."

"There must be more to it, then. Perhaps if I access the archives—"

"No."

The sharpness of the single word startled Verchiel. She stared at the Highest Seraph, at the way his gaze remained focused on his desk for a long moment before rising to meet hers.

"You have enough to look after with this hunt," Mittron said. "If it's that important to you, I will assign someone to look into the matter further. Should anything of significance surface, which I doubt, I will let you know."

Verchiel held the Highest's stare for a moment longer and then, keeping her demeanor carefully neutral, she nodded her acceptance. "Thank you," she said. "I will keep you apprised of Aramael's situation."

"Of course."

Verchiel stepped out into the hallway, closed the heavy wooden door behind her, and then sagged against the wall, her pulse racing.

He lied, she thought, her astonishment almost too great to comprehend. The Highest Seraph lied, and not very well, either. He had no intention of looking into anything. He made empty assurances designed to placate her, to prevent her from pressing for answers, and to keep her from finding out—what?

Verchiel crossed her arms and raised one hand to tap gently on her lower lip. Did she dare? Did she have the nerve to disobey what she knew had been meant as an order?

Aramael's words came back to her: *Just for a moment, think for yourself.*

She remembered the raw vulnerability she'd felt when the mortal woman had seen her, and thought of what the experience could do to Aramael, to a Power already damaged by his past, by the demands made on him by his very existence. Then she stood away from the wall, arranged the folds of her robe with precision, and turned to face the hallway that led not to the library, but to the archives nestled within the heart of the building.

Oh, yes, she thought. She dared, all right. And the Highest could blessed well blame her persistence on whatever overdeveloped sense of responsibility he liked.

Her steps faltered. Wait. If she was truly going to think for herself, she needed to look at the bigger picture: the hunt itself. It could take days, even months, to find the answers she sought in the archives, assuming they even existed. In the meantime, Aramael's hunting ability remained hobbled by the woman unless Verchiel could think of a way to assist him, preferably without Mittron's knowledge.

Bloody Hell, she thought, and then blushed. Wonderful. Going behind the Highest's back *and* stooping to Aramael's level of language. She pondered the issue at hand, and then pinched the bridge of her nose between thumb and forefinger.

No. She couldn't.

But who else was there? This whole mess had started because Aramael had been the only angel they could think of who might protect the woman, but maybe they just hadn't thought far enough. Maybe there was another. Not an angel, exactly, but still capable and trustworthy.

At least for now.

MITTRON STARED AT the office door long after it closed behind Verchiel. She hadn't believed him. It may have been almost five thousand years since the cleanse of their soul-mating, but she still knew him better than any other angel. Well enough to know he had lied to her.

The question was, what would she do with the knowledge? Her capacity for compassion was enormous, and capable of engendering considerable guilt, especially where it concerned Aramael. Would that be enough to let her ignore her innate desire to obey, let her defy his order?

The answer settled into the space beside his heart, cold and dark and hard. As well as she knew him, he knew her, and he should have known from the start she might prove difficult.

Damn her to Hell for complicating matters.

Damn him for not foreseeing the complication.

He pushed back from his desk and stood, turning to stare out the window. A female figure in a purple robe strode across the gardens, headed for a building on the opposite side. At least she wasn't going to the archives. Yet.

Not that it would be long before she did. Now that her suspicions had been raised, it wouldn't be easy to put them to rest again. Doing so might even prove impossible. Mittron's heart stalled for a second. He hadn't expected resistance, but he had still taken the precaution of hiding the records. Had he done so well enough, or would she find something he had missed?

He curled his fingers against the window frame. Damnation, why had he not thought to assign a different handler to Aramael? But even as the question formed, so did the answer, making his mouth twist. Because he'd become arrogant, that was why. And arrogance bred carelessness—a fatal flaw.

Unless he took steps to correct it.

"GOOD MORNING."

Alex spun to face Trent, the coffee in her hand spilling over its cup and onto her skin. "Shit! What the hell are you doing here? I told you to leave."

Trent leaned against the door frame. "You'll need a ride to the office."

She wondered if he had spent the night in spite of her order, but decided she'd rather not know. She set the cup on the counter and reached for a tea towel. "I can drive myself."

A muscle went tight in Trent's jaw. He crossed his arms and looked down at the floor. On the wall near his head, the kitchen clock quietly ticked off the passing seconds. Twenty-eight of them before he raised his gaze to hers again.

"I'm not leaving."

And that answered the question of whether he had done so last night. A quiver started deep in Alex's belly. "I don't want you here."

"I know."

The quiver became a vibration and Alex bit her lip. She'd spent most of the night trying to add the kitchen scene she'd witnessed to the list of things that hadn't happened, couldn't have happened. She hadn't been entirely successful, but she had reached an uneasy compromise: denial. It wouldn't last forever, but it worked for now, because as long as she could believe none of last night—hell, none of yesterday—had happened, she didn't have to face the creeping, horrifying prospect that Jennifer might be wrong, that she might actually be going insane.

Or the even more horrifying prospect that she was sane and the events she'd witnessed were—

No. Not real. Never real, because angels only existed in places like her mother's head.

Didn't they?

What's going on, Trent? Last night, in the alley and in the kitchen, what was it I really saw?

The question hung between them, waiting for her to speak it.

Instead, she lifted her chin. "I'm asking Roberts to put you with someone else."

Trent's eyes narrowed and the little muscle in his jaw flexed. Before he could say anything, however, the doorbell rang and Alex heard the front door open. She stiffened instinctively. No one she knew would just walk in like that—

"Yo, Jarvis! You home?"

Except maybe Delaney.

Trent turned his head and called out, "In the kitchen." He looked back to Alex. "Sorry. I forgot to mention she called while you were in the shower. She said she had something for you and I told her I'd leave the door unlocked."

He'd stayed the night, answered her phone, and invited Delaney into her house? Alex couldn't even bring herself to respond. Not civilly, anyway.

Heels clacked down the hallway and then Delaney breezed past Trent, flashing him a quick smile before turning her attention to Alex. "Wow. You look like hell."

"Thanks for noticing," Alex said.

"Shouldn't you still be in bed?"

"Four hours of fighting off my attacker every time I closed my eyes was enough, thanks."

Not that reality was any better than her nightmares had been. Alex's gaze rested on Trent's crossed arms, lifted to his stony face, moved back to Delaney.

The fraud detective glanced between her and Trent. "I'm sorry, did I interrupt something?"

Alex tensed at the sudden interest. Great. That was all she needed, Delaney's office grapevine getting involved in this mess. "Just a disagreement about me going to the office today," she lied. She motioned at the manila envelope Delaney held in fuchsia-tipped fingers. "For me?"

"I was in the neighborhood, so Roberts asked me to drop it off and see how you're doing."

More like she'd asked for the errand so she could check out the damage for herself. Alex reached for the envelope, trying to think of a way to extend the conversation. As little as she and Delaney had in common, she didn't want the fraud detective to leave just yet. Didn't want to have to face Trent alone again.

She cleared her throat. "So how did that complaint turn out yesterday?"

Delaney waved a dismissive hand. "A crank call, just like I figured. The complainant didn't even keep our appointment. Apparently he had more important business. It wasn't a complete loss, though."

"Oh? How so?"

"I followed up with the other party just to be safe. Turns out he's good-looking, single, and interested. Not to mention interesting. In fact," Delaney added, glancing at an oversized watch on her wrist, "I have a breakfast date with him, and I'm going to be late if I don't get moving. Roberts says you're not to turn up until at least noon, by the way. He also says he'd prefer you didn't show at all, but he knows better than that."

Alex opened her mouth to point out the potential conflict

of interest should Delaney's fraud complainant resurface, and the ethical questions that could be raised, then she shook her head. She was way too tired for a discussion of that nature this morning. She held up the envelope.

"Thanks for dropping this off."

"No problem." The other detective cocked her head and favored Alex with a probing look. "Are you sure you're all right?" she asked. "You look—"

"Like hell," Alex said. "You already told me."

Delaney rolled her eyes. "I was going to say pretty fragile, actually. Maybe you should take your partner's advice. You won't be much good to anyone if you come apart at the seams."

CHRISTINE PAUSED INSIDE the restaurant door and pushed her sunglasses up onto her head. She surveyed the tables and then wrinkled her nose when she found him at the back, near the kitchen doors. She would have preferred something a little quieter, but let's face it, if this gorgeous, fascinating male had suggested they meet in the middle of the freeway at rush hour, she'd have agreed. She smiled, shook back her hair, and started toward him.

His gaze settled on her instantly, its impact almost physical. Anticipation coiled through her and her heart rate kicked up a notch. He was every bit as delicious as he'd seemed last night when they'd met and he'd bent low over her hand in a courtly gesture she'd only ever read about. Every bit as exhilarating as he'd been later when she had—when they had—

Christine felt her cheeks warm. She still couldn't wrap her head around the way she'd broken her own rules about first dates like that, the way she'd so completely abandoned control. And it hadn't even been a real date.

He stood as she neared the booth, moving into the bright sunlight that streamed in through the skylight above, drawing the attention of everyone within viewing distance in the restaurant. Waiting for her.

Christine's heart swelled with pride as she took in his full magnificence. Tall, perfectly proportioned, his black hair immaculately groomed, his features exquisitely carved. He reminded her of—her steps faltered.

Christ, how the hell had she missed that? The man's resemblance to what's-his-name, Alex Jarvis's new partner, was downright startling. She stared as he strode forward to take her hands and lift them, one at a time, to his lips. She searched his features, met the intensity of his dark eyes. Blinked away a sudden blurriness and then studied him again.

She relaxed. No, he looked nothing at all like Trent—how bizarre that she should think so.

"Is something wrong?" Her companion raised an eyebrow.

"It's nothing. You just reminded me of someone for a second." She felt sudden watchfulness in the way he stilled.

"Really?"

She shook her head and smiled. "I was wrong. I'm not even sure why I thought it. Must've been the light."

He didn't move for a moment. His gaze cooled and seemed to reach inside her to places she would prefer not to share, and she felt her smile fall away. Tension crept across her shoulders, but before Christine could act on an urge to pull her hands from his, he tugged her forward into an embrace, and into memories of the night before. She stiffened, aware of the stunned hush that had spread among the other patrons, certain of their disapproval, but then a flush of need returned to spread through her belly and she twined her fingers into his hair and raised her mouth to his. Eagerness gave way to disappointment when he brushed his lips against her cheek instead.

"I'm glad you could make it."

Her heart gave a bound. "Me, too, but I can't stay for long. I have to be back to the office for a meeting at noon."

"Then we should make the most of our time." His lips found the crook of her neck. "How hungry are you?"

Christine swallowed. "Very."

"For food?"

She shook her head.

He pulled back to look down at her. "Say it."

Desire spread through her veins, heating her blood, shocking her with its speed. Its ferocity. She bit her lip, watched his eyes fasten on the movement. Felt an answering flare in response. She struggled for control.

"We're going so fast—"

"Say it!"

She jumped at the harsh command. Disquiet slithered through her. He was so intense, so— Her breath caught as his thumb found and traced the pulse in her throat. A wave of wantonness washed over her and she sagged against him, ignoring the stares, objections fleeing in the face of sheer need.

"I'm hungry for you," she whispered. She reached up to trace her fingers along his jaw, paused to finger the stiff band of white tucked into his upright black collar. "Father."

NINETEEN

Verchiel looked up from her desk as her door opened. A black-clad figure strolled across the room and dropped into a chair across from her.

"Do come in," she said dryly.

The Appointed grinned at her without repentance. "Just obeying your summons, oh esteemed one."

"Really, Seth—" Verchiel broke off, realizing the Appointed teased her with his usual irreverence. "Thank you for coming so quickly."

"It's not like I have a lot else to do."

No self-pity lay behind the words, but Verchiel felt a pang at their truth. "Perhaps not yet, but one day—"

"Oh, please." Seth rolled his eyes toward the ceiling. "Don't you start with that one-day-you'll-fulfill-your-destiny crap. I've heard quite enough of it from Mittron, especially lately."

Verchiel flinched at the Highest's name and interest flared in the Appointed's gaze. He settled back into the chair, resting one ankle atop the opposite knee and waggling his eyebrows.

"Having issues with His High and Mightiness, are we? How intriguing." His gaze narrowed with sharp perception. "What exactly was it you wanted to see me about, anyway?"

Verchiel hesitated, and then got up to close the door. She returned to the desk and took her seat. "A favor. A very quiet favor."

One dark brow ascended. "I see. Am I to take it you'd prefer a certain Seraph didn't know about this favor?"

She nodded.

"Go on."

In a few brief words, Verchiel outlined Aramael's dilemma and her solution. The Appointed remained silent for a long moment when she had finished, appearing to study the toe of his shoe with great interest. At last he looked up.

"There's no way you can keep this from Mittron. You could face exile."

She swallowed. "I know."

"Why?"

"Why what?"

"Why do you care so much about Aramael? Why are you willing to risk your own existence on this?"

Verchiel's throat went tight. She wanted to look away from the dark intensity of Seth's gaze, but wouldn't let herself. "I was the one who sent Aramael after Caim the first time. I thought their closeness as brothers would give Aramael an advantage, an edge. Let him find Caim faster. I was right, but it was more difficult for him than I had anticipated. It did something to him and he has never been the same."

Black eyes watched her for another few seconds, weighing, considering, seeming to know she hadn't told him the whole truth. That it had been Mittron's idea, not hers, and she had allowed herself to be swayed by something that had no longer existed between them. Then Seth uncoiled from the chair and stood tall again.

"I'll do it on one condition. I take full responsibility."

"I can't let you—"

"Verchiel, he can exile you. But me?" Seth stuck his hands into his pockets and strolled toward the door, tossing a grin over his shoulder. "He has no choice but to put up with me. Let me know when the Guardians have been informed of my arrival."

Verchiel stared after the Appointed for a long moment, and then closed her eyes and massaged the now perpetual ache in her temple, hoping she hadn't made yet another error.

ROBERTS WAS ON the phone when Alex and Trent arrived in the office at the appointed midday hour, but when Alex would have passed by his office, he rapped on the window and motioned her in. She obeyed, only too glad to get away from her partner and drop into one of the chairs across from her staff inspector while he finished his call.

She cradled her wounded arm across her chest, willing the throb to subside and cursing her lack of foresight in not bringing any painkillers. Even with Trent doing the driving, an ache had settled into the limb that put her teeth on edge. Now the headache had returned, too.

Roberts covered the receiver's mouthpiece. "Bad?" he asked.

Alex produced a smile she hoped wasn't as wan as she felt. "I'll live," she said.

Roberts lifted his hand from the mouthpiece. "Yeah, I'm still here. Go on," he said into the phone. He opened his top left hand drawer, rummaged in it, and extracted a plastic bottle. He leaned across and set it in front of Alex. "Keep them," he murmured, then ended his conversation, "Okay, Dave. Thanks for getting back to us so fast on this one. We owe you one." He reached over and dropped the receiver back onto its cradle.

Alex picked up the bottle and opened it, shaking two caplets into her hand. Her trembling hand. She frowned at the appendage, willing it to be still. The tremor intensified. She slipped the pills into her mouth, forced herself to swallow, and tucked the offending hand into her lap, still clutching the bottle of painkillers. The caplets lodged at the base of her throat.

Roberts regarded her balefully. "You should be at home."

"I'm fine." Alex ignored his snort. "So? What do we have?"

His sandy eyebrows ascended. "Other than what I sent you?"

Sent her—? Ah, hell. The envelope. She envisioned it sitting on the table in her entry, still unopened, where she'd set it when she'd gone upstairs to escape the partner who wouldn't go away. She rested her good elbow on the arm of the chair and cradled her cheek in her hand. "I forgot to look at it," she admitted. "Sorry."

"Never mind, it was just the autopsy results. You can look them over later, but in a nutshell, yesterday's body matches the others to a *T.* Pattern of cuts, weapon, everything. That was the lab on the phone just now." Roberts inclined his head toward the instrument on his desk. "Some of the blood we found on your attacker last night matched the victim's."

Alex felt herself blanch. She hadn't wanted to think about the possibility last night that her attacker might be connected to the murders, and didn't want to hear evidence now that supported the idea.

"Of course," Roberts continued, "that's the good news."

"And the bad news?"

"The knife used on you isn't the murder weapon, and while your blood was in the expected spray pattern on the suspect's shirt, the victim's was smeared."

"So, what, unless our boy went home and changed his shirt halfway through the slicing, we're looking for a second person?"

"Are you surprised?"

Professionally speaking? No. With the number of victims they'd found, more than one killer was entirely within the realm of possibility. If she listened to Trent's certainty about the issue, on the other hand . . .

She rested her good elbow on the arm of the chair and leaned her chin in her hand. "Did the suspect wake up yet? What did he say? And who is he, anyway?"

"Martin James, age twenty-eight, unemployed. He's done

time for break and enter and narcotics possession, but nothing more."

Alex frowned. "He doesn't sound much like he has the makings of a serial killer."

"Neither did Ted Bundy at first," Roberts pointed out. "Anyway, he did wake up and Bastion and Timmins went by the hospital to talk to him this morning, but he was tanked on sedatives. They've reduced his dosage, so he should be coherent soon. If you're up to it after the meeting, would you like to take a shot at him?"

Alex's stomach recoiled a little at the idea of facing her attacker—and their potential killer. She glanced at her bandaged arm and thought of the damage inflicted on the victims so far. *There but for the grace of God . . .*

She shut down the latent possibilities behind the thought and nodded. "Of course."

"Take Trent with you, and let him do the driving."

Well. She supposed now was as good a time as any to tell Roberts she wanted out of the partnership. "About that—"

Roberts's office door opened and Joly stuck his head in. "Channel Six news, Staff. You should see it."

It was a report on their serial killer, now dubbed the Storm Slasher, and the journalist had been busy. She knew about the posing of the bodies, and what she lacked in actual detail beyond that, she'd more than made up for in wild speculation. Silence reigned for a long moment when the report ended and the television went dark.

"Fucking hell," someone murmured behind Alex. "The *occult*? Where in God's name did she get that from?"

She heard Joly reply, "Maybe she's not that far off. You have to admit this one is about as weird as we've ever had. I mean, come on. A storm every single time the guy hits? We haven't been able to find so much as a flake of skin with usable DNA. He has to at least be some kind of weather psychic or something."

Alex looked over her shoulder at her colleague.

Joly shrugged. "Be honest, Jarvis," he said. "You've felt it, too. There's something about this guy that just isn't natural."

Her gaze swept past him to Trent. Met the watchfulness in his expression. Felt the pull of his presence. The image of a winged man among flames flashed through her brain.

Whack on the head, drugs, stress, lack of sleep, she told herself, repeating the mantra she'd come up with on the ride to the office. The explanation for the last twenty-four hours of her life. An explanation that didn't even begin to fit but was all that stood between her and the alternative.

Either of the alternatives.

"All right, knock it off," Roberts growled. "It's bad enough having the media and the public going off the deep end without us following suit." He fixed a grim look on the group as a whole. "What I want to know is how that reporter knew about the posing of the bodies. If anyone in here has been talking to the press about this case, writing tickets for jaywalking will be the high point of his or her pathetic career, is that clear?"

Nods and scuffles all around.

"Good. Now let's get our heads out of the fantasy world and back into reality. We have a killer to catch."

Alex trudged toward the conference room with the others, careful to keep to the back of the group and well away from Trent. She took up a position near the door, leaning her shoulder against the wall and cradling her injured arm against her side.

Overnight, the task force had tripled in size, now filling the room to overflowing. Many of the people Alex didn't recognize, but assumed were detectives from Toronto's surrounding municipalities where the killer had struck; others were uniformed officers and detectives called in to assist from other sections within the city's own force. On the opposite side, Delaney squeezed in between Bastion and Timmins, looking flushed and uncharacteristically disheveled, rather like her breakfast date had gone better—and longer—than expected.

Alex shifted her arm and turned her attention to her staff inspector as his voice boomed through the room.

Despite the number of personnel working the case, the meeting went quickly. Roberts reviewed the attack on Alex, focusing on the possibility they were looking for more than one suspect. With respect to the other victims, there was little to report. Two of the bodies remained unidentified. Apart from a general assumption regarding their killer's sex, age, size, and fitness levels, the psychological profiler was stumped, and the geographic profiler didn't yet have enough data.

"We must have something else," Roberts said. "We have tips coming in by the hundreds. Hasn't anything panned out yet?" Silence met his query and he threw himself back in his chair impatiently. "Come on, people. We're up to nine bodies—"

Alex blinked. "Nine?" she interrupted. Last she'd counted, there were seven including the one tied to her attack.

Across the room, a pencil snapped in two with a muted crack. Alex stared at the two slender pieces of wood in Trent's hands. No one else seemed to notice. She forced herself to look away again.

Roberts spared her a brief look. "We had two come in last night. One in Aurora, the other in Peel." He returned his attention to the group at large. "Well? Nothing else?"

Shit. The claw. She'd forgotten to tell him about the claw. "The what?"

Alex saw that all attention had riveted on her. She realized she'd spoken aloud, and that Trent's gaze had narrowed to that uncomfortable intensity again. She swallowed.

"The claw," she repeated. "When you sent us to the coroner yesterday, that's what Jason Bartlett wanted to show us. He thinks it may be part of the murder weapon."

Roberts looked as if he didn't know whether he was being fed a line or should have her committed on the spot. He looked to an impassive Trent, then back to Alex.

"What is this, a bad joke?" he asked. "Exactly how hard did you hit your head, anyway?"

Alex glared at him. "Not that hard," she retorted, forgetting that she herself had just used her injury to explain away certain anomalies, "and it's not a joke. Joly and Abrams saw it, too. The coroner found what looks like a claw in victim number four, our Jane Doe. They're still waiting for DNA results, so they haven't been able to identify where—or what—the claw is from, but they have an expert on big cats coming in from the zoo today to give them a hand. Bartlett's supposed to call me when he has something."

She considered adding the weird temperature part to her revelation, but given the tension now permeating the room, decided to keep that detail for Roberts alone, especially on the heels of the news report. Judging by Joly's tightened mouth, he was no more eager to share the information than she was.

Roberts ran a hand over his buzz cut. Opened his mouth to speak. Closed it again. Then he rose from his chair and threw down his pen, sending it skittering the length of the conference table. "Fuck it," he said. "I'm going for coffee."

TWENTY

Aramael followed Alex down the hospital corridor, stopping beside her as she held up her shield for inspection by the uniformed officer stationed outside a room.

"Is he awake?"

"On and off, from what I gather. I don't think he's said anything yet. They check on him about every half hour." The young cop—he didn't look more than twenty—indicated Alex's arm. "You the one he nailed? Lucky thing for you, that lightning."

Alex went white and, without another word, pushed open the door and stepped into the room beyond. Aramael followed. He didn't expect much from the interview. Witness reports had placed Martin James at the victim's side with another man, which told Aramael the mortal had probably faced Caim, and most likely in at least partial killing-form. They'd be lucky if Martin remembered anything at all, let alone anything of use. No human had ever emerged with mind intact from a full-on encounter with a Fallen One in demon form.

Folding his arms, Aramael leaned a shoulder against the

glass and settled in to wait for Alex. He stared out, beyond the hospital grounds, to the city where Caim would already be stalking another mortal, another victim. Wondered how long it would be until he failed, again, to stop his brother.

Behind him, he heard Alex cross to the lone bed occupying the room. She cleared her throat. "Martin, I'm Detective Jarvis from Homicide Squad. I need to ask you some questions."

As Aramael had expected, the man in the bed did not respond. Aramael tried to focus on sensing Caim's energy, but found himself unable to shut out Alex's words.

"Martin, last night you attacked me in an alley off Dundas Street. Do you remember that?"

Aramael pushed his awareness outward. Nothing. Not so much as a hint of his brother's whereabouts. His mouth twisted. Not that it mattered, because even if he knew where to find Caim, he couldn't go after him. No matter how much he wanted to.

And oh, how he wanted to. Desperately. Twice last night he had felt Caim's rising bloodlust; twice he'd known his brother had slain another mortal; twice he had been unable to pursue him, held back by the thread that connected him, unforgivably, to a Naphil woman. The thread that made him aware, even through Caim's depravity, of Alex's restless sleep in the room over his head, of her every breath, her every toss and turn.

Bloody Hell. Aramael raked a hand through his hair.

Alex's voice continued. "You had a knife, and blood on your clothes. A lot of blood. Some of it came from the body of a man found at a construction site—"

Her words broke off and Aramael turned to see Martin James's eyes blink, shift to Alex, and then return to looking past her. Surprise twisted through him, and he straightened away from the window. Could he have been wrong? Could the mortal have retained something? Might he remember where he'd met Caim, or perhaps who the Fallen Angel pretended to be?

Aramael filtered swiftly through the potential caught up in the idea. No Power had ever worked a hunt from concrete facts, or even needed to consider such an option, but what if it were possible? What if he could figure out how Caim was choosing his victims, where he might be tracking them from?

Alex leaned over the bed, her face inches from that of James. "Martin," she insisted, "there was someone else at the construction site with you. Someone besides the man who was killed. Who was there, Martin?"

The man in the bed shuddered. His eyes widened, rolled back in his head. Tanned, callused fingers clawed at the sheet covering him, and the metal stand beside the bed rocked sideways as the tube connecting him to a bag hanging from it pulled taut.

Aramael hesitated a moment, and then stepped away from the wall and moved to stand behind Alex. In a way utterly alien to him, he extended a sense of calm outward from his center to envelop the man, fighting the innate impatience threatening to swamp his efforts. Grudging as the effort may have been, however, the terror that stood in Martin James's way began to ease and he loosened his fisted grip on the covers.

"Martin?" Alex prompted.

Slowly, very slowly, the man focused on her, his mouth working as if he might speak. Then his gaze slid past her to settle on Aramael, and his face contorted with soul-deep, unstoppable horror.

Aramael watched in resignation as the rest of the man's mind disintegrated beyond reach.

IT TOOK ALEX a moment to realize where the low keening came from, and another few seconds to react. By the time she reached out to the man in the bed, he'd already ripped out his IV and was fighting with the sheet that covered him. She grabbed for him with her good arm, her hand closing on a fistful of hospital nightgown, and braced herself against the bed. Martin James's first lunge told her she couldn't hold on long.

From the corner of her eye, she saw Trent move to help her. James's keening escalated, becoming a loud, nearly inhuman wail. His thrashing nearly took them both to the floor and Alex realized that the closer Trent got, the more frenzied became James's efforts to escape. She tried to shout over the chaos, to steer Trent away, but James's voice rose to a banshee-like shriek, drowning her out, his words running together in an endless babble, impossible to untangle.

Then, when she didn't think she could hold on for another second, Trent veered off and Alex saw a flood of people pouring in the door behind him. Doctors, nurses, orderlies, the cop who had greeted them at the door. Her hold failed as others took her place; then a nurse was steering her toward the door along with Trent, pushing them both out, shutting the door behind them. Alex sagged against the wall, arm throbbing with fire, and listened to the screams that wouldn't stop.

Trent's hand closed over her shoulder and she started, glancing up at him.

"Are you all right?" he asked.

All right? She had no idea. She was still reeling from what had just happened. Hell, she still wasn't sure what *had* happened. She swayed, feeling the strength in his touch, fighting the impulse to turn and shelter in it. She pulled away.

"I'm fine," she lied. A white lie, really. When she stopped shaking, she would be fine. Maybe.

Inside the room, their suspect's cries diminished, then faded altogether. A few minutes later, the door opened and the medical staff began filing past her. The cop brought up the rear.

"What the hell happened in there?" he asked, shock in his voice. "What'd you guys say to him?"

Alex roused herself. "Very little, actually. And we got nothing from him."

The uniform snorted. "You won't, either. Not today, anyway. They gave him enough to knock him out for hours, they said."

Damn. Damn, hell, shit.

Alex peered through the open door at Martin James, lying deathly still under the restraints that held him in the bed, his eyes the only indication of life. Eyes that tracked past her to the man standing at her side. Eyes that lost their drug-dulled haze and focused with sudden intensity and—recognition? A shiver spiked down Alex's spine. She glanced at Trent, found him rigid and equally focused on the man in the bed.

What the hell—?

She pivoted back to James and, stunned, watched him mouth a single, unmistakable word.

"You," Martin James said.

She waited until they reached the car before she rounded on Trent. "He knew you," she said without preamble.

Trent shrugged as he unlocked the driver's door. "I've never seen him before last night."

"He knew you," Alex repeated, "and he was afraid of you."

Perhaps because James, too, had seen wings? She squashed the thought. Other than that brief flare of unearthly blue light, it had been too dark in the alley for James to have had a good look at Trent. He had to have known her partner from somewhere else.

"Was he?" Trent opened the door and reached in to touch the electric lock button. Alex's door clicked in response.

She scowled. "He was terrified, and you know it. Why?"

"I'm a cop and he's a murder suspect," Trent pointed out with an edge of impatience. "Does he need another reason?"

No. Yes. Maybe. But whatever response Alex might have decided on died unspoken. Behind her, and far above, came the sound of shattering glass. She turned and looked up, searching for the source. A shower of glints and sparks rained down, brilliant in the afternoon sun, landing in a discordant, tinkling chorus over cars and pavement. She hadn't fully registered their meaning when foreboding drew her attention upward again—

In time to see a man in a hospital gown tumble from a ninth floor window, free-falling silently, horribly, through the air.

TWENTY-ONE

Verchiel paused outside the Highest Seraph's door. She did not want to be here, did not want to speak to Mittron again—did not want to deal with any of this. She rested her forehead against the oak barrier between her and certain confrontation. How could she have allowed this? Could she not have foreseen what would happen? No matter that Mittron commanded the obedience of nearly every angel in Heaven, herself included, she should still have fought harder against what her every fiber had told her was wrong.

Should have, but once again hadn't.

She sighed, raised her head, and knocked.

"In," came Mittron's disembodied voice.

She pushed open the door.

"You look unhappy," Mittron greeted her from beside the window, his bearing aloof, his eyes cold.

"The mortal who attacked the woman—"

"Is dead. I know."

Verchiel's heart missed a beat. The event had only just occurred; did Mittron have another angel monitoring Aramael? Monitoring her? "You know?"

"I ordered it."

She felt for the door frame behind her and leaned against it. "You! But that would be"—she caught back the word *murder* and finished instead—"interference of the most direct kind."

"I didn't order him killed, for goodness' sake. Only that he be allowed to do as he wished, to take his own life."

"But—"

"The man's mind was destroyed by what happened, Verchiel. He would never have recovered. Allowing his death was a mercy rather than interference. It will have no effect on the pact. Besides, we couldn't risk him telling the woman what he had seen. It would have raised too many questions."

Verchiel's lips tightened. The Highest Seraph's shortsightedness astounded her sometimes. "Perhaps, but his death will raise other questions. Many others. The woman already suspects something about Aramael's presence there, and this will only make matters worse."

"Really, Verchiel, you worry too much. Our only concern with the Naphil is keeping her out of Caim's hands. She is of no import beyond that."

Verchiel glowered at him. "And Aramael? Is he of no import either? With all due respect, Mittron, your interference makes an already impossible hunt even more difficult for him."

Mittron's gaze sparked amber fire. He drew tall. Threatening. "You overstep, Dominion."

Verchiel wrapped her hands into her robe and gritted her teeth against a retort. Former soulmate he might be, but he was also her superior, and continuing to question his judgment would only lead to a formal reprimand and certain suspicion regarding Seth's imminent involvement in the whole mess. If she truly wanted answers to the increasing number of questions she had, or to assist Aramael, she would do well to back down while she still could.

Swallowing her indignation along with her pride, she inclined her head. "You're right, Highest. Forgive me."

"Are we going to have a problem with seeing this assignment through, Verchiel? If so, perhaps you should consider removing yourself and letting someone else take over."

Verchiel raised an eyebrow. As if any other Dominion would agree to take on Aramael. She was the only one of her choir who wasn't petrified beyond words by him. But when she opened her mouth to share the observation, she hesitated. Wait. Mittron knew full well how wide a berth the others gave her charge. He had to know that none of them would agree to the task, and that he would have to take it on himself. So why would he even suggest the idea? Unless that was his intent. But why?

"Well?" Mittron asked.

Verchiel buried her reaction to the question under an ingratiating smile and a reassurance. "That won't be necessary, Highest," she murmured. "I'm quite capable of finishing this."

She'd better be, because Mittron's heavy-handed approach might well put Aramael over the edge—and turn the idea of all hell breaking loose into a reality.

ALEX MADE A beeline for her desk the moment she and Trent arrived back at the office from the hospital. Trent could deny it all he wanted, but she'd swear on her own sanity that her so-called partner and Martin James knew each other. She paused, remembering the current, questionable state of said sanity, then shrugged irritably. The point was, if Trent had lied about knowing James, what else was he keeping from her? She couldn't put it off any longer: she needed to know what the fuck she was dealing with.

A picture of wings flashed through her mind as she reached for the phone. Her hand jerked sideways, knocking over a container of pens.

Whom, she corrected herself. *Whom she was dealing with.*
She dialed staffing.

"Hey, it's Alex Jarvis from Homicide. I need you to access a file for me."

A presence loomed over her and she looked up to find

Trent, his brow like one of the storms plaguing the city. She put her hand over the receiver and fixed him with a level stare. She didn't even pretend politeness.

"Private conversation," she stated.

For a moment she thought he would object, but then, his face going cold, or colder than it had already been, he retreated in silence toward the coffee room. Alex turned her attention back to the phone. Three minutes later, as un-enlightened as she'd been when she began her mission, she slammed the receiver back into its cradle. Classified? They had to be fucking kidding. Since when was a homicide detective's entire service record classified?

She flopped back in her chair and leaned without think-ing on her injury. Pain lanced through the abused limb and into her shoulder. She bolted upright again. "Goddamn son of a bitch!"

"Bad day?" Joly inquired, looking over from his desk.

"You have no idea," she muttered, waiting for the pain to recede and the blood to return to her face.

"Jarvis!"

Alex jumped at the bellow and turned to see Staff Roberts in his office doorway, looking about as happy as she felt. She sighed and raised her hand, the one that wasn't throbbing in time to her heartbeat, to let him know she'd heard.

She pushed herself to her feet. "Apparently it's just going to keep getting better, too," she muttered to Joly. She threaded her way through the maze of desks to Roberts's office and tapped on the door frame.

"You wanted to see me?"

Roberts motioned her in, continuing with the paperwork on his desk. "I assume there's a reason a call to staffing is more important than filling me in on what happened at the hospital?"

Sometimes she hated how fast news traveled in this place.

Alex straightened her shoulders, knowing there was no point to lying. "I wanted to follow up on Trent's file. I'd still like to find out about his background."

"And I would like you to focus on the goddamn case."

Roberts slammed the pen he held onto the desk. "How many ways do I have to tell you to deal with this, Jarvis? Trent is your partner. Whatever his service record is has no bearing on the fact that he will *remain* your partner, and continuing to fight me on this will affect your *own* record. Now, are we finally straight on this matter?"

"Of course," she said through her teeth.

"Good. Tell me about the hospital."

She shrugged, immediately regretted doing so, and fished in her pocket for the painkillers Roberts had given her earlier. "There isn't much more than what I told you on the phone. James went ballistic, they sedated and restrained him, we left, he got loose and threw a chair through the window, and then he jumped after it."

She popped the cap off the pill bottle and shook out two tablets into her palm. She considered the building headache and throbbing arm and added a third pill.

"You need to go home?"

"I'm fine."

"Sure you are." Roberts locked his hands behind his head. "So our only suspect offed himself. Why?"

To her mind, the better question was how. How had the heavily sedated James slipped his restraints in the first place, let alone found the strength to smash a chair through a plate-glass window and then follow in its wake?

"All I know is that the man took one look at Trent and lost it, Staff. Completely and totally. I've never seen anything like it—he was terrified."

"Of what?"

She grimaced. "Trent?"

Roberts's brows formed a solid slash above his nose. "Damn it, Alex—"

"Just telling you what I think, Staff."

Her supervisor raised his eyes to the ceiling. "Then why don't we try confining it to what you *know* instead? As in, do we have anything more on the murder weapon? What did Bartlett say about that, anyway? Is there any chance James's knife is a match to any of the vics?"

The very thought of James's knife had Alex protecting her injured arm with its partner. As for the idea that the weapon might have been used on others . . . She waited for the slight roll in her stomach to subside, then addressed Roberts's question. "I haven't heard yet, but I can—"

"Staff?" Joly leaned into the office beside her. "We have two more."

"Two—" Roberts stared at Joly for a second, then stood up and reached for the jacket on the back of his chair. "When?"

"Sometime in the last twelve hours."

Roberts paused with one arm thrust into a sleeve. "What, both of them?"

"Looks like. One out in Etobicoke, the other downtown."

"Christ." Roberts scowled and thought a minute, then sighed. "All right. You and Abrams head to Etobicoke and see what they have. Call me when you get there. I'll head out with Bastion and Timmins to the other one."

"Um—Staff?" Alex held up her hand for Roberts's attention.

"You're done for today." Roberts shrugged the rest of the way into his suit jacket.

"But—"

"I mean it, Alex. It's nearly five o'clock, you're injured, and you are done for the day. Write up your reports from the last couple of days and then go home. That's an order."

"But—"

Her staff inspector brushed past her with a look fierce enough to make her clamp her lips together and swallow the rest of her objection. She and the others might occasionally joke about the Wrath of Roberts, but the phenomenon was real enough—and not something she cared to trigger. Her arm gave a twinge and she shifted its position. Besides, there was always a chance that Roberts might be right about leaving her behind this time.

She realized her staff inspector had stopped to speak to Trent and she moved toward them, unashamedly eavesdropping. Hearing her supervisor invite Trent to ride along, her heart gave a little leap. *Go,* she silently urged her partner. *Please go.*

Trent looked at her. "I think it's better if I see Detective Jarvis home safely," he said.

Alex bridled, forgetting she wasn't part of the conversation. "I don't need looking after."

If I'm to protect Alex . . .

Again those words from last night. Alex felt the blood drain from her face and she swayed slightly, just enough to make Roberts raise a skeptical eyebrow and turn to Trent again.

"Good idea. When she's finished her paperwork, you can run her home." Roberts gave her a tight, frosty smile. "And yes, Jarvis, that's another order."

ALEX PASSED BY the conference room on her way to get a coffee, paused in her step, and returned to the open doorway to confirm what her eyes told her she'd seen: Jacob Trent, settled into a chair, with files spread across the table in front of him. Appearing to do the kind of police work for which he'd expressed such disdain just yesterday.

She blinked. Then she leaned her good shoulder against the door frame. "You look busy," she said, her voice guarded.

Trent's gaze barely brushed over her. He pulled a file toward him and flipped it open.

She tried again. "May I ask what you're doing?"

"Research."

"Something in particular?"

"More of everything in general." He scanned the file, made a note, and shoved the folder away. He selected another.

Alex watched him in silence for a few minutes. She should leave him alone, she thought. She didn't care in the least what he was up to; had decided, for the sake of her nerves, to limit any interaction with the man to the bare minimum. So she should just go and get her cup of coffee, and then continue with her own paperwork instead of contemplating another attempt at conversation. But she remained where she was until Trent set the second file aside and curiosity overcame her better sense.

Pushing upright, she wandered into the room to stand beside him. He went still at her approach, and for a moment that heightened awareness moved again between them, making her suddenly aware of the heat rising from him, the softness of his hair near her elbow, the shift of his body so near her own. She swallowed and shuffled sideways, and then made herself look at the notebook in front of him.

With an effort, she focused on the words he'd written and saw he was listing everything they knew of their victims. She cleared her throat.

"What?" He flipped open the third folder.

"You could save yourself some trouble," she said.

Trent looked up, his expression grim and unfriendly. Alex ignored it and pointed to the enormous dry-erase board hanging on the wall opposite, covered in notes on all the victims.

She strolled toward the door again. "We've already wasted our time on that."

His voice stopped her in her tracks, cold and clipped. "Detective Jarvis."

She hesitated, then half turned to him, her eyebrow raised in inquiry. "Yes?"

"I said forensics was a waste of time," he said, his head bowed over the file on the table. "I've come to believe linking the victims together may be of some value, however."

Alex chewed the inside of her bottom lip and studied his bent head. *Coffee,* she reminded herself. *You wanted coffee, not an argument.*

She tucked her injured arm against her side, supporting it with her other hand. "Detective Trent, we have some of the best forensic people on the continent working this case," she pointed out. "They haven't left so much as a grain of sand unturned. How in God's name can you call what they're doing a waste of time?"

"Have they found anything yet?" he asked, continuing with his notes. "Fingerprints, DNA?"

"Not yet, but they will."

"No, they won't."

She huffed. "The killer can't be this careful forever, damn it. Or this lucky. Sooner or later he'll screw up and leave something behind—a hair, an eyelash, skin under a fingernail—and it won't rain all over the scene and wash away the evidence. We'll find what we need, Trent. We always do."

"The weather has nothing to do with it. You'll find nothing, Detective, because there is nothing to find."

What had started as simple irritation flared into real annoyance and Alex felt her hackles rise another notch. "Oh, really. I don't suppose you'd like to tell me why not?"

"You already know."

"Excuse me?"

Granite-hard eyes lifted to stare at her. "I said you already know why not. You just don't want to admit the possibility."

The hairs lifted on the back of Alex's neck and, suddenly, she was back in the alley at the scene of the third murder, crouched beside the victim, holding the tarp away from the body. Seeing again the disregard for human life.

It was obscene, she'd thought. *Depraved.*

Evil, a voice in the back of her mind whispered.

It was evil.

Alex lifted her chin. "Are you trying to spook me?"

One dark eyebrow rose. "No," he answered. "I'm not. *Are* you spooked?"

A shiver crawled down Alex's spine. She caught back the *Go to hell* hovering on her lips and turned to leave.

"No," she lied over her shoulder in parting. "I'm not."

She stomped toward the coffee room. Why in God's name could she not learn to keep her distance from that man? Or at least keep her mouth shut? She sidestepped a cleaning cart and brushed past a woman emptying a garbage can.

What the hell was he hinting at, anyway? How was she supposed to know why they wouldn't find forensic evidence?

Wings. Invisible power surges. A glimpse of something standing over the victim in the alley in Chinatown. A suspect freeing himself from his restraints and plunging out a window to his death. Evil.

Alex shuddered. Screw coffee. What she really needed was a good stiff drink.

Or two.

TWENTY-TWO

Frustration rose in a tangle in Aramael's throat and he glared after Alex's retreating figure. Damn it to hell and back, this was *not* going to work. Not like this.

He'd been so hopeful that logic would be his salvation in the midst of this decidedly illogical existence in which he found himself. The idea had seemed sound when he'd thought of it in Martin James's hospital room, but after two hours of reviewing paperwork, all he'd managed to do was thoroughly confuse himself. He didn't have the first idea how to go about bringing order from the chaos of information in these files, and the board Alex had so kindly pointed out to him might as well have been written in the Principalities' tongue for all the sense he'd been able to make of it.

Yet Alex and her colleagues made it look so easy.

Bloody, bloody—

He paused in mid–mental curse. Alex. Alex knew what she was doing in this investigative morass. What if he—what if she—?

It seemed almost too simple. Too obvious. But if he could

get Alex to cooperate, it might just give him the edge he needed. A way to figure out a pattern to Caim's movements or, failing that, at least a hint at the identity his brother had assumed.

If he could get Alex to cooperate.

He balled his hand around the pen he held. She would have questions. More questions. She always did. How much would she want to know? How much would he be able to tell?

He thought about Caim stalking the streets, already seeking a new victim. Thought about it, but felt no more than a faint awareness through the greater thrum of energy that had become Alex. This was it. This was all he had left of his hunting prowess when in her company. Somehow she had overshadowed a Power's instinct and dragged him down to an unprecedented level.

Cooperation with a mortal. A Naphil.

With Alex.

The pen in his hand snapped in two, sending a spatter of ink across the files.

Bloody Hell.

HAVING DECIDED IT would be wise to hold off on alcohol until after she'd finished her reports, Alex continued her quest for coffee, only to meet Christine Delaney in the coffee room doorway. The fraud detective's smile brightened at the sight of her.

"Alex, I'm so glad I ran into you."

Alex? Since when were they on first-name terms?

"Delaney," she responded.

"Oh, please. Christine. We're working together now, after all."

Alex remembered seeing Delaney in the briefing, one of the many recruited to the task force until they caught their killer. She skirted the other woman and headed for the coffeepot. "We're on the same case," she allowed. "But I'd hardly call it working together."

"Whatever," Delaney said. "I just need you to go over things with me. Bring me up to speed."

Alex paused, pot hovering over cup, and shot a look over her shoulder. "We covered everything in the briefing. I don't have anything more."

A hint of pink washed over Delaney's cheeks and her gaze slid away from Alex's. "Yeah, well, I wasn't a hundred percent focused in there, I'm afraid."

Alex remembered the uncharacteristic dishevelment she'd noted earlier. She turned to hide a smirk. "Your breakfast date?" she hazarded.

She gave a little start of surprise as Delaney suddenly hefted herself onto the counter beside her. Meeting the gleam in the fraud detective's brown eyes, she felt her heart sink. Oh, hell. Please don't let Delaney think that was an invitation—

"Actually, yes," Delaney said, her voice conspiratorial.

Alex swallowed a groan. She didn't like girl talk at the best of times, but with Delaney, the idea took on a whole new level of *ick*. Now she really needed a drink.

She sought frantically for a change of subject as the other woman leaned in.

"I've never met anyone like him," Delaney confided. "He's so . . . intense. So consuming. I never expected that from someone like him. I always thought priests were ultra-conservative and uptight."

"He's a *priest*?" Alex's hand jerked, and a black puddle spread across the counter toward Delaney's cream-linen-clad backside.

The fraud detective gave a yelp and hopped down to retrieve a handful of paper towels.

"You're dating a *priest*?" Alex asked again, certain she had to have misheard.

Delaney nodded and spread the towels over the spilled coffee. "Shocking, isn't it?" She grinned, wiping Alex's cup dry and passing it back to her. "I tell you, if they all looked the way he does, church attendance would skyrocket. He is *so* totally hot."

"A *Catholic* priest?"

"I've no idea. The subject hasn't had a chance to come up, if you know what I mean." Delaney pitched the wad of paper towel into the trash can. "Does it matter? We can just call him a man of the cloth, if it makes you more comfortable."

"Comfort has nothing to do with it." Alex frowned. "What about the fraud complaint against him?"

"That? I told you it didn't pan out." Delaney shrugged.

"You could give it a little more time," Alex pointed out, an edge to her voice. "What happens if the complainant resurfaces and demands an investigation? Don't you think you're being a bit shortsighted?"

Delaney's brow creased with thought. The creases deepened to confusion. Then she scowled. "I didn't come to you for a lesson in how to do my job, Jarvis. All I want is a crash course on this case. I'm meeting William for dinner in an hour and I don't have time to read through all the crap."

Alex stared. Had Delaney really just called their case files *crap*? In addition to blowing off an investigation and dating an alleged suspect? While she'd never held the fraud detective in particularly high esteem, Alex hadn't expected to discover the woman was a complete idiot.

She snapped her teeth shut and schooled herself to silence. She had enough to worry about without taking on the fraud detective's issues. Or covering for her. She added cream and sugar to her coffee, then stirred.

"Well?" Delaney asked as the spoon clattered into the sink.

"The files you need are in the conference room." Alex picked up the cup. "In case you weren't paying attention to that part either, they stay there."

"But I told you I have a date—"

"You also have a job. Your choice."

Alex stalked from the coffee room, still shaking her head about the priest idea, only to jolt to a stop as a sudden presence loomed in front of her. She watched coffee drip down the mug and onto the floor. She sighed. What was it with her and coffee these days?

She lifted her chin and regarded Trent. A belligerent Trent. Her shoulders sagged. "Now what?"

"I need your help," he announced.

More liquid sloshed over Alex's hand. She set the cup on a nearby desk.

"And I," she said wearily, "need a drink."

"WHAT'LL IT BE?" Alex asked Trent over her shoulder as she led the way down the hall. "Iced tea, water?"

Scotch? she added mentally, but kept the offer to herself. As much as she really did want a drink, she preferred not to mess with her inhibitions around her partner. There was no telling what she'd say or do under the influence.

Or see.

She dropped her keys on the kitchen counter and turned to Trent, who remained in the doorway, looking as if he very much regretted his suggestion to continue their conversation at her house. Almost as much as Alex regretted agreeing to it.

She reached into the cupboard for two glasses. The idea had seemed sensible enough at the time. Alex's arm and head had both begun throbbing again—especially her head, after that conversation with Delaney—and she'd given up any notion of completing Roberts's requested paperwork, so there had been nothing to keep her at the office. Now, however . . .

Alex's gaze drifted toward the corner where she'd seen the purple-robed woman the night before, and memories rushed back. Trent's gentle tending of her injury, the voices that drew her downstairs, the torment in her partner's eyes that very nearly made her reach out to him in spite of the wings.

Toes curling against the tiles, she forced her attention back to Trent. "Well?"

"Iced tea. Please."

She pulled open the fridge and took out a pitcher. "You can come in and sit down, you know."

Trent's mouth tightened, but he moved into the room and took a seat at the pine table. Alex poured the iced tea and carried the glasses to the table one at a time, and then settled into a chair opposite. She unclipped the cell phone and gun holster from her waist and set them beside her glass.

She'd keep the conversation short, she decided. Find out what he wanted, answer his questions, and make sure they stayed on topic and didn't wander off into the bizarre the way they usually did. How hard could it be?

"So. What is it you want help with?"

"I need to find the connections between the victims. Tell me what you look for. How you look."

Alex raised an eyebrow at the *I*, but decided not to pursue it. She tapped a fingernail against the glass. "That's pretty basic stuff."

"Humor me."

"All right." Alex settled back in her chair, sweeping her hair over one shoulder. "We look at friends, neighbors, workplaces, lifestyles—"

"Be more specific."

"About lifestyles, you mean?" She shrugged. "We find out everything we can. Who their doctors are, where they service their cars, where they go to church, where their kids go to school, what schools *they* went to, what grocery stores they use, what route they take to work, what vet vaccinates their dog—"

"And you still have nothing to link any of them?"

"Apart from the fact they're all human?" she asked tartly.

Trent inclined his head, acknowledging the jab. "Apart from that, yes."

"Nothing."

He frowned. "Then you must be missing something."

Alex bristled. "We're still gathering information—look, why this sudden interest in police procedure, anyway? Yesterday you said it was a waste of time. Said you could catch him because you could—" She broke off, clamped her mouth shut, and looked away, remembering her intention to stay away from the bizarre.

"Feel him?" Trent finished softly. "I still do."

Then what changed? she wanted to ask. *If you felt him last night, why didn't you go after him?*

Even as she framed the questions, however, she knew what his answer would be. Had heard him speak it last night in this very room. Still felt its echo in her belly. *If I'm to protect Alex . . .*

Alex stood, carried her iced tea to the sink, and dumped it. She took out the bottle of thirty-year-old Scotch she kept in the lower cabinet by the fridge and poured a good three fingers into her glass, then tossed back the amber liquid in one swallow. The alcohol burned a path down her throat to her gut, trailing rawness in its wake. She tightened her grip on the glass, waited for her eyes to stop watering, and poured a second drink. Bracing her uninjured hand against the counter, she stared out the window over the sink. Felt, acutely, Trent's attention on her as the Scotch's warmth reached her toes and turned them fuzzy.

The clock in the living room chimed nine times.

So. Trent hadn't gone after the killer because he'd been tied to her, had been protecting her. The real question, then, was why? Except if she asked that, it meant acknowledging what she'd heard—and seen—the previous night. And if she acknowledged *that*, she'd also have to acknowledge, at least to herself, the rest of it.

The wings.

The raw connection between them.

The undeniable parallel to her mother.

Trent cleared his throat and Alex slugged back the second Scotch. She'd reached a crossroads. Ask or not? Continue to deny that the tidy little compartments in her mind weren't quite as defined as they used to be, or begin to accept? Where the hell did she draw the line?

The psychic thing, real. His connection to the killer, also real. The connection between him and her, undeniable. But the wings and other stuff? Ice trickled into her belly, dispelling the Scotch's lingering warmth. God, how she wanted to continue believing the wings were just her own special brand of reality. As much as the similarity to her mother terrified her, the alternative was a thousand times worse. A thousand times more frightening in its possibilities.

"Shit," she muttered.

"Alex."

Her name, spoken in Trent's low, rough voice, reverberated through her entire body. She tightened her grip on the counter. He'd never called her by name before. She could have done without him doing so now. And sure as shit could have done without the urge it triggered to turn, tear open her blouse, and offer herself to him right here, right now.

She swallowed hard. "You should go."

"We need to talk."

"No."

"Alex."

Again she felt the impact of her name all the way down to her alcohol-blurred toes. She scowled. "I can't," she said. There. She'd admitted it. "I get that there's more going on here than I understand, but I don't want to know. I can't. There's too much—it's too close—" She broke off and swallowed. Finally let herself look at him. "Please. Just go."

He shook his head.

"Because you have to protect me?" The question escaped before she could catch it back.

Trent's jaw went tight. "Yes."

She lifted her chin. "Even if I don't want you to." A statement this time.

"It's not your choice to make."

Alex tensed. She focused on the streak of pain running up her arm. No. No way would she ask. She'd told the truth when she said she didn't want to know, didn't want to understand. Whatever he might tell her, she didn't trust herself to process it. Worse, feared she might process it, but her already stretched-thin sanity wouldn't survive.

She poured a third drink, watching the tremble in her hand. Nope. No more questions. No more anything. Not tonight. She lifted the glass and turned to tell Trent exactly that.

The doorbell rang.

TWENTY-THREE

Alex stared at the man standing on her front porch in a pool of light, his powerful back turned to her, hands shoved into the pockets of black jeans that had seen better days. A stranger. A very large, very imposing stranger.

Her first impulse was to close the door and walk away. Her second was to return to the kitchen, grab the Scotch, and get shit-faced enough to end any chance of more thinking tonight. She did neither. Instead, she reminded herself she was a cop, a professional, and made herself take stock of her visitor. From midnight black hair caught back in a haphazard ponytail, to the black T-shirt and jeans, right down to the cowboy-booted feet.

Weariness gave way to wariness. "Can I help you?"

The man swung around to face her and Alex had to force herself not to step back. Imposing from the back, he was nothing short of overwhelming from the front. This was one *very* big man, and not just physically. Presence-wise, he had an aura about him that made her feel the size of an insect. A particularly small one.

"Alex Jarvis?" His voice rivaled the throaty growl of a police dog on alert and had the same effect of inspiring extreme caution.

She settled into a more solid stance and wished for the reassuring presence of the sidearm she'd left in the kitchen. "Who's asking?"

"I'm looking for Jacob Trent. I was told he might be here."

"I'll ask again," she said coolly. "Who are you?"

"Seth Benjamin. I worked with Jake a while back." He must have seen her disbelief, because he chuckled, a low rumble of sound, and added, "Undercover Narcotics," as he held out his hand in greeting. Amused eyes regarded her, surprisingly warm despite their darkness. "Dispatch gave me your address. I hope you don't mind my dropping in like this. I wanted to surprise Jake."

"So you have," Trent's voice said behind Alex before she could decide whether to accept Seth Benjamin's outstretched hand or demand ID first.

"Jake." The stranger's grin widened. "I heard you were working again."

"Indeed."

Working again? As in hadn't worked for a while? Alex peered over her shoulder at Trent. If not, why not? Was that what made his service record classified? And what was with the animosity sparking between these two? Seth Benjamin made it sound as if they were friends, but she'd never have guessed it from Trent's less-than-welcoming tone. Or from the annoyance he made no effort to hide. She looked back to Benjamin, who seemed oblivious to any undercurrents and in no hurry to break the silence.

She cleared her throat. "I don't suppose either of you would like to tell me what's going on?"

Benjamin's gaze flicked to her and then back to Trent. "I just need to talk to my colleague for a minute."

Trent's face turned to stone. "I'm not interested in any messages you have."

"No message. Just an offer of help."

"I don't need help."

"You cannot hunt and protect the woman at the same time."

Hell, not him, too. Alex bit back a groan. This was no better than the conversation with Trent in her kitchen. She scowled at the newcomer. "Excuse me."

Benjamin shot her a look that suggested he had forgotten she was there.

"The *woman* is standing right here," she informed him, "and I neither want nor need protection." She turned to Trent, all trace of alcohol-induced fuzzies driven out by sheer irritation. "And just what the hell does he mean by *hunt*, anyway?"

The two men exchanged glances.

"Perhaps we should continue this discussion elsewhere," Benjamin suggested.

Trent's response was unequivocal. "No. I'm not leaving her."

Alex bristled. "I said—"

"Do you mind giving us a minute?" Benjamin asked as if she hadn't spoken.

Alex nearly choked. She did sputter. "You—you—yes, damn it! You bet your ass I mind. This is *my* house, and as I recall, you weren't even invited!"

Seth Benjamin blinked at her, then turned to Trent. "You really do have your hands full, don't you?"

She pivoted away from the newcomer and jabbed a finger into Trent's chest, trying not to notice just how solid he felt beneath her touch. Or how her finger tingled from even that brief contact. She decided against a second jab and let her hand drop back to her side. Maybe the Scotch hadn't entirely disappeared from her system after all.

"Get out," she told her partner. "And take your friend with you."

"I can't."

"You'd better, because in thirty seconds, I'm calling for backup. I don't care how badly I screw my career. I'll press charges against you for—" Alex broke off as her cell phone, still on the kitchen table, trilled a summons. "Oh, for the love of God!" she growled. "Will this fucking day never end?"

ARAMAEL WAITED UNTIL Alex had shouldered past him and stomped down the hallway to answer the phone. When her snarled greeting reached them, he rounded on the Appointed, his fisted fury one step short of violent.

"What the hell is going on?"

Still on the porch, Seth gave him a lazy smile and leaned a shoulder against the door frame. "I told you. I'm here to help. Judging by what I interrupted just now, my timing couldn't be better." He eyed the Power curiously. "Would you really have told her?"

"You saw her. Do I have a choice?"

"She'll never believe you."

"I'll make her."

"No." Seth shook his head. "There are things in her past that won't let her believe, and telling her might destroy her."

"How do you know? She's had no Guardian to record her life."

"She is Nephilim. Apparently Mittron was still keeping track of them, at least at a cursory level. Verchiel couldn't find anything more than a chronological history, but we were able to read between the lines."

"And?"

"The woman—"

"Alex."

"What?"

"Her name is Alex," Aramael snarled, silently daring the Appointed to comment.

"Of course. Alex." Speculation gleamed in Seth's eyes, but he kept his thoughts to himself and continued, "Alex's mother was mentally ill. She saw things, heard voices. She called them her angels."

Aramael stared at him. "She was Nephilim, too? Is it possible what she saw was real? Is that why Alex—?"

"The Nephilim blood flowed through the father's veins, not the mother's. The mother's illness was just that. She was normal enough when she took her medication, but rarely did so. When Alex was nine years old, her mother killed her father and took her own life. Alex found the bodies. Because the illness, schizophrenia, can be inherited, Alex fears becoming like her mother."

Aramael did some of his own reading between the lines and felt his stomach knot. "Bloody Hell, she thinks she's imagining me?"

"Part of you, yes. If you tell her the truth, she may see it as proof of the illness. She doesn't have schizophrenia, but she can still be driven to madness."

"Bloody Hell," Aramael said again, remembering the fragility he had sensed in Alex. The desperation. He thought of her reaction to the murder scene they'd attended before her attack and how she had refused to hear the answers to her questions this evening. So much made sense now. A hollowness formed beneath his breastbone. "Then the best thing I can do for her is to find Caim and be out of her life."

"Of course." Seth sounded surprised that it even needed to be stated.

The hollowness grew to encompass Aramael's entire chest. He had always known his ultimate goal was Caim's capture. From the moment he'd accepted the assignment, it had been about protecting the Naphil while hunting his brother. It had been simple.

Until he'd met Alex. Until he'd touched her, and felt her, and—

"You have feelings for her." Seth's expression was a mix of intrigue and accusation.

Aramael stared at the Appointed, denial rising in him. Feelings for a mortal? A Naphil? Impossible, he wanted to say, but his tongue cleaved to the roof of his mouth. The angel in him would not allow him to refute what he knew to be true. He stayed silent.

"Does she know?" Seth asked.

"I didn't realize *I* knew," Aramael growled. "How could she?"

"Do I know what?" Alex's voice intruded between them with all the subtlety of Judgment. She looked between Aramael and Seth and held up her hand. "Never mind. I don't *want* to know."

She turned to Aramael. "That was the coroner on the phone. They came up dry on matching the claw's DNA to anything in the database. They've put out a call to the science community at large, but Bartlett doesn't sound hopeful."

Aramael said nothing. He didn't think he needed to; she already knew what he thought. The haggard lines around Alex's eyes deepened. So did the unhappy ones about her mouth. He watched her straighten her shoulders.

"Well. That's it, then," she said. "I'm going to bed."

She'd reached the halfway point on the stairs before he found his voice. "What about us?"

Alex paused. "Trent, for all I know, we have a fucking werecat tearing apart these people. You want to watch my back tonight, be my guest. I'm too goddamned tired to argue anymore."

She took two more stairs then looked back at him. "Just do me a favor and lock up after yourself if you change your mind, all right?"

Aramael watched her climb the rest of the stairs and listened to the tread of her feet down the hall. A door closed. He waited a moment and then turned to Seth.

"So. Exactly how is it you're supposed to help?"

TWENTY-FOUR

Alex intercepted her staff inspector at his office door the instant he emerged. "I need to talk to you."

Roberts paused, looked at her warily, and then strode toward the conference room and the morning briefing. "Is this another complaint about Trent?"

She swallowed a sharp retort. All things considered, she probably deserved that. At least from Roberts's perspective. "No."

"Then what do you want?"

Alex glanced at their surroundings. Too many ears for this kind of conversation. "In private," she said.

"Fine. This afternoon. Three o'clock."

"It's important—"

"Three o'clock, Detective. You'll have five minutes."

He pulled open the conference room door and stalked in, leaving her to follow. Alex tipped her head back and put a hand up to massage a knot in her left shoulder. Hell. Trust Roberts to be in one of his bulldozer-type moods. She'd been up half the night, wrestling with herself over this decision. One minute she'd be certain it was the right thing—the only thing—to do, and the next she'd convinced herself it wasn't necessary, that she was fine.

She was a fighter, not a quitter. She'd never run away from anything in her life, never allowed her past to interfere with her present, never used it as an excuse, never let herself be weak. But this—this case, this untenable situation with Trent—it was too much. With every incident, she came a little more unraveled, a little less able to keep herself stitched together. Regardless of whether or not his wings were a part of her imagination, a decision she'd decided was best to simply avoid, the stress of this case would put her over the edge if she stayed.

She knew that, and still it had taken everything she had to persuade herself she had to do this, had to remove herself from the case. It had taken even more to make herself go through with it, only to be shut down cold before she'd opened her mouth. Shit.

"Jarvis! You planning on standing out there all day, or can we get on with this?" Roberts bellowed from the room.

Alex gritted her teeth against the desire to tell her boss what he could do with both his meeting and his three o'clock appointment. Reassignment would continue to pay the bills. Suspension without pay wouldn't.

She stepped into the conference room and scanned the gathering. One chair sat empty on the other side of the table, right beside Trent. Her gaze locked for an instant with his, noting the anger there, and then she took up a position by the door and leaned against the wall, determined to ignore him. He could be as pissed off as he liked that she'd left home without her alternate bodyguard; it wouldn't be nearly as pissed as she'd been when she'd woken to find Seth Benjamin ensconced in her living room and Trent himself missing.

She glowered at the memory and her spine went stiff with indignation. If she hadn't made up her mind during the night to take herself off the case, she'd have done so this morning just to be rid of her self-appointed wardens.

Roberts rapped on the tabletop, cutting through the murmur of conversation in the room. "Okay, people, let's get this show on the road. What do we have that's new? Ward, anything on the victim in Etobicoke?"

"Nothing. We're still waiting for the prelim autopsy."

"ID?"

"Nada. But we do have IDs on the construction site victim and one of our John Does from downtown—and it turns out they're connected." Ward looked down at the notebook in his hand. "An Arthur Stevens, age fifty-five, and his son Mitch, age—"

A sudden crash outside the conference room door cut off Ward's words and made them all turn. Alex, closest to the door, saw Christine Delaney with briefcase in hand and a shattered vase of flowers and spreading water stain at her feet.

Roberts heaved a aggrieved sigh. "Christ, Jarvis—first you and now Delaney. What are you, contagious? Someone get some paper towel and let's help her clean up."

Alex watched a half dozen people move to help Delaney—or rather, do the work for her, because Delaney herself stood rooted to the spot, white-faced and silent. Alex edged past the others to touch the fraud detective's shoulder.

"Delaney? You all right? Do you need to sit down?"

Delaney twisted away. "I'm fine. Thank you," she mumbled.

Alex regarded her doubtfully, half convinced the other woman might join the flowers on the floor. "You sure?"

Delaney jerked her head up and down in what Alex presumed was a nod. "Don't bother," the fraud detective said harshly to Joly, who was trying to pick the flowers out from amidst the shards of glass. "I don't want them."

Alex stared at the blossoms scattered at their feet. "Are you sure? They're orchids, aren't they? They look expensive—"

"I'm sure. I'm allergic. Keep them if you like. They're from— I was bringing them to show—" Breaking off, the fraud detective whirled on her heel and stumbled away.

Alex looked down and met Joly's eyes, finding her own puzzlement mirrored there. "What was that all about?"

"Beats the hell out of me." Joly waved the flowers in his hand at her. "You want 'em?"

Alex took the flowers from him. The orchids were truly gorgeous. Huge, exotic-looking black blooms, they might have been just plucked from a tropical island somewhere. But for all their perfection, something about them made Alex's skin crawl. She shook her head.

"Thanks, but I'm not the flower type." She dropped the flowers into the trash can alongside the broken vase and stared after Delaney. Marble white, the fraud detective disappeared down the corridor that led to the elevator and stairs.

Alex frowned. That girl was seriously twisted up about something. It occurred to her someone ought to go after the fraud detective and make sure she was all right, but Roberts's voice hailed from inside the room and, with a last look after Delaney, Alex turned back to the meeting.

CHRISTINE JABBED BLINDLY at the elevator button. Missed. Tried again. Connected. She stared at the display over the doors and fought to control her breathing, the shaking in her chest that had begun when she'd heard Ward: *Arthur Stevens, age fifty-five, and his son Mitch—*

A coincidence, she told herself harshly. It had to be a coincidence. The names weren't all that uncommon. They didn't have to be connected to the fraud file she'd brushed off so easily. The file that had led her to William.

Her stomach spasmed, forcing bile into her throat. No way could the two files be connected. William couldn't possibly be involved. It would be too bizarre for words. It would mean— She swallowed a bubble of hysteria.

It would mean she'd been dating a serial killer, for fuck's sake. That she'd been—she thought of her time with William and cringed. In only two days, she had explored facets of sexuality she had never even dreamed of, let alone imagined she would participate in. Surely to God she would have known if her lover was a killer. Surely she would have sensed something . . .

She shuddered, remembering the intensity behind William's touch as he took possession of her, the way she seemed to lose a little of herself to him each time. The emptiness that remained in her when they were done, never quite filled. An emptiness she saw reflected back at her in his eyes.

But a serial killer?

The elevator doors slid open. She stepped inside, made herself nod to the uniform already there, pushed the button for the parking level.

She thought of the file she'd opened in response to Arthur Stevens's complaint. A file that had sat untouched on her desk for the last two days while she screwed the alleged suspect. Even if William wasn't the killer, her negligence was bound to come to light at some point. Christine pressed her fist into her mouth and slumped against the elevator wall, ignoring the curious look from the uniform. Any way she looked at this, she was fucked.

She fought down the seethe of panic in her belly. There had to be some way to lessen the impact, something she could do or say. The elevator door hissed open on the second floor and the uniform exited, leaving her to continue her descent alone.

Jarvis. She could call Jarvis. Alex already knew about the fraud complaint, and about William, more or less. If Christine passed on what she knew, if she begged Jarvis not to tell anyone about the personal relationship between her and an alleged suspect—

The elevator jittered to a stop on the parking level and Christine pulled herself upright, reaching for her cell phone as the doors opened. She didn't have Alex's number, so she called dispatch, waiting impatiently for them to patch her through as she walked through the cavernous underground lot to her car. Swearing when the call went straight to voice mail.

"Shit—Alex, it's Christine Delaney. Look, I need to speak to you about something, so call me back when you get this, will you? It's—" Christine swallowed and leaned her elbow on the car roof. "I've really fucked up, Alex. It's urgent." She gave her number, repeated it, and then flipped the phone closed and rested it against her forehead.

There. Now she just had to wait. If Jarvis found no connection between William and the killer, no one would ever need to know about Christine's personal involvement with him. She'd still face a reprimand for her sloppy investigative work, but that would be all.

But if there *was* a connection—

The scuff of a shoe on pavement broke through her agitation. She tucked the phone into a pocket and brushed her hair back from her face. Going to pieces in the parking lot would solve nothing. Better to get out of here, go for coffee somewhere, make notes of everything she needed to tell Jarvis, get her head straight. She turned, ready to smile at whoever approached and pretend that her career hadn't just taken a major dump.

William's cold eyes stared into hers.

ALEX SURVEYED HER desktop with its neat stacks of completed files. Everything she knew about the case, committed to paper. Everything she'd rather not think about, safely tucked away in her mind where she wouldn't have to deal with it anymore. At least not after she'd seen Roberts in— she glanced at the clock on the wall—ten minutes.

She wondered what he would assign her to. With luck he'd keep her on the squad, maybe working other files no one else had time for. She hoped he wouldn't be pissed enough to transfer her out; she preferred to keep her job, knew she was good at it. Liked it.

From the desk abutting hers came the sound of Trent clearing his throat. Alex's heart gave an unwelcome thud.

Most of the time she liked it, she corrected.

She looked at the clock again. Nine minutes. She wiped damp palms against her trousers. She'd avoided Trent the entire day, keeping her head bent over her desk, steadfastly crossing t's and dotting i's and even forgoing lunch so he wouldn't have a chance to speak to her.

Trent *ahemm*ed again, the sound reaching out to set off the now-familiar quiver in her belly.

Alex pulled the top file from the stack and flipped it open. She didn't need anything from it, and couldn't have read the words if she'd tried, but it gave her something to do. Something besides facing Jacob Trent. Or the sense of emptiness she'd battled in the last few hours at the idea of being without him.

She scowled at the papers in front of her. She'd wanted to be rid of the man since the moment she'd met him. Now was not a good time to be having second thoughts.

"Detective—" Trent began.

Alex cut across his words. "I'm taking myself off the case." She didn't look up.

"No."

Now she looked. And raised an eyebrow. Of all the responses she might have expected, that one wasn't even on the list. "Excuse me?"

"I told you I need your help."

"There are others—"

"I'm not trying to protect *others*," he growled. "I'm trying to protect you. And this hunt is damned difficult enough without you adding to my grief any more than you already have."

Alex gaped at him. "*Your* grief?" she hissed, aware of the many people within hearing distance. "How in the hell have I added to *your* grief?"

Heat flashed through his gray eyes, reaching out to lick along her veins in a decidedly shocking manner, and then disappeared so fast that she had to have been wrong. Hoped to God she had been wrong, because matters were fucking complicated enough already.

"You refused Seth's company this morning."

"I was capable of driving myself."

"That's not the point, and you know it. I told you—"

"I know what you told me, Detective Trent. I told *you* I don't need your protection. Or Benjamin's. Once I take myself off the case, it will be a moot point anyway. I'll be out of your hair and you can focus on finding the killer instead of whatever it is you think you're doing for me."

Trent's voice dropped to a harsh, angry snarl. "Do you really think you can sidestep him that easily? He doesn't give a damn about the case. The rest of these people mean nothing to him. I doubt he's even noticed them. It's you he wants, and leaving the case won't even slow him down."

"And I'm just supposed to take your word for that? What about the other victims? If the killer is after me like you say, then why kill so many others?"

"To find you."

"That doesn't make sense. He either knows me or he doesn't. You can't have it both ways."

"He didn't know you at first. But once he saw you in the alley, he did. If I know him, he is stalking you even now."

"Do you?" she asked. "Know him?"

The soul-deep anguish she had seen before was back, accompanied this time by a stark honesty. "Yes," he said. "I do."

Alex went still. Stared at her partner. Tipping point. If she continued asking questions, she would be caught up in whatever world Trent inhabited. Might never extricate herself. Might never have another chance to walk away.

"Jarvis! You want your five minutes or don't you?" Roberts's bellow reached across the office and thrust itself between them.

For a long second, Alex couldn't respond. Couldn't look away from the very man she most wanted—needed—to avoid. Roberts called her name again. Drawing on a strength she hadn't known she possessed, Alex forced herself to her feet and lifted her chin.

"I'm taking myself off the case," she repeated and, turning her back on Trent, she made her way to her staff inspector's office.

TWENTY-FIVE

"No," said Roberts. He didn't look up from the papers he was signing.

Consternation shafted through Alex. Son of a bitch, she wished she'd seen this coming. In all her agonizing over the decision to remove herself from the case, it hadn't occurred to her that Roberts might say no—the same response Trent had given her.

She scowled. What was this, a bloody conspiracy?

"You know I wouldn't ask if I didn't need this."

"I do know that." Roberts laid aside his pen. "And I wish I could do it, Alex. But this case is too big and I need you too badly. Without a medical certificate, I simply can't justify taking you off the file."

"You want me to see a shrink?"

"If you're finding things this difficult, maybe you should." Her staff inspector studied her, linking his fingers behind his head and leaning back. "You're sure you're telling me everything? This doesn't have something to do with Trent?"

Alex looked away from her staff inspector's too-perceptive

eyes. It had everything to do with Trent, but she was damned if she'd say so. If Roberts thought she needed to see a shrink based on what she'd told him so far—that the case was dredging up too many memories and causing serious stress in her life—then she could just imagine what he'd think if she confessed the rest of it. One whisper of wings and otherworldly presences and he'd pull her off duty altogether and declare her unfit. Her career would never recover.

Worse, she'd have no choice but to seek the help he only suggested now. The kind of help that required delving into her past, reliving it, and facing each and every one of the demons she'd spent a lifetime denying. The fingernails of Alex's good hand drove so deep into her palm it was a wonder they didn't scrape bone.

"I'm sure," she answered her staff inspector. "It's not about Trent."

Roberts regarded her in tight-lipped silence for a long moment. Alex shifted in her seat.

"Then I have to ask, Detective: do you think you're a danger to yourself or anyone else?"

Alex glowered. "I'm not about to go postal or do myself in, if that's what you mean. I'm not that far gone."

"Like I said, I have to ask."

She put a hand to the back of her neck and kneaded the ache there. Gave her supervisor a weary nod. About to rise from her chair, she paused when he spoke again.

"Alex—" Roberts broke off, fiddling with a pen on his desk. A furrow settled between his eyebrows. "For what it's worth, you're not the only one struggling with this file. I think we've all figured out this isn't quite our ordinary, run-of-the-mill serial killer."

He paused, seeming to expect a response, but Alex said nothing. Roberts shook his head. "I really do need all the help I can get on this thing. I'm sorry." He sighed. "Bring me a medical certificate and I'll take you off the case. Until then—" He broke off as Bastion stuck his head into the office through the partially open door.

"Sorry to interrupt, Staff, but have either of you seen Delaney kicking around anywhere?"

"Not me." Roberts raised an eyebrow at Alex.

She shook her head. "Not since she dropped the flowers this morning. She headed for the elevators right after that."

"Something urgent?" Roberts asked.

"Nah. Just following up on something. I'll try her cell phone again." About to withdraw, Bastion paused. "Oh, Jarvis, I'm supposed to tell you there's a call holding for you. Your sister, I think."

The door closed.

Roberts returned his attention to Alex. "Look, I know it's not much, but if you think it might help, I can put you and Trent on the desk end of things. Maybe things won't get to you quite as much if you don't have to go out to the scenes."

A lump settled into Alex's chest. That was it? She'd worked herself into a lather all night and most of the day for an offer of desk duty that included the partner she so desperately didn't want? Was there no way to rid herself of Jacob Trent?

She swallowed hard, not knowing whether to laugh or cry. Face Trent across a desk all day, or sit beside him in a vehicle? View the murder scenes in person or go over the color photos in minute detail?

Lose her mind slowly or just get it over with?

"No desk duty," she said. "Being cooped up like that would definitely put me over the edge."

Roberts nodded. "Let me know if you change your mind. And when you get that appointment."

Alex pushed out of the chair and crossed to the door. Trent waylaid her just outside.

"Well?" he asked.

She favored him with a baleful glare. "You win."

"He refused?"

"Outright, unless I produce a medical certificate attesting to the fact that I'm losing my mind."

Trent's mouth tightened. "I'm sorry."

She snorted and began to walk away. "Right."

A hand on her shoulder stopped her, heavy and warm. Alex waited but didn't turn back.

Trent's voice deepened. Roughened. Washed over her in a wave that drew her in, folded around her. "I *am* sorry, Alex. More than you'll ever know."

She almost faced him then. Almost gave in to the compassion she heard, almost turned to him for the answers she had denied the night before . . . at least the ones she thought she could handle. But then something changed, shifted, and her lungs deflated with a tiny hiss.

Wings, she thought. *If I turn now, I'll see wings again.*

And still she wavered. It would be so easy. Easier than continuing to fight, to deny what increasingly felt inevitable. She'd turn into that powerful chest, his arms would go around her, she'd feel his wings envelop her . . .

Alex pulled away from her partner's touch. "I have a call waiting," she said.

HOW COULD I?

Aramael watched Alex cross to her desk, her steps jolting, out of sync. His stomach rolled at the thought of what he had just done; of what he had, for a split second, wanted to happen more than anything else in the world. A shudder ran through him.

To open himself to a mortal like that—to deliberately set aside the veil that hid him from her; to wish for her to turn, to see him not just as a man, but as his true self, as an angel . . .

The absolute wrongness was staggering.

The regret that she hadn't done so, indefensible.

He drew a ragged breath. He was losing it, he thought with faint astonishment. Acting outside the parameters that guided his presence here on Earth; knowingly breaking the cardinal rule of noninterference with a mortal. How much further would this go? How much further would he *let* it go?

He watched as Alex reached her desk and picked up the

phone. Her gaze met his for the space of a heartbeat and then moved away, simultaneously filling his soul and leaving it barren. Aramael closed his eyes.

No further, he thought. He could let it go no further. Somehow he had to find a way to regain his focus, his purpose. Had to find a way to finish this hunt and return to Heaven before he destroyed her.

Before she destroyed him.

"HEY, JEN," ALEX said into the receiver. From the safety of her desk, she risked a peek at where she'd left Trent and found him watching her in a decidedly hostile—and wingless—manner. Her pulse had skipped a beat.

She realized her sister had stopped speaking. "Sorry. I wasn't listening. What was that?"

"I *said*," replied her sister tersely, "when the hell were you planning to tell me you'd been hurt?"

Hurt. Alex looked down at her bandaged arm. She'd all but forgotten the injury. A sign of healing, or one more indication of her lack of touch with reality?

"I'm fine," she assured Jen. "Just a scratch. How did you find out?"

"Good God, when was the last time you read a newspaper? You were on the front page yesterday morning and I've been trying to reach you ever since. Don't you ever check your voice mail?"

Alex pulled a face and sat down. She sensed a lecture coming on; she might as well make herself comfortable for it. "It's been a little busy around here."

She tugged her cell phone free of its holder and flipped it open. Shit, the damned thing was dead. No wonder it had been so quiet today. She opened her desk drawer and rummaged for the charging cord. Jen hadn't said anything more and Alex paused. "Jen? You still there?"

"I'm here." Jen's voice went soft. "Al—how are you holding up on this thing? Really."

Alex swallowed past an unexpected snag in her throat. "I'm doing okay. Not sleeping much, but neither is anyone else."

"What about the other stuff?"

"Other stuff?"

"What you wanted to talk about the other day. I wasn't a very good listener. I'm sorry."

"It's fine, Jen, don't worry about it."

"But I am worried. You haven't asked questions like that in more than twenty years. Something must have happened to trigger it now."

Alex looked to Trent, now standing in the conference room doorway and glaring at the victim board. *You have no idea,* she thought, but she answered, "It's just the case, Jen. I've seen so many knifing victims in the last week, it's bound to bring up some stuff I'd rather not remember."

Alex plugged in her cell phone, switched it back on, and set it on her desk, making a mental note to check her voice mail later and erase the multiple messages Jen had almost certainly left. From the corner of her eye, she saw Joly waving for her attention. She looked over at him and he held up the receiver and two fingers. She nodded. "Look, Jen, I have to go. I have another call."

"But—"

"I'm *fine,* Jen. I'll call you when I can—maybe you can feed me dinner one of these days. Give Nina a hug for me. Love you." With no small relief, Alex reached out and punched the button for line two of the office phone. "Homicide. Detective Jarvis."

"Have you missed her yet?" a man's voice asked.

Alex frowned. "Missed who? Who is this?"

"One of your own is gone, and you haven't even noticed." He *tsk*ed. "I'm disappointed, Naphil. I thought you would be at least slightly more astute than other mortals. That something of the divine might have survived in you."

Naphil. She'd heard that word before. In her kitchen. Spoken by a winged Trent to a purple-robed woman. Alex's

initial confusion gave way to cold, certain instinct and her
heart kicked against her ribs. She whirled in her chair and
snapped her fingers for Joly's attention, pointing to her
phone. His eyes widened a fraction and then he nodded,
reaching for his receiver, understanding she needed a trace
on the line. His partner stood and jogged across to Roberts's
office, banging on the window for the staff inspector's attention.

Alex steadied herself and returned to the conversation.
"I'm sorry I disappointed you—"

"No matter. I'm sure I'll still find what I need in you. The
question is how I'm going to get to you. Christine was kind
enough to provide me with your details, but I still have to
find a way past *him*."

"Get to me?" *Christine? How the hell does he know
Christine?* Her throat dry, Alex scanned the office for Trent.
She saw him on the far side of the room, striding toward
her, and quailed from the fury that told her he knew who
was on the other end of the line.

"So he hasn't told you. Then I wonder what it is that
draws you to him, that makes you accept him into your life?"
The voice took on a musing tone. "If you don't look to him
for protection, then what— Oh, my. Really? This is an unexpected bonus, especially if he reciprocates." The voice
sharpened. "Does he?"

Trent was halfway to her, fiery wings unfurling in his
wake.

"Does he what?" Alex's gaze locked with her partner. *If
I'm to protect Alex . . .*

"No, of course he won't have said anything. It's utterly
forbidden. I'll tell you what. When you do find her, when
you see what I've done to her and what I'm going to do to
you, make sure he goes with you. I'll be there, watching, so
that I might judge for myself. Can you do that for me,
Naphil?"

Trent reached her desk, focused, intent, every inch a
predator. A winged hunter. He held out his hand for the
phone and Alex tightened her grip on the receiver. The

conversation had come full circle and she could not end it now.

"When I find who?" she whispered, knowing. Dreading.

"The lovely Christine, of course."

The line went dead.

TWENTY-SIX

Alex left Roberts cursing the tech support guy in his office and walked across to where Trent had all but paced a trench into the floor by the file room. His body stilled when he saw her coming, but the energy poured off him in waves. Raw, harsh, chaotic. Thick enough that, as Alex drew nearer, it took every ounce of willpower to keep moving toward him, every step feeling as if she drew a foot up from half-set concrete.

"Are you all right?" she asked when she reached him.

He stared at her, his hands on his hips, jacket shoved back. Surprise glinted from his turbulent eyes and for a breath, the energy around him edged down a notch.

It surged back up again immediately.

"I didn't feel him," he grated. "Not even a whisper. I have *never* not felt my prey."

Prey. Alex looked away and, with an effort, managed not to turn tail and run. She nodded toward the empty file room beside them. "Let's go somewhere quiet."

Again the energy subsided. This time it stayed that way,

still a moving, almost living force between them, but diminished. Trent regarded her wordlessly, then nodded and followed her into the room. Alex closed the door.

"The tape of the conversation is pure static," she said without preamble, "and the trace was useless. Christine's vehicle is still in the parking lot, she isn't answering her cell phone, and she's not at her apartment. How do we find her?"

Trent expelled a blast of air and started pacing again. "I don't know. I told you, I can't—"

"Feel him," Alex interrupted. "I get that. But you know him. You know how he operates, how he thinks. That makes you our best chance for finding him. And her."

Trent stopped in front of her. "You're different," he announced. "Something has changed."

Alex looked away. "I don't know what you mean."

Her partner was quiet for a moment. Then he asked, "What did he say to you?"

"He said he had Christine—"

"What else?"

She licked dry lips. From the corner of her eye, she saw him track the movement. Torment flared across his face and sudden heat joined the energy still radiating from him, finding an answer low in her belly. *Focus, damn it.* She edged away.

"Alex." Trent's voice stopped her mid-sidle. "What else did he say?"

Alex folded her arms across herself. Wished herself somewhere far, far away. Gritted her teeth and made herself answer. "He called me Naphil. Wondered how he was going to get past you to me."

"And?"

Heat scorched her cheeks. "He wanted to know why I allowed you in my life if I wasn't looking for your protection, and if you felt the same way. He said that when we do find Christine, he'll be watching you to judge for himself."

Silence.

"You don't want to ask questions." A statement.

"No." The word came out as a bare thread of sound. Alex cleared her throat. "No. I just want to find Christine. And the killer."

"As do I."

Alex thought about the voice mail message Christine had left for her, the clue that had to be in the fraud detective's words, if she could only decipher it. If *they* could only decipher it. She tightened her arms around her stomach and reached deep for the fortitude she needed for this next part. The part where she did what had to be done if they were to ever find their killer: she turned, faced Jacob Trent, and finally accepted him as her partner.

"Then let's do it," she said.

ARAMAEL SWALLOWED A snarl and heaved his pen across the room. "We're wasting time. This is getting us nowhere."

Alex looked up from the files she'd spread across the conference table, frustration stamped in the stubborn, weary lines of her face. "You have a better idea?"

He shoved back from the table and prowled the room's perimeter. "You know I don't, but there must be something more than this"—he waved his hand—"this endless going over and over the same things. You can't tell me this works. That *this* is how you hunt."

"Rather successfully, actually." She tacked yet another annotated sticky note onto the wall among dozens of others. Flashed him a look of profound annoyance. "This is real police work, Trent. Meticulous, grinding, dry as dust, and nothing like the movies. But it does work, so until you figure out an alternative, suck it up."

Aramael drew himself to his full height, towering over her. "Excuse me?" he breathed. He didn't care how much of a bond he felt with this woman, no one spoke to a Power like that.

But Alex showed not the slightest sign of intimidation. "You heard me. And for the record, we don't hunt, we investigate, and if you have nothing to contribute, then go find something else to do."

He actually felt his wings begin to unfurl, his indignation was so great. He glowered at her, searching for words that would even begin to express his irritation, and then felt himself falter when she looked away from him. He stared down at her in surprise. She had never backed down before. Why—?

She reached for a file and his gaze locked on her hand. Or more precisely, on the tremble in her hand. His anger drained from him in a rush. She was afraid. He berated his stupidity. Of course she was afraid. She'd spoken to Caim, had seen what he was capable of, knew the threat against her was real. She was terrified, and with good reason.

Aramael turned and stalked to the other side of the room. What an unholy mess. What a fucking, unholy mess. His hands twitched with frustration and pent-up energy. Energy that should be aimed at his brother in fury and retribution, but instead longed to be directed toward Alex in comfort and reassurance and all manner of things he dared not contemplate.

He heard the soft clearing of her throat behind him. Gathered himself. Made his hands unclench. Turned.

Alex stared down at the table. "You can stop him, right?" she asked.

He didn't answer for a moment. Then, even though she couldn't see, he nodded his head. "Yes," he said. "When we find him, I can stop him."

Because the alternative was unthinkable, and not just for the reasons Heaven imagined.

She weighed his words, and he saw her want to believe them. But when the door opened and her supervisor came into the room, followed by several other detectives, doubt still shadowed her eyes.

"Well?" Roberts asked.

Alex shook her head. "Nothing. You?"

"Dick all." Roberts stared at the sticky-note-covered wall. "Where the fuck is the connection? With this many vics, there has to be *something*. These people wouldn't all just go off with some random stranger, not with all the media coverage on this thing. We can't even get a decent profile on the son of a bitch."

"Maybe we're making it more complicated than we need to," one of the other detectives muttered. "If it *is* as random as it looks, maybe we just ask who all these people would go with."

"You mean, like someone they trusted," Alex said, coming alert and straightening up from the table.

"Uniforms," someone else offered. "People trust uniforms."

A sudden thrill of interest buzzed through the room. Ideas spilled over one another.

"A cop."

"Firefighter."

"Armed forces."

"Paramedic."

"Priest," Alex said.

The room went silent and Aramael, along with all the others, turned to Alex. She looked stunned. Sickened. Horrified. "The bodies. They were all posed like a crucifix. Delaney was dating a priest."

The moment she said it, Aramael knew it to be true. Caim would love the irony, would take enormous pleasure in the idea of thumbing his nose at Heaven in that way.

"A *Catholic* priest?" Roberts asked.

"She didn't know. He'd been accused of fraud, but the complainant never followed up and Delaney decided to close the file." Alex pressed her hands to her temples. "Shit, that's what her message was about. Why didn't I see this before?"

Roberts's face had turned a brick red. "She was dating a *priest* accused of *fraud*?"

"The flowers," Alex muttered.

"The what?"

She lifted her head. "The flowers. When Delaney dropped the flowers this morning, we'd just started the meeting. Someone— Ward." Alex whirled to face another of the men. "You'd just given the ID on two of the vics, father and son."

"Stevens. Arthur and Mitchell. Arthur Stevens was the

complainant on a fraud file Delaney had. Bastion was trying to get hold of her this afternoon to follow up on it."

A handful of seconds ticked by while those in the room processed the information. Worked through the implications. Then Roberts strode toward the door.

"Find Bastion," he directed the man named Ward. "Get that fraud file from him. I want the name and address of the priest on my desk in five minutes along with a warrant. Alex, call tactical."

SETH PULLED OUT a chair across the table from Verchiel, swung it around, and straddled it. "You've been hiding," he said cheerfully.

He watched the Dominion turn over her papers and cover the page of the record she had been reading. An old record, he noted. Very old.

"Not hiding," she said. "Just busy."

"Too busy to respond to your messages? I've been trying to reach you for some time now."

"My apologies."

"You haven't asked why."

Verchiel rested an elbow on the table, cradling her cheek in her hand. "I know why, Seth. I just don't know that I have the answers for you."

"Or for Aramael, apparently."

She looked away. "Or for Aramael."

"You know he has feelings for the woman."

Seth watched Verchiel twist a strand of hair around a finger, saw the tiny lines between her brows deepen. He probed a little further. "There is a difference between not having answers and not sharing the ones you do have, you know."

"You're not going to let this go, are you?"

"No. Aramael deserves better than this. If you don't have answers for me, then I will find them elsewhere."

Verchiel's expression reflected an inner struggle, and then

hardened as she seemed to reach a decision. "What do you want to know?"

"What went wrong?" he said. "Why does Aramael have feelings for the woman? Why can she see him?"

Verchiel's hand twitched atop the papers in front of her. Seth reached across the table to place his own hand beside hers and, after a moment's hesitation, the Dominion withdrew. Seth slid the papers aside and pulled the thick sheaf of fragile, yellowing papers toward him. "What page?"

"All of them." Verchiel nodded toward a stack by her elbow. "Those, too."

"I don't suppose you could summarize for me?"

"I'm not done yet. I've barely started, in fact, but if I'm reading these right, Aramael and the woman—" Verchiel took a deep breath. "I have no idea how it happened, but there's a possibility they may be soulmates. It's really the only possible explanation for the connection between them."

"Angels don't have soulmates."

"Not now, no. But we did once. In the beginning, when Lucifer sat at the One's side, all of angelkind loved and were loved, and we knew great happiness. We were sisters and brothers, mothers and fathers . . ." The Dominion's voice trailed off.

After a moment, she roused herself. "Then the One created the mortals, and Lucifer's descent began. He was so very jealous. So resentful of the time and attention the One paid to them. At first the One tolerated his interference; I suppose she thought he would come around, but it only became worse. Lucifer persuaded the Grigori to share knowledge with mortals that they weren't prepared to handle. Humans began to fight among themselves, to use their new skills to gain power over one another. Wars broke out. Then Lucifer encouraged the physical unions between Grigori and mortal, and the Nephilim were spawned."

Seth held still, sensing that she wasn't done. So far the story was a familiar one all of Heaven knew, but the yellowed paper in his hands suggested there was more to be learned.

As if she'd read his mind, Verchiel smiled tightly. "You know all this, of course. We all do. The One cast out the Grigori and Lucifer, one-third of the host followed, war ensued between us." She nodded at the paper he held. "The rest of the story is in there. All of it. The pain of battling our loved ones, of losing so many of them to Lucifer, very nearly destroyed us, and so the One did the only thing she could. She removed our free will, took away our responsibility for our own actions, made it her decision that we go against our mates, our children and siblings. And she removed our memories of love. Our capacity for it."

Far away, in the bowels of the room that housed the entire history of angelkind and mortals alike, Seth heard the thud of a book dropped to the floor. Listened to its muffled echo die away.

At last he spoke, surprised at the gruffness in his voice, "Familiar stories, even those. But you speak of those events as if you remember them."

Verchiel's eyes clouded. "I've always remembered. It's distant, muted, but I know what it was like to love, to have a soulmate. I know the pain Aramael will endure in losing the woman."

"Even if you're right, you're hardly responsible."

"Aren't I? If I'd stood up to Mittron, refused to send Aramael after Caim a second time, I might have prevented any of this from happening."

Surprise stirred in Seth. "But you would have been disobeying an order—an action like that would require free will."

Verchiel blanched. Looked ill. "Yes. It would."

Seth sat back in his chair and tapped a finger against his top lip. "How long have you known?"

"Mittron—" She paused. "Mittron was my soulmate. I thought that my ambivalence toward his authority was because of our familiarity. I've only just realized it is more."

"Are there others like you?"

"I don't know. If there are, they wouldn't talk of it."

"I suppose not." Seth fell silent. Verchiel might be an

anomaly, but with nearly three hundred thousand angels in Heaven, it was unlikely she was the only one who struggled with this. Which begged the question of how many others had harbored the same secret, and for how long? Not to mention how it had happened in the first place.

He touched the stack of papers. "And this? What is it you're looking for in this?"

"I don't know yet. Connections, I suppose. Reasons."

"Was it not the Highest who saw to the Cleanse?"

Verchiel folded her hands on the table, knuckles white with strain. "Yes."

"So I'm guessing he didn't sanction your research?"

"No."

Seth rose from his chair, turned it around, and pushed it into place at the table. He slid the papers across the desk toward Verchiel. "Keep looking. I want to know more. Tell Mittron I set you to the task, and that I'd like to know what he plans to do about this mess."

Verchiel looked startled. Horrified. "You want me to tell the Highest Seraph he is to—"

"Report to me? Yes. Tell him I said I'm pulling rank on him. It's about time someone did." Seth began strolling back the way he'd come through the rows of documents that made up the archives, then he paused and turned back to Verchiel. "You need to tell Aramael."

"He won't take it well."

Seth held back a snort. Verchiel had no idea. "Probably not," he agreed. "But it may be our only chance to temper what we can no longer control."

TWENTY-SEVEN

Alex watched three projectiles punch through the painted-over plate-glass window. Loud pops followed in their wake, and then the brief, brilliant glare marking them as flash grenades. Another smaller explosion followed at the mission door as the charge set by the tactical unit blew apart the lock. Before the puff of smoke had even formed, the unit went into action, the first through the door bearing a shield that would protect him and those following from whatever lay on the other side. In seconds, all the team members had passed through the doorway and into the building.

She waited, gun in hand, crouched to one side of Father William McIntyre's street mission. The bricks pressed into her back. A few meters away, Trent paced the sidewalk. He had refused to don a bulletproof vest; refused to join the team waiting to penetrate the building; refused to let Alex out of his sight.

Roberts hadn't seemed to notice. Alex hadn't argued.

The earpiece she wore crackled to life.

"Clear."

"Clear."

"Clear."

Alex tightened her grip on her gun, her palms clammy with anticipation. No difficulties encountered so far. No surprises. No killer. No Christine.

From inside, she heard the crash of wood giving way. The rattle of heavily equipped Emergency Task Force members moving forward in another rush. Silence. Alex straightened up, her intestines slithering over one another to form a knot in her belly. Her throat tightened. Where were they? Why didn't they say something?

As if she'd conjured it, the team leader's voice sounded in her ear. Tight, shaking, hoarse. "Holy fucking hell. You guys better get in here. Now."

The smell of blood hit before she cleared the doorway. The gut-emptying stench of rotting meat came next. Alex gagged and buried her nose in her sleeve. Odor became taste as she breathed through her mouth and fought a wave of nausea. What the hell was in here? She waited for a moment to let her eyes adjust to the dim light, and then made herself take stock of her surroundings.

A half dozen cheap, waiting-room-style chairs sat against one wall, a desk, littered with broken glass from the grenades' entries, faced the entrance. No blood. No bodies. She focused on a door hanging from its hinges in the opposite wall. Flashlight beams crisscrossed the darkness beyond, but not a sound emerged, not even the clump of boots. As if everyone there moved on tiptoe.

A fine, creeping quiver crawled along Alex's skin. She lowered her arm. There had to be two dozen street-hardened cops in the place. Cops who had seen it all. Why the hell was there not so much as a whisper from any of them?

Light flared suddenly in the other room as someone found a switch. A bare instant later, one of the tactical team members, stone-jawed and pasty, bulldozed through the doorway and onto the sidewalk. Alex heard him retch and the quiver along her skin became a tremble in her gut, her lungs, her heart. Death's scent permeated her every pore, wove its way into her soul, became an icy slag-heap of fear. She looked again toward the room beyond the lobby. Toward what the killer had invited them to find, what he hinted would happen to her.

No. Not hinted. Said.

A hand touched her arm. She jumped and looked up into her partner's flinty eyes, saw the uncompromising promise there: *He won't get you.* For a moment, she almost believed him. Then she looked toward the room beyond the lobby.

Eleven bodies to date, and now this. Christine missing, the toughest cops in the city silenced and brought to their knees. She wanted to trust Trent to protect her, but how could he? How could anyone be safe from this monster?

She stepped away from Trent's hand and into the other room, and saw what had made the tactical team go so silent. Understood why one of their own had bolted from the scene. Might have followed, but shock and disbelief paralyzed her feet.

Alex reached for the support of the wall, remembered she stood in a crime scene, and caught back her hand. She struggled to take in the mayhem before her. The gore. Blood was everywhere: splashed across walls, spattered on the ceiling, pooled on the tile floor, tracked into every corner by cops' booted feet. Its scent rose to clog her throat; its vivid crimson flooded her vision. Air became fire in her throat, her chest. For an instant, every memory, every fear that had ever tormented her loomed in her mind and blotted out the real with the remembered. She crossed her arms and dug her fingers into her ribs in an attempt to hold herself upright, to stave off the urge to crumple onto the floor and fold in on herself and give up.

Trent's presence loomed at her back and she wavered, feeling the draw of his strength, the promise of his protection. *No,* she told herself fiercely. *You've made it this far, no way will you fall apart now.*

She looked away from the blood-bathed walls toward the center of the room and the rows of neatly arranged, still-occupied chairs. Her jaw went slack. Resolve cracked, crumbled, began to dissolve. Horror attained a whole new definition.

The bodies. Dear God, so many, many bodies.

She didn't want to look, didn't want to see the defilement of human life, but she couldn't seem to stop herself. She scanned the victims, pausing on each as a distant part of her mind counted, catalogued, recorded.

One, a fresh-faced young man in a courier's uniform; two, a thirtyish black woman in a business suit . . .

. . . seven, a vaguely familiar girl with tattooed arm sleeves and a half dozen facial piercings . . .

. . . twelve, an unkempt middle-aged man, his skin color obscured under layers of street living . . .

. . . twenty-one, an elderly Asian man; twenty-two, a young woman with a swollen, pregnant belly.

Twenty-two victims. All sitting in chairs lined up to face the front of the room, throats gaping, eyes blank. Lifeless. Without so much as a rumpled shirt or skewed chair to indicate a struggle.

Alex tried to swallow but couldn't get past the lump in her throat. Her eyes burned hot and dry in their sockets as she stared at the rows of dead. Sweet Jesus, how could they have just sat there, waiting their turn at death? Why hadn't they fought back? How in God's name had the killer made them sit and watch and—

"Jarvis." Roberts's voice echoed in the unnatural stillness of the room, jarring her out of her horror, and at the same time further into it.

Alex looked toward the front of the room where her supervisor stood on a raised platform, beckoning her forward. With Trent following as her own shadow would, she walked toward Roberts. Halfway there, she saw it.

A crucifix, mounted on the wall behind a flimsy wooden dais. Upside down. The body on it not of plastic or wood or plaster, but of bone and tendon and shreds of putrid flesh—recognizable as human only by its general shape. Alex tried to halt her steps, but the awfulness drew her forward even as it repelled her. She stopped at the edge of the platform and stared up at the atrocity, gagging anew at the reek. At the idea of a mind capable of this kind of malevolence.

A mind that had targeted her.

She tried to draw a steadying breath, but couldn't. Couldn't breathe at all. Panic stirred in her chest, trickled lower, turned her belly to liquid, became the stirrings of terror. Then Trent's hand pressed into her back, warm and solid and strong, and she focused everything she was on the touch, taking his strength into her as her own, letting him become the glue that kept her together, that kept her from spinning away into oblivion, right here, right now.

Alex stared past her supervisor. It would be so easy to give in to the collapse that hovered, to give herself the excuse she needed to walk away from all this. Roberts wouldn't even be able to say she hadn't warned him.

But even as she considered the possibility, her staff inspector cleared his throat, drawing her gaze back to meet his, and ice streaked down her spine at the bleakness there. It spread to claim her limbs as Roberts looked toward his feet, even before she followed his gaze.

Even before she saw Christine Delaney's carefully posed body and looked into her dull, dead eyes.

CAIM PACED THE sidewalk behind the gathered gawkers with tight steps. How much longer would they remain in there? Surely the hunt would drive out Aramael soon. Caim snarled softly. This wasn't what he'd had in mind. The three minutes the Naphil and Aramael had spent on the sidewalk before entering the mission had told him nothing. The woman had barely acknowledged his brother, and the Power had remained well away from her. Caim needed more, much more, if he wanted to confirm his suspicions.

Because if he was right . . .

If he was right, it changed everything. If Aramael had feelings for the woman, then it became more than Caim finding a Naphil and a back door into Heaven. It became perfect justice. Retribution against the brother who had betrayed him. Taken away his freedom. Spurned him.

Caim balled his hands into fists. He willed Aramael's reappearance, but the mission's front door remained occupied only by the uniformed cop guarding it.

Fuck. All that trouble, all that effort, for this? A spot on the sidelines, watching the mortals' clumsy, bungling efforts to catch a killer they couldn't even begin to conceive of?

He'd have been better off going after that mewling female. The one who'd entered the mission as he'd finished the slaughter and then fled before he could turn his attention to her. Not that the girl was any threat to him. She might be physically unharmed, but her mind would have sustained serious damage when she'd looked on him and what he did. There was nothing like stumbling on life's darker realities to screw with the fragile mortal brain.

Still, he didn't like loose ends any more than he cared for idleness, and this was the second time someone had seen and escaped him. Maybe he should just track her down and—he scowled. No. He had to stay disciplined. Focused. Had to follow through on what he'd started. He would remain here, be patient. Aramael and the woman would emerge at some point, and he would be waiting, watching, learning.

Just as he'd promised the Naphil.

ALEX STARED PAST the beat cop Roberts was talking to, unable to look away from the bloodied place of worship. Snippets of conversation washed over her, meaningless in the face of the atrocity with which they dealt.

". . . truly dedicated to the street . . ." the beat cop's hushed voice murmured. ". . . saw him just yesterday . . ."

Behind her she heard the Forensics team lower the cross with the putrid body to the floor. Most likely Father William's remains, identified by the cross he wore around his neck, engraved with his name and the date of his ordination. An autopsy would be needed to confirm the identity for the record, of course, but Alex knew it was him. Knew it deep down, in her cop's gut. Which raised the question of whom, exactly, Christine Delaney had been dating—and how he'd made himself look enough like Father William to fool a cop who saw him nearly every day.

A muttered prayer reached Alex's ears. She blocked it out and studied the pregnant victim in the front row of chairs. The woman looked to be about six months along. No wedding ring. Maybe there wouldn't be anyone to notify about the loss of both a wife and a child in the same awful day.

". . . don't understand how he could look like this now . . ."

Over the beat cop's shoulder, she saw Trent at the back of the room, pacing, his face drawn into lines of rage and torture, his body taut. Alex's insides shifted. She so didn't want to have to do this next part, but it was time. She'd run out of options.

She looked again at the victims lined up in the chairs and closed her eyes. Drew strength from some nether region of her mind she'd never before visited. Never had to visit. Then, with a mumbled aside to Roberts and the beat cop, she skirted the chairs and the bloody floor beneath them and headed toward Trent.

Her partner spoke first, before she'd even reached his side, his voice harsh. "He's taunting me."

Alex tripped over a floodlight cord. Righted herself. Paused a few feet away and twisted her hands into her jacket pockets. "The others think there's more than one killer."

"But you know better."

It was a statement, not a question. Alex steeled herself. This was why she'd come over here. "Yes. I know better."

Satisfaction flared in his expression.

"Now I want to know what you're going to do about it," she added.

The look of torture returned to his face. "I don't know."

"Can you feel him?"

"No."

"Why not?"

"Trust me. That part you *don't* want to know."

Alex pressed her lips together against an automatic objection. She looked away from him. He was right. She should keep her questions pertinent, focused on the case. Like a good cop. Like a cop who believed they could actually catch the killer.

"We know he's made himself look like Father William. Maybe if we put out a description—" Her voice trailed off.

"And if you find him, what then? You'll arrest him?"

The grisly scene in which they stood pressed in on Alex. She felt Delaney's accusatory eyes boring into her back along with those of twenty-two witnesses to the fraud detective's death and Father William's desecration. No, she thought. None of them would be able to stop the monster who had done this. The monster who was after her.

Again Trent seemed to tap into her thoughts. "You're not responsible for what happened here," he said quietly.

Alex's throat tightened. "Aren't I? Del— Christine told me about the priest. I should have said something then. Should have realized—"

"You didn't make her ignore her Guardian," Trent interrupted. "She chose to do so. And you didn't fail in your purpose. I did."

Guardian? Purpose? Alex felt the beginnings of a desire to hyperventilate. She looked over at Roberts. She'd give anything to return to his side and have this be a normal case where she could do the job the way she was supposed to. Where she could gather evidence and follow leads, and face a dozen killers instead of one who had somehow held twenty-two people in place while he murdered them one at a time; who had kept them from caring about what happened in front of them, or from seeing it at all. Or worse, had let them remain cognizant of every horrific moment.

Alex rested her hands on her hips and chewed at her bottom lip. There had to be *some* way of catching this son of a bitch. "Maybe if you tell me how this psychic thing of yours works, I can help."

"Psychic thing?" One of Trent's eyebrows ascended.

"Your connection to the killer. Is it stronger when you're somewhere quiet? If you meditate?"

Trent's other eyebrow joined the first. "Meditate?"

"I'm just trying to help, damn it."

"There's nothing you can do."

"Why not? Why can't you at least let me try? Why—?"

"Because," a new voice interrupted. "You are the problem, Alexandra Jarvis. Not the solution."

Alex saw a murderous glint in Trent's eyes even as she recognized the voice. She turned her head and fixed hostile eyes on Seth Benjamin. "You again."

"Despite your earlier efforts to be rid of me, yes." Benjamin's gaze moved past her to Trent. "Your presence is requested. I'll stay with her until you return."

Trent's dark brows had become one. "The way you did last night? If he'd known where to find her—"

"He didn't. And you have my word that I won't let her out of my sight this time." Benjamin's confidence made Alex lift her chin. He smiled at the gesture. "Not even if I have to tie her down," he added, as much for her benefit, she was sure, as for Trent's. "Verchiel waits for you. I think you'll want to hear what she has to say."

Alex saw Trent waver, then dip his head in agreement. "Wait," she said. "You can't leave now. I need—we need you." She felt a flush climb into her cheeks at her slip. A flare in Trent's eyes told her he'd noticed, but he answered without inflection.

"I won't be long. A few minutes at most. Promise me you'll stay with Seth."

Alex shot the other man a look of dislike. Something about Trent's former partner—if that was who he really was—set her teeth on edge. "I'll be fine," she told Trent, turning her back on the man lounging against the wall. "With all these people around, how could—?"

Trent grasped her shoulders and whirled her to face the bloodied room. "Enough," he snarled in her ear. "You cannot keep pretending you don't see what is before you, Alex. Damn it, open your eyes and look!"

She closed them instead. She didn't need to look. Didn't need to see any of it again to know he was right. To let what she had toyed with intellectually settle into her core, her center. To make the ultimate admission to herself that this wasn't just any killer. It wasn't even human. It was monstrous and obscenely powerful and evil beyond comprehension.

And it was bigger than her—bigger than all of the cops in this room put together.

And it had decided to come after her.

And the only thing standing in its way was the man holding her. The man whose heat burned against her back, whose strength once again folded itself around her and made her want to lean into it. Become one with it.

Alex opened her eyes. She could feel Seth Benjamin's disapproval and knew that he knew her thoughts. She lifted her chin in defiance and turned to Trent, schooling herself not step into the arms that had returned to his sides as she asked the question burning uppermost in her mind, "How am I the problem?"

"What?"

"*He*"—she shot Seth a look of dislike—"said I'm the problem, not the solution. How am I the problem?"

Trent's own glance in Benjamin's direction held much more than simple dislike. "He didn't mean it—"

Without thinking, Alex put her hand up to her partner's mouth to stop his words. She pulled back even as she brushed against him, but not before the sensation of his lips burned into her skin. Not before shocked heat flared in gray depths and found an answer in her belly.

She swallowed.

Detached her tongue from the roof of her mouth.

Scrabbled together the remains of reason.

"He did mean it," she croaked. "Now I want to know *what* he meant."

Trent shook his head. "I can't explain."

"Then I can't promise."

"Damn it, Alex—"

"Tell me."

War waged across his features. "You ask the impossible."

"So do you."

Benjamin cleared his throat behind her. "You should get going, *Jacob*," he said. His emphasis on Trent's name seemed to be a message of some kind, for it made Trent stand taller and glare at him in defiance.

"She needs to know."

"It is forbidden."

Alex rounded on the other man. "Shut up," she snapped, and felt immense satisfaction at his surprise. "You don't get to waltz into my life and turn it upside down without explanation. No one does. You want my cooperation, I want answers. It's that simple."

Benjamin studied her for a long moment in silence, probing, measuring, thoughtful. Then he looked at Trent again. "Think of the consequences."

"What if she refuses cooperation and he gets to her?" Trent responded, his voice gruff.

Benjamin shrugged. "Touché." He quirked an eyebrow at Alex. "You're certain about this, Alexandra Jarvis?"

Alex shored up her crumbling resolve and wiped her palms against her jacket. Roberts called her name. A part of her, desperate to finish the conversation before she lost her nerve, wanted to ignore her supervisor's summons, but a second bellow made her respond with a wave of acknowledgment.

She looked up at Trent. "I have to see what he wants."

"But you'll stay with Seth."

"You'll explain later?"

"You have my word."

She swallowed at the fierce promise in his eyes. "Then you have mine, too."

TWENTY-EIGHT

Hollow as she knew it to be, Alex found a certain comfort in going through the motions of an investigation. Seth Benjamin's presence, however, was another matter.

Every note she scribbled, every scrap of evidence she stooped to examine, his black eyes never left her. It was downright unnerving, not to mention irritating.

Even more annoying was the way none of the others questioned his being there. They didn't even seem to notice him. It was as if he didn't occupy actual space against the wall near the raised dais. As if he existed only in her head, except she didn't believe that anymore. Not after all she had seen and couldn't deny. Not after that phone call.

Alex tightened her grip on her pen. Crouched beside the pregnant woman, she looked toward the front of the room and saw one of the Forensics team edge between Benjamin and the platform. A little hiss of relief escaped her. So others did see him. That was good, because despite her recently formed opinion that she hadn't completely lost it, it was nice to have proof.

With gloved hands, she opened the woman's handbag and tugged the wallet from the jumbled contents, and then stood and flipped it open. The woman's photo stared back at her from the exposed driver's license. Elizabeth Anthony, born August 17, 1990.

August 17.

Alex glanced at the date on her digital watch and felt her throat tighten. Shit. She stood and looked down at the woman, taking in the carefully made-up face and tidy hair, now sprayed with blood, and the swollen belly that had become a grave rather than a haven for the unborn child within.

"Happy birthday, Elizabeth Anthony," she whispered.

Roberts joined her. "You doing all right?" he asked.

Alex handed him the wallet, her finger hooked over it to point at the date on the license. Roberts's face went a shade grayer than it had already been.

"Fuck," he said.

Alex jotted the woman's name and address into her notebook and stooped to retrieve the handbag from the floor. She dropped the wallet into it, slid everything into an evidence bag, and sealed the bag.

Roberts cleared his throat. "I've been thinking about what we talked about earlier. This one's pretty big, so if you'd rather sit it out . . ." His voice trailed off.

Hope flared in her, then sputtered out. Why couldn't Roberts have seen it this way before the killer had placed a personal call to her? Before Delaney went missing? Before Alex had seen this mayhem and slotted away the memories with all her others? She took a marker from her pocket and held it in a grip that numbed her fingers. It was too late to back out now. Hell, if she were to believe Trent, it had been too late for her all along.

She uncapped the marker. "I'm okay."

Her supervisor shuffled his feet. "I mean it, Alex. There's something about this one that makes my skin crawl. Given your background, I can only imagine how much worse it must be for you."

"I mean it, too. I'm fine."

Roberts stared at the floor. "You wouldn't keep anything from me, would you?"

"Like what?"

"Like information pertinent to the case." Her supervisor held up a hand to stave off her objection. "Like the fact he's after you."

Shock removed the guard on her tongue. "How did you—?"

"I've been a cop for thirty-two years, Alex, and I've known you for six of those. You were way more shaken than you should have been when you got off the phone with him earlier."

Alex looked to Benjamin and saw his eyebrows draw together in warning. Rebellion flared in her, but sputtered out almost immediately. She couldn't defy him even if she wanted to, because she didn't know anything yet. Didn't know if what she found out *could* be shared.

"You're wrong," she lied to Roberts, hearing the bitterness in her voice. "You would have been shaken, too, hearing about Christine like that. Like you said, I have more reason than anyone else to be affected by this whole mess. So no, I'm not withholding information, and no, he didn't threaten me."

Her staff inspector's piercing gaze held hers for a long moment, rife with questions, doubts, uncertainty. Then his face tightened. "I don't believe you. I'm putting a watch on you."

"You can't."

Roberts raised an eyebrow.

Alex bit her lip. Struggled for the right words. "This case makes my skin crawl, too, Staff. But not because of my history. The killer isn't— I'm not sure he's—"

"I know about the DNA results on that claw."

She blinked at the sudden change in subject.

"I know it was unidentifiable."

Alex stared at her supervisor and watched him carefully not acknowledge all that stood behind his statement, all that stood behind her clumsy attempt to explain what they dealt with. Roberts looked away first.

"I'm putting a watch on you."

"Don't. If he is after me, he'll go through whoever is in his way. You won't be able to stop him." *And I don't want anyone else to die.*

"What if someone else on the team was his target? What would you do?"

Alex's silence spoke for her.

Roberts nodded. "I thought so. But if it makes you feel any better, I'll ask for volunteers."

ALEX LEANED AN elbow on the roof of her sedan and threaded her fingers into the hair at her temple. She surveyed the dozen ambulances on the street, and twice that number of cop cars, all with their dome lights flashing. Yellow tape cordoned off half the city block, and farther away, wooden barriers held back the usual gawkers. The scene had all the earmarks of a Hollywood setting, complete with an air of make-believe, because surely the events here were too surreal to have actually happened.

Two paramedics came out of the building, carrying a stretcher with yet another body bag on it, their faces grim. Alex's grip tightened on her hair. She wished to God she *could* take Roberts up on his offer to let her sit this one out. No one on the squad would question the decision, and she sure as hell wouldn't miss seeing the carnage.

On the other hand, she'd be left with nothing but time on her hands. Time to sit and think about being hunted by a killer she could no longer believe was human; about being protected by someone about whom she harbored the same thoughts.

No, as useless an exercise as this investigation might be, at least it kept her occupied. Kept her—Alex's thoughts halted as, over the heads of the crowd gathered beyond the barriers, one face suddenly stood out. Trent. Tall and strong and watchful, his attention on the proceedings, he had returned from his meeting with the mysterious Verchiel. Alex frowned. But what was he doing out there? Had he seen something? Felt it?

Irritation stabbed. He'd promised her answers, damn it, and should have come straight inside to her and Seth. Speaking of whom . . . She straightened and glanced over her shoulder at the doorway, feeling a prickle of guilt. Her watchdog wouldn't be impressed when he realized she'd slipped away from him like this, but it served him right for taking that holier-than-thou attitude with her. Besides, she hadn't gone far, and eventually he'd figure out where she'd gone and come after her.

She located Trent again in the crowd. He hadn't moved. She hesitated. Part of her wanted to go to him—even needed to—but that still didn't make it easy to do so.

So much sat between them, barely acknowledged, let alone explained. So much that moved like a vast, dark, endless sea she wasn't sure she wanted to explore, despite her earlier, confident words. She studied him for a long moment. Wondered if she was ready to hear his secrets. To finally know who—or what—he was.

No more lies, no more pretense of any kind. Just him and her and . . . Alex looked at the chaos of emergency vehicles surrounding her, lights splintering the night. *And that.*

She watched another body bag being loaded into a waiting ambulance. Wondered who would face the task of removing Father McIntyre's remains from the inverted cross. Her stomach twisted. She turned back to the crowd, steeled herself, and walked across the street to the barrier. Pushing her way through the gathered throng, she reached Trent's side and said without preamble, "It's time to talk."

Trent tensed and stared down at her in shock. He peered around as if to see at whom she directed her words and then frowned.

"All right," he said warily. "About what?"

She scowled. "What the hell do you think? About this." She jerked her chin toward the murder scene and lowered her voice. "You promised, damn it. You said you'd give me answers."

The confusion cleared from her partner's expression and

it turned thoughtful. Attentive. "Yes. I think that would be good. But not here."

Alex took stock of their surroundings. It was unlikely that anyone would overhear them, or even notice their presence, but he was right to be cautious. She nodded. "I'll need to finish up here—" She broke off as the cell phone at her waist rang. Unclipping it, she glanced at the display and then flipped it open. "Jen, this isn't a good time—"

"Alex. Thank God," Jen whispered.

Alex's entire being tuned in to the edge of hysteria in her sister's voice. The cell phone turned to lead in her grip, weighing down her arm. "What's wrong? Is it Nina? Is Nina all right?"

"I don't know. She came home covered in blood and won't talk to me. I don't think she *can* talk. She's sitting in the living room just staring at the wall and not moving, and I don't know what to do."

Ice trickled through Alex's veins. *What the hell—?* She moved away from Trent and the cluster of people near him, trying not to make Jen's panic her own. She lowered her voice. "Have you called the police?"

"I'm scared to. What if she—what if—" Jen's voice choked off into a strangled sob and then a hiccup. "Alex, just come. Please."

"I'm on my way. Just stay with her until I get there. Don't touch her or let her wash—"

"She's my *daughter*. I'm not going to *not* touch my baby."

Alex tried to separate her professional self from the person her sister needed her to be right now. The person her niece would need when she got to their house. "Of course. But no washing. We'll need her clothes as evidence."

"Whatever. Just get here."

SHE THOUGHT HE was Aramael.

Caim clenched his fists at his sides, struggling not to snatch the phone from the woman. Not to grab her arm and pull her into the alley with him and slice her open then and there; to find out, finally, if he was right. If the soul of a Naphil could be the key to his return.

So close.

He breathed in her scent, warm, clean, with a hint of vanilla. He could take her now, but he wanted more. Much, much more. He wanted Aramael to witness his success, and to feel firsthand the agony of his own defeat, of loss. Wanted him to live an eternity with that loss.

The woman snapped the phone shut and moved close. "I have to go," she said, her voice low. "That was my sister. Something's happened to my niece."

Sister? She had a sister and a niece? Caim's heart raced and his mind followed suit. Any blood relation to the woman would be Nephilim, too, which meant three within his reach. Could he really be that fortunate?

He tried to still his thoughts, to sort out the possibilities. He had three, but needed only one. Wanted only one. One whose demise would inflict on his brother the kind of damage he'd endured himself. He mustn't lose sight of that.

Neither, however, should he assume that want would guarantee success. Despite Aramael's erratic behavior, the Power could still outmaneuver him without warning. A backup plan wouldn't be at all amiss.

"Let me take you," he said quickly, trying to temper his eagerness with the appropriate concern.

"As if you'd let me out of your sight," she muttered, but the look she flashed him was one of gratitude.

And something more.

Caim's heart thudded in his chest. So he hadn't been mistaken on the phone. She really did have feelings for his brother. *Oh please, please let Aramael return those sentiments the way I think he does.*

He cleared his throat. "Give me the keys," he suggested gruffly. "I'll drive."

"I'm okay, and it will be faster if I do the driving. I know the shortcuts." She looked over her shoulder, away from the irritation surging within him. "I'll just let Roberts know what's up and—"

"Give me the keys."

The woman blinked at the command. "Excuse me?"

Caim forced his shoulders down, his arms to relax. He stared at her, formulating the thoughts he needed to back up his words, the ideas he wanted her to accept. "I will get you there. You can call whoever you need to from the road while I drive."

Still she hesitated. Annoyance reared in him. He was so close. *So* close. He gathered himself to press in on her mind a little harder. Without a Guardian to interfere with him, it shouldn't be this difficult to influence her. Was it because she was Nephilim? Or because of her relationship with Aramael?

Sudden warning prickled along his spine and he jerked his head up, away from the woman, and stared across the street. Someone watched him.

His gaze passed over a tall man standing beside the doorway to the mission, hesitated, moved back, and met brooding black eyes. Caim inhaled slowly, studying the man, sensing his curiosity. His puzzlement. The man's scrutiny intensified. Caim's palms grew damp as foreboding teased at the edges of his mind. The man wasn't mortal. But he wasn't an angel, either. He was something else entirely. Something—

Abrupt recognition flared in the other's face, along with an ugliness Caim had only ever seen in one other being, a being who had dared to defy the One herself.

For an instant, shock paralyzed Caim. Then, as the other's black brows slammed together, desperation struggled to his rescue. He would *not* lose. Not now. He reached for the woman in front of him.

"Alex!" the other shouted, running toward them.

As if privy to some secret signal, the woman dropped to the pavement, out of Caim's reach. Caim hesitated, gauged the other's proximity, and, with a snarl, shifted his energy and left the scene.

TWENTY-NINE

Alex stared at Seth's outstretched hand, noting the squared fingertips and lean strength. Her gaze traveled up his arm, across his leather-clad shoulder, and settled on his eyes. Calm eyes. Concerned eyes. Eyes that looked nothing like the fierce, infinitely powerful ones that had commanded her to fling herself away from Trent. Eyes she had obeyed without question.

She knocked the hand aside. Levered herself off the sidewalk. "What the *fuck* was that about?"

Seth hesitated and she glowered at him. She didn't have time for this; she'd get her answers from Trent on her way to— She scanned the area in disgust. Great. He'd disappeared again.

"God damn it to hell," she muttered. "*Now* where did he go?"

"That wasn't Jacob."

Alex paused in her check to make sure she still had cell phone, badge, and gun in place after her concrete-dive. "Of course it was."

"No." Seth shook his head, his voice oddly compelling. "It wasn't."

"Then who—" The words stilled in her throat. In the space of a heartbeat, she went over the few minutes she'd spent with Trent on the sidewalk. Recalled his wary surprise at her approach, her own unease at his reaction to her sister's phone call. Felt bile rise into her chest at the realization he had somehow changed his appearance to that of her partner . . . and then remembered.

Her sister's phone call.

Sweet Jesus, he knew about Jen.

"SOULMATES?" ARAMAEL ECHOED. He ceased pacing the gravel path and frowned down at Verchiel, seated on the stone wall surrounding the fountain.

"You're familiar with the concept."

"Passingly." He waited, but Verchiel remained silent, rearranging the folds of her robe across her lap. Aramael's temper edged upward. "I am in no mood for guessing games, Dominion. Tell me what you need to and be done with it."

Verchiel folded her hands together. "You and Alex."

"Me and Alex what? Damn it, Verchiel—" Aramael stopped. Stared. Felt his jaw go slack. "Soulmates? She and I are— But angels don't have soulmates."

"Not now, no. But they did once. Along with free will." Verchiel held up a hand to forestall another outburst. "Surely you remember the stories, what it was like before the mortals."

"My purpose is not to listen to stories."

"No. No, I don't suppose it is." The Dominion sighed. "Before the One created the mortals, we existed much as they do. Well, without the famines and wars and such. But we had free will and a full range of emotions, and we had soulmates. When Lucifer left and took the others with him, we went to war. The agony of having to fight our loved ones nearly tore us apart and, to make it easier on us, the One took away our free will and the capacity to feel love for those near to us."

Aramael frowned. "Why don't I remember any of this?"

"You never had a soulmate to remember."

"If all this was taken from us, how can I have one now?"

"I don't know." Verchiel shifted her seat on the stones. "Perhaps the woman's Nephilim bloodline has something to do with it. If she retained enough of the divine, maybe it triggered your recognition of one another."

Aramael thought back to the first time he met Alex, the first time he touched her and felt the explosion of energy between them that had rocked his entire universe. That had been one hell of a recognition. It made him wonder: if she really was his soulmate and they were to come together—

Heat engulfed him with a ferocity that shocked him, setting his body aflame. He turned away from Verchiel and gritted his teeth.

"Why are you telling me this?" he asked, struggling for control, knowing the hoarseness of his voice gave him away.

"You need to understand the seriousness of your situation."

He laughed, a short, bitter bark. "Believe me, Dominion, no one understands better."

"And you need to leave her."

Fury surged. Aramael whirled. "No."

"Aramael, listen to me. You cannot hunt Caim like this. Your feelings for the woman, for Alex, interfere with everything that you are, everything you need to be. You must put distance between you. You have no choice."

"I will not leave her alone while he stalks her."

"I'm not asking you to. Seth has agreed to remain with her until your hunt is complete. She will be safe with him, you know that."

Aramael tipped back his head and stared at the sky, bearing witness to the debate raging in his heart. The two hungers warring within him: the hunt, and what he felt for Alex.

For a moment, he thought he might physically rip in half under the strain—and then a cleared throat, not Verchiel's, claimed his attention. He looked over to see another angel, a Virtue, standing a few feet away.

"Pardon the interruption," the tiny female said. "But Seth requests that you return to the woman at once. He says it is urgent."

As acute as the heat had been a moment before, the cold that ran through Aramael now was a thousand times more intense, freezing every cell in his body. Holding him prisoner in a grip of ice.

"Aramael?" Alarm pitched Verchiel's voice higher than normal. Broke through his imagined shackles.

He spun around, found she had stood up from the fountain wall. He towered over her. "Why could he not reach me directly? What did you do?"

"I needed to be certain our conversation remained private. There are things I haven't told you, things—"

"If anything has happened to her—" Aramael broke off, leaving the unfinished threat hanging between them. The muscles in his arms and shoulders knotted with his efforts to control his anger.

No wonder love had created such chaos on the heels of Lucifer's departure. And no wonder the One had chosen to remove it from those who remained at her side.

With a last snarl, Aramael pulled back from Verchiel, gathered himself, and stepped out of the heavenly realm.

JEN AND NINA. That monster knows about Jen and Nina.

Alex squared off against Seth, who leaned against the driver's door of her car. She wanted to throw herself at him, to pound on that implacable face and demand to know how the killer could look like Father McIntyre yesterday and her partner today; wanted to give in to the terror rising in her chest, a terror so huge she didn't dare acknowledge it for fear it might paralyze her.

The knowledge that she had put Nina and Jen at risk held her back. Held her upright.

She pushed back her jacket to expose her gun. "Move out of my way or, so help me God, I will shoot you."

Seth settled more firmly against the car and folded his arms across his chest. "You know that won't work."

Alex bit down on the inside of her lip. There was so much more in that statement than she could deal with right now. She lifted her chin. "Maybe not. But it will draw a lot of attention you don't want and I'll get away in the confusion. Your choice."

"I'm just asking you to wait for a few seconds until Ara— until Jacob gets here."

The killer knows about Jen and Nina.

"No."

"Be reasonable, Alexandra Jarvis. You can't just disappear without telling him where you'll be. A moment or two won't make a difference."

Two strides took her to within inches of him. Anger rolled through her in waves. Her hand settled on her weapon.

"That murdering son of a bitch knows I have a sister," she grated through clenched teeth, "and a niece. And I don't care how livid Trent will be, I'll be damned if I stand here while a monster goes after them. So get the *fuck* out of my way, Benjamin. Now."

Black eyes studied her calmly and it took all her strength not to back down from them, not to hide from their too-canny perception. "If he does find them, you can't stop him. Not alone."

"Yes," she said. "I can."

Something dark crossed Seth's features and she knew he understood her meaning. What she intended. Long seconds ticked by before he spoke again. "I cannot let you sacrifice yourself."

"Damn it, Benjamin—"

He shook his head, cutting her off. "My job is to keep you safe when Jacob cannot. No more, no less."

Alex whirled away. She released her grip on the gun

and raked hands through hair before settling them on her hips. She stared at the scene she had walked away from and thought about her fellow cops still dealing with the insanity behind the brick walls and plate glass, clinging to the belief that they could find the killer. That they could catch him. Stop him.

The belief that he was human.

Her fingers dug painfully into her hip bones. She turned back to Seth, her terror now a quiet desperation. If she couldn't save Jen and Nina, at least she could be there for them. "They're the only family I have, Seth. Come with me if you want, but let me go to them. Please."

Seth looked away. Hope struggled to life in Alex's chest. Had she found a chink in that damnably impenetrable armor? She crossed the sidewalk and placed her hand on her bodyguard's forearm. "Please," she said again.

Seth stared down at her hand and a sudden tingle crawled along her skin. A frisson of awareness. Alex felt him tense beneath her touch and she drew back, flustered by his response. Shocked at her own. Heat rose in her cheeks.

Seth stood without moving for a moment, then shoved his hands into his pockets. Shook his head. "We wait."

Her shoulders slumped. Hell. That put her back to shooting him, then.

Even as the thought crossed her mind, however, Seth looked past her and relief flashed across his face. "Took you long enough," he said.

Alex glanced around to see Trent step out from a recessed doorway behind her. He swept a narrow look over both her and Seth and she wondered what he'd heard. How much he'd seen.

Why it should matter.

She looked to Seth. "You're sure it's him this time?"

Trent frowned. "This time?" he echoed. "What does she mean, *this time*?"

"We had an incident," Seth told Trent.

Trent took a threatening step in Seth's direction, his eyes glittering. "He was here? You let him talk to her?"

"I didn't *let* him do anything," Seth growled. "As soon as I realized it wasn't you—"

"You should have been watching her. I trusted you."

Seth straightened up from the car and stepped onto the sidewalk, leaving the car door unprotected. "I kept her safe."

"You let him get to her. How is that *safe*?"

Alex stared at the car. Did she dare—? Trent's chest suddenly filled her field of vision, cutting off her escape, and she took a startled step back.

"Are you all right?"

His voice, gruff with concern, reached inside her and laid bare the vulnerability Alex had tried so hard to ignore. The terror.

"Alex?"

The killer knew about Jen and Nina. Knew, because Alex had told him. Her throat constricted and she gulped for air; felt her mind begin to part company with her body. She crossed her arms, certain that she literally held herself together, that she would fly apart into a thousand pieces if she released her hold. Was she all right? No. She might never be all right again. Strong fingers took hold of her chin, lifted, tightened.

"Look at me," Trent commanded softly. "Tell me what happened."

In a few brief words, Alex told him of her encounter with the killer who had looked like him. A cold mask of fury settled over his face and the unmistakable rustle of feathers sounded behind his back. She closed her eyes.

"Did you tell him where your sister lives?" he asked.

"No." Her voice cracked on the word. She swallowed. "But he'll still find them, won't he?"

"Yes. But we have a little time."

The air wheezed from her lungs. She opened her eyes again. "How little?"

She could tell that he tried to soften his gaze for her, tried to look reassuring, but he failed. Miserably. For a single heartbeat, terror won and only Trent's grip on her chin kept her upright. Then she locked her knees. Clung to his words. Stepped away from his touch.

"I'll drive," she said.

Because a little time was better than none.

It had to be.

THIRTY

Aramael said nothing for the first few minutes of the drive, not sure he could be civil to the backseat passenger. Instead, he contented himself with glaring daggers over his shoulder at Seth, mutely promising their confrontation was far from over.

He told himself it was Seth's negligence alone that disturbed him, but he lied. His anger stemmed not just from the averted threat to Alex, but from what he had witnessed when he joined her and Seth on the sidewalk.

Her hand on the Appointed's arm.

Seth's reaction to her.

Hers to him.

Sourness twisted in his belly. He met Seth's hooded gaze; knew the Appointed read his thoughts. Distrust crackled between them. Aramael turned away again and, with an effort, made himself focus on the "incident" he had missed.

He shuddered.

Caim. Here. With Alex.

His brother had found her. Could have killed her then

and there. Could have ended everything with a single swipe of his hand. Aramael felt Alex's sideways look and knew she sensed his rising tension. The way she sensed everything about him. *Soulmates.*

Aramael stared out the window. Caim could have ended everything, but he hadn't.

Why not?

Because of Alex's sister and niece? But why would he need another Nephilim target when he already had Alex? What game was he playing? Aramael's thoughts stilled. That was it. Caim played a game. With him.

How could he not have seen it? Caim had all but spelled it out for him in that phone call to Alex at the office, asking if Aramael felt the same way about her as she did him. Saying he would be watching them, would judge for himself. Because he knew. He knew Aramael had feelings for Alex.

But still—why not just kill her outright? Why wait? Aramael snarled under his breath. He was missing something, but what? He turned to Alex. "Can we go any faster?"

Alex reached for a switch under the dash and a siren wailed to life.

JEN FLUNG OPEN the front door before Alex rang the bell.

"Thank God!" she exclaimed, grabbing Alex's arm and hauling her into the brightly lit entrance. "I thought you'd never get here. She's in the living room. She still hasn't said anything and she hasn't moved. I don't know what's wrong—" Jen's babble died away as she looked past Alex's shoulder. "I thought you were coming alone."

Alex glanced at the two men she hadn't been able to convince to remain in the car. A taxi rolled by on the street behind them and turned the corner. "Colleagues," she said, for lack of a better description, and then added to Trent, "You should come in. It's not safe to stand in the open like this."

The two men joined her in the front entry and Alex peered past Jen into the lamp-lit living room. "I don't see her."

Jen's face drew tight and she pointed into a corner behind the sofa, just outside the circle of light. Alex made out a drawn-up pair of knees and a curtain of dark hair.

Nina. Looking small and vulnerable and very, very fragile.

Alex's heart skipped a beat. She pitched her voice low. "Has she said *anything*?"

Jen shook her head. Bit her lip. "Not a word."

"All right." Alex shrugged out of her blazer and laid it across the back of a chair. "Why don't you make some tea while I talk to her?"

"She might need me—"

"She might need to talk to me first."

The sister in Alex ached as she watched Jen struggle with hurt and fear, but she knew from experience that kids her niece's age tended to be more forthcoming without their parents hovering over them. She wondered if that had been the case when Delaney had spoken to Mitchell Stevens; if Delaney had ever had the chance to do so. Then she pushed away questions that no longer mattered and nudged her sister toward the hallway. "I'll come get you when I'm done."

With Trent and Benjamin hovering in the living room doorway, Alex crossed the room and settled onto the floor beside her niece, near but not touching. "Nina?" she said softly. "It's Alex."

Nina had dropped the "Auntie" title a few months before, declaring herself too old to use it. Alex hadn't argued, seeing at the time an emerging, confident young woman in her niece. No trace remained of that young woman in the crumpled figure beside her now. The crumpled, bloodstained figure. She took in the details of her niece's appearance and felt her heart jump into her throat. Blood had soaked both of the girl's running shoes and all of what Alex could see of her jeans, and had dried to a crust in strands of Nina's hair. *What the hell?*

She bit her lip, trying to decide who Nina most needed her to be right now, cop or aunt, and then looked up as a darker shadow fell over her.

Trent scowled at her. "You didn't tell me she'd seen him."

"What?"

"Your niece. You didn't tell me she'd seen Caim."

Caim? Alex frowned. "I don't know what you're talking about. Jen called me because she arrived home like this and wouldn't say what—" The rest of her words piled up in her throat, mixed with bile, choked off all possibility of sound. She stared again at her niece. Jesus, no.

She took in Nina's runners a second time and then examined the rest of her niece, from the girl's legs to the huddled shoulders, the matted hair. That was a lot of blood. An awful, frightening amount of blood. The kind of blood that came from multiple bodies. Multiple victims. Then she remembered the one with the tattooed arm sleeves and piercings who had seemed vaguely familiar . . . and how she had seen the girl in Nina's company once when she'd picked up her niece from school. Every cell in Alex's body went still with horror. Denial.

No.

Of its own volition, her hand reached for Nina, slid beneath her chin, forced the girl's head up and around to face her. She looked into the familiar, bright blue eyes and saw—

Nothing.

The same nothing she'd seen when she had looked into Martin James's eyes yesterday. *Sweet Jesus, no.* The parting of Alex's mind from her body, begun outside the mission, became a little more pronounced. A little more defined.

Trent's hand closed over her arm, tugged her hand away from her niece. Nina's head lolled forward again. Trent raised Alex to her feet, his face set in grim lines.

"It's time to talk."

"Nina—"

"Seth will stay with her." Trent shot a glare at the other man that dared him to object.

Seth hesitated for a fraction of a second, then looked at Alex. He nodded. "Go," he said quietly. "You've earned your answers."

* * *

ALEX WATCHED TRENT prowl the perimeter of her sister's dining room. Once again he had the look of a predator about him, but this time one that was caged and desperate to find a way out. One she would have preferred not to provoke, if she'd had the choice. But with Jen and Nina now at risk, no choice remained. If she wanted any chance to keep her sister and niece safe, she had to know what was going on. All of it.

Even if it involves wings.

She retreated into a corner of the dining room, crossed her arms, hunched her shoulders, and tried to ignore the doorway that yawned invitingly to her left. Trent stopped pacing. Alex swallowed.

"Are you sure you want to do this?" he asked.

She studied the oak floor at her feet. "I'm sure."

"There can be no turning back. No way to undo—"

He stopped midsentence as she raised her gaze to his. Gray eyes stared into hers, so many thoughts and emotions churning in them that she couldn't begin to sort them out. Somehow she found it comforting to know he suffered as much angst about this as she did.

She nodded. "I'm sure."

Trent watched her in silence for a second and then nodded. "Very well. My name is Aramael." He lifted his head. "And I'm an angel."

As much as Alex had expected the words, they still rocked her world to its very foundation.

She had known for a while now that something out of the ordinary was happening; that she could no longer deny her partner was more than he seemed and the killer more than they thought. This afternoon, when the killer called, she had turned her back on any last lingering doubts about her sanity. But still—

An *angel*?

She bit down on her lip. Couldn't he have been something

else? Anything else? An alien, maybe? Hell, she would have preferred he declare himself to be Supreme Tooth Fairy.

But her very own, couldn't-get-much-more-fucking-crazy-than-this angel? A tremor began in her chest. Maybe she'd been wrong. Maybe she had followed in her mother's footsteps after all, and this was just part of it. Part of the insanity. Maybe—

"You're not her, Alex."

Her head snapped up and she stared at Trent—Aramael—whoever the hell he was. "How do you know about—?"

"It goes with the territory."

Of course it did. Silly her. She flexed her fingers, stiff from the tension that seemed to own her, and studied him. He was dressed in the same suit he'd worn when she first met him—how had she not noticed that he never changed?—and he looked so . . . normal. So not like she imagined an angel might look. No heavenly glow, no shining white robes. He didn't even have wings at the moment, for God's sake.

Her other thoughts piled up behind the last one like a train wreck. If he was an angel, then God—? Heaven—? She reached for the back of a chair to support herself. So many questions. She didn't know what to ask first. Or what to avoid.

"Sit," her former partner said. "I'll start at the beginning."

Alex did as he suggested, mostly because she no longer trusted her own legs to support her, and in less time than she would have believed possible, what little remained of her reality was turned on its head. She learned of the One's creation of a human race, nurtured throughout its evolution, and of Lucifer's intense envy of the One's attachment to those humans. Of the splitting of Heaven and the formation of Hell. Of the downfall of those angels who chose to follow Lucifer. The resulting noninterference pact. The appointment of a handful of those who remained loyal to the One as Powers when not all of the Fallen would abide by the agreement.

Learned, absorbed, and then sat in silence for a long, long time after he finished.

Footsteps approached on the wooden floor and stopped in front of her. "Well?"

She stared at his feet, humanly clad in leather dress shoes, and then lifted her gaze and flinched from a glimpse of fiery golden wings. "What kind of angel are you?"

"Not the nice kind. I'm a Power, an angel of the Sixth Choir. And a hunter of the Fallen Ones."

"So the serial killer is—?"

"One of those who followed Lucifer. Yes."

A buzzing started in her ears. One of Lucifer's followers. A Fallen Angel. Stalking her. Stalking Jen and Nina. Alex fought down the urge to hyperventilate and drew on the shreds of her training. Being a cop might not help if she came up against Caim, but it could at least keep her thinking. Maybe keep her and Jen and Nina away from him long enough for Aramael to do his job.

So think, damn it.

She frowned. "Wait a minute. If you're an angel, can't you just do some kind of miracle thing and find him?"

"I wish it worked like that, but I can only sense him in his demonic form, the one he becomes when he attacks a mortal."

"Demonic—" The buzz in Alex's head became louder. Shit. "What about the rest of the time? Can he look like whoever he wants?"

Trent—no, Aramael, he'd called himself. Would she ever get used to that? Aramael flexed his hands at his sides. "He can make you think he looks like someone else, but his true form is the one you saw tonight," he said. "Caim is my brother, Alex. My twin."

The dining room door swung inward and Alex jumped in her seat, then stared at her sister. Jen's gaze darted from her to Aramael and back. "Alex? Nina—"

"She's with my colleague," Aramael said brusquely.

Discontent fluttered across Jen's brow.

"She's fine, Jen." Alex forced the reassurance through stiff lips. "We're just discussing the situation."

Discussing the total upheaval of everything I held to be true in life.

"Did Nina say something? Have you called someone?" Again Jen's eyes did the darting thing. "You haven't, have you? Why not? What's going on, Alex? Has Nina— Oh, God—" Her grip went rigid around the edge of the door. "Did she hurt someone?"

"No!" Rousing herself from her own shock-induced stasis, Alex went to her sister's side, pried her hand loose, and led her to the chair she'd just vacated. "Nina could never hurt someone, Jen. You know that."

Brown eyes, wide with shock, met hers. Jen nodded. "Of course. I do know that. It's just—" Her voice dropped to a whisper. "There's so much blood. Where did it all come from?"

Alex crouched down on one knee. "We think she may have witnessed something, sweetie. Something pretty awful. That's why she's not talking."

Her sister's head bobbed. "Shock will do that," she agreed. "We've covered that in class. But she'll get better."

Alex bit her lip, seeing more than a little shock in Jen's own face at the moment. Not wanting to add to it. Remembering Martin James.

Jen's fingers dug like claws into her arm. "She will get better, won't she, Alex? We can get her help—"

Alex looked to Aramael for an answer, but found only a reflection of her own misgivings. Her heart lurched. He looked haggard, she thought. She hadn't known angels could look haggard. Not that she'd known angels at all until now. And still didn't—at least, not as well as she needed to if she was going to protect her family.

Rising from beside her sister, she leaned back against the windowsill, her hands braced on either side of her, and returned to where she and Aramael had left off. "He's really your brother? Couldn't they have sent someone else after him? You're not the only one who does this, are you?"

"No. There are others. Seventeen in all."

"Then why send you— Wait—*seventeen*? That's it? How many angels did you say fell?"

"Alex, what the hell—?" Jen broke off.

Aramael answered as if Jen hadn't spoken. "A third of the host. A hundred thousand, give or take."

Alex thought of the destruction wrought by Caim in the last few days and swallowed. "You're telling me only seventeen of you stand between humanity and a hundred thousand demons?"

A hundred thousand Caims?

"All of Heaven stands between you. But with the agreement between Lucifer and the One, only seventeen of us have been necessary to . . . keep the peace, I suppose you could say."

Jen almost fell off her chair. *"Lucifer?"*

Alex ignored her sister. "You're kidding me. You're only here for the ones who break some pact? What about the others? They just get to walk around freely, indistinguishable from the rest of us?" She shuddered at the thought. Her cop habit of seeing nearly everyone she met as a potential criminal had been bad enough; she didn't know what she'd do with the possibility that any one of them could also be a Fallen Angel. "Doing what, exactly?"

"Whatever they can within the limits. They attempt to influence the choices mortals make, and Guardians try to counter that influence."

"That's it. That's just how it is. Angels and demons playing tug-of-war with human beings. I thought God—the One—was supposed to be all-powerful."

Aramael leaned his weight against the table and shook his head. "That's not the point."

"Then what is the fucking point?" she demanded. "People are dying because of these monsters and—"

"They're not all like Caim."

"For chrissake, you just told me they're trying to wipe out humanity!"

"Only with your permission."

Alex shook her head to clear it. "What?"

"The One gave mortals free will, Alex. Each of you has the ability to choose, to determine your own path. Both good and evil have always existed in your lives, only you can decide which to follow."

"That is such a complete cop-out it's not even funny. Can your One destroy these demons or not?"

"Demons?" squeaked Jen.

Alex sent her sister a quick look. Angels, demons—how the hell was she going to explain any of this? Especially given their mother's delusions?

Irritation crept into Aramael's voice. "I'm not here to debate theology with you. All I can tell you is that the One is ultimate good and does not destroy."

"Right. And droughts, volcanoes, wars, earthquakes— what would you call those if not wholesale destruction?"

"Mortals choose where and how to live. The One does not impose that on you."

"No, she just lets demons walk among us and sends you to kill the ones who step too far out of line."

"To hunt the ones who step out of line, yes."

Jennifer rose from her chair and, giving Aramael a wide berth, edged to Alex's side and put a hand on her arm. "Alex, for God's sake, what is going on?" she hissed. "What the hell are you talking about? Angels? Demons? This is insane!"

"Not now, Jen. Please." Alex shrugged off her sister's touch. Aramael's last correction hadn't sounded like semantics. "Hunt. Not kill."

"I am an instrument of the One. If I were to destroy in her name it would alter the balance of the universe in ways I don't think any of us would care to explore. But rest assured Caim will be exiled to a place far removed from the mortal realm."

"So that's it? After all that monster has done, he gets to live?" She paced in front of the window. "Damn it to hell, you saw what he did in that mission. What he did to those people—to Christine and Father McIntyre. How many more does he have to kill before you do more than exile him?"

"That isn't my decision to make. My job is to stop Caim from interfering in your realm. Nothing more, nothing less."

"Then why haven't you?"

Aramael angled his body away from her, every line shouting tension. Misery. "There are complications."

From the kitchen came the sound of a teakettle's whistle building to a scream. It ended abruptly as someone lifted it from the stove. Seth, probably. Seth, whose words rang again in Alex's memory: *You are the problem, Alexandra Jarvis. Not the solution.*

Her. Aramael meant her. She was the complication. Because of the Naphil thing Caim had called her? No. If Aramael had been sent to protect her, he would have known about that beforehand.

Aramael's gaze grazed hers and sudden comprehension snaked through her belly, became more. Became aware. Became connected. To an angel. Alex felt the blood drain from her face and then surge back again, hot and prickly and . . . complicated.

A hand touched her arm and she looked down at it, then back up at her sister. Borderline hysteria and a million questions stared at her, along with the steel-clad control that had seen Jen through so many crises in her life. So many crises in Alex's life.

Jen straightened her shoulders. "I'm trying really, really hard not to panic right now, Alexandra. Whatever's going on, I know this isn't the time to explain it, but you're scaring the hell out of me and I just need to know if Nina is going to be all right."

Aramael shifted his stance, his suit rustling into Alex's silence. A silence that marked, profoundly, her inability to answer her sister's plea. The kitchen door swung open to Alex's right and a fourth presence entered the room.

Alex slipped an arm around her sister's waist and hugged her sibling fiercely. "I'll do everything I can," she promised into her sister's hair. "Everything."

Then Seth was there, tugging Jen from her arms and

steering her toward the kitchen. Alex met his eyes, glittering and aloof, over her sister's head.

"I'll watch them both," he told her. "You need to finish here." He looked at Aramael. "Soon," he added, and pushed through the swinging door.

THIRTY-ONE

The instant the door swung closed behind Seth and Jen, every nerve in Alex's body fine-tuned itself to the man who remained across from her, separated only by the width of the table. *No, not the man,* she reminded herself, *the angel. An angel who, no matter how attuned you are to him, to his scent, to his very existence, will remain an angel. So whatever you're thinking, don't.*

"Alex."

Aramael said her name in a deep, rich tone that made her want to crawl out of her own skin because the sensations it triggered were almost too much to bear. A tone that demanded she look at him. She felt the energy surge between them and her heart slowed into long, heavy beats, sending heated blood to parts of her she didn't think she had ever known. Aramael stalked toward her, his eyes fastened on hers with an inhuman intensity.

He stopped, mere inches away, and cleared his throat. His voice remained husky. "You and I—we can never be."

Alex tried to ignore his nearness. His heat. She didn't pretend not to understand. "Then why are we?"

"A mistake."

Alex shook her head. No. Something this big, this true, could never be a mistake. "I don't believe that."

Naked pain flared in eyes that had turned the color of long-cold ashes. "I'm an angel, damn it. You shouldn't even know me."

"But I do."

Long seconds ticked by. A muscle flexed in his jaw. "I can't feel this way about you," he muttered at last. Embers glowed among the ashes now. "I *can't*," he snarled. "Don't you understand? You have become the most important thing in my existence, and I am crippled by your very presence. Caim remains free because I cannot track him, cannot feel him. Because all I can feel is you."

Aramael raked both his hands through his hair, making a visible effort to restrain himself. "I am a Power, Alex. A hunter. It's not just who I am, it's *what* I am. There is no room in my existence for anything else."

Anger hit, hot and sudden and tangled in Alex's belly. "Then why the hell put me through this? Why tell me about you, about everything, when you knew you couldn't—when you knew I felt—" She struggled for words. Struggled not to strike out at him in her fury. Her loss. "Why?" she asked simply.

Frustration rolled off Aramael in waves, pushing her away. Then her angel reached out to her and brushed back the hair from her face with a gentleness that laid bare her soul.

"Because as much as I cannot feel this way, Alexandra Jarvis," he whispered, "neither can I stop myself from doing so."

Time, and Alex's heart, stood still. For what seemed an eternity, she felt nothing but Aramael's hand against her cheek. His truth. And then, with a ferocity that stole her capacity to breathe, elation exploded through her entire being and the universe narrowed until it encompassed just the two of them. Until she herself became nothing more than the heat of his body, the whisper of his breath against her face, the longing that flooded her veins.

Need ached in her every fiber.

Agony stared back at her from Aramael's eyes.

"Do you see?" His voice was hoarse. "This is what I cannot have. Not while Caim remains free. If I let myself give in to this, if I lose myself in you—"

He didn't finish. Didn't need to. Alex tried to shut out the specters raised by his words, but a memory of the mission murder scene rose in her mind, more effective than a deluge of ice water.

All those bodies. Christine. Father McIntyre.

The heat in her veins subsided.

The killer still roaming the city. A demon loose among mortals.

Her heart slowed.

Nina.

She clenched her fists and buried the last of her need in a quiet, private place within her. Aramael was right. His priority—*their* priority—had to be stopping Caim. She stepped away from his touch, ignoring the way it followed her until she moved beyond his reach, clinging to his words: *Not while Caim remains free.* Words that left open the faintest possibility of *after.*

After Caim was captured.

After this nightmare had ended.

She drew herself up to speak, but the sound of shattering glass crashed between them. Jen's scream followed.

"*Nina*—no!"

Even before Alex shoved past Aramael into the living room, she knew what she'd find, knew the emptiness she'd seen in Nina wasn't the only thing that had paralleled Martin James. But expectation did nothing to dim the reality of a jagged hole gaping in the living room window, punctuated at its edges by great slivers of razor-sharp glass. Did nothing to lessen the horror of seeing Nina, her bloodied hands hanging at her sides, slowly crumple to the floor, a shard of glass protruding from her belly.

The contents of Alex's stomach rose into her throat and her hands started to shake. *Dear God, no.*

"She's still alive," Aramael said in her ear. "But she needs help."

As if to confirm his words, Nina raised her head and looked toward Alex, her eyes calm but puzzled. "Auntie Alex?" she whispered.

Alex started forward again. Nina wasn't just alive; she was cognizant, too. She looked to a struggling Jen, held back by Seth from running to her daughter's side and worsening Nina's injuries. Or injuring herself.

Skirting the fragments of glass that had flown into the room instead of exploding outward with the lamp and remainder of the window, Alex snapped over her shoulder, "Call nine-one-one. Tell them we'll need the paramedics and the fire department. Then find a blanket—something warm but not too heavy."

Jen struggled against Seth and Alex didn't think she'd obey—wasn't even sure she'd heard. But her sister nodded. "Nine-one-one," she whispered. "And a blanket."

"Good girl," Alex said. "Go."

She turned to her niece. Felt her stomach clench at the sight of the blood-slicked shard protruding from Nina's stomach. Trying to recall her first-aid training, Alex crouched and brushed back the hair from the girl's face. "Ssh," she whispered as Nina tried to sit. "Stay still, sweetie. Help is coming."

Nina went quiet and Alex swallowed as she looked into blue eyes once more emptied of all expression. *Not again.* She grappled briefly with despair and then pulled her thoughts to heel as she assessed the damage to Nina, calculating that at least three inches of glass protruded from her niece's belly. She had no idea how many more inches were buried inside her. Hopelessness threatened.

A hand closed over her shoulder and she looked up at Aramael. "You can't—?"

He shook his head. "I'm sorry, I don't have that power."

"What about Seth?"

Silence.

Hope sputtered out. "I see. No interference, right?"

"I'm sorry," he said again.

No interference, not even to save a life. That just fucking figured. She stroked Nina's dark hair, fear mingling with fury and the bile of betrayal. She remembered the day she'd knelt in the pool of blood at her father's side and prayed for his life. There had been no angels with her that day and so, she supposed, no possibility she might be heard. But for God to allow two angels to stand by Alex now and forbid them to intervene while they watched life drain from Nina?

Benevolent being, my ass, you coldhearted bitch.

A blanket appeared in her peripheral vision, trembling violently. She reached to take it from her sister's hand, standing as she did so. She gave Jen a quick hug and then pulled back to look into the tear-streaked face. "Sit with her," she directed. "Keep her calm and don't let her move too much."

"Shouldn't we take out the glass? Do something?"

"The glass may be slowing the bleeding. If we move it and there's an artery involved—" Alex stopped as Jen swayed on her feet. Too much information. "Let's let the paramedics have a look first," she finished.

A siren wailed its approach. Jennifer nodded and folded herself up to sit beside her daughter, taking over where Alex had left off. Alex spread the blanket over her niece, hoping it would stave off some of the shock. Outside the gaping window, she saw a fire truck lurch to a halt beside the little crowd of neighbors gathered on the sidewalk.

Help had arrived. *Thank God.*

No. Thank humanity. Because apparently God, or the One, or whatever the hell Aramael wanted to call her, didn't want to get involved.

THE ONE STOOD for a long time after Verchiel's words had faded into silence, unmoving, giving no indication she had heard any of it. No indication she cared. Verchiel bit her bottom lip to keep from demanding a response. Twisting her hands into the folds of her robe, she waited.

"You're certain," the One said at last. She turned from her surveillance of the gardens and forests spread below the balcony. For the second time since coming into her presence, Verchiel had to suppress a start of shock at the Creator's appearance, at the weariness in the faded silver eyes. When had the One become so old, so worn? Had the decline been so gradual that none of them had noticed, or had they just not wanted to see it?

Not dared to see it?

"No," said Verchiel with the honesty that was—or should have been—innate to all angels. "I have no proof yet, only suspicion."

"Suspicion strong enough to bring to me."

"Yes."

"And to involve the Appointed in your concerns."

Verchiel swallowed. "You know about that?"

Sorrow shafted through silver eyes. "Have I been so very remiss that none of you think I pay attention anymore?" The One shook her head. "Yes, Verchiel, I know you asked Seth for his help. Did you really think I wouldn't notice the absence of the Appointed?"

Without waiting for an answer—one Verchiel wasn't sure she would want to give in the first place—the Creator paced the length of the balcony railing and back. She made three such trips before pausing to regard Verchiel again. "Have you told anyone else?"

"Just the Power. I thought it best he be aware."

The One made another trek along the railing, stopping this time at the far end.

Verchiel waited for as long as patience held out and then cleared her throat softly. "Do you know what you're going to do?"

"Nothing."

"Nothing? But—"

"You've said yourself that you have no proof, Verchiel. There's a chance you may be wrong. Until I have evidence to the contrary, I must honor Mittron's potential as I do that of any other of my creations. And if you're right, then choices have already been made that I cannot change."

"If I'm right," Verchiel countered, "you could stop him."

Of course the One could stop Mittron. She was the One. The Creator of everything. The ultimate power. She had to be able to set things right. It was why Verchiel had left the research to which Seth had assigned her, why she had risked untold disciplinary measures by vaulting over Mittron's head to the greatest power in the universe. But as the One gazed out over Heaven's landscapes once again, her eyes distant and her shoulders bowed, apprehension whispered through Verchiel's veins. This was not the bearing of the Almighty. Interminable seconds passed, threatened to become an eternity.

At last the One turned, her face set, her eyes resolute.

"Even if I could, it's not him I'm worried about."

THIRTY-TWO

Aramael watched Alex slip an arm around her sister's shoulders and hand the other woman a cup of coffee. The niece had been in surgery for almost three hours, but he had no idea if that was good or bad. Seth had been gone for the same time. Again, bad or good?

He thought back to his short—very short—conversation with the Appointed while they waited for the paramedics to load the girl into the ambulance. It had started with his own cryptic warning to Seth, ripped from him despite his better judgment.

"You cannot have her."

"Who said I wanted her?"

Aramael's wings had flexed involuntarily and only with difficulty had he held back the accusatory words, the demand to know more about the touch he'd interrupted on the sidewalk. The Appointed had eyed him with seeming laziness, but a sharp edge to his demeanor had pierced to the center of the ugliness curling in Aramael's core.

"You do know that you can't have her either," Seth had

observed. "She is mortal, Aramael. And one of the Nephilim. Even if you were permitted a soulmate, it could never be her."

Aramael lifted a hand to where denial had burned—still burned—acidlike in his chest. He knew. He knew the truth of Seth's words, but knowing shredded all that was rational in him and held the potential to destroy him. The very volatility that made him a Power, that enabled the hunter in him to access Heaven's rage in the span of a heartbeat, now threatened to be his downfall.

The pity in Seth's expression hadn't helped.

Just when he'd felt himself teeter on the edge of reason, however, Seth had looked away and dropped his voice. "How well do you know Mittron?" he asked.

Surprise had jolted Aramael out of his seething. "The Highest? Well enough to know he's a pompous ass."

Seth's lips had twitched. "An accurate description. But I want to know if you've ever crossed swords with him. Done anything to make him go after you in some way."

Aramael had frowned. "Not that I'm aware of, no. Verchiel is my handler and I've never had to deal with him directly. Why? What is this about?"

"I'm not sure. A theory. A hunch. Tell me, has any Fallen One ever escaped Limbo before?"

"Never."

"Doesn't it strike you as strange?" Seth watched him. "The only one to ever escape is your brother. He turns up in a place where it's only a matter of time before he runs into a Naphil whose job it is to capture him. The same Naphil who turns out to be your soulmate. The one Mittron sent you to protect while you hunt Caim."

Aramael's entire being went still under the sheer enormity of what Seth suggested. He took a lungful of air that felt thick, tasted sour. "That's one hell of an accusation you're not quite making," he said.

"It's one hell of an accusation I'm trying my damnedest not to even imagine," Seth retorted in a flat voice. "But I'm seeing way too many coincidences to be coincidental."

"But why? To what purpose?"

"Damned if I know."

"Can you find out more?"

"Not here."

Aramael had looked down the corridor to Alex and her sister. Then he'd pulled himself inward, centered himself, reached out with every scrap of awareness he could scrape together, straining past Alex's presence to search for his brother. Nothing.

Or nothing that he could feel, anyway.

"Go," he told Seth. "I'll stay with Alex. And the others."

"DETECTIVE."

Alex, leaning forward in a chair, elbows resting on knees, looked up from the magazine she wasn't reading. She met her supervisor's scowl and felt her stomach drop. Time to face the music.

Roberts jerked his head to the left and she nodded. She set her magazine aside and reached to give Jen's hand a squeeze. Jen returned the gesture but didn't seem able to let go again, and Alex felt her heart constrict at the rigid lines of control etched into her sister's face.

She extricated herself gently. "I have to talk to Staff Roberts," she said, pointing. "I'll just be over there, and I won't be long."

Jen stared at her, visibly swallowed her need, and nodded. With a reassuring pat on her sister's knee, Alex pushed out of the chair and went to join Roberts in the corridor outside the ICU waiting room.

"How is your niece?" he asked without preamble.

"Alive for now. She punctured her bowel. They've repaired it, but it'll be twenty-four hours before we know if they've stopped the infection."

Roberts's lips tightened. "What the hell is going on, Alex? You leave the crime scene without a word to anyone, your niece is soaked in enough blood to fill a slaughterhouse, she impales herself on a broken window . . ." He trailed off, angry and bewildered.

She scuffed the toe of one shoe against the gleaming floor. "You wouldn't believe me if I told you."

He snorted. "Trust me, Detective, at this point you have nothing to lose by trying."

Alex weighed her options. She wondered what the repercussions might be if she simply refused. Then she wondered if she cared. "She was there."

"Who was where?"

"Nina. She was at the mission. She saw the killer. Saw what he did. That's why she tried to kill herself. Like Martin James."

"She—James—" Roberts broke off and rocked back on his heels. He remained silent for a long time, staring over Alex's head, a muscle flexing in his jaw. Then he looked down at her again, his gaze flat, steady. "Can she give us a description?"

"No."

The muscle in front of Roberts's ear twitched again. "I'm posting two uniforms at the elevators and two at each set of stairs. Joly and Abrams are on their way here to sit with you and your family."

"Staff—"

Roberts cut across her objection. "You need to know something."

The hairs on the back of Alex's neck prickled to life. "What?" she asked.

"It may not be connected," he hedged, "but I'm not taking any chances."

She only just stopped herself from seizing her supervisor's shirtfront. "*What?*"

"They found a cab a block from your sister's house. The driver's throat was slit."

Before he'd finished his sentence, Alex was already running, shoving a startled nurse out of her path, sending a supply cart crashing into a wall. Aramael met her halfway, his fiery wings spread behind him, flexed and powerful; his arms going around her as they came together.

"He knows," she gasped. "He knows where we are."

SETH RESTED HIS cheek against his loosely fisted hand, his elbow on the paper-strewn table. He stared at the dozens of records spread before him. He'd been at this so long it was a wonder he hadn't gone cross-eyed. What a complex, convoluted trail. For every path that brought him closer to the answers he sought, a dozen others led him so far astray it took hours to reorient. It didn't help that everything was written in the complex tongue of the Principalities, the Keepers of Divine Records.

He lifted his hands and smoothed them over his hair. Hours of research, and not a single shred of evidence to prove—what? He didn't even know what allegation he should be making. Bloody hell, he would get nowhere this way, and without something tangible, could enlist no other help. Mittron was the highest level of authority in the entire realm other than the One herself, and without good reason to question the Seraph's actions, the One would be content to leave him in exactly that position. Mittron, who had already declined to answer Verchiel's questions and forbidden her from looking for her own answers.

"Interesting research," observed the object of his interest.

Seth stiffened and masked his expression before looking up. "It is, actually."

The Highest of the Seraphim Choir reached out and lifted one of the papers from the table, scanned it, and dropped it back into the morass. His hands went behind his back. From the tension in Mittron's arms and shoulders, Seth guessed that they were clasped there. Tightly. His interest ratcheted upward.

He let the silence draw out for a few seconds, and then cocked an eyebrow. "You wanted something?"

"Verchiel gave me your message."

"Ah."

"Pulling rank? You have no rank."

Had the Highest Seraph just sneered at him? Seth leaned back in his chair, lifted his booted feet onto a clear spot on the table, and interlaced his fingers behind his head, his attitude one of bored disrespect. Mittron's nostrils flared in response.

"Technically, no." Seth shrugged. "But my understanding is that, technically, neither do you. Yours is a position of trust, is it not, rather that one of power?"

"My position is none of your business." Dislike flashed across Mittron's face and ice crystals settled into the amber eyes. "None of this is your business."

"I disagree. I think secrets in Heaven should be everyone's business."

To his surprise, Mittron laughed with real amusement.

"You've no idea how ironic those words are, coming from you," the Highest told him.

Seth frowned, sensing a loss of advantage in a game he still didn't understand. "I have no secrets."

"It's not the secrets you have, Appointed, it's the ones you *don't* have."

What the hell was that supposed to mean? Seth scowled. "Spare me the dramatics, Seraph. If you have something to tell me, just say so."

"It's not that easy, I'm afraid. You see, I would be in a great deal of trouble if I were to tell you."

"More trouble than you'll be in if this pans out?" Seth indicated the paper-strewn table. "Which secret is more dangerous, Mittron?"

"Which is more valuable to you?" the Seraph countered.

"Truthfully? Whichever one lets me live with myself. Which I doubt I could do if I climbed into bed with you." Seth dropped his feet to the floor and scooped a sheaf of papers together and tapped them into a tidy stack. "So thanks anyway, but I'll pass on knowing my secret and settle for finding out yours."

Mittron's expression turned hard again. "You're making a mistake."

"But retaining my integrity."

A muscle flickered in the Seraph's tight jaw. "You won't find what you're looking for."

"You wouldn't be trying to stop me if you believed that." Seth manufactured an indifferent yawn. "Don't you have something else to do? Someone else to harass?"

"Even if you find the answers you seek—" Mittron's hands curled at his sides.

"What? You'll stop me from telling the One? Banish me from Heaven?" Seth mocked. "You forget who you're talking to, Seraph. You may hold sway over the host, but I'm not one of them, remember? You have no control over me."

"I was going to say that you won't find them in time," Mittron responded. "Events have been set in motion that cannot be stopped. Not now. Not even by you."

The Highest Seraph's footsteps retreated. The slam of a door echoed through the cavernous hall and faded into silence. Seth inhaled the scent of dust and old ink permeating the rows of records that stretched in every direction, records he hadn't yet begun to examine. Records Mittron had just told him he didn't have time to examine.

Just what the hell had the Highest Seraph done?

MITTRON BRUSHED PAST the queue of angels waiting outside his office without a word and slammed the door against questions for which he had neither patience nor time. Questions for which he had no stomach in the face of seeing his carefully constructed plan come apart.

He crossed to his desk and flung himself into the chair. Stood again and paced the room with quick, staccato strides. His lungs burned. Damn Verchiel to eternal Limbo. First her suspicions, then her decision—behind his back—to involve the Appointed. The one variable Mittron had failed to take into account. Failed to foresee. How could he have been so blind?

Now his former soulmate had disappeared, leaving behind a note that said she'd decided to remove herself from

Aramael's case after all, and had gone on sabbatical. The sour scent of his own anxiety filled his nostrils.

If only she could have made that decision before she'd gone to Seth.

Mittron pressed fingertips to lips, cool against warm. The sound of laughter floated through the open window behind his desk, a harsh counterbalance to the thread of desperation intertwining with his thoughts. Until now, everything had moved forward as he'd hoped, come together as he'd envisioned, impelling Heaven and Hell toward what, really, had been inevitable all along. He'd been absolutely certain he had covered every eventuality, every possibility, and now it all came down to timing. Hinged on whether Seth could find the proof he sought before matters came to a head and the final piece of the plan fell into place—

And Mittron silenced him forever.

ARAMAEL STOOD TO one side of the girl's bed, facing off against Alex on the other. Seth watched them both from the foot of the bed, his arms folded across his chest. Aramael alone could feel the Appointed's influence, exerted to help the Guardians keep the ICU nurses at bay, and he alone bore the full brunt of Alex's fury.

"What do you mean, you're leaving?" she hissed. "If he's after Jen and Nina, how in bloody hell will it help for you to go off chasing him somewhere else? You said yourself you don't even know where to start."

Aramael felt weariness creep over him. "It's the only way to end this. Caim won't come after you as long as I'm here; he knows I'll capture him before he gets within twenty feet of you. He'll just keep killing until I go after him. You'll be safe with Seth. All of you will be."

Alex rested her hands on her hips. Then raked them over her hair. Then fisted them and leaned on the bed, staring down at her niece. "You're sure there's nothing else we can do?"

"I wish there was."

With every fiber of his being, he wished. But he'd been over it a thousand times in his head, from every possible perspective, only to conclude that Verchiel was right. He had to leave Alex, put distance between them so he could feel something other than her presence. So he could fulfill his purpose.

So he could remember it.

He watched Alex's struggle for control and felt the iron constraints she placed on her fear, her determined efforts to retain her humanity in the face of that fear. Ignored the twist in his gut as she looked to Seth for confirmation and sagged at the Appointed's nod.

A nurse approached, her lips pursed and her brow furrowed. Seth turned to her and shook his head. She hesitated, looked confused, and then changed direction. Seth turned back to Alex and offered her a half smile. "He's right. It's the only way. I will keep you safe. I promise."

Aramael's spine tensed as Alex considered the Appointed's words. Then she relaxed a fraction and he sensed the beginnings of her trust.

In Seth.

Aramael reined in a surge of something he thought safer not to identify and made his shoulders drop. "I'll never be far," he said. "If Caim should come after you in spite of Seth's presence, I will know about it."

Doubt shadowed Alex's face. "But if you don't feel him . . ."

He reached across the narrow bed and covered one of her hands with his own. "Even if I fail to feel him, I will feel *you*. That *I* can promise."

She stared at him for a long time before she nodded. "All right. But we can't stay here."

A sharp inhale heralded her sister's return from the hospital cafeteria. "You're not leaving me here alone with Nina, are you? Alex—"

Alex pulled free from Aramael's grip and turned to her sister. "Of course not, Jen. I'm not leaving either one of you until this is over. I promise." She gave the other woman a quick hug. "But we can't stay here. None of us can." She looked over her shoulder at Aramael. "If he comes here, even if he doesn't get to us, there will be a bloodbath—and the kind of attention you can't afford. We'll take her to my house."

"No," said Aramael. "Your colleague—the one he killed—will have told him where you live."

"He'll be watching her, Aramael. He'll know where she is no matter where she goes," Seth pointed out.

Most unhelpfully, judging by the way Alex turned the same color as the bed in which her niece lay. But she lifted her chin and met Aramael's gaze steadily.

"He's right," she told him. "It's as safe as we'll get until you nail him."

Jen inserted herself between Alex and the girl in the hospital bed. "Are you insane? You can't move her, she'll die!"

"No, she won't."

Aramael met Alex's determination. He knew she was right, but hated it. Too many already knew too much. He swore viciously and turned to Seth. "Do it."

The Appointed's jaw dropped. "Are you out of your mind?" He came around to where Aramael stood and, keeping his back to the women, said in a low, hard voice, "Think about what you're suggesting, Aramael. Three mortals already know of our existence—we've no idea what consequences will stem from that alone. But to add a healing? That goes beyond just breaking the cardinal rule, that's openly flouting it."

"From what you've told me of your conversation with Mittron, we have no alternative. We're on our own here, Appointed. We do what we must."

"Or what that damned Seraph is hoping we'll do," Seth muttered darkly.

The possibility had crossed Aramael's mind as well, but at this point, he saw no choice. Not when Verchiel had disappeared from their situation and the One herself seemed to be paying no attention.

"Fine." Seth heaved a sigh. "I'll do it, but only to the point where she's safe to move. And this one *you* get to claim responsibility for, Power."

ENOUGH.

The word filled the One, weighing her down with its intent. Its truth.

The door clicked shut behind the Dominion Verchiel and the One let the stiffness slide from her spine. She leaned her forehead against the cool wood of the bookcase by which she stood. Enough, she thought again.

Enough struggling to maintain an impossible balance. Enough tiptoeing about in the world of her own creation as if everything might crumble if she so much as breathed the wrong way. Enough of this infernal dance between her and the one who had once sat at her side.

More than enough, if her own angels had begun to turn against her. Betrayal sat bitter on her tongue, alongside disgust at her own blindness. She could see it so clearly now, how Mittron had angled for this for four thousand years, how he had taken advantage of her distraction.

Or had she just let him do so?

She closed her eyes against the second, even less palatable truth. The truth that said she had been blind only to what she had not wanted to see. Known that Mittron attempted to catapult Heaven and Hell into the final war. Known, and failed to heed. Chose even now to ignore what was so obvious. But why? Why would she have not wanted to see one of her own trying to cause what she herself had worked so hard to prevent?

A third truth whispered through her, underpinning the first two and twisting her very core of being into a knot of denial. The One tried to push away the thought, to bury it again, but it pushed back, demanding acknowledgement, refusing to retreat.

Waiting patiently.

Implacably.

Until the One raised her head and opened her eyes and faced it without flinching. Until she recognized it, accepted it, and gave it the voice she had withheld for so many millennia.

"Because I am tired," she whispered, and felt a single tear slide down her cheek.

THIRTY-THREE

Alex dabbed the water from her face with a tea towel and struggled to steady her heartbeat. Her every fiber tuned in to the presence behind her, to the gray eyes following her every move. She kept her gaze fixed on the sink, refusing to allow it to rise to the darkened window and the reflection she knew she would find there.

With Seth using that strange influence of his to run interference with the nurses, they'd managed to get Nina out of the hospital and home to Alex's living room. She was settled on the couch now, with Jen beside her and Seth standing watch over both of them, leaving only Alex and Aramael in the kitchen.

Alex, Aramael, and the conversation they'd begun at Jen's.

A conversation that loomed between them, demanding closure.

Alex crushed the tea towel in her hand and stared into the bottom of the sink. She didn't need to see Aramael to know how he would look, leaning against the kitchen door-post with his arms crossed over his chest, jacket and tie discarded, snowy shirt open at the neck. Wings folded behind him.

She closed her eyes and tried to ignore her bounding pulse, to listen for sounds from the living room where she had left Jen and Seth with a physically healed but still mentally absent Nina. Measured footsteps crossed the kitchen floor.

Alex gripped the edge of the sink so hard that little needles of pain shot through the injury she had almost forgotten. The footsteps stopped. So did her breathing.

"Are you all right?" Aramael asked.

Hysteria burbled up in her throat. She couldn't have spoken past it if she'd wanted to. Sparks lit the backs of her eyelids. Behind her, she felt the heat of his body, inches from her own.

"I'm sorry you were pulled into all this. It should never have happened this way."

Alex swallowed. "You want to know something funny?"

"What?"

"My whole life I've worried I'd inherit my mother's schizophrenia. Now I realize it would have been easier if I had, because insanity would make one hell of a lot more sense than any of this does."

He exhaled a long, slow breath that stirred her hair, and only sheer determination kept her upright. Kept her from leaning back into an angel's embrace. She opened her eyes and stared at their shared reflection. At the raw pain reflected in the lines around Aramael's mouth and the gaze that met hers.

Outside, thunder rumbled ominously. Restlessness joined the shadows in Aramael's eyes. "I have to go," he said.

Alex folded her arms over her belly. "He's going to come after us, isn't he? Even with Seth here."

A tattered flash of lightning lit the night.

"Perhaps. We don't know for sure."

Thunder rolled past again. Alex thought about all the storms that had coincided with the bodies and wondered if she'd been right about a connection. She decided it didn't matter. Not anymore. "Can Seth really stop him?"

"He can slow him down until I get here."

"And you're sure you'll feel him? If he does come here, I mean?"

Gray eyes met hers again, savage with promise. "Even if I don't feel him, I will feel you. I will always feel you."

But will you feel me in time?

She bit down on her lip, holding back the question, knowing he could give no guarantees. Knowing they had no choice but to take the risk. She and Jen and Nina might become sitting ducks without him here, but Caim wouldn't stop killing until Aramael went after him. Three lives weighed against countless others. No guarantees. No choice.

In the window, Alex watched Aramael turn and walk away. He made it to the middle of the kitchen before she stopped him.

"Aramael." His name felt foreign on her tongue, and she realized with a jolt that it was the first time she had spoken it aloud. "What about after?" she asked, giving voice to the question that had plagued her since their conversation in Jen's dining room.

"After?"

She stared at the wings framing his broad back, mouth parchment dry. She should stop, she thought. Before she got in any deeper. Before either of them did. She should just let it go.

But she couldn't.

She turned from the counter. "After you catch Caim," she whispered.

Had any being ever moved more slowly? By the time he faced her, she had lived a thousand lives, died a thousand deaths. And loved him a thousand times over.

"I don't know." His mouth twisted. "No, that's not true. I do know, but I don't want to think about it."

It was the answer she had expected, of course, but it still sliced into her heart and left her bleeding inside, quietly, invisibly, mortally. "Damn it," she whispered. "This is so not right."

Aramael's wings flexed, but he said nothing. Alex felt the few feet separating them grow to a chasm and sudden anguish gripped her. She couldn't let him leave like this. Not with that distance between them; not when she might never have another chance to breach that gap.

"I need to tell you something before you go," she said. She gripped the counter behind her and dredged up the last bit of strength she possessed. Sucked in a scant lungful of air. "I—"

She got no further. Aramael suddenly stood in front of her, a single finger pressed against her lips. "Don't," he said. "Please." He rested his forehead against hers. "If you say it, I don't think I'll be able to leave."

Then stay, her heart whispered.

As if he'd heard, Aramael's hand moved, feathering across her jaw to her throat, tightening around the back of her neck. Alex breathed in his scent and felt his heat envelop her; felt yearning stir in her belly. She waited, not daring to move. Aramael's harsh exhale exploded against her lips.

"By all that is holy, Alex, I cannot—" He stopped and raised his head to stare down at her, and primal need burned in his eyes. "Bloody Hell," he grated.

Then he crushed her against the counter, his powerful length pressed against her every inch. His lips found hers, fierce with hunger. The ache in her belly turned molten and, in a single beat of his heart against hers, ignited into wildfire that spread to her every fiber. Need became a demand for more. A demand for everything.

Her hands twisted into his hair with the desperation of all the times she had held herself back from reaching out to him. The desperation of knowing that, no matter how much she might hope, there would be no *after*. Her mouth opened to his, felt his tongue slide against hers, tangle with it, possess it. His hands slid from her shoulders, spanned her rib cage, splayed against her lower back, fitted her to him so closely that, for a moment, they might have been one. One body, one mind, one soul—angel and mortal, destined to mate for eternity.

Alex's whole being sang with completion.

And then he was gone.

She stumbled at the loss, caught herself before she fell, sagged against the counter. Little by little, the heat in her veins cooled, changed to ice crystals that settled in her core beside the agony that had become her new companion. She sank to the floor, her back against the cupboards, forehead resting on bent knees. On the wall, the clock ticked with cold impartiality, counting the passing seconds, and then the minutes.

OUTSIDE THE WINDOW, Caim scowled as his brother embraced the Naphil. Bitterness filled his mouth and trickled down to his gut. So. He'd been right about everything. About Aramael, the woman, their relationship, and all the possibilities that relationship held for him. He had everything he needed to make his revenge complete. So why the hell did he feel this weariness instead of elation?

He watched the two figures merge and remembered how it had felt to be a part of that passion, that completion. What it had felt like to lose it, to have it torn from him. He reminded himself it had been Aramael who had testified against him, Aramael who had ultimately denied him his return and made certain he would live with the memory of his loss for all eternity.

But still doubt tasted flat on his tongue. He risked so much, killing the Naphil in the presence of his brother. He would have a far greater chance of success if he took her while Aramael was gone. Distracted. Did he really need to take this to the next level? Could he not be satisfied just knowing the pain he would inflict on his brother, his hunter?

He watched Aramael pull back from the woman, saw him disappear from the kitchen, felt the price he paid to do so. Vicious satisfaction permeated Caim. Gave him his answer. Folding his wings against his back, he withdrew into the shadows.

Did he want Aramael to suffer as he had? Yes.

Did he want to bear witness to that suffering?

A hundred thousand times, *yes*.

ALEX STOOD IN the doorway, surveying the occupants in the living room. Her niece, asleep under a blanket on the couch; Jen curled up likewise in a chair nearby; Seth, arms folded and face brooding, standing guard at the window.

He looked around at her entrance, his face enigmatic. "Are you all right?"

She nodded. "He— Aramael is gone."

"I know. I felt him go." His jaw tightened. "I suspect the whole damned universe felt it."

Alex frowned. "What do you mean?"

"The two of you—" Seth paused. "Suffice it to say you generate considerable energy together."

Heat scorched her cheeks. Did he know—had he felt—? Shit. She went across to Nina and straightened the already smooth blanket over her niece's shoulders. "How is she?"

"Physically she's fine. She'll still need recovery time, but there will be no complications."

"Thank you for that. I know you weren't suppose to, but thank you."

Again the muscle in Seth's jaw moved. "I don't know that I did you any favors. Or her. She may not recover from seeing Caim the way she did, and if she does, she'll never be the same."

"But she won't try to kill herself again."

"No. I was able to do that much for her. The rest will be up to her."

"Then I mean it. Thank you."

A faint smile curved his lips. "You're welcome."

Alex left Nina and Jen and joined him at the window, leaning a shoulder against the opposite frame. She stared out at the dark lawn. "Can I ask you a question?"

"You can ask, but I reserve the right not to answer."

"Caim called me Naphil. What is that?"

"Aramael didn't tell you?"

"We had a lot to cover, what with the whole existence of angels and demons and all," she said dryly. "We didn't quite manage to get to this."

"I see."

She sensed his hesitation. "If I am what he said, I think I should know."

"And I think you should be careful what you ask for." Seth replied. "But in this case, you may be right." He rested his shoulder against the wall. "The One assigned a choir of angels, the Grigori, to watch over the mortals during their evolution. Unfortunately, with Lucifer's encouragement, they did more than just watch. Much more. They shared knowledge humans weren't ready for, mentally or morally. Knowledge that led to wars, poverty, every decay human history holds. And they mated with humans; begetting offspring called Nephilim—half angel, half human."

"Half—" The enormity of the idea choked off her words.

Seth continued as if she'd said nothing. "The One would have nothing to do with them and, without Guardians, most didn't survive the first generation. The few who did, however, went on to procreate and their descendants walk this realm even today. Caim believes that one of their souls, with its divine roots, might pass through Heaven—however briefly—upon the death of its vessel, and that he might be able to accompany it there. To return."

Alex would have liked to swear, but no words seemed strong enough. She grappled with her new awareness of herself, decided she wasn't quite ready to go there just yet, and settled for another question. "Would it work?"

"We don't know for certain, but it's possible."

"Are there others who want to return?"

"Yes."

"So if he succeeds, others might try the same thing."

"Yes."

"Shit," she said. *All those victims.* She left the window and crossed—stumbled—to the fireplace. Leaning both hands on the mantel, she stared into the previous winter's cold ashes. She really should clean those out and call a chimney sweep before autumn set in again.

Steady, Jarvis. Don't lose it now.

She turned back to Seth. "But if he knew about me, then why would he kill all those other people? Why not just come after me?"

"That's one of the things I've been trying to figure out." Seth turned his back to the window and sat against the ledge. "The best I can come up with is revenge. Caim changed his mind shortly after following Lucifer and petitioned for forgiveness. The One rejected his plea when Aramael testified against him. I think he recognizes Aramael's feelings for you and wants to see him suffer the same loss he did. The loss of a soulmate."

Soulmate.

Only when the room swam before her did Alex realize she'd stopped breathing. She inhaled quickly. Coughed. Groped for the chair by the fireplace and sank into it. Stared at Seth.

He sighed. "Let me guess. You didn't get that far, either."

She shook her head. Silently marveled that one could go so numb that they couldn't feel their own movement anymore. Couldn't even feel their limbs. "I didn't—I never—I didn't know angels had soulmates."

She hadn't given much credence to the notion where humans were concerned, either, but that was another matter.

"They don't. At least, not anymore. Lucifer's fall wreaked havoc among those who remained loyal, especially when it came to battling their loved ones. The One's solution was to cleanse all recognition of soulmates from her angels."

"Wasn't that a little harsh?"

Seth regarded her without expression. "Feeling what you do for Aramael, would you be able to fight him? To destroy him?"

Alex's brain wouldn't even let her go there on speculation. "Point taken," she said softly. "So none of you can love?"

Seth hesitated, and then turned to the window again. "Not the kind of love you're speaking of, no."

"Then what happened? How is Aramael different?"

"That, Alexandra Jarvis, would be the mystery."

On the couch, Nina stirred and murmured. Alex watched her settle again, and then glanced at Jen, noting the lines of worry that creased her sister's brow even in repose.

She turned back to Seth. "A minute ago you said something about Guardians—did you mean Guardian angels? They're real, too?"

"For most people, yes. But not for you." His looked toward the couch and chair. "Or for them."

"This One of yours really takes her grudges seriously, doesn't she?"

"A Guardian doesn't guarantee a trouble-free existence. Nephilim descendants make their own choices, their own decisions, just as anyone else does. Free will comes at a price for all mortals."

Nina moved again on the couch and Alex looked over to find the girl's eyes open and staring in their direction. She shivered at the emptiness that occupied the blue depths. Free will might come at a price for all mortals, but what higher price for those like her niece and sister?

Or her?

WHERE THE BLOODY Hell was Caim?

Aramael turned left at a corner and picked up his pace. Nothing. He felt *nothing*. Because he hadn't yet put enough distance between him and Alex? Or because his brother was lying low, biding his time? Perhaps watching Alex even now, as Aramael stalked the streets in search of him.

Disquiet crawled over his skin. It went against every fiber of his being to leave Alex's side like this. To turn her into bait. Because no matter how he tried to convince himself otherwise, that was what he'd done. Because he knew— bloody Hell, they all knew—it was the only way to draw Caim out. He had to leave her, to get far enough away that Caim would go after her, and hope to Heaven he'd get there in time to stop his brother. But no matter how many times

Aramael told himself she'd be safe with Seth, that the Appointed would be on high alert, no amount of reassurance made it easier to entrust her life—and his very soul—to the care of another.

Because if Caim were to somehow get to her in spite of the precautions . . .

He shook off the very graphic scenarios his recently formed imagination saw fit to provide. The muscles across his shoulders knotted, causing the feathers along his wings to ruffle. He stopped in an office building doorway. *Focus, damn it. The only way you'll keep her safe is to get to Caim before he gets to her, and you're not going to do that by standing on a sidewalk whining about how hard it is. You know your purpose, Power. Now find it. Use it. End this game.*

With every ounce of self-control he possessed, he turned himself inward. Stilled his thoughts. Fought to rediscover what had once been so natural for him, what had *been* him. Waited for the tremor in his own energy that would signal Caim's presence. Seconds edged by.

Nothing.

He straightened his spine and flexed his wings, and then tried again, straining to feel the slightest hint, the faintest vibration. Frustration twitched in his core, eating at his concentration and his confidence.

What if he didn't find him in time?

What if—?

Aramael slammed his fist against the wall beside him, shattering a brick in its mortar setting. One last effort. A desperate push past the limits he'd once thought he had—

And still nothing. He couldn't feel a damned thing.

Except the woman who depended on him to make this right.

To protect her.

ALEX JOLTED AWAKE to the soft chiming of the mantel clock. Six chords, marking the start of a new day, confirmed by the sunlight streaming in through the living room window. The window beside which Seth still stood, still stared out. Alex straightened protesting knees from under her and struggled into a more comfortable position. Her gaze fell on the deserted couch and chair opposite.

Before she'd had time to even process the fact that Jen and Nina were missing, let alone panic about it, Seth's low rumble reached across the room to her. "They're fine. They moved up to your room about three hours ago."

Alex stood up stiffly, catching the blanket as it fell from her lap. She stared at it. She was sure she hadn't covered herself. She hadn't even intended to fall asleep—she looked across at Seth. "Thank you."

He shrugged.

"Has Aramael been back at all?" She laid the blanket across the chair arm.

"Not yet." He smiled a faint reassurance. "He's a Power, Alex. Caim may have been his equal at one time, but not now. Not since he fell almost five thousand years ago."

"But what if he's caught by surprise? He said himself he can't feel Caim, said there are . . ."

"Complications. Yes, I know, but trust me, Caim won't be going after Aramael. He doesn't have the courage to precipitate an all-out war."

"A what?"

But Seth's face had closed over as soon as the words left his mouth. "Nothing. Forget I said that."

Like hell she would. Alex moved to join him. "War between whom?"

"I said forget it."

"I'm not very good at that, so you may as well just tell me now and save us both a lot of trouble."

"There are some things you really are better off not knowing, Alexandra Jarvis."

She frowned. "Why do you do that? Call me Alexandra Jarvis all the time?"

Mild annoyance entered Seth's expression. "You ask a lot of questions, don't you?"

"It's my job to ask questions. And that's not an answer."

He turned his head from her and stared through the window. "You're not what I expected. As a mortal, I mean. I'm surprised at how engaging you are, and how much I find myself drawn to you. The formality of your full name reminds me to maintain distance."

Oh. Alex felt her cheeks heat at the unexpected and, in her experience, unprecedented honesty. The awkwardness of their shared touch on the sidewalk at the mission returned tenfold, and she shuffled her feet. "Um . . ."

Seth slanted her a sideways look that was half amused and half way-too-serious for her taste. "Relax. I'm in no better position than Aramael to pursue a relationship with a mortal."

She pulled away from the wall. Now, there was a path she didn't want to travel, she thought. Not from the perspective of Seth's blatant declaration of interest, and sure as hell not from the perspective of any potential relationship with Aramael—or lack thereof.

She shifted her posture, trying to ease the knifelike pain that had slid between her ribs and into her heart. Coffee. She'd make coffee, take some time to herself in the kitchen—

A crash overhead reverberated through the living room. Alex froze for an instant and then met Seth's startled look.

"Nina," she whispered. "Jen."

THIRTY-FOUR

"Alex, wait!"

Alex took the stairs two at a time. Seth's bellow—and his footsteps—followed. She yanked her gun free of the holster she'd scooped up from the coffee table and tossed the holster aside. Gaining the top, she skidded to a halt in front of Jen, emerging bleary-eyed but seemingly unscathed from the bathroom. "Are you all right?"

Jen blinked at her, and then at Seth. "I'm fine. What's going on?"

"We heard a crash—"

"Oh, that. I owe you a new soap dispenser." Jen pulled a face. "I picked up the pieces, but there's soap everywhere."

Alex sagged against the wall. It wasn't Caim. Nothing mattered except that. She waved away her sister's apology. "Don't worry about it. I just thought—we thought—"

Jen's swallow was audible in the silence of Alex's inability to finish the sentence. Then she forced a sad caricature of a smile. "Nope, just clumsy me. I'll finish cleaning up. Excuse me."

She disappeared back into the bathroom and closed the

door, and Seth's hand instantly seized Alex's shoulder, dragging her around to face him.

"*Never* do that again," he hissed, shaking her none too gently. "Not even I can protect you if you run right into Caim's arms, and that"—he fixed an angry look on the gun in her hand—"is useless against him. Do you understand?"

Alex's heart skipped a beat. What did he mean, he couldn't protect her? Seth gave her a little shake, as if he'd read her thoughts.

"As long as he doesn't get hold of you, I can put myself between you long enough for Aramael to return."

"And if he does get hold of me? Can you not stop him then?"

Seth's face turned grim. "Only a Power can remove him to Limbo. But . . ."

Swallowing had never been so difficult. "But what?"

"Alex, if Caim gets hold of you, Aramael could well lose control. He might not be able to stop himself from killing Caim, and if that happens . . ." His voice trailed off again and his fingers tightened on her shoulder. "If that happens, it will break the peace between Heaven and Hell."

She shivered and moistened dry lips. "That's the war you mentioned?"

"Mortals call it the Apocalypse."

Alex stared into the black, bottomless eyes and felt something deep inside her turn utterly still as Seth's words settled into her core. *The Apocalypse.* An angel's soul had become entangled with hers and he had sworn to protect her against all odds, against all rules, and if she allowed him to do so, the world would face the end of days? She shook her head in silent, sick denial and Seth's hand on her arm gave a gentle squeeze in response.

"We won't let it get that far," he said. "I promise."

Jen came out of the bathroom again, wiping her hands against the seat of her jeans. "I got the worst of it, but watch your step if you go in there. It's still a bit slippery." Her gaze darted between them. "Am I interrupting something?"

Alex felt Seth's hand slide away. She looked away from

her sister's too-perceptive stare and, with the automatic movements of the robot she felt she'd become, tucked the gun into the waistband in the small of her back. Dredged up the ability to speak again, to pretend the rest of her reality hadn't just shattered at her feet.

"No," she answered Jen. "You're not interrupting. I'm going to make coffee. You interested?"

"Lord, yes. I'm just going to grab a shower first. I'll be down in a few minutes."

Alex hesitated. She eyed a still seething Seth, who had just so forcefully underscored her sense of vulnerability. Seeming to understand her thoughts, he gave a slight shake of his head. She turned back to her sister. "Actually, Jen, I think we should stay together."

"But we are together."

"In the same room together."

"Isn't that just a little paranoid? We'll hear if anyone tries to get into the house—"

"It's not paranoia." Alex suppressed a surge of impatience, reminding herself that Jen hadn't seen what she'd seen. Knew only a fraction of what she knew.

If I were to destroy in her name it would alter the balance of the universe in ways I don't think any of us would care to explore.

"That might be too late," she told her sister. "We stay together. We'll bring Nina back downstairs with us."

Jen looked as if she might object further, but then she sighed. "Fine. Can I at least have a clean T-shirt first?"

"Third drawer in the dresser."

Alex waited until her sister stepped into the bedroom and closed the door again, and then she faced Seth. Chewing at the inside of her bottom lip, she reached back to adjust the gun resting against her spine. "Do you really think he'll try anything? He must know you're here."

"I'm sure he knows. But that doesn't mean he cares."

"He's that desperate?"

"Yes. And that determined."

The murmur of Jen's voice came from the bedroom.

Good. She was waking Nina, which would make it easier to move her. Downstairs, the mantel clock chimed quarter past the hour. Fifteen minutes since Alex had woken up; four hours since Aramael had left her in the kitchen. How much longer—?

"I'll go help Jennifer," she said.

Leaving Seth leaning against the wall, hands in pockets and ankles crossed, Alex pushed open the bedroom door. Jen looked around at her entrance, T-shirt in hand.

"You should have told me your friend was back. Surely with all of us here it's safe for me to take that shower."

Alex paused in the doorway, hand resting on the knob, eyes adjusting to the semigloom created by the drawn blinds at the windows. "What?"

"Your friend." Jen nodded toward the bed. "He says he'll watch Nina for me."

Splinters of ice shot through Alex's heart.

No.

She tried to swallow, but too great a lump sat in the way. *Dear God, no.*

For what felt like an eternity, she stood, unable to look in the direction Jen indicated. Unable to move. Unable to think. Incapable of reacting. At last her hand crept toward the light switch beside the door and flicked it upward. She blinked against the brightness and then, finally, looked at the bed where Nina still slept, her body a lump under the covers, identifiable only by her long, dark hair splayed across the pillow. Her gaze shifted a fraction to the right, to *him*.

Caim.

Lounging beside her niece, torso propped against the headboard, feet stretched out comfortably, hands tucked behind his head. Looking every inch like he belonged there. Looking so much like Aramael that Alex hesitated. Doubted.

Until he smiled.

Until his eyes turned from gray to obsidian, and he reached out a hand to stroke Nina's hair, and Alex saw the ragged, bloody place where a fingernail had been ripped from its bed. In the space of a single, ponderous heartbeat, a dozen thoughts flashed through her mind. A dozen certainties.

Aramael's hand, stretched out to touch her face only a short time ago, had been marred by no such blemish.

A claw, the only physical evidence they'd found at any of the scenes, still lacked identification.

A claw, broken from the hand of a demon, might leave behind a mark such as this.

And if any doubt remained, there, tucked behind him, were his wings. Unkempt, yellowed, and lacking in any of the glory of Aramael's—but wings nonetheless.

Horror replaced Alex's doubt. Turned to terror. Became a cop's instinctive bid to protect the vulnerable—and to survive. With fingers numbed by fear, she pulled the gun from behind her back and trained it on Caim's chest. She had no misconceptions that a bullet would stop him, but maybe she could slow him down enough to get Nina and Jen to safety—

Caim laughed. A loud, genuinely amused laugh. "Seriously?" he asked. "Haven't you learned anything about us yet? Or are you really as stupid as the rest of them?"

The gun wavered in Alex's hand. She gritted her teeth and steadied it through sheer force of will. Demon or no demon, he was still scum. "Get the fuck away from my niece, you son of a bitch!"

"Son of a bitch? Me?" Caim chuckled again, letting a lock of Nina's hair slide through his fingers. "You have it wrong, Naphil. I'm just a lowly Fallen Angel. Now, *he*, on the other hand"—he jutted his chin in her direction—"he truly does qualify for the title."

Seth's hand closed over the gun in Alex's hand and pushed it down to her side. "Get behind me," he ordered. "Now."

"Listen and she dies, Naphil." Caim's hand snaked out and lifted Nina, limp as a rag doll, upright by her hair. All trace of amusement had disappeared and his eyes glittered with a cold, bright light.

Seth raised his left hand, palm toward the bed, and Alex's

skin prickled under the energy building around him. Caim pulled back Nina's head to expose her throat and curved his other hand across the pale skin there.

"What if you're not fast enough, Appointed? Or strong enough? What if you can't hold me until the Power arrives and the girl dies and I was right all along?"

The fingers of Seth's extended hand flexed wide.

Jen fell to her knees on the carpet, her shriek turning from shrill to muffled as she slapped a hand over her own mouth. Alex launched herself at Seth's arm.

"Seth, no!"

"Listen to her, Seth." A single nail on Caim's hand had grown and turned black and polished and curved. It pierced the fragile skin of Nina's throat, drawing a tiny trickle of blood. Malevolent black eyes held Alex's without wavering. "You know, don't you, Naphil? You know there's no way out of this, that someone will give up their life to me today."

Alex felt Seth's arm contract under her hold. She gripped tighter. Nodded. "I know."

"Then it's all about choices, isn't it? Her"—Caim looked down at Nina with an almost tender adulation, and then lifted his gaze to Alex again—"or you. Free will's a bitch, isn't it?"

Alex stared at him for a long moment, searching for any hint of uncertainty. Found only a cornered animal made unpredictable by desperation. Caim might want Aramael's defeat more than his own return to Heaven, but with every passing second, they risked him changing his mind and deciding to go with the sure thing he already held in his hands.

Which would open the door to a hundred thousand others like him, each seeking his or her own Naphil fast track to Heaven. A hundred thousand serial killers, give or take, unleashed on Earth.

She turned to Seth. "If you try anything, she'll be dead before you blink," she whispered. "You know that."

"And if I leave you with him," he growled, "we risk Aramael's return. You know *that*."

"Not if you find another Power to stop him."

"Another Power will go right through you, Alex. Without hesitation."

"I know."

She waited for Seth to sift through to the truth she had already reached. Watched comprehension turn to denial in his gaze, then darken to bleak acceptance.

"Caim is powerful," he said quietly. "He can make you call out to Aramael, to summon him. What if I can't move fast enough?"

Alex steeled herself not to flinch. "We have to try. There's no other choice. Get Jen and Nina out of the house and then go," she said. "I'll hold out as long as I can."

She pulled her sister up from the floor and shoved her toward the door, away from the chance of an embrace she wasn't sure she could end. "Go," she said. "Seth will bring Nina."

Beyond argument, Jen stumbled through the doorway, her expression dazed. Shell-shocked.

Alex met Seth's grave gaze one last time and then turned to face Caim.

"Me," she said. "You can have me."

THIRTY-FIVE

Caim moved faster than Alex could blink, depositing Nina in a heap on the floor at Seth's feet and grasping Alex by the throat so tightly that the very air itself scraped her windpipe. Dragging her away from the others, he shoved her against the wall, ragged wings outspread behind him. Then he looked over his shoulder at Seth and lifted his chin in defiance. "Do what you're thinking of doing and she dies before you can draw breath. Now leave us."

Alex met Seth's helpless fury and fought down the wave of panic that threatened to swamp her, to make her change her mind and beg for help. This was the only way, she reminded herself. All they could do now was prevent Aramael from triggering the unthinkable.

"Go," she croaked. "Don't let him win."

Not until she heard the front door close and the car start did Alex breathe easily again. Or as easily as she could with Caim's fingers digging into her throat. She tried to pull back from his grip a little, but stopped when his nails pressed harder.

His nails—or his claws?

His face swam into focus through tears of pain.

"Now, Naphil, before Seth is able to put your little plan into motion—" He paused at her involuntary start. "What, you didn't think I could hear you?"

His face moved closer, until his cheek rested against hers. Until his lips moved against her ear, his breath hot and moist. "You truly have no idea the power you're dealing with, have you? Your puny mortal brain just can't stretch far enough to grasp what lies outside you, and anything of the divine in you is long gone, too diluted to make any difference. So what is it that he sees in you, then?"

Alex pressed her lips together, refusing to answer. Or to release the agony building in her throat. The claws pressed a little harder and she felt one pierce the skin.

"Did you know that I loved someone once?" Caim asked softly. "Not just someone. My soulmate. She didn't follow when I left the One, and when I tried to return to her, Aramael stopped me. I lost her forever because of him."

Alex swallowed against his grip. She could think of nothing more bizarre than discussing a demon's love life right now, but she needed to keep him talking. Needed to give Seth time to find another Power. "But I thought soulmates were taken from all angels," she rasped. "Even if you return, she won't remember you."

"But I would finally find the same peace that she has." His face twisted. "Nearly five thousand years I have lived with the memory of her loss. Five thousand years of feeling my soul slowly bleed to death, because my brother denied my return. Denied my cleansing."

Alex tugged in vain at Caim's hand and struggled for air. She willed herself not to black out. Not yet. "I'm sure he didn't mean—"

His hand left her throat, wrapped into her hair, and threw her to the floor. Her head cracked against a baseboard and explosions of light and fire went off inside her skull. She clenched her teeth against the wave of nausea that washed through her and struggled to sit up. A foot shoved into her face, sending her to the floor a second time. Her nose shat-

tered with an audible crack and a fresh jolt of agony ripped
through her. She gagged on the blood flooding her throat
and remained down, staring up at her captor through the
tears streaming from her eyes.

Caim stooped and grasped her chin in a cruel grip, a
yellowed feather dropping from a wing and brushing against
her cheek in its descent to the floor.

"Never, ever think that your angel is any less merciless
than the one he serves, Naphil," he grated. "He knew. He
knew, and he told me my memories would be just punishment. Told me I deserved to suffer for my actions against
the One." His eyes became like chips of black ice. "He knew,
and now he will know more. He will understand what he
sentenced me to with his betrayal."

He grasped her hair again and hoisted her to her feet as
if she had no weight, no substance. Then he slipped behind
her, one hand at her throat, the other resting over her heart.
"Call him," he commanded. "I want him to see you die."

"I can't—"

He jerked her against him. "Call him."

"I don't know how."

"Say his name!"

Alex thought of the torment she had glimpsed in gray,
turbulent eyes during unguarded moments. Thought about
the war that might be triggered by the pain of a Power's loss,
and what new level of agony would be added to that pain if
he had to witness that loss. Knew that she could not allow
that to happen. Would not.

"No," she whispered. *Please let Seth have found someone. Please let him be on his way back . . . please.*

"The Appointed was right, you know. I can make you."

Caim's voice had roughened and the texture of his skin
against hers had changed. Alex did not want to know why.
She stood tall, closed her eyes, and braced for the worst.

"No," she said. "You can't."

"Poor, naïve mortal," Caim whispered in her ear. "You
really don't understand, do you?"

Three distinct, icy-cold points dug into Alex's chest over

her heart and her eyes flew open. Heat followed the cold, as the points raked across her, shallow at first and then deepening, gouging, tearing through tissue and bone alike. Agony pierced through to the very core of her sanity. The next time Caim's voice growled its command to call Aramael, she did so—obediently, instinctively, mindlessly.

ARAMAEL STOOD AT the edge of a roof, thirty-four stories above the streets, and watched the city come to life below him. Hundreds of thousands of mortals beginning their day, going about their business, all oblivious to the drama playing out in their midst.

Oblivious to an angel's torment.

He raised his head and glowered at the morning sky. Damn it to hell and back, how he ached to be with her. Ached for this hunt to be over, so he could return to her. Hold her, feel her presence mingle with his, discover how complete the melding of their energies might be.

His mouth twisted. But as much as he desired the end of this hunt, he dreaded it, too. It would only be a matter of time before he was cleansed as the others had been; before his recognition of a soulmate was removed from him and she became nothing more than a distant memory. There, but without context. Without meaning.

Aramael bit back an oath and he turned to pace the roofline. Froze in mid-swivel. His head snapped up and he stared out at the sunrise, focused, rigid, waiting. A long moment slid by, then another. He frowned. He was sure he'd felt—yes. There. A ripple along the edge of his consciousness. The stirring of an awareness that he'd almost missed amid the chaos of his thoughts. An awareness he'd almost forgotten, it seemed so long since he'd felt it.

Caim.

Savage exhilaration filled him. Head high, he tensed, centered himself, willed himself to stillness. Caim's energy surged through the air, bold, vile, and entirely traceable as he transitioned to his demon side. Sudden thunder rolled overhead, a low, ominous growl that signaled Caim's interference in a universe he had no business toying with. The city's sounds faded into the background. The fire of the hunt licked along Aramael's veins, kindling the cold rage he carried in him. The rage that *was* him.

Satisfaction snarled through his center.

I'm coming, Brother.

But on the verge of increasing his energy vibration to give chase, he went still. Something was wrong. He fought back the fury, struggled to control the instinct that would overtake him. No, not wrong. Missing. His center turned to ice.

Alex.

He could feel Caim, but where the hell was Alex?

Aramael forgot to breathe. Forgot, for a moment, how to think as his heart collapsed inward, drawing every fragment of his attention, every atom of his energy. He felt no Alex.

The impossibility of failure loomed in his mind, all encompassing, all consuming. Then, even as agony began to rip him apart from the inside out, a scream of anguish tore through his mind. Pierced to his core.

His name.

Alex's voice.

ARAMAEL TOOK IN the scene before him, missing nothing. Caim, half changed to demon, holding Alex's limp body; the gashes across Alex's chest spilling a frightening amount of blood over her captor's withered arm and curved, deadly claws.

A haze of red descended over Aramael's vision and he fought to see through it. To see the truth, and not to lash out mindlessly. Brutally. Alex wasn't gone yet. As soon as he'd arrived here, he'd felt her presence again. Weak, thready, but clinging to its earthly vessel. He could still save her.

If he maintained control.

He tamped down the ferocity that boiled in him, demanding release. He flexed his wings. Inhaled deeply. Felt his nostrils flare.

"Caim."

"Aramael," his brother rasped in return. "Glad you could make it."

Caim shifted his grip and Aramael heard a tiny gasp from Alex. Her eyes opened, met his, clouded with pain and regret. Aramael's heart contracted.

"You're here," she murmured. "I'm sorry. I tried not to call."

Her words ended on a groan as Aramael's twin gave her a rough shake. Pain spasmed across her face and her eyes drifted shut again. Aramael's rage battled the prison he imposed on it.

"How touching," Caim drawled. "A mortal trying to protect the great Aramael. Have you become that weak, Brother?"

Aramael unfurled his wings. Struggled grimly to hold on to his temper. "Release the woman," he snarled in return, "and let's find out."

Caim's own tattered wings flexed wide at the challenge and, for an instant, he seemed to consider the idea. Then he shook his head. Smiled. "Oh, I've no doubt you can still overpower me. You carry the full force of Heaven behind you, after all. But there's more than one kind of weakness, isn't there?"

He forced Alex's chin up and back, exposing the curve of her throat. His claws extended, reaching their full, deadly length, and his skin drew tight and thin over the bones of a body that had lost its substance. In an instant he became fully demon—a living, skin-clad skeleton, his flesh consumed by the evil and hatred that had eaten away at him since his downfall.

The same hatred that burned in his eyes now.

"Even now you hesitate, Power. You can stop me, but your feelings stand in your way. What do you call that, if not weak?"

For the first time in Aramael's existence, impotence held him immobile. He felt the truth of Caim's words like a blow to his gut and struggled for words that would buy him time.

That would buy Alex time. "You don't even know this will work," he said. "And even if you do succeed, you'll never be allowed to stay."

Weak as the words were, momentary doubt crossed Caim's expression. Then he shook his head. "She'll understand," he said. "If I can just talk to her, I can make her understand what it's like in that prison. The emptiness. The nothingness. An eternity with no touch, no thought, nothing but the memories of all that I have lost."

Caim straightened and his claws slowly sank into the skin of Alex's throat. "I'll make her understand what she sentenced me to. I'll make *you* understand."

"Caim—"

"Oh, please do, Aramael. Please beg. I'd like that." Caim's hand tensed and began to pull back. "Beg as I once did, when I asked to return and you refused me." His claws ripped through Alex's flesh as if through an overripe plum.

Aramael saw Alex's eyes go wide, heard air gurgle in her throat. Shock reverberated through him, carrying with it a horror that pierced to his core. He extended a hand to his brother. "Caim, no!"

Caim regarded him calmly. Sadly. "I never wanted this, Aramael. I wanted only to go home. To go back to the way it was. But none of you would let me." He shook his wizened head. "You may be right that I cannot succeed, but whether I do or not, I will find a certain peace in knowing that I leave you suffering as I have suffered. That I have taken from you what you denied me."

Aramael felt Alex's life force waver, her presence fade. The red haze he'd fought turned black and slipped between him and his brother. Between him and reason. With a speed he had never known, an iciness he had never encountered, Heaven's wrath swelled in him, strained against the confines of his control, and then broke free.

His wings lifted high with a thunderous crack, flames licking along the edges, igniting each and every feather. Golden fire turned bloodred, streamed along his limbs, set his body alight, threatened to consume him. Aramael clenched his fists at his sides in an effort to slow the fury, to control what threatened to control him. Then he raised a hand and sent a blast of divine energy across the room, knocking his brother into the wall, startling him into releasing Alex's throat.

Caim's eyes went wide, but after only a split second, he dug his claws into Alex again. Aramael sent a second surge into his brother, tearing Alex from his grip. Then, still grappling for mastery over his fury, a third. And a fourth.

His center began to give way under the strain.

Blast after blast hammered into Caim, channeled by Aramael's hand, driven by his loss. Flames joined the energy leaving his body, scorched his brother's withered frame and wings, licked along the blackened edges of the wall and across the floor toward Alex. Pooled blood sizzled in the heat. Aramael's restraint slid another notch and he hurled Caim through the wall into the room beyond.

The effort it took not to follow nearly ripped his soul from him. He fought through the agony to deny his purpose, to deny the need to finish the capture and tear Caim from the mortal realm and cast him into Limbo. Instead, he staggered to the broken, bloodied body of the woman who had so briefly completed him. The anguish of defeat, of failure, felled him to his knees.

Hand shaking, he pushed back blood-soaked hair from her face, groping for the fragile spark of her life's presence somewhere in his awareness. It was there, but only just. Floating weakly in a well of emptiness and betrayal that he had ignored for almost five thousand years. Aramael sucked in a quick breath and centered himself, reaching clumsily to steady the spark. She was still there. If he was careful, he might still—

The spark dimmed. Guttered. Disappeared.

Aramael stared at the empty vessel that had been Alex. His soulmate. The other half of the whole he'd never known he could be. From a place far distant, he watched Caim lurch through the flames to stand over him, swaying, gloating, triumphant.

"I guess you were right," his brother croaked. "It didn't work after all. What a shame. But not a complete loss, I think."

He stepped across Alex's body and crouched down until he was on a level with Aramael, the skin below his eye swollen and split. Blood trickled down to the corner of his mouth and he licked it away.

"I've taken her from you, Aramael. Taken away the only thing you've ever loved. The way you took my life from me. How does it feel?" He reached across Alex and touched the center of Aramael's chest. "Do you feel it here, the way I did? A great, gaping hole where your heart is no more?"

Aramael flinched from his twin's touch and tried to shake his head, to deny the words. The truth. The hatred he had seen in Caim found purchase in his own belly. He swallowed against it. Searched desperately for his connection to the One. Felt it slip in his grasp, tightened his hold.

He saw Caim reach out to Alex's face and stroke a single finger down the curve of her cheek. His own hand shot out. Encircled his brother's wrist and snapped it like a twig.

Unflinching, Caim smiled. "Go ahead," he said. "Send me back. Not even Limbo will be unbearable now. Not with this memory to sustain me."

Aramael didn't answer. Couldn't. Not past the coldness he felt rising in his soul, the blackness that belonged to a part of him he didn't recognize. He sucked in a great, shuddering breath. Looked down again at the lifeless woman before him. Felt the emptiness engulf him.

Alex.

He rose to his feet, fluid and powerful, and yanked Caim upright. Thrust him away. Threw back his head and drew all the fury of Heaven into himself. Readied it, balanced it, held it close.

Stared into the eyes of the one he had once called Brother and cringed from the satisfaction there. The gloating. The connection to the One began to fray. Aramael struggled to retain his hold on it for a moment more, just long enough to complete his task, to fulfill his purpose—and then Caim stretched out a booted foot and nudged Alex's body and a barely discernable whisper of air escaped her lips.

Life.

Caim went stiff and raised a startled gaze to Aramael's. For the barest instant, neither moved. And then, before Aramael could raise a hand to stop him, Caim dived toward the woman between them—toward Alex.

The already-fragile connection to the One snapped and, in a single, massive surge, Aramael's full power slammed outward, shattering Caim's body into a million shards that hung, suspended in the air, as if startled to find themselves there. Startled to find themselves separated from one another; from their host. From a broken place inside himself, Aramael watched flames flow from his outstretched wing tips, turning the shards to blackened bits that fell to the floor, greedily seeking the tiny shimmer of Caim's immortality at their center. Enveloping it. Destroying it.

Then, before he could go to the woman who had been his soulmate, the woman who was still alive, Aramael felt the rush of other wings.

Felt his arms and legs pinioned.

Felt himself ripped from the human realm.

THIRTY-SIX

*H*ot.
  "Alex?"
  No. Not hot. Cold.
  "Alex."
  Cold inside. Hot out. Odd.
  "Open your eyes, Alex. Give me some indication you're still alive, because I'm not permitted to bring you all the way back and I sure as hell can't face telling Aramael you're dead."
  And tired. So tired.
  And smoke? Not good. Should move. Get out.
  But so tired . . . and heavy. The sensation of heat contrasting with cold grew stronger. She cracked open her eyes and watched the flames licking at her blackened extremities. Frowned. That didn't look good. She needed to move. But how? Maybe if she rested for a bit—
  "Damn it, Alex—"
  Wait . . . that voice. She knew that voice.
  She forced her eyes a fraction wider. Saw more flames. The beginnings of fear twisted through her. *Out, Alex. Get*

out. She tried to force her limbs into action, but no part of her responded with so much as a twitch. Inside her grew colder.

She felt a gentle touch on her cheek.

"Oh, Alex," the voice said sadly.

Seth. It's Seth. Talk, Alex. Say something to him.

She tried to swallow. Agony screamed through her, her throat its epicenter. She waited until the world righted itself and the dark faded. That *hurt.* She released the breath she'd held in a long, low groan, barely audible to her own ears. The hand on her cheek went still, then cupped her jaw with utmost care.

"I heard that," Seth said, "and it's good enough for me. Hold on. I'm going to make some of this better."

Alex felt a hand at her throat. Fragments of memories crowded in on her, black with terror, but her attempt to struggle resulted only in the barest lift of her chin and another jolt of pain. The hand covered her throat, accompanied by an intense heat . . . and then a slow lessening of the pain there. A tear trickled from the corner of her eye and pooled in her ear.

The hand lifted away.

"Is that any better?"

She considered the question. Swallowed cautiously. Tried her voice. The odd sound that emerged was nowhere near the *yes* that she intended, but it made Seth chuckle.

"I'll take that as an affirmative."

The hand returned, spreading over her chest. More pain accompanied it, radiating outward, making her grunt. More heat. Another slow ease. A steadying of her heartbeat, whose threadiness she hadn't noticed until now, and a gradual sensation that her limbs once again belonged to her.

"I know I'm hurting you, but I don't dare move you until we look after at least the worst of it," Seth said. "I won't be able to do everything, though, or it will raise questions. Can you bear with me for a minute more?"

Alex shook her head. All the while Seth had tended to her, she'd sensed her extremities growing hotter and hotter, and now they felt like they were in an incinerator. "Feet," she croaked. "Hands. Hot."

"What? Oh, Hell—"

Instant relief. Alex looked past the figure crouched at her side and saw that the flames had retreated several feet and that her skin was no longer charred. The overall heat seemed to have decreased, too, as if a bubble had been created around her and her rescuer.

"Sorry about that. I think I need practice at this nurse-maid stuff." Seth slid an arm under her shoulders and levered her into a sitting position. "Let me take care of your nose and your head, and then I'll get you out of here, all right?"

"Wait—Jen? Nina?"

"They're safe. Both of them."

He reached for her nose, but Alex put a scorched hand over his.

"Aramael?"

Seth went quiet for a moment, staring at their hands. Then he looked down at her. "I don't know."

A new wave of cold washed through Alex. In the distance, she heard the wail of sirens. "Caim didn't—he didn't—" She paused and made herself form the question she needed to ask. "Aramael is all right, isn't he?"

Seth's black eyes went soft. "I thought you saw."

"Saw what? Damn it, Seth—"

"Aramael killed Caim, Alex."

Relief, hot and heavy and sweet, would have made her collapse if she hadn't already been on the floor. Aramael was alive. And the monster was dead.

"Thank God."

Seth remained silent, his jaw flexing. The sirens grew nearer.

"Seth? What is it?" Alex realized that he hadn't actually said that Aramael had lived and her belly turned liquid. "He is alive, isn't he? Seth?"

Seth sighed. "It's not that simple."

She wondered if she had enough strength in her arms yet

to smack him. She scowled. "Nothing is ever that simple with you people."

The sirens died into silence outside her house. Seth lifted his head to listen and took his hand out from under hers.

"They'll be coming in soon. I need to get you out of here."

Alex smacked at the hand heading for her nose. "Not until you tell me what the hell is going on with Aramael."

"I don't have time—"

"Make time."

He glared at her. "No wonder you've caused so much trouble. Fine. He's alive. Now let me get you out of here so we can take care of things before the place is overrun with firefighters."

Alex pushed away the distraction arising from the *take care of things* idea. "That doesn't tell me anything, and you know it. Where is he? Is he hurt?"

Quiet sympathy emanated from Seth.

"Aramael destroyed another being, Alex. He committed the unforgivable in the One's name. The repercussions—" Seth broke off and then finished, "The repercussions are immeasurable at this point."

She remembered then. Swallowed painfully. "The pact with Lucifer—he broke it."

"Let's just say he opened doors we would have preferred to keep closed."

She sat in silence, still cradled against him, listening to the sound of splintering wood downstairs, the muffled shouts from her lawn, the roar of flames that surrounded but did not touch her. Seth placed his hand over her nose and she winced at the crunch of cartilage moving back into place. A little more strength trickled back into her body. She thought about the repercussions Seth had mentioned.

More monsters at large in her world, undoubtedly. Monsters, and a war beyond mortal imagination. The Apocalypse. All because an angel and a human had dared to touch, dared to connect.

"Where is he now?" she asked quietly.

"Hold on."

Seth wrapped his other arm around her and a sudden explosion shook the house. The flames along the hall fell back for an instant and then flared anew, higher than before. Alex shrank back into the shelter of Seth's body. The shouts on the lawn receded.

Seth looked down at her reassuringly. "We need to keep the firefighters out," he explained. "It will look as if you were attacked by the killer"—he touched her throat—"and that he died in the fire. There will be questions, but when the killings end, the investigation will close."

"My house—" Alex stopped. A war between Heaven and Hell loomed and she worried about her house? "Never mind. Tell me where Aramael is."

"The Archangels have him."

She wouldn't know an Archangel from a Guardian, but something in Seth's tone made her heart go cold. "I take it that's not good."

"No."

"But you'll help him."

"I'm sorry, Alex—"

She pulled away and turned on him. "He killed Caim because of me."

Seth nodded.

"He told me that he and I—that we were a mistake."

"Yes, but—"

"So this is how Heaven handles its mistakes? By punishing the victim? How the hell is that ultimate good?" Alex threw her arms wide. "What the *fuck* happened to justice?"

"I told you, it's not that—"

"If you say it's not that simple one more time, Seth Benjamin, I swear to God I will kick you in the balls—angel or no angel."

Seth raked his fingers through his hair, his forehead furrowing. "This is out of my hands, Alex. What do you want me to do?"

"I want you to help him."

He stared at her, frustration stamped between his brows. "Fine. I'll try."

"Not try. Help."

"Damn it, Alex—"

"He doesn't deserve this, Seth."

Seth's angry gaze held hers for another moment and then he closed his eyes briefly, opening them to regard her in defeat. "You're right. He doesn't, and I will do everything in my power to help him."

Alex released a long, unsteady breath. "Thank you."

"*Now* can I please get you out of here?"

"I want to see him again."

"You're joking." Seth stared at her and then groaned. "You're not joking."

"I want to say good-bye. I should have that much."

Seth was silent for so long that she wondered if he'd heard her. Then a gentle hand stroked her head. "Yes," he said. "You should."

He carried her down the stairs, removing whatever protection he'd placed over her as he descended the last few steps, he explained, so that the heat would sear her skin and her lungs and the smoke would sting her eyes. So that she would emerge from the fire looking like she'd been caught in it and there wouldn't be questions about how she'd emerged unscathed. He set her down in the front hall, steadied her, sheltered her from the worst of the heat as she coughed and struggled for air. Wiped away the tears streaming down her cheeks.

"I'll try my best," he said. "For everything."

Then he stilled the flames between her and the door and pushed her through the smoke, and she stumbled across her porch and into the waiting arms of a half dozen firefighters.

THIRTY-SEVEN

They took him to Mittron's office, depositing him with a telling lack of care in the middle of the floor. Aramael staggered, righted himself, and threw himself at his winged captors.

"Damn you both to hell!" he snarled. "She's still alive! I have to go back to her—"

The Archangels' wings meshed together, forming an impenetrable wall. A barrier no one short of the One could breach. Where Aramael was strong, backed by Heaven's wrath, the One's enforcers were stronger—their power rooted in her Judgment. Cold, compassionless, absolute. The chill from their touch would linger on his soul for a long time—and he would beat himself bloody and senseless against their might before they moved a feather from his path.

With a roar of frustration, he gave up his assault and stood in the center of the room, hands fisted, chest heaving with exertion, heart shredding within him. "Bastards!" he spat.

One of the Archangels—Raphael—turned glittering eyes on him, then crossed his arms and stared into the distance.

Aramael glared at him for a moment more and then spun to face the door as it opened to admit the Highest Seraph.

New fury, ugly and personal, rose in him. "You son of a bitch!"

He leaped for Mittron's throat. Heard the rustle of a wing that wasn't his own. Picked himself up from the opposite wall. Swiping the blood from his nose with the back of his hand, he glowered at Raphael, now standing between him and the Highest.

"You've no idea what he's done," he told the Archangel. "This—all of this—is because of him." He turned his glare on Mittron. "I'm just not sure if it was accidental or deliberate."

Mittron raised an eyebrow. "Serious accusations, Power. I assume you have evidence to back them?"

Aramael wiped another drip from his nose. He didn't know what, if anything, Seth had found, but the Highest's supreme confidence told him that a search for information had probably been wasted in the first place. He stayed silent.

"I didn't think so." Mittron looked to the Archangels and inclined his head. "Thank you for bringing him so quickly. If you wouldn't mind waiting outside—" He broke off and glanced at Aramael. "But bind him first."

Aramael fought, but the skirmish with the Archangels was brief and ineffective, ending with his wings held motionless and his hands bound before him with a length of soft but unbreakable rope. Panting, he sent Mittron a murderous look as the door closed behind the Archangels.

"So," Mittron said. "The business of your future."

"No," Aramael snarled. "Alex first."

"The woman is the least of your concerns, Aramael. But if it will allow us to move forward, she lives. Apparently the Appointed shares some of your regard for her."

The relief flooding through Aramael turned confused, complicated by a dozen other emotions: gratitude for Seth having saved her; jealousy at the idea she would wake in the Appointed's arms and not his own; wrenching loss at the knowledge he hadn't had the chance to hold her again. That he never would.

He forced muscles to relax. She lived, he told himself. For now that was enough. *Had* to be enough. He had more pressing matters to pursue. "Why?" he asked. "Why have you done this?"

He thought the Highest might keep up the denial, but without the Archangels present, Mittron seemed willing to relax his guard. Happy to share.

"Change, Aramael. You were a perfect, predictable catalyst for change. With the help of your brother and the Naphil, of course."

"Change? What change?"

Mittron's face turned reminiscent. Brooding. "He was never good enough to sit at her side," he murmured. "I tried to tell her that. To warn her he could not be trusted. She didn't listen to me, of course, and she was broken. Destroyed by his betrayal. I was the one who held her together through it. I advised her, guided her, watched over her. I did everything for her. Without me, the mortals would never have survived."

Aramael shook his head to counter his confusion. Mittron seemed to be speaking of Lucifer, but Aramael didn't remember the events the way the Highest described. The One had been devastated, yes, as had they all. She had even been compassionate to a fault, perhaps, but she had never been less than the One, the ultimate power in the universe. Had never been weak in the way Mittron described. Had she?

He thought of the One's marked and continued absence from her angels' lives; how more and more of her instructions and wishes had been filtered through Mittron over the millennia. His blood ran cold, chilled his heart. Had they really missed something as monumental as the One's slow breaking down?

"But it made no difference," Mittron continued. "She relied on me, yes, but never really saw me. Never saw that it should be me at her side, that it should have been me all along."

Aramael's wings gave an involuntary twitch against their bonds. He thought he might choke. "This was about *ego*?"

The Highest's brows became an angry slash. "Careful, Power. I haven't yet meted out your sentence and it can still change."

"I don't give a damn about my sentence. The One's decision had nothing to do with you. She swore she would never place *anyone* that high again."

"She will have no choice once Lucifer declares war."

"He can't. Not with the pact—" Aramael stopped. He stared at Heaven's administrator, and in a single, awful instant of clarity, understood his part in Mittron's drama. Saw beyond the pain of losing Alex, the grief of denying his brother, and the anguish of betraying the One. Saw the impact of his actions on the universe. His voice went hoarse. "I broke the pact."

"With an act of war against your own brother," the Highest Seraph agreed. "Just as I knew you would when I conceived of this idea four and a half millennia ago, when Caim wanted to come back to the fold and your testimony swayed the One to deny him. You were both so angry with one another, so betrayed. You were on the verge of striking out at him even then. You only needed a little motivation. A little guidance."

"But how?"

"Your soulmate had not yet been given a vessel, it was an easy matter to arrange for that vessel to be Nephilim. Easier still to tamper with your cleansing so you would recognize her when the time came. Easiest yet to convince Caim there might be an alternative route to his return." Mittron stood up from his chair and stretched, looking smug. "Once events were put in motion, it was a matter of patience. The mark, I might add, of a brilliant tactician."

He picked up a paper and came around to hand it to Aramael. "Not the kind of tactics I can reveal to the One, of course, but I will have ample opportunity to prove myself against Lucifer."

"Aren't you forgetting something?"

"The agreement?" Mittron waved a careless hand. "Covered. Remember, I've had several millennia to work out the details. I must admit to a qualm or two when the Appointed became involved in matters, but I've used the opportunity to ensure that I've erased all my tracks now, and when the time comes, Seth will no longer pose a problem."

"No." Aramael shook his head, ignoring the paper in the Highest's outstretched hand. "This is insane. You're talking about the end of the mortal race and possibly our own."

"The mortals are expendable, and I am more than capable of looking after our own."

The Highest's sheer conceit defied description. Defied understanding. Aramael's wings strained to extend, to respond to his need for power, but the Archangels' bindings held fast. He could do nothing. He would be exiled to Limbo knowing what Mittron was, knowing what he planned, and be completely helpless to do anything about it.

"Someone will find out," he told the Highest. "Someone will stop you."

"No one dares move against the Highest Seraph, Aramael. Except you, perhaps, and you will be safely removed from any interference. And now"—he waved the paper he held under Aramael's nose—"it is time."

Aramael stared at the parchment. A decree. He saw the seal on it. "That's—"

"The One's mark. Yes. She took a special interest in your situation." Mittron's voice was casual, but a tenseness around his eyes told Aramael the Highest wasn't as relaxed about this as he wished to portray. He jiggled the paper again. "Take it."

The moment the document touched Aramael's skin, it burned its intent into his soul. Marked him forever as having broken faith with the One. Branded him as Fallen.

His stomach heaved and his hands shook. Fallen. He hadn't thought of it that way. Hadn't stopped to consider that, in choosing to betray the One's trust, he would follow in the path of those he had existed to hunt.

But there was more. He forced himself to look at the jumbled words on the page, to bring them into focus. Bypassed the phrase about his sins. Found the one about his sentence. Stared. Blinked. Read it a second time, and then a third. He looked to the Highest for confirmation. "Not Limbo?" he asked. "Just cast out? Where am I to go?"

"Unless you choose to throw yourself on Lucifer's mercy—and given your track record with his followers, I wouldn't recommend doing so—you will spend your eternity in the mortal realm. You will have no access to Heaven or anyone in it. No connection to the One. And—"

Mittron hesitated, not out of compassion, Aramael thought, but a desire to draw this out as much as possible. And to draw as much pleasure from it as he could.

"What?" he demanded bitterly. "What more can there possibly be?"

The Highest looked pensive. "I must be honest with you, Power. The very qualities for which I chose you as my pawn worry me now. Your instability makes it difficult to predict what you might do if I leave you to your own devices. Even without a connection to any of this realm, you might still do damage. I think it best that I strip you of your powers, as well."

Aramael would never have imagined himself capable of destroying a second life, but if he'd been able to spread his wings and access his powers just then, been able to channel the rage that filled him, he didn't think Mittron would have survived. The careful distance Mittron maintained from him said the Highest knew it.

"Only the One can remove an angel's powers," Aramael growled through clenched teeth.

"Given the number of your infractions on this last assignment, she has left it to me to decide whether or not you can be trusted to retain them. I find you cannot."

Mittron strolled to his desk, picked up a second parchment, and returned. Aramael stared at the document and the seal stamped upon it. He tensed, his wings aching with the strain of trying to break free. An angel, stripped of his powers, cast into the mortal realm for eternity. Could there be any worse punishment?

He felt Mittron's anticipation. The Highest expected him
to plead for mercy, he realized. Wanted him to beg. His
throat closed against the urge to do just that.

Never.

The mortals managed to survive without divine powers.
He would learn to do the same. And he'd have all of eternity
in which to do so.

Head high, jaw clenched in defiance, he stretched out his
hands and snatched the parchment from Mittron's grasp. He
felt its impact immediately. Felt it snake through him, an
inferno burning in its wake. He tried to release the paper,
but it clung to his open palm. Melded with him. Became
him. Then, when he didn't think he could endure a minute
more, it fluttered to the floor. The internal fire disappeared,
leaving cold emptiness wherever it had touched. Nothingness where there had once been a great energy.

The bonds holding his wings and hands fell away.

Mittron strode to the door and pulled it open to readmit
the Archangels. "We're done," he said. "You may take him."

Aramael swayed under the weight of his new weakness,
but stayed on his feet. He would *not* fall before Mittron, he
told himself fiercely. Wouldn't so much as stumble. Straightening his shoulders and lifting his head, he went to meet
the Archangels.

But in brushing past the Highest, he felt fingers burrow
into the feathers of a wing. He stiffened as the Seraph
stepped behind him and grasped one wing in each hand.

"I almost forgot these. With no power to hide them anymore, I'm afraid you won't be able to keep them." Mittron's
fingers dug in cruelly and he leaned close, dropping his voice
to a whisper. "Nor, I'm afraid, will you keep your awareness
of your soulmate. She turned out to be responsible in great
part for that unpredictability of yours going beyond what
I'd expected. I think you'll be safer without her."

Aramael stiffened, but the Highest's grip prevented him
from turning. He tried to shake it off, but his wings barely
moved in response, powerless to rid him of the traitor on his
back. Mittron's will flowed into him and the exquisite aware-

ness of Alex faltered, and then faded by slow degrees, first into nothing, and then into less than nothing. Until he could remember her, but no longer feel her. Until the emptiness that had begun with his fall, with his turn away from the One, became complete.

Until he stood, depleted and beaten and more barren than any being should ever be, and felt his wings ripped from his body.

Agony drove him to his knees. Pure and physical and absolute, it wrenched a guttural roar from a place so profound and dark that he hadn't known its existence. Filled his head, his chest, his body with its force. Finally spent itself in a lack of air, leaving him gasping. Shaking. Hating.

He dug his fingers into his thighs, willing himself back to control, back to his feet. But before he could summon the strength needed, he heard Mittron's order above his head.

"Take him," the Highest said. "Anywhere will do."

Once again, cold, talonlike hands lifted Aramael from the floor.

THIRTY-EIGHT

S he knew. One look at the shadows darkening her silver eyes and Seth was certain she knew. He steeled himself against the urge to confess his doubts and beg her forgiveness. Calmed his thoughts. She couldn't know, because he had only toyed with an idea. Wondered at it.

Had no intention of following through on it.

He swallowed. "One."

The slender, silver-haired female brushed the dirt from her hands and looked with satisfaction at the potted plants on the greenhouse table. Then she smiled wistfully. "I should have stuck with plants," she said. "They're a great deal less trouble."

Seth made himself return the smile. "You'd miss the challenge."

"Perhaps," she agreed and looked up again. "Are you ready, then?"

Seth slid his hands into his pockets and worked to control his features. "As ready as I can ever be, I suppose."

"Do you have any questions?"

He thought about all that had been allowed to pass, about

the secret Mittron had hinted at, about the inexplicable and confusing feelings he had for a mortal. About how he could know and accept his destiny for thousands of years, only to falter now. About his promise to Alex to intervene on Aramael's behalf.

"No," he answered. "No questions."

The One glanced down at the pockets that hid his clenched fists. He thought she might comment, might probe further, but after a moment she turned away to fill another pot with soil.

"You understand that I may not interfere with you once this is done," she said. "No communication of any kind. That was the agreement."

"I understand."

"Then as soon as things are finalized, we will proceed according to schedule."

Seth's fists tightened. "You're certain this will work? That Lucifer will honor the agreement?"

A tiny smile curved the One's mouth. "I'm very certain of Lucifer."

He flinched, hearing a message for himself in her words. Or maybe it was his guilt speaking. To cover his reaction, he cleared his throat. "Will you still have Mittron oversee the transition?"

"Unless you have an objection."

Now. Now is the time to tell her, to show her what you found and stop the Seraph. Now is the time to remove temptation.

"No. No objection." Seth resisted the desire to withdraw his hands from his pockets and wipe his palms dry. "I should go."

The One gave him a long, searching look. "So much rests on your shoulders, Seth. You know you have the right to refuse this task we have set you, that you may choose to remain here instead. You need only say."

Seth stared at her, stunned. How much had it cost her to make that offer, knowing the outcome if he abdicated his destiny? Sudden, fierce love gripped him, filling him with determination. He stepped forward and grasped the One's hands in his own, ignoring the dirt that soiled them both. "I will fulfill the destiny you have set for me, One. And I will make my choice with the love and compassion you have taught me. I promise."

For the instant it took to draw a single, quick breath, sadness hollowed his mother's eyes. Then Seth blinked and the look was gone, replaced by gentleness. Calm. The One returned the squeeze on his fingers.

"You will do everything you must, my son. I have never doubted that."

Seth walked out of the greenhouse, holding fast to his certainty that he would keep his word. Clinging to it with both hands.

Believing it even as he prepared to lie again to Alex.

THE ONE WATCHED the Appointed's departure from the greenhouse and then turned. "You heard?" she asked a row of tall plants.

Verchiel stepped from behind the greenery, hands tucked into her robe. "I did."

"You don't look happy."

"Mittron, One? Are you certain he can be trusted?"

"I am certain the decision is mine."

Verchiel went pale. "Of course. I only meant—"

"I know what you meant, Verchiel, but you need to believe that what I do, I do with good reason." The One quirked an eyebrow. "I think this might be where faith comes in."

"Of course," the Dominion said again. She remained quiet for a moment, her internal struggle obvious, and then straightened her shoulders. "Forgive me, One, but Seth is your son, and after all I've told you about the Highest—if you think he might do something—"

"I have spoken, Dominion."

"But should we not at least assign a Guard—?"

"I *said* I have spoken."

Verchiel flinched as if she had been struck, and bowed her head. "Yes, One."

"Then you have your instructions. Monitor the Highest and advise me when preparations are complete. And, Verchiel—whatever happens, remember this conversation. Remember that, above all else, I demand faith from my angels. Not just trust."

The One waited until Verchiel had departed the greenhouse before she sagged against the potting bench and raised hand to chest. She thought of what she had set in motion, what she could still stop now but wouldn't, because it needed to be. Should have been thousands of years before. Then she closed her eyes and squeezed her hand into a fist over a heart heavy with grief and guilt.

"Forgive me, my son."

"DID YOU EVEN try?" Alex asked.

She stared out her sister's newly repaired living room window at a cat prowling through the neighbor's flower bed. Jen had insisted on taking her in after the fire—Alex would have preferred the privacy of a hotel, but hadn't had the strength to argue. It hadn't been as bad as she'd expected, living here. Jen seemed to sense that Alex needed to be left alone to heal, and hadn't asked any of the million questions she had to have. Or maybe Jen was just too busy trying to put her daughter's mind back together again to worry about her sister's mental state.

Seth said nothing, but Alex didn't need his words to hear his truth.

Her arms cradled her belly, protecting her from the future looming in the face of that truth. A future without Aramael, without the chance to even say good-bye. A band of iron settled around her heart, tight enough to make a tiny stab of pain the companion to each beat. She put a hand to her throat and traced the wound healing there, then the ones across her chest. Bruised ribs protested the breath she drew. She turned to face Seth. "So that's it, then. It's all over."

Seth hesitated.

"I meant my part in this," she said.

"Yes. Your part is over." Seth regarded her with a compassion that made tears threaten. "Will you be all right?"

"Do I have any choice?" Alex grimaced at the bitter note in her voice. She ran a hand through her hair, careful to avoid the tender lump that remained from her run-in with Caim. Restlessly, she moved away from the window. "I'm sorry," she muttered. "I know none of this is your fault—it's just so . . ."

"Unfair?"

"Wrong."

Seth stood up from the sofa and tucked his hands into his front pockets in a gesture shockingly reminiscent of Aramael. Alex swallowed a lump in her throat and turned away from him.

"Try to remember that it could have been much worse for him, Alex. Limbo would have destroyed him. At least this way he has a chance at a semblance of life."

"Something we have in common."

"Your job—"

"Is waiting for me when I'm ready to go back."

"Will you?"

"I don't know. I don't have anything else to do, so I suppose I should. It just seems somewhat pointless with everything else that's going on."

"Everything—you mean what's happening between Heaven and Hell?"

"The thought had occurred to me, yes." She cast a dark look over her shoulder at him. "Do we mortals even stand a chance of survival?"

A smile tugged at the corner of Seth's mouth. "I don't think you have to worry about extinction just yet."

"With the emphasis on *yet*?"

"With the emphasis on not worrying."

"Not worry about a potential war between Heaven and Hell. You're kidding, right?" Alex glared at him. "Is there some part of being mortal that you're unclear on? We die, Seth. Bad things happen and we *die*."

"I know, but I still think you're worrying too much."

Alex carefully and deliberately set aside the tangle of pain sitting in her chest and took a mental step back to examine Seth's words. She fixed him with a hard stare.

"You're not telling me something."

Seth remained silent for a long moment, looking past her and visibly grappling with something inside himself. Alex crossed her arms, fixed him with an unwavering stare, and waited.

"There's a contingency plan," he allowed at last.

"A contingency plan."

"Another way to avoid war and decide who will have dominion over the mortal realm."

"I see. And this plan would be—?"

Seth stared down at the carpet at his feet. Dug his hands deeper into his pockets. Then raised resigned eyes to hers. "Me," he said. "I'm the plan."

EPILOGUE

War.

Aramael sat on the hard, sun-baked earth long after the last he would see of his kind had abandoned him in a silent rush of wings.

Heaven and Hell locked in the final, ultimate battle that would decimate the mortal race.

And he could do no more than watch from the sidelines. He stared out at the barren landscape. Knowing what was coming, knowing who stood behind it, he could do nothing to prevent it. Couldn't warn anyone, couldn't stop it, couldn't even take part.

Sweat trickled down the back of his neck and between his shoulder blades. The sun, at its zenith in a cloudless sky, beat down without mercy.

The Archangels had picked their dumping ground with stunning appropriateness. He would die a dozen deaths by the time he walked out of this hell. Die, and because of the immortality he retained, be resurrected into the same hell, over and over again. A hell where Mittron had won a battle Aramael hadn't even known they waged until it was too late.

Wiping his forehead with his shirtsleeve, he thought about the woman he'd known as soulmate for so brief a time and wondered what she would do when the war came. Would she be able to remain as strong as he remembered her? A few humans would undoubtedly survive. Would she be among them?

Perhaps it would have been better if she hadn't fought so hard to stay alive through her encounter with Caim. If she'd died then, she wouldn't have to face what the rest of humanity would endure. Aramael's stomach clenched at the thought, bringing him up short. That almost felt as if he still cared . . .

Impossible. He'd never forget how his awareness of Alex had faltered and then faded into nothingness. Until emptiness was all that remained in him. All he knew.

He frowned. Except it wasn't all he knew. Because he still knew her, still knew exactly what he'd lost. Surprise made him grunt softly. He closed his eyes, pushed past the loss that sat heavy in his heart, and dredged up everything he could remember about Alexandra Jarvis. Stubborn courage further defined by vulnerability, hidden wells of compassion and strength, skin like silk beneath his fingers when at last he'd given in to the need . . .

His eyes shot open and he stared at his hand, feeling the imprint of her skin on his flesh. He dusted his fingertips together and the tingle from them flowed into his arm. He still had the memories. Clear memories. Vivid ones. What the hell—?

Free will.

The thought slithered through his mind so quietly he almost missed it. Almost ignored it. Then he seized on it. He could remember because he wanted to, because no one had directed him not to, and even if they had, he could refuse the order. Because he had free will.

Possibilities jangled in his brain, clamoring for his attention. Aramael raised his face to the sky and felt the sun burn against his skin. His mind slowed, settled, sharpened.

Alex, he thought. He could return to Alex. If he remembered her this clearly because he chose to, what more would he feel if he found her again? If he deliberately tried to reignite what he had felt for her? The ache of loss in his center deepened at the idea.

Then he remembered Mittron and his jaw went tight. He might not be able to out the Highest Seraph the way he'd like, but maybe he didn't need to completely discount himself just yet. Maybe he could still do something to stop the Highest— or at least slow him down until someone else clued in.

Alex or Mittron. What a hell of a choice.

Aramael raked his hands through his hair and winced at the scrape of fingernails against his sunburned scalp. If he stayed here much longer, he would die his first death on the spot. He stood and dusted himself off, and then made a full revolution where he stood, squinting against the desert's glare. He grimaced. *Bloody Hell.*

In every direction, the land stretched as far as he could see, lifeless and littered with dried bits of scrub. He pushed away the memory of previous, easier travels, chose a direction, and began walking. At least he'd have time to decide where his priorities lay. And maybe—

He stumbled over a stone and stopped in his tracks. Wait. Maybe he didn't need to choose. He grappled with his thoughts, forcing himself to recall those agonizing last moments in Mittron's presence. What was it the Highest had whispered, just as he had ripped Aramael's wings from him?

She turned out to be responsible in great part for that unpredictability of yours going beyond what I'd expected. I think you'll be safer without her.

Aramael stared ahead into the vast emptiness, remembering how his purpose had once filled him, had defined his existence. Remembering how the power of Heaven itself had channeled through him and how his feeling for a mortal woman had taken all of that and magnified it and given the control of it to him. Power now lost to him, unless he could find a way to reconnect to it. Find someone who might be able to provide that connection.

Unpredictability beyond the expected.

Mittron sure as hell wouldn't expect that.

From national bestselling author Ann Aguirre

AFTERMATH

A Sirantha Jax Novel

Dead heroes get monuments.
Live ones get trials.

Sirantha Jax has the right genes—ones that enable her to "jump" faster-than-light ships through grimspace. But it's also in her genetic makeup to go it alone. It's a character trait that has gotten her into—and out of—hot water time and time again, but now she's caused one of the most horrific events in military history . . .

During the war against murderous, flesh-eating aliens, Sirantha went AWOL and shifted grimspace beacons to keep the enemy from invading humanity's homeworld. The cost of her actions: the destruction of modern interstellar travel—and the lives of six hundred Conglomerate soldiers.

Accused of dereliction of duty, desertion, mass murder, and high treason, Sirantha is on trial for her life. And only time will tell if she's one of the Conglomerate's greatest heroes—or most infamous criminals . . .

Now available from Ace Books

M850T0711

**From National Bestselling Author
Jeanne C. Stein**

CROSSROADS
AN ANNA STRONG, VAMPIRE NOVEL

*As a bounty hunter, Anna Strong knew how to find trouble.
But now that she's vampire, trouble seems to have a knack
for finding her . . .*

The death of Anna's old vampire mentor is causing ripples
in the mortal world. His forensic report has brought up some
anomalies, and people are asking questions—questions that
no vampire wants to answer.

Anna needs to lie low, but with the sudden discovery of a
slew of drained bodies near the Mexican border, and some
stunning news from an unexpected source, she soon finds
herself on a journey that may threaten her existence—and
that of all vampires.

"[Anna is] a heroine with the charm, savvy and intelligence
that fans of Laurell K. Hamilton and Kim Harrison will be
happy to root for." —*Publishers Weekly*

"I cannot wait to see where Anna's adventures take her
next . . . an excellent book." —*Bitten by Books*

penguin.com